BROKEN BONDS

REALMS OF ASARA

V. BRICKER

BRICKER
NOBLES

Cover Illustration by Audrey Hotte

Editing by Holloway House

Paperback ISBN 978-1-963455-14-4

Hardcover ISBN 978-1-963455-11-3

ebook ISBN 978-1-963455-13-7

www.brickerandnobles.com

For Nicole

Thanks for putting up with all my whining. Never gonna stop lovin' you, b—

CONTENTS

ACKNOWLEDGMENTS

I would like to express my gratitude to my family and friends for their support throughout writing this book. Your love and ability to pretend to listen to my rambling kept me going when the path seemed uncertain and I didn't want to continue.

To my editor, Shelley, thank you for your invaluable insight and meticulous attention to detail. I am incredibly grateful for your expertise and dedication to making this book legible.

I would also like to thank my beta readers: Nicole, Brenna, Simona, Katherine, Rhett, and Baylee. Your thoughtful feedback and support were crucial in the first draft.

Finally, to every reader who picks up this book, thank you for taking this journey with me. I hope you enjoy Broken Bonds as much as I enjoyed writing it.

CHAPTER 1

"Are you sure about this, Kai?" Ruby asked as she handed her friend a slender metal hook.

"Ruby, this was your idea!" Kai hissed. "Now give me the tension wrench."

"Umm…"

Kai sighed. "It's the one that looks like an 'L.'" She held her hand out behind her, waiting for the tool without looking at Ruby.

Ruby carefully picked out the tool Kai desired from the leather holder sitting flat on her lap and placed it in Kai's palm. Both women were on the floor, Ruby sitting while Kai knelt close to the keyhole of a handsome mahogany wardrobe.

The two women were in a small study, decorated with a plush, dark-green carpet on a gray stone floor and paintings of different animals adorning the walls, from lions to griffins. A writing table and chair sat near the far wall, the desktop tidy with a fountain pen and inkpot on one side and a stack of papers on the other. Next to the wardrobe was a silver cage where two lemurs peered at Ruby from their hammocks, with their luminous yellow eyes. There was a fireplace near the door, but no wood burned in the hearth, leaving the room chill and dark.

Ruby moved the oil lamp from its place on the floor next to her, holding it aloft to shed light over Kai's shoulder while she worked. It was past dinner time, and they should have been doing homework and preparing for the night's rest, but here they were, breaking into a professor's supply of herbs and ointments.

If they were caught… Well, she didn't want to think about that.

There was a loud click in the empty study, and Kai let out a satisfied breath. "There we are." She turned the handle, and the door of the wardrobe swung open with the creak from hinges that needed to be oiled. "Archaic methods, my ass."

Professor Morel had said Kai's way of going about solving problems was archaic and "only suitable for beggars and thieves," all because she didn't have the more refined education that many of the other students had.

That was why they were here, breaking into the professor's study. Payback.

Ruby and Kai both attended Valwen College, a place of learning housed in a mountain castle on the western edge of the Andrean Empire. Valwen was where the country's mages were taught, men and women who could learn to focus their abilities to cast spells and enchantments. Magic was commonplace in Andrea—many people could perform simple tricks—but there were few who were strong enough to gain admittance to Valwen.

Signs of magical ability began showing at the start of adolescence, and Ruby had been as surprised as anyone when she'd been able to move her toys and brushes around without needing to touch them. After terrifying a few maids, her parents realized what was happening and summoned a local mage to teach her how to control her abilities and not hurt herself or others. As her power grew throughout her teenage years, the young woman had wanted to learn all she could and had begged her parents to let her attend Valwen when she turned nineteen, the minimum age for the renowned college.

They had denied her request, but in the end, she had not needed *their* permission.

Glass bottles lined the wardrobe, sealed with corks and a string tied to the necks, labeling each of their contents. Professor Morel taught zoology. Animal fur, bones, and other parts could serve as components for potions or arcane focuses for rituals. It seemed cruel to Ruby, who was able to cast her spells without the need for such focuses, but not everyone was so lucky. The mages at Valwen taught that the more difficult the spell, the more mental focus it required, and for many, having a physical object to represent the type of spell they were casting alleviated the strain on the mind.

Many mages worked this way, while others did not. She didn't know why it worked like that, though the professors said it was a matter of intellect and study.

"Do you have the ivy?" Kai asked, glass clinking as she shifted through the small vials. Most held no more than a few fronds of herbs or seeds.

"Yes, right here." Ruby dug into the pocket of her gown, producing a small bundle, carefully wrapped in a silk handkerchief. Kai was two years her junior, but the two had become fast friends when Ruby had helped her out of a tight spot. Ruby had had few friends and found upper society dull. Everyone looked at her for her title more than for who she was as a person—everyone except Kai. "Be careful. If you touch the leaves directly, you'll have a rash for days."

Kai scoffed. "Save your concern. Who has more of a precise touch than I do?"

She had a point. Kai's magic may not have been as strong as some of the other students, but the young woman was exceedingly dexterous. Having spent her life working, Kai had skills that the pampered nobles in attendance couldn't match, both impressing and infuriating the professors. Having first served as a scribe's apprentice, she was only one and twenty and in her first year at Valwen, but if she stuck out her education, she would be a formidable mage indeed.

Ruby had turned three and twenty this year, and her time at Valwen was almost up. In a few months' time, she would graduate, and then she would have to marry Mikel. That was the deal she and her fiancé had struck, which allowed her to attend the prestigious college of magic.

If Ruby was being honest, she did not want to get married, at least not yet. She wanted to continue learning. Four years was not nearly enough to hone her skills and her mind in the arcane arts. There was so much more she could be taught. If it were up to her, she would be perfectly fine with waiting a few more years, or perhaps in her heart, she desired a different groom.

But it made no difference what she wanted. This marriage had been arranged when she was a little girl, and Mikel had not inherited his title yet. She had met her betrothed at her debutante ball in the summer of her eighteenth year, though they had already been engaged for eight years by then.

He was handsome, charming, and kind. Everything she had dreamed he would be—or so she thought. Ruby only learned of his true nature later.

Locating the bottle of ground mint, Kai removed it from its perch. Ruby had heard from one of the maids that the professor liked to make a salve of mint and sage to rub on his skin most nights and had shared her idea with Kai. The next thing they knew, they were breaking into their professor's office.

Kai removed the cork on the bottle and carefully replaced the mint with the leaves of poison ivy from Ruby's bundle, dumping the harmless mint into a pouch at her waist. She didn't take all of it. The professor might get suspicious if the aroma of the mint leaves did not come from the bottle when he uncorked it.

Their task finished, Kai closed the cabinet and stood, brushing dust off her knees. She positively beamed as she turned to Ruby.

"Mission accomplished. Let's get out of here before someone comes along and notices the light."

The young women headed toward the door, but Kai slowed to a stop as they passed the professor's desk. There were a few textbooks and papers stacked neatly on the desktop. Papers from last week's lecture on hippogriffs, if one could judge by the top parchment.

"One last trick," Kai muttered as she perused the stack of papers on the desk.

"Last?" Ruby asked. "Are you giving up your life of crime? Ready to become a model student like me?"

"Like you?" Kai scoffed. "Let me remind you—again—that this was *your* idea."

"I know, I know," she said, feeling her cheeks reddening. "It is a harmless prank, yes? He can get healed in the infirmary."

"Yes, but the rash will be a sight to behold," Kai replied, barely containing her glee. "Serves him right for being such a prick."

Kai did not have a good relationship with Professor Morel. The man was in his sixties, and from what Ruby had heard, he had been the fourth son of the previous Lord Morel. Having three older brothers meant there would have been little for the professor to inherit, but with his magical prowess, he had been invited to teach at Valwen. Ruby would have had no qualms with his parentage, but he tended to favor noble students over common-born ones and seemed to have a particular dislike for Kai.

Though Ruby had asked, Kai didn't like to talk about where she'd come from. Her family resided in Valkea, the capital of the Andrean Empire, and she was an only child, like Ruby. She had the feeling that her friend's childhood had not been a happy one, and Ruby wouldn't force her to talk about a subject she found painful. Kai was here now, and that was what was most important.

"About this being your last trick," Ruby began, as Kai pilfered. "What did you mean by that?"

Kai smiled at her, but the expression didn't touch her eyes. "It's nothing for you to be concerned about, Ruby. Like you said, I'm giving up my life of crime. Everything should be much smoother from now on." She opened the top drawer of the desk, taking out more pieces of parchment and examining each one before moving to the next. It almost seemed like Kai was looking for something.

"Forget to turn in a paper?" Ruby asked, making her way to the opposite side of the desk and picking up a small bottle Kai set on the desk as she dug through the drawer. It was filled with tiny white shards. Bone, maybe.

"Something like that."

Ruby ground her teeth. Kai was keeping something from her.

Kai opened the bottom drawer, and her eyebrows rose. When she straightened, she was holding a large scroll of fading old parchment. She unfurled it on the desk, revealing what looked like architectural plans. She stared at the diagram, her green eyes flicking over every line.

"Is that the layout of the inner sanctum?" Ruby asked,

moving to peer over her head. She'd recognized the rough drawing of a ward at the center, a sort of magical trap. The only place she had seen a ward like that was in the vault in the headmage's office, the inner sanctum.

"I'm not sure," Kai said as she turned away from the diagram, her tone high and disinterested. That made Ruby pause. She had known Kai for a little over six months, and the younger woman was curious by nature. If that was a diagram of the headmage's inner sanctum, where all the most powerful, dangerous, and rare artifacts at Valwen were housed, Kai wouldn't just ignore it. Something told Ruby that her disinterest was feigned. But why would she hide that from her?

"I am fairly certain that it is," Ruby pressed, leaning around her short, blonde friend to examine the parchment. She reached out to press a finger to the pentagram in the middle, marking the heart of the inner sanctum, but Kai snatched her wrist before she could touch the drawing.

"Are you crazy?" she snapped, all indifference forgotten. "What if the paper is hexed?"

"Do you really think Professor Morel would hex something that a student could find so easily? Besides, you've already touched the scroll. If it were hexed, it would have triggered."

Kai didn't argue, instead staring at the ward. "What do you think is—?"

The study door slammed open, making both women jump. In a flash, the scroll was rolled back up and behind Kai's back.

"Miss Valestris! Miss Soumarei! What in the name of all the gods are you doing in my office at this time of night?!"

Ruby started, dropping the jar in her hands. It shattered, the contents spilling out all over the stone floor. A firm hand gripped her arm and spun her around, bringing her face to face with an older man, his gray hair receding from his temples. The man was tall and skeletal, with cheekbones sharp enough to cut parchment and cold, pale-green eyes. Normally, his face was as pale as the rest of him, but tonight, it was flushed red in anger.

Professor Morel.

"Ah, Professor," Kai managed to get out. Ruby saw out of the corner of her eye that her friend had dropped the scroll back into the drawer behind her back so the professor wouldn't see it. Then she raised her hands in a placating manner. "What are you doing up so late? It's not good for your health."

"I will ask you one more time." The professor's face looked thunderous. "What are you doing in my office, and why are you going through my desk?"

Ruby shrank back from the man, but Kai plowed on as if this were just any ordinary conversation. "I realized that I made a mistake on my paper. I hoped to find my essay and fix it before you started grading, but I couldn't find it."

Morel's expression grew darker. He didn't believe her for one second. "Miss Valestris," he began, turning his glare to Ruby. "Why are *you* here?"

"Helping, of course," she said, trying to sound as blasé as Kai but failing miserably. She just sounded meek and awkward. "I would hate for my friend to receive a low mark."

If it were possible, Morel's face reddened further. "You are to be a duchess! You would do well not to associate yourself with people of undesirable status."

Ruby blustered, but Kai threw her a don't-rise-to-the-bait look. The young noblewoman clenched her jaw shut.

"Out! Both of you!" He moved a step to the side to allow the women to exit the room, following them out and shutting and locking the door behind him.

"We are going straight to the headmage," the professor

growled, prodding the women in the back. "I would have expected something like this from Soumarei but not from you, Miss Valestris. Did she talk you into this? Threaten you?"

Ruby felt a flush creeping up her neck. The only reason the professor was suggesting that was because Ruby was of noble birth and engaged to a duke, and Kai was a commoner.

"No, it was my idea," she said defiantly. The professor was behind her, so she couldn't see his face, but she heard his scoff.

"There's no need to protect her," he cooed in amusement. "After this, I'd be surprised if she didn't get expelled."

"You know I'm right here?" Kai growled, glancing over her shoulder. "I can hear you, if your eyesight is so bad that you can't tell who you're pushing along."

Professor Morel cuffed the back of Kai's head. Ruby wanted to turn around and punch him in the face. He would have never dared to do that to one of the noble students. What made him think he could abuse the common-born ones instead?

They made the trip up two floors and to the headmage's office in silence, Professor Morel breathing down their necks. The women didn't dare speak. Ruby didn't know what would happen to them, but if he got the rash from the poison ivy now, they would know exactly who had switched the herbs.

They reached a large door with an intricate design inlaid in gold adorning the wood. The lines all coalesced in the center, forming a pentagram with the dragon of the Andrean Empire in the middle. The symbol of Valwen and the headmage's office.

Professor Morel stepped in front of them and loudly rapped three times on the door.

"Maybe he's asleep," Kai said after a minute went by with

no answer. "Oh well, we'll have to take our punishments in the morning."

"Don't move," the professor growled, throwing Kai a scathing look over his shoulder. He knocked again, more vigorously this time.

After another thirty seconds or so, there was a soft click, and the door creaked open to reveal a short, aging man with gray streaking his once-black hair. The man was Theodore Marcovici, the headmage of Valwen. The older professor was a man of renown. He had been the court mage to the previous emperor and was considered to be the person to go to for all questions about the arcane. He was a man Ruby greatly respected, even though he'd had a personal friendship with her fiancé. Professor Marcovici always seemed kind, which was more than she could say for many of the people at Valwen.

"What is going on here?" Marcovici asked, looking down at the two women. "Petar, why are you knocking on my door so late?"

"I found these two breaking into my office mere minutes ago, Headmage," Professor Morel said with a disdainful sniff. "I believe that Miss Soumarei has dragged Miss Valestris into whatever scheme she had been planning.

"That's not what—"

Ruby's breath came out in a huff of expended air as Kai elbowed her in the side. The young noblewoman glared at her friend and rubbed her side as it throbbed in pain.

"I'm sorry, Professor," Kai said, looking down at her feet and adopting an expression of chastisement. "It was just a prank. Ruby came along to make sure I didn't do anything too egregious and get myself in trouble. Please don't punish her."

Ruby stared at her. What was she saying? The idea had been Ruby's all along!

The headmage surveyed both women. He sighed and shook his head, then turned back to Professor Morel. "I will deal with Miss Soumarei, Petar. Miss Valestris, please go back to your room. You are dismissed."

Ruby opened her mouth to argue, but while the teacher's eyes were on her, Kai shook her head. The young noblewoman had to bite back her retort before it left her lips. Clenching her jaw, she dipped into as graceful a curtsey as she could manage, shaking with anger as she was.

As she turned from them, she caught the triumphant look on Petar Morel's face. It disgusted her.

She was halfway down the corridor when Ruby heard Kai speak.

"I have something I need to tell Ruby, Professor Marcovici. Please. I won't run off."

"Very well, but make it quick, Miss Soumarei."

"Ruby, wait!" Kai called as she bounded down the hall.

But Ruby was angry, and when Kai caught up to her, she whirled on her friend. "Why did you do that?" she snapped. "Why did you take all the blame yourself?"

"Don't worry about me. I'll be all right," she said with a grin. "I'll probably just be scrubbing pots for a week."

"It does not matter. I should be scrubbing pots with you. It was *my* idea."

Kai sighed. "Ruby, they would have never let you scrub pots. You heard Morel. *You're a future duchess!*" she said, imitating the professor's nasally voice. "It was only ever going to be me scrubbing pots. You might have gotten lines, but that's about it."

"That is not the point, Kai!" she hissed, trying not to let her voice carry to the professors who were waiting for Kai to return. "It is not right for them to think you are the mastermind just because you were born into a lower status than me!"

"That's how the world works, Ruby. We don't get to dictate what society thinks is right and wrong." Kai looked back over her shoulder. "As much as we might want to." When she faced Ruby again, she had a strange, resigned expression. "I'll see you… later."

Ruby couldn't explain it, but the look on Kai's face scared her more than the wrath of their teachers. "We have class at nine tomorrow."

"I know."

"I will see you in the morning, yes?"

"Of course. Good night, Ruby."

Fear clutched at Ruby's stomach as Kai turned back to the headmage's office. Ruby stared down the corridor for a few seconds before turning around and heading back to her room. She took a deep breath and rubbed her arms, trying to ward off the sudden chill and still her racing thoughts. *I will see Kai in the morning*, she told herself.

Even after she reached her room and started undressing and preparing herself for bed, she couldn't stop thinking about the look of resignation on Kai's face as she bid her goodnight.

Why had her words sounded like a "goodbye?"

CHAPTER 2

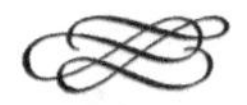

*Y*ells echoed off the stone walls and resounded throughout the halls of the old castle as the night turned stormy. Kai gripped the windowsill, her knuckles white, as she hung six stories over the castle grounds. Those shouts had been for her, rousing the other guards and commanding that everyone locate the young woman who had infiltrated the inner sanctum and stolen the headmaster's treasured key.

Even in her precarious situation, she smiled to herself. It hadn't been difficult to bypass the old man's safeguards—especially after finding that parchment drawing in Professor Morel's desk. No one suspected that a student, hidden among the new wave of enrolled for the autumn term, was a spy. They'd even taught her some valuable tricks that she'd employed to steal the headmaster's most protected posses-sion. Traps of magic and fire had awaited her, but grounding out the power in such things was one of her specialties. The old wizard really was losing his touch.

She'd be able to collect her fee a whole two months early and would now get as far from this place as possible. Maybe she'd go south to Langard. Langard was known for its temperate climate and inviting landscape. That sounded like a nice change.

Her stomach gave an uncomfortable twinge, and sadness gripped her heart, but she banished the feeling, focusing on the task at hand. The wind had begun to pick up, and the sharp scent of ozone stung her nose, foretelling the approaching storm. Even though she had a decent grip in her current position, if it began to rain, it would become slippery and dangerous. She needed to get to the ground floor before that happened.

Kai pulled her legs up and out of view of the window beneath her. Her shoes found purchase in the cracks between the stone, and she slowly began her climb down to the next row of windows. A second later, she heard a door slam shut and male voices arguing. She paused to listen to what they were saying. It might come in handy.

"—how could this happen?" the deeper of the two voices asked. "How did they get past the wards?"

"Who was it?" the second voice asked, and she recognized the speaker. It was the history professor, an ancient Andrean man by the name of Harold Trellis. She could almost imagine the old man intertwining his long fingers and folding his hands in front of him as he spoke. "Did the guards outside see anyone? They haven't—"

Distant thunder rumbled, drowning out the rest of the conversation as the wind ruffled Kai's hair.

Her grin widened as she continued shuffling along the wall. It seemed they still didn't know that the thief had been one of their precious students. Not many people tried to steal from Valwen College.

Valwen—also referred to as *the* Academy—was where nobles sent their sons and daughters who showed magical aptitude for learning. For the common folk, going to Valwen was normally out of reach. Only the nobility could afford the tuition rates that the college charged.

But it wasn't *all* nobles. The empire sponsored and sent people to Valwen who they deemed would make excellent court mages, learning alongside the nobles they would eventually serve. It created an eclectic mix of students and a clear divide between the haves and the have-nots. There was no official difference in what was taught to the two groups, and many of their classes were integrated, but the teachers seemed to favor the students with powerful connections over those of low birth. Go figure.

Kai used some of her magic to grip the stone better, drawing in power from the electrically charged air dancing on her skin to fuel her spell. Her fingers found purchase where they otherwise should not have, and she made a slow but steady climb down and to the right, to another window ten feet away from her previous position.

This descent had not been part of her escape plan, so she didn't know whose window this was, but it would belong to a student. Students occupied the third through fifth floors on this side of the castle. The room was dark inside. With any luck, its occupant was still asleep.

Kai placed one foot on the sill and then another, holding her arms out to her sides, trying to use them for balance. She cautiously braced herself in the small space as she reached into her pocket and pulled out a little metal hook, like one that would be used to crochet. With a steady hand, she carefully slipped it into the space between the window and the frame, lifting the latch that locked the panes of glass together.

A sudden burst of wind pushed Kai into the window, throwing her off balance and making her fall forward. She tumbled as the panes parted, and sprawled on the floor, the windows banging sharply on the wall as they rebounded off the stone and slammed closed again. It was a good thing that the glass was enchanted. Otherwise, it would have shattered.

Kai pushed herself into a crouch almost instantly. The dim glow of embers in the hearth allowed her to see her surroundings. On instinct, she drew the small silver dagger she kept in her right boot, her eyes scanning the dark room around her for any sign of a threat. There was the outline of a vanity, dresser, wardrobe, two chairs by the fireplace, and a four-poster bed, all standard issue in the rooms of the nobles. The plush rug had cushioned Kai's fall, and a dressing gown lay over one of the chairs. Two trunks sat in one corner, and while she couldn't read the name inscribed on the metal latch in the darkness, she recognized the coat of arms with the depiction of a horned elk embossed in the leather. Her eyes settled on the form stirring from her slumber in the four-poster bed, and her heart sank.

"Kai? Is that you?" A spark of magic filled the air, and an oil lamp sputtered to life, revealing the confused and tired face of Ruby.

If Kai looked like an underfed tomboy—not her words—with her straw-colored hair, button nose, and green eyes, Ruby was a lady in every sense of the word. The young woman was elegant and dignified, beautiful and refined. She was tall for a woman and well-proportioned, whereas Kai was short and skinny. She had long, silky, dark-brown hair, a cupid's bow of a mouth, and eyes the blue of a clear summer sky.

They couldn't have been more different.

There was also the fact that Ruby was rich. She was from house Valestris, and her father was a baron. Her house was not of particularly high standing, a baron was nowhere near the top of the social ladder, but her engagement made up for that in the eyes of her peers.

Ruby was engaged to Mikel Belmont, the Duke of

Ayrilon, and had been since she was ten years old. From Kai's experience, women who were in love talked about the object of their affections with gentle voices and knowing smiles, punctuated by long-suffering sighs, but she suspected that the daughter of house Valestris was not fond of her fiancé. Ruby didn't talk about the duke at all. She had told Kai that it was an arranged marriage, something her parents and his had put together when she was a child, and that was all she would say on the matter. That meant that she'd been engaged for almost thirteen years—an inconceivable about of time to Kai.

Maybe Kai was reading too much into it, but she suspected that the duke had hurt or offended Ruby in some way, and, unable to go against the wishes of her family, the young noblewoman had resigned herself to her fate as his wife. The thought made Kai sick to her stomach. She would have never been able to accept other people deciding her future.

Despite all of that, Ruby was Kai's friend. Unlike the other nobles that attended the Academy, she wasn't stuck up and rude to the people who were of a lower station than her. The other men and women of standing mostly pretended the commoners didn't exist or treated them no differently than they would a member of the staff, there to serve them. Where the other nobles only pretended to be generous and caring, Ruby actually was.

When Kai had first arrived at Valwen, some of the other nobles had decided it was their mission to make her life hell. Their reasoning was equally idiotic, saying that she didn't deserve to be there since she was of low birth, even though there were plenty of other students attending Valwen on an imperial scholarship. The ancestry that the Guild had set up for her hadn't been an illustrious one, being of common parentage and an assistant to a scribe. It was better than the truth, that she'd been an urchin on the streets of Valkea, the capital city, when the guild master found her eight years ago.

The ones tormenting her, a lordling by the name of Tobias Sarlus and his cronies, had tried to get her into trouble with the professors. They'd accused her of purposefully destroying the alchemy lab by brewing an unstable potion that had exploded, a sure way to get her punished or even expelled. But Ruby had stepped in, claiming that she had been helping Kai study at the time of the accident. It was an obvious lie, but since no one would dare gainsay a future duchess, Kai didn't get expelled. The mages still made Kai clean the alchemy lab, saying that it would help curb her attitude, which was grossly unfair. Sarlus got off without so much as a warning.

To her surprise, Ruby insisted on helping her. They had never spoken before that incident, and Kai had assumed she was aloof and haughty due to the fact that she didn't socialize much, but she couldn't have been more wrong. When Kai asked why she—a noble lady—had helped her, Ruby simply responded, "Lord Sarlus is an ass."

That was the beginning of their unlikely friendship. Kai liked Ruby a lot. She was naive and pampered, but she was also funny, clever, and had helped Kai out of a few other sticky situations with the teachers and students. Under that dignified facade was someone who liked to play pranks, sneak out after hours, and wasn't afraid of standing up for what she believed was right, even if everyone around her sneered behind her back.

They'd known each other a little over six months, and she felt a connection with her.

But now, she'd have to sever that tie.

"Go back to sleep, Ruby," Kai hissed, her eyes flicking toward the door. There was light coming from under it, but that didn't mean that the faculty was rousing the students. Yet.

Kai crept forward, listening. She couldn't hear anything from the hallway beyond.

"What is the matter?" Ruby asked instead of heeding Kai's words. She pushed her blanket off and rose to her feet, her nightgown brushing the carpet, staring at Kai as though she had grown a second head. "Why are you coming through the window? Did something happen with the headmage?"

So many questions.

When Kai didn't answer right away, Ruby picked up the oil lamp and started to move. "Let me get one of the professors—"

"No!" Kai whispered as she sprang at Ruby, snatching her wrist and pulling her away from the door she'd taken a step toward.

Ruby dropped the oil lamp, her eyes wide in shock. The lantern shattered on the carpet, and the room was plunged into darkness again.

"Don't scream," Kai said, her voice flat. She didn't want to scare Ruby, but she couldn't let her call the guards.

"What is happening, Kai?" Thunder rumbled, and the wind blew the window open again.

It was too dark to see Ruby's expression, but Kai suspected that if she could, it would be one of sheer terror.

This hadn't been in the plan. Kai was supposed to have gotten out of the inner sanctum and gone left in that hallway, which would have led her straight to the stairs. Even if she'd been blocked off there, she could have gone through a window and come back inside through another below it and to a different hallway that also had a set of servants' stairs, evading the guards easily.

But that wasn't what happened. After Kai had knocked out the headmage, she'd stolen the key and gotten out of the inner sanctum, only to run straight into a professor and six guards in the corridor, so she'd had to run in the opposite direction and take a different window than she'd planned. One that had been closest to the student quarters. The window could have belonged to any student, but of course she just *had* to break into the room of the one person she'd hoped not to meet again tonight. Hurting Ruby was the last thing she wanted to do.

Kai cursed under her breath and let go of Ruby's arm, slipping the dagger back into her boot. "Sit," she ordered, and her frightened friend obeyed without a word. Kai waved a hand and concentrated, making the shattered pieces of glass reform. It took an effort. Kai was better at breaking things with her gift than fixing them. She picked up the oil lamp and relit the wick with her magic, then set it on the table and turned back to Ruby, her hands on her hips.

Ruby's blue eyes were wide, and her hair was mussed, dark brown strands sticking out of her loose braid. It had only been two hours since they'd parted, but it was clear that she had been fast asleep. Jewels sparkled at her ears and from a pendant around her neck, items that were small and simple enough to be worn comfortably while asleep. Even roused from slumber, she was still pretty. Her cheeks were flushed, and she fidgeted with the hem of her sleeve, a nervous gesture. Her confused look was even more endearing. It made Kai want to laugh.

"Don't look at me like that," Kai snapped, trying not to smile. Ruby immediately averted her eyes, which only served to annoy Kai. "Don't just do what someone tells you, Ruby!" she said hotly. "What if I actually wanted to hurt you?"

"Do you want me to follow your orders or not?" Ruby shot back and crossed her arms over her chest, the nervousness in her body language replaced with anger. There she was, the real Ruby, not the good little girl that everyone else saw. "You are the one who burst through my window in the middle of the night like a mad woman. What kind of mess have you gotten yourself into that you cannot get back out of, Kai?"

"You know, I would be hurt by your accusations, if you weren't right." Kai glanced at the bedroom door again. She thought she heard voices beyond and quieted her own. "I'm leaving here tonight, and I can't be seen by anyone else."

Ruby blinked at her, almost as if she didn't believe what she was hearing. Her lips moved, but it took her a few moments to form words. "Why? Where are you going?" She looked down at her hands briefly and then back up to Kai's face. Her brows furrowed. "Do you have to?"

Oh, hells. Kai was a guild thief and a good one, so why was it that when she looked at Ruby, she felt like she was kicking a wounded animal? More important, why did she care? Ruby was one of the nobility, one of the people who had held her in scorn all her life, keeping her down and oppressing the people around her. Kai had nothing, while this woman before her had everything. Kai's guild had gotten her into Valwen. This was just supposed to be a job. So why did she care about one stupid noblewoman, a future duchess at that?

But she did care, even if it was idiotic. It felt wrong to just leave her here, alone. Ruby had other "friends," if you could call the conniving ranks of young lords and ladies anything but rivals, but there was no one else for her to confide in. She wasn't close to her parents, and though the duke sent her gifts every few weeks, she tossed most of them into her luggage, never to be brought out again. Though they hadn't known each other that long, Kai knew that she was the closest thing Ruby had to someone who cared about her.

It was Kai's fault. She wasn't supposed to get attached, but she had, and now, she had to leave her behind.

Then Kai had an idea, and she immediately knew it was a stupid one.

"Come with me," Kai said before she could think about the words. "Don't you want to live your life on your own terms instead of the way everyone else has laid out for you? Don't you want to be free, Ruby?"

If Ruby had looked shocked before, her look now was nothing short of incredulous. "Are you seriously suggesting that I abandon Valwen? What about my studies? My obligations?"

My marriage to the duke. Kai could almost hear those words swimming in Ruby's head. She knew that was what Ruby was thinking. Responsibility. Honor. It was all the nobility ever talked about.

Kai opened her mouth to speak, but shut it, her attention being drawn to the door. There were voices right outside the bedroom this time. Kai cursed, stepping over to it and checking that the lock was firmly in place. It wouldn't keep the guards out for long, not when any professor could unlock the door with magic.

She turned back to Ruby. "Look, if you want to continue being a good little girl and doing whatever mommy, daddy, and the duke say, then stay here. But I know you, Ruby, and I know that you would rather do anything other than marry the man you are betrothed to. That's why you came to Valwen in the first place, isn't it? To postpone the wedding for a few years? You don't want to be his wife, but you're too afraid to do anything about it."

While she talked, Kai made her way over to the window and looked down. They were on the fourth floor, and it was hard to see the ground in the darkness, but there should only be grass and maybe a few lavender bushes below. Her plan had her slipping out through the kitchens, but there was no way she could do that now. In her line of work, one needed backup plans for their backup plans.

Pulling her travel pack off her shoulder, Kai started rooting around in it. She hadn't wanted to use up all her magic before she'd even left the castle grounds, but she didn't see another way of escaping now. She would have to rely on her wits instead of her power to get through the Wytchwood.

"You should think very hard, Ruby. I'm offering you a chance at freedom. No more titles, no more duties, and no more betrothal. Just you and me and whatever adventure we can find." Kai pulled out a length of rope and a feather. Tying one end of the rope to the bedpost, she gave it a sharp tug to ensure it was secure.

Ruby was silent, thinking, and Kai worked quickly, sensing her friend was going through an internal struggle, one that would decide her future. Kai gave her time to think, but she couldn't wait long. The voices outside the door were growing louder and more numerous. It seemed the students were finally waking up to the commotion. Kai opened the window again. The night air was still charged with the coming storm, but it seemed less intense than before. Maybe the wind had changed, and they would not see the rain this night. That would be ideal for their escape.

As she stared down into the darkness below, a chill went up her spine. If she was wrong about what was below them…

There was no time for doubts. Kai stepped onto the sill, the rope in one hand and the feather in the other. Breathing deeply, she drew energy from within herself to fuel her spell and concentrated. Kai opened her palm, and the feather dissolved into tiny motes of blue light that swirled above her hand. The casting was simple. Using the feather as a focus, she would use her magic to make herself lighter, which in turn would make it easier to climb down.

She held the spell there, the magic swirling above her

fingers, and gazed at Ruby again. "You have a choice. Take your fate into your own hands."

Ruby looked back at the door and to Kai again. She looked stricken, torn between the life she was supposed to lead and the life that she wanted. This was the most important decision that she would ever make, and she only had a few seconds more in which to decide.

In a move that surprised even Kai, Ruby took a step toward her, then another, and then she was stepping up onto the stone next to her.

Kai grinned. Excitement coursed through her veins, and she felt energized by it. She didn't need to say goodbye to her friend at all. Ruby was coming with her.

"Are you ready?" Kai asked, holding the hand with the blue motes out to her.

Ruby looked around the room again, and her expression changed from wry amusement to one of grim determination. The dim blue glow of Kai's spell enhanced the shadows around her face, making her seem older than her years. Then Ruby took Kai's hand, amplifying the spell with her own magic until the light from the motes was almost blinding, and stepped off the windowsill.

CHAPTER 3

In hindsight, this was a bad idea. Ruby had known that when she'd taken Kai's outstretched hand and led them down into the dark night that awaited. Valwen had been alive with guards and soldiers looking for Kai, and they had only been able to get off the castle grounds without getting caught due to Ruby's magic covering them in shadow and Kai's quick thinking. The thrill that Ruby had felt during their escape had worn off during the long trek through the woods in the pitch-black night. Branches and low brush grabbed and tore at her nightgown, and she wished she had thought to put on proper shoes instead of her slippers. Her toes were so cold that she could barely feel them.

What had she been thinking? She was a woman of noble birth and had no experience whatsoever navigating the outdoors. Had she expected them to take off in a carriage bound for lands outside of Mikel's influence?

What concerned her most was that even if she'd known that she would be walking through the Wytchwood in the pitch-black night, shivering and longing for a fire, she would have taken the same action. Had she taken leave of her senses?

"Do you know where we are going?" Ruby asked for what must have been the hundredth time that night. "I am not sure how much farther I can walk in these conditions."

"For the *millionth* time," Kai began crossly, the lantern light making her frown and furrowed brows much deeper than they actually were, "we're heading in the right direction, and you'll keep walking if you don't want the Academy mages to find us." She adjusted one of the straps on her traveling pack and looked around. "Dammit. At least, I think we are still on the right path."

"You think? You just said we were going in the right direction."

Kai reached into her pocket and pulled out a small compass in a brass housing and held it up to the light of her lantern. "It's too dark to tell, but we are still heading to the northeast. It will be easier to pinpoint our exact location once the sun rises."

That wouldn't be long from now, Ruby hoped. The air had that pre-dawn feeling to it, when the world went quiet and still. Their breath fogged out in front of them in the chilly early morning air, and Ruby shivered, rubbing her arms with her hands. The storm that had been brewing earlier that night still had not reached them. The sounds of rumbling thunder faded, and she hoped that meant that it would miss them entirely. She didn't know if she would survive if it started raining.

Kai looked back at her and cursed again. "I'm an idiot. I should have told you to grab your things or at least a change of clothes." She unfastened the cloak around her neck and held it out to Ruby, revealing the belt of weapons she had donned once they'd reached the safety of the trees. Two large daggers hung from one side and a sword from the other. "Here, use this."

Ruby took the cloak gratefully and put it on. "It's not as if we had a lot of time. I doubt I would have been able to grab much of anything before they figured out you were in my room." She sighed as the remnants of Kai's body heat warmed her. "What did you do that made the guards chase after you?"

Kai didn't answer her right away, picking her way through the brush.

"I'll tell you once we get somewhere safe," she said after a time, then left it at that.

"It sounded like the whole castle was being roused," Ruby said thoughtfully. She wanted to ask Kai again, to pick at the subject until her friend told her what was going on, but by Kai's uncertain tone, Ruby had the feeling that she needed to let Kai tell her in her own time, as annoying as that was. "They will know that I am with you. My door would have been the only one to remain closed."

Kai grimaced. "It was stupid of me to ask you to come, but I don't regret it. The farther we get from Valwen, the more certain I am that it was the right thing to do. We just need to get you a change of clothes the first chance we get." Glancing down, Kai winced. "And shoes. I'm sorry, Ruby. I don't have a spare set, and I doubt they would fit you anyway."

Ruby managed a small smile. "Are you saying that I have large feet?"

Kai rolled her eyes and continued forward, holding back a branch as she passed. It occurred to Ruby that she was picking the path that had the least amount of brush and debris for them to push through, and for that, she was grateful. The less she had to wade through the foliage, the better for her decency.

They continued walking for some time in silence, Kai carefully watching their footing and checking the compass every so often while Ruby followed clumsily after her. With the added warmth provided by the cloak, Ruby's eyes began to grow heavy. Her feet were numb with the cold, and she couldn't feel much from them anymore. She yawned. Were they going to walk until dawn?

She didn't notice when Kai stopped, and trudged right into her.

Ruby gasped and opened her mouth to apologize, but Kai placed a hand over it before she could speak. Quickly crouching down behind a bush with large, spikey leaves, she pulled Ruby in beside her.

"I think I see a light ahead. Maybe a campfire," Kai said under her breath. "We should be careful. This part of the forest isn't traveled much. So who knows what we'll find? It could just be a hunter, but it could be a group of bandits or outlaws. Maybe you should get your best attack spell ready." Kai extinguished her lantern, then reached down and pulled a dagger from the belt at her waist, and pressed a finger to her lips, indicating for Ruby to be quiet.

For her part, Ruby mentally went through the offensive spells she'd practiced back at the Academy. They taught these spells to all the students, but no one had really used any of them in earnest. Why would they? Most of the students were the sons and daughters of the country's nobility and were unlikely to ever experience a real fight. Even so, she knew a few that she thought would aid them if it came to that. She exhaled slowly through her nose, reaching down into herself, and focused on bringing forth the energy that she needed to fuel her spells.

In the darkness, Kai nodded at her, then turned back to the situation at hand and moved forward, still in a crouch.

She was like a shadow in the night, making no sound. Her footsteps were light, and each movement was sure, as if she had practiced it so often that it had become second nature. Ruby couldn't emulate Kai's grace and ability, but she did her best to step in the same places she had and move in the same way as they approached the flickering firelight.

They crept forward, and the trees thinned as they entered a small clearing free of brush and roots.

As Kai had predicted, there was a campfire burning in the center, where the long grass had been cut back. A steaming pot hung by a hook from a metal contraption placed over the fire, and what looked like several large leather bags were stacked neatly a few feet from it.

One of the largest horses Ruby had ever seen grazed on the uncut grass not too far away. It was hard to tell what color it was in the firelight, but it seemed to almost shimmer in the darkness. Its mane and tail were thick and full, and long hair almost covered its hooves. It was a beautiful creature, with a dappled coat and a muscular body.

There was a saddle resting on a rock not too far from where the horse grazed, but the rider was nowhere to be seen. Could this person have been a hunter like Kai had suggested? It seemed unlikely that it was some lone bandit. From what she had read of them in stories, they were a rough and uncouth bunch and would never have a horse like that.

Seeing that the clearing was empty of the owner of the horse and supplies, Kai relaxed her stance and looked around, then sidled over to the fire and peered into the pot. With one hand, she waved Ruby forward while she sheathed her dagger with the other.

Ruby joined her and inhaled deeply, smelling rosemary and garlic. It made her mouth water. Having never been allowed to observe the cooks in the kitchen back home, she knew nothing of the process of making food edible, but even she could tell that this was the handiwork of an expert.

Kai looked around again, then stepped over to the leather bags, shifting them around as she looked through them.

"Perhaps we should wait for the owner to return. I cannot imagine they would be gone long, with their food cooking." Ruby said, staying close to the fire. The heat it provided felt heavenly, and she reached out her hands to warm them.

"It's weird that someone would be camping all the way out here," Kai said as she opened and dug through the second bag, ignoring Ruby's comment about waiting. "I mean, there are no towns nearby—besides the one outside Valwen—and those villagers are too scared to come into the forest at night." She pulled back a blanket, revealing another large bag and a bow with a quiver of arrows. Kai lifted the flaps of the bag and peered into it. "There are a lot of provisions here. I don't think this person lives in the town. If I had to guess, this camp was built by one of those people who migrate from place to place and live off the land." She straightened, finished with her perusing, and tapped one finger to her bottom lip in thought. "I think I've heard them called *wilders*."

"Yes, that's right," came a male voice from behind them.

Quick as lightning, Kai drew her dagger again, whipping around to face whoever had snuck up on them. There was a flash of steel, and her blade flew across the clearing and into the trees close to where they'd entered from.

The man who had appeared out of the brush took a step to the left, easily dodging Kai's throw as if he'd been expecting it, and the *thunk* of the blade burying itself in a tree echoed throughout the clearing. He wasn't close enough to the fire for Ruby to see him clearly, and the hood of his cloak hid his features in darkness, but it hung open, and she could see that he wore a loose-fitting shirt, a belt with a scabbard, and dark breeches. He was at least twenty feet away, and from that distance, he wouldn't have been intimidating, save for what was in his hands.

He raised the rifle and pointed the firearm at Kai's chest.

Kai froze. She'd been in the middle of drawing the sword on the other side of her belt, but at the threat of the rifle, she released the hilt of her weapon and raised her hands in the air, palms out, with an angry and defeated look on her face.

The whole altercation had been only a few seconds, and Ruby had been too stunned to react. She'd lost her focus on her magic. She could have called on it again, but if this man was a mage, he would be able to sense it, and she didn't dare do anything that would put her friend in danger.

The cloaked figure stepped closer to them. "Who are you, and what are you doing here?" he demanded, his voice low and gruff.

Kai narrowed her eyes, hands still above her head. "We are only travelers passing through. We saw your fire and were merely waiting for you to return."

"Is that why you snuck in and started rifling through my supplies?" he snapped back. "Those are the actions of a thief, not a traveler. Are you thieves?" The barrel of the gun never wavered.

"Please, sir," Ruby started talking before Kai could answer him. Kai was not one to control her temper, and this situation called for diplomacy, not more violence and threats. "She speaks the truth. We have been walking the forest all night, and the sight of your camp was a relief to our tired bodies. It was never our intention to cause you trouble, and we will leave if you insist upon it."

His head turned toward her, and she could feel his scrutinizing gaze. The rifle stayed pointed at Kai, but he took a few steps closer to Ruby, presumably to get a better look at her. She held her head high, as one of her rank should. Intimidating as this unknown man was, she would not let him see her tremble. He was only a dozen feet away now, and the light from the fire at her back gave her a glimpse of a sharp nose and dark eyes under the hood of his cloak.

"Who are you?" he asked her, and there was confusion in his voice.

"As I said," Kai broke in with a growl. "We are just passing through."

As if a spell had been broken, he turned away from Ruby and back to Kai. "Where are you going then? There are no roads through this forest, and the closest town is back in the opposite direction from where you came."

Kai lifted her chin in defiance. "We are going to Issalden."

"It would be faster and safer to go back to Helwyd and take the road from there. Why are you cutting through the Wytchwood to get to Issalden?"

"We have our reasons," Kai replied. "I know what I'm doing."

The man scoffed, clearly doubting her words. He then glanced back at Ruby, seeming to consider her. Reluctantly, he pointed the rifle at the ground near Kai's feet, but there was no mistaking the continued threat. It would take less than a second for him to lift it to a more vital area and shoot.

Ruby relaxed a little. At least he wasn't pointing the firearm directly at Kai anymore. Maybe they could get out of this in one piece. Kai lowered her hands, still watching the wilder.

"Are you all right, miss?" the man asked, and it took Ruby a moment to realize that he was talking to her. Concern was heavy in his voice. "Did this one force you into the woods?"

"*Excuse me?*" Kai asked indignantly. Her hand twitched, and Ruby thought she might go for another one of her daggers. "Why would you assume that I kidnapped her?"

The wilder turned an angry look on her. "Because,

unlike you, she is out here in little more than a night dress, cloak, and slippers, which, I might add, have been ripped almost to shreds. How could someone with no ill intentions convince her to walk through the forest in such conditions?"

Ruby looked down at her feet. The man was right. The cold had not only numbed her feet but masked any pain she'd been feeling. In the firelight, she could see that the delicate fabric had been ripped in many places and the once pristine white silk was stained with dirt and blood. Her blood. She didn't want to know what her feet looked like under that mess.

"Ruby," Kai began, bringing her focus back to the conversation at hand, "tell the nice psychopath that you are not here under duress." Kai's eyes never left the weapon pointed at her feet.

"I have not been abducted," Ruby said immediately, her gaze shifting to the man with the rifle. "I chose to go with her. You need not worry about my safety."

"In your night clothes?" he asked doubtfully.

Ruby felt her cheeks warm. "I did not really think that part through. It was sort of a spur-of-the-moment decision, as they say."

He gave her a look like she was an idiot, and despite her resolve not to show fear, she shrank a little under that gaze. She agreed with his unspoken assessment of her.

"You do not have to leave," he said after a long and tense pause. "I'm willing to share my food and fire, so long as you behave as guests and offer me no threat."

It was Kai's turn to scoff. She crossed her arms over her chest, glaring at the man. "You ask that after pointing your own weapon at me?"

"If I remember correctly, it was you who attacked me with your dagger first," he said, then lifted the rifle into a relaxed position on his shoulder and took a few more steps toward them and into the light of the campfire.

The wilder was tall, just over six feet from the looks of it. His face lacked the roundness of youth and there were tiny lines around his eyes that were accentuated by the shadows, making Ruby put his age closer to thirty than twenty, and sported a beard that was trimmed short. The man pulled the hood of his cloak back and shook out dark hair that brushed his shoulders. There was a smudge of dirt on his cheek. His hazel eyes were focused on Ruby, and she shivered. Those eyes reminded her a little of Mikel's. He had that same intense gaze.

"My name is Serik Belin, and as your companion guessed, I'm a wilder. I live out here in the Wytchwood."

"I am Ruby," she left off her last name. It was unlikely that the wilder had heard of her family and even less likely that he would recognize it, but on the off chance he did, it didn't seem prudent to inform him that she was the baron's daughter. "And this is Kai. It is a pleasure to meet you, Serik," she said with a graceful nod that was so ingrained in her that it was automatic.

The side of Serik's mouth twitched up in a smirk, and Ruby felt herself blush. She was used to speaking and acting properly when addressed. If she wanted to blend in when they reached Issalden she would have to work on that.

"The Wytchwood is a dangerous place, Miss Ruby. You really should go back to Helwyd." He brushed past them and over to the fire, looking into the pot hanging over it and giving it a quick stir with a wooden spoon that had been lying on a rock nearby. "It's easy to get turned around here. You'll need a guide that knows these trees well."

Kai had moved closer to Ruby while Serik spoke. She'd opened her mouth to say something to her, but at the wilder's words, she turned her eyes to him. "And let me guess. You are just such a guide who can get us to Issalden safely?" Her tone was not friendly.

He chuckled, stirring the contents of the pot again, and glanced at Ruby, making a point to eye her from head to toe. "You're obviously not prepared for the week-long journey through rough terrain and the cold weather."

There was no arguing with that. Kai may have had the supplies to make the trip alone, but now that Ruby was with her, they would need help.

Kai must have come to the same conclusion as she didn't immediately snap at the wilder. "If we were to take you on as our guide, how much would you be charging us for your 'help'?" she asked the large man, her eyes narrowed.

Setting the spoon back on the rock, Serik turned away from the bubbling contents of the pot. His head tilted as he thought it over, gazing first at Kai, then at Ruby. "Twenty crests should suffice."

Kai's eyes bulged, and her mouth fell open. "Are you joking?! Twenty crests for an escort? Why don't you just gut us and steal everything we have right now and be done with it?"

Ruby stared at Kai, feeling at a loss. She knew what crests were, of course, but she didn't understand how much the coin was worth to those outside of the upper class. Being the largest denomination of money in the empire, she imagined it was valuable. The next coinage down was a mark, which was one-fourth of a crest, and then a bit, which was one-eighth of a mark. The way Kai spoke made it sound as if a single crest was a lot of money, but that had been less than what she'd received in a week's allowance when she was living with the duke. This was just another shortcoming of hers she would need to work through.

"Twenty crests is a *bargain*," Serik continued patiently, as if Kai's outburst didn't bother him, "to guide two young women who just happened to stumble into my camp before dawn out in the middle of nowhere. The closest thing to civilization is Valwen, and I'm going to assume you don't want to go there. Otherwise, you already would have done so." He smiled, and the expression looked sharp. "So, you're desperate, and Issalden is days out of my way. That adds to the price. If you want to proceed on your own, feel free. I'll tell the mages where to find your bodies."

"You expect us to trust someone we just randomly met in the woods?" Kai argued.

"I don't think you have a choice if you want to get to Issalden safely."

The look on Kai's face indicated that she was close to violence, but Ruby put a hand on her arm.

"It is all right," she said and reached up to her ears. Kai was in this situation because of her, so the least she could do was pay for the wilder's services. She unfastened her earrings and held them out to Serik. "Will this be an adequate form of payment?"

The man's features softened considerably as he took the earrings from her, examining them in the firelight.

"I will admit," Ruby began, watching the wilder as he turned the jewelry over in his palm, "I do not know how much they are worth, but those are diamonds. It should fetch what you are asking, yes?" She glanced at Kai for the last question. Her friend looked like she'd eaten something foul, but she gave Ruby a curt nod.

"Are you sure you want to give these to me?" Serik asked. His eyes assessed her again.

"Yes, if you will escort us to Issalden." Ruby had no sentimental attachment to the earrings. The duke had given them to her during her last break from the Academy. Kai had been right. She did not want to marry Mikel. Leaving Valwen had signaled the end of the engagement, so it felt wrong to keep the jewelry. His necklace was still around her neck, tucked beneath the nightgown. She'd have to get rid of that as well.

Serik made a thoughtful sound and placed the earrings in a pouch on his belt.

"We'll leave at sunrise." Turning away from them, he walked over to the pile of supplies near the fire. "I suggest the two of you eat and get some sleep." He opened one of the bags and dug around for a few seconds, then pulled out a small leather pouch and three wooden bowls. "Miss," his eyes met Ruby's. "Go sit by the fire."

"Why?" she asked, drawing the cloak in closer and eyeing the bag in his hands.

One eyebrow quirked up. "Because you won't be able to walk far on those feet. I need to clean and bandage them so that they don't become infected, or would you like to lose some toes?"

Ruby's lips parted. No one had ever talked to her in such a way. Well, no one besides Kai. All her life, it had always been "yes, miss," or "if you please, miss." She wasn't sure if she should be offended by the casual manner in which he treated her, or if this was common outside of the country estates and sprawling manors she'd been raised in.

Still, she didn't like his tone. Lifting her chin, she said, "And do you know what you are doing? Are you a trained physician as well as a wilder?"

"Just sit and let me tend to your wounds," he said gruffly. Kai took the wooden bowl Serik handed her and spooned some of the food he'd cooked into it. She didn't appear to be bothered by their exchange.

As much as Ruby was loathe to admit it, he was right. She couldn't continue on with her feet in this condition. Letting out a long breath, she gingerly made her way over to the fire and looked around for a decent place to sit. She decided to set the cloak Kai had given her on the ground as padding between her bottom and the grass. It wouldn't do to have her nightgown soaked through before they could find other clothes for her to wear.

Serik watched her, an amused look on his face. "Not used to being out in the wilderness, miss?"

His mirth irritated her. "My name is Ruby, not *miss*," she said as he knelt in the grass next to her. He touched her ankle, lifting her foot gently to get a good look at it in the firelight. Holding the skirt of her nightgown to avoid indecent exposure, she tried to ignore the feel of his skin against hers. "And no, I do not make a habit of wandering around wooded areas in the dark with only my nightclothes." That got a chuckle out of Serik, and she winced as he peeled what remained of her right slipper off her skin and tossed it aside. The cloth was in tatters.

It was a small mercy that she couldn't see how bad her wounds were. The wilder fished a small bottle containing clear liquid out of the bag and uncorked it. The strong smell of alcohol stung Ruby's nose. Most of the damage must have been on the bottom of her foot because Serik poured some of the liquid onto a clean cloth and started dabbing at the skin there.

Ruby sucked in air through her teeth and involuntarily tried to jerk her foot away, but Serik held her firmly. "You'll need to keep still Miss Ruby. It will be over soon."

By the time he finished cleaning and wrapping her feet, there were tears in her eyes, and she was trembling from pain rather than the chill air. Serik gave her a bowl of hot rabbit stew to eat. The fire and the food warmed her body, and it was all she could do not to lay her head down on Kai's cloak and fall asleep. It had been a long and exciting night, and now that she could stop and rest, she was exhausted.

Ruby watched Kai set up her own sleeping arrangements. As she laid out a thick blanket near the fire, she looked over at Ruby and grimaced, then turned to Serik. "Do you have an extra blanket? I hadn't originally packed for two." Red tinged her cheeks as she spoke.

The wilder nodded and pulled a neatly folded wool blanket out from under his supplies. "What would you have done if you hadn't found my camp?"

"Slept in shifts," Kai said simply as she spread out the blanket next to Ruby so she wouldn't have to get up and walk on her bandaged feet.

Ruby frowned as Kai showed her how to tuck the blanket in so that she didn't end up lying directly on the ground. She looked up at her friend, feeling guilty that she was causing her to worry. "I am sorry, Kai. I am going to be a burden to you on this journey, and I should not have come." Ruby knew she was feeling sorry for herself, but she couldn't help it. As much as she longed for her bed back at the school, she didn't regret the decision that she made, but feared that Kai might be regretting the choice to bring her along.

Kai knelt in front of her and put her hands on either side of Ruby's face. "You aren't a burden. It was my idea to ask you to come and not give you any time to think it over. I'll just have to teach you how to survive outside of manors and castles. So don't give up on me, and especially not on yourself. A month from now, you'll be a pro at this." She grinned at her. "Besides, we have the most expensive guide in the empire to show us the way."

Ruby laughed at her words and nodded.

"Now, get some sleep," she said as she stood. "I'll be up for a while to make sure the wilder doesn't try to murder us while we slumber." Kai threw Serik a scathing look. He'd been watching them and just shrugged at her glare.

"It seems a waste to go through the trouble of cleaning and bandaging my wounds if he wanted to murder us." Ruby smiled.

"Maybe he just wants to murder *me*," Kai mused, her expression relaxed. "Sleep, Ruby. I'll keep you safe."

"Thank you, Kai," Ruby murmured as she laid down and wrapped herself in the blanket. It took her a while to find a comfortable position, but she eventually drifted off to sleep listening to the crackling of the campfire.

CHAPTER 4

*S*erik roused them just after sunrise. Every inch of Ruby's body ached from sleeping on the hard ground, and her feet felt tender from the wilder's earlier ministrations. Her magic would help her heal faster and made the chance of infection slim, but she had no experience using healing spells and couldn't mend those wounds with her own powers. Recovery would be faster for her than someone without magical ability, but she'd still have to wait for her wounds to close, just like everyone else.

Kai looked tired, but she was quick to her feet, much quicker than Ruby, and had her things packed up and ready before Ruby had fully awoken. The storm that had been threatening them the previous night had passed, and sunlight sparkled off the fresh morning dew. The daylight revealed the shadowy clearing to be surrounded by tall evergreen trees and dotted with yellow and purple wildflowers. While the morning air was still cold, it was warm for this early in the spring. Ruby hoped that it was a sign that their journey would be a smooth one.

Once they'd eaten what was left of the rabbit from the

night before, Serik started gathering the bags and saddled his horse. Standing at least sixteen hands tall, the magnificent steed was a mare, and in the daylight, Ruby could clearly see her silvery dappled-gray coat with a white mane and tail. She had never seen another horse like her and knew many members of the upper class would have coveted her. Even more astonishing was how well-trained she was. After ignoring their presence the previous night, the mare had trotted right up to Serik when he whistled for her.

"Miss Ruby," Serik began as he finished securing his belongings to the saddle. "You'll ride with me."

Kai had been lying on the grass and snoozing while Serik had been getting ready, but she jumped right up at his words.

"Why?" she asked, her tone bordering on hostile.

"Her feet are still healing, and she has no shoes," he replied in annoyance. He seemed more irritable with Kai than he'd been the night before, and Ruby wondered if they had talked more after she'd fallen asleep.

"I'm asking why you are riding with her. *Your* feet are fine."

"Because you are perfectly capable of walking. And it's *my* horse." They stared at each other, but eventually, Kai scoffed and turned away, shouldering her pack. Ruby approached the gray horse, eyeing it warily. How was she supposed to climb onto *that?*

The wilder murmured an apology, then put his hands on her hips and lifted her onto the horse. She let out a squeak of surprise and grabbed onto the saddle, steadying herself so as not to fall off the other side. Serik helped her get settled before climbing up behind her.

It wasn't proper for a young woman to sit astride wearing only a nightgown, much less with a wilder to her back, so Ruby sat side saddle, one leg bent in front of her. If her mother could have seen her, she would have had a fit. The thought made her smile. Her mother had sought to instill the customs of high society in her daughter from a young age and was so stringent in her teachings that anything less than perfection was unacceptable. To be in such a compromising position as this one, well, Ruby was glad that she would never know of it.

Serik's arms around her kept her position stable, and Ruby tried to keep her body as far from his as possible. The arrangement was awkward enough already without having him lean against her or vice versa. If he thought anything of the way she rode, he said nothing, leaving her the space and her honor. Perhaps they could trust him after all.

With the mare's snow-white mane clutched tightly in her hands, they set out from the clearing. Serik had picked up everything that they used and left the area clean of any debris. The only sign that they'd been there were the ashes from the campfire.

"What is her name?" Ruby asked as she watched one of the horse's ears twitch.

"Dream," he said fondly. "I called her that because her coat looks like starlight, and when the light of the moon hits it, she could have walked straight out of a dream."

"Dream," Ruby repeated, stroking the mare's mane. "That is a good name for her."

"I'm glad you approve."

They rode through most of that day, keeping a slow and steady pace that Kai could easily keep up with. Sunlight filtered in through the branches of the evergreen trees, warming the forest floor, and small woodland critters dashed out of their way as they navigated a path through the Wytch-wood. Through the breaks in the trees, Ruby saw snow-capped mountain peaks poking out in the distance. Recalling a map she'd seen of the area, she knew there were mountains to the north and west of Valwen.

Serik-the-wilder had been a good investment, as he seemed to know where he was going. He would stop every so often to dismount and check the area around them, pulling out a compass much like the one Kai had used the previous night.

He was a good riding companion. The wilder didn't talk much, but the silence between the three of them wasn't awkward. Kai seemed too preoccupied with her hike to keep up any sort of conversation. It gave Ruby time to contemplate what she'd done.

Had she really thrown everything away on a whim? Her family would disown her, and the duke… he would be angry, but she would never see it, and for that, she was grateful. By choosing freedom, she had lost the security that came with being someone of status. She would need to make her own way in the world now, without any aid from her family.

The warmth that Ruby had enjoyed during the early part of the day's ride passed as the sun moved across the sky and clouds began to fill its place. They made camp not long before sunset, choosing another clearing with ample room to spread out. Kai was so tired that she went to sleep immediately. Ruby was not far behind her. Any concerns they had about her situation or Serik's intentions seemed insignificant in the face of their exhaustion. The wilder woke them to eat, and Kai was much more alert, but Ruby went back to sleep soon after.

The next day was easier, but Ruby still hadn't slept well. There was just no comparing the cold, hard ground to the feather beds she was accustomed to. Throughout the day, she caught herself leaning back into the wilder, but he either didn't notice the closeness or didn't mind. As much as she wanted to pay attention to where they were going, the lack of sleep left her tired, sore, and having a hard time sitting straight in the saddle.

"You don't need to be so stiff," Serik said as she tried to adjust her position again. "If you need to rest, we can stop for a while."

"Thank you for your concern, but I am fine. All I have been doing is sitting here." She looked over her shoulder, but he was too close to get a good look at his expression without it being awkward. She didn't like not being able to see his face when he spoke. "Nothing I have done warrants a rest."

"Just because you're not holding the reins doesn't mean you haven't been riding all day," he replied mildly. When she didn't answer him, he chuckled. "You can rest against me if you're feeling tired."

Ruby felt her lips pull up into a smile. "Are you actually concerned for my well-being or are you just trying to get me to lean against you?" she teased.

"I'm afraid you've figured out my plan." He sounded amused with the direction the conversation had turned. "It is very lonely living in the woods by myself."

"How dare you, sir!?" Ruby said in mock outrage. Glancing back at him, she saw the grin tugging at the corner of his mouth. "I did not know that wilders such as yourself would try to trick innocent young women into compromising positions."

"Only the pretty ones," he said in a flat tone that was betrayed by the glint in his eyes.

"So, you think I am pretty?"

Serik laughed.

"Hey!" Kai said, looking up at the two of them, mouth set in a disapproving frown. "No flirting. You don't know who this guy is or why he's living in the Wytchwood, Ruby. He could have been doing anything out here."

"Is she calling me dirty or uncivilized?"

"That is the question, is it not? I would say that it is probably both," Ruby said seriously.

He laughed again, and Kai made a frustrated grunt.

"It's all right, Kai," Ruby said to placate her. "Serik appears thus far to be a trustworthy individual. I am sure he is not going to try to wrest any more wealth from me—which does not exist, if you were curious," she added for the wilder's benefit.

Serik, for his part, made no comment.

Kai was being particularly prickly. Judging by how the sun had already dipped below the canopy of densely packed trees, they had to be stopping soon.

"Are you hungry?" Ruby asked Kai, having another hunch about the reason for her peevishness.

There was a short silence before Kai replied, "Yes."

"My friend gets irritable when she goes without food for too long," Ruby explained to Serik in a low, confiding tone. "It can be quite unpleasant, and it would be best to get something into her stomach before she murders the two of us and eats Dream."

"Ruby! You're terrible!" Kai exclaimed. "Remind me, why did I agree to bring you along?" Despite her tone, she rolled her eyes and tried to hide the smile that threatened her lips.

"Because you love me."

"We'll be stopping at the next clearing," Serik said, looking down at Kai. "I want to get a fire going before the sun sets anyway. There are wolves and other creatures in this part of the forest. A strong campfire will keep them away." He scanned the trees ahead of them. The area was already heavily shadowed, and with dusk fast approaching, it would only become harder to navigate. Branches and leaves swayed in the light breeze, creating a low rustling sound, but nothing else moved that Ruby could see. "We should be coming to one within the next hour. You'll have to hold out until then."

They rode in silence again after that. Ruby thought about what it would be like to see a wolf. Wolves were dangerous, she'd read enough books to know that, but she was more curious than fearful. Were they like big dogs? Would beasts like that approach their group when hunting should be plentiful at this time of year?

"Are you going to tell me why the two of you were out wandering around the Wytchwood in the middle of the night?" Serik asked next to Ruby's ear, startling her out of her thoughts.

His sudden question shouldn't have surprised her. The wilder hadn't asked them many questions up 'til now.

"No, I do not think so," Ruby said, turning her head away. If he was trying to catch her off guard in the hopes that she would reveal something she shouldn't, he was going to be disappointed. Kai hadn't instructed her to keep quiet, but Ruby was pretty sure that Kai wouldn't want her to reveal where they had come from. They had only been traveling with the wilder for three days, and despite her earlier teasing, they didn't know if Serik was trustworthy or not yet.

Though, Kai *had* trusted him enough to have him guide them through the forest. Serik seemed capable, but Ruby wasn't the best judge of that. Her life experiences had been minimal. She'd had more adventures in just the few days since leaving the Academy than in her whole life. Meeting a stranger in the woods. Sleeping outside for the first time. Riding a magnificent horse.

"Even if it helps me get you to Issalden safely?" he asked. His lips were now next to her neck and his breath tickled her skin.

She made a thoughtful "hmm" before continuing. "It really is not any of your business. Perhaps you should sate your curiosity elsewhere."

"You know," Serik began, sounding amused again, "there's quite a mouth on you for a gently bred lady. Didn't your governess teach you better manners?"

Ruby glanced over her shoulder at the wilder. Was he insulting her? "Whatever gave you the idea that I am gently bred? For all you know, I grew up on a farm."

Kai snorted from beside them. "No one would ever believe that."

Ruby looked down at her. "Why is that?"

Serik was the one who answered. "Well, for starters, you don't talk like one of the common folk. Your statements are too wordy and precise for you to be anyone other than a young lady who was raised with the nobility. Then there's the way you walk, with your back straight as an arrow. You've never had to carry anything heavy or slink in the shadows."

Ruby remained silent. She could feel her cheeks heating up as Serik listed off observations he'd made.

"Your nightgown is made of silk, which is not a material that any one of the lower classes could afford. Then there's the fact that you were wearing diamond earrings while you were strolling through the woods. Earrings worth about twenty crests, no less."

"Very well! Your point has been made," she huffed. Ruby was beginning to feel stupid. Why hadn't she thought to grab anything useful before jumping out of that window?

But Serik wasn't finished with her. "Someone could easily look at you and think, 'My, what a ransom she'll fetch.' You'll need to blend in better if you want to make it to Issalden. Perhaps, we should roll you around in the dirt a bit more to make you look less prim and proper. Though, if you speak, you'll still give yourself away."

"I have the distinct impression that you are poking fun at me, sir," she growled back at him. She looked down at Kai, who was covering her mouth. Apparently, her friend was finding this entertaining to watch.

Serik didn't respond to that. He directed Dream around a tree that was in their path.

"Kai, I do not think I like your guide. Perhaps we would do better on our own," Ruby said once it became apparent that Serik was ignoring her.

"You're the one who paid him, so he's technically *your* guide," she reminded Ruby, trying not to laugh.

"There are no refunds," Serik said, amusement lacing his voice.

Ruby pinched her lips together. While it was embarrassing to have the disparities between them so readily pointed out, she couldn't deny that she liked the wilder. Maybe that would change with time, but right now, she felt incredibly lucky that they had met Serik and that he was willing to help them.

Sighing, she shifted in her seat. The saddle was not made for two, and having ridden this way for two days now, working so hard to maintain a proper distance from the wilder, she was discovering muscles she didn't even know she had, and they all hurt. The wilder's hand on her thigh steadied her when she wobbled, but if he thought it a nuisance, he didn't say it. Ruby felt herself blushing again for an entirely different reason.

Serik had been right. Within the next hour or so, the trees gave way, and they came upon a clearing, a little smaller than the one they'd found the wilder in the first night. Leading the horse into the middle of the glade, he dismounted from Dream and helped Ruby down, then started untying his bags from the saddle.

Long grass grew around them, and in the fading sunlight, Ruby saw a few squirrels flicking their bushy tails as they darted up trees and sat on branches, staring at the unknown creatures that had invaded their sanctuary. One chittered at her, then dashed across the branch to hop to another tree.

Dream began nibbling on the long, green stalks while Serik unstrapped the saddle.

Dropping her pack, Kai flopped down and lay on her back in the grass. "Don't bother me for at least an hour. My legs feel like they are going to fall off."

Ruby looked around the clearing and then down at her hands. She blinked as she noticed the dirt under her fingernails, then took a closer look. Not just her hands, but her arms and legs were also covered in dirt marks and grass stains. Her once white nightgown was now a brownish gray from the dirt and dust, green in the places it had rubbed up against the plant life. This was the dirtiest she'd ever been. A hot bath sounded divine, but that was one luxury she was unlikely to find in the Wytchwood. She would have to settle for a cold one.

"Is there a water source near here?" she asked Serik.

The wilder set the saddle down on the ground and tugged the drawstring open on one of his bags. "Yes, there is a stream just past those trees and down a small hill," he said, pointing to his left. "I'll need to fill our canteens in the morning before we set out."

A stream would do. This close to the mountains, the water would be just shy of freezing, but it was the only thing she had to work with. Ruby took a few steps over to Kai and leaned over her.

She opened one green eye. "Didn't I say not to bother me?"

"Do you have anything I could use to clean myself?" She gestured down at the dirt stains. "Soap or anything else?"

"Yes," Kai said, sitting up immediately and reaching for the pack that she'd thrown on the ground. She frowned as she dug to the very bottom of the pack. "I should have thought about this earlier." Pulling out a small leather pouch, she handed it to Ruby. "Everything you need should be here, well, except the change of clothes."

Ruby nodded her thanks and started making her way over to the tree line.

"Where do you think you're going?" Serik's gruff voice said from behind her.

Pausing, she glanced over her shoulder at him. "Over to that stream to freshen up. I daresay I need it in the state I am in."

Serik held a large dagger in one hand. He had set out the pot they had seen the first night and had been clearing a small area of grass, presumably to make the campfire. "If you can wait a few minutes, I will accompany you."

Ruby bristled. He was treating her like a child who needed constant supervision. It wasn't even fully dark yet. It reminded her of the maids and servants who would follow her around when she was little. She had been no better than a prized flower, tended to and cared for to the point that she had no will of her own. She hated it.

"I am three and twenty, not some ignorant babe who needs an escort to bathe, sir," she said indignantly. "I can care for myself for the length of a few minutes."

Kai snickered, and Serik gave Ruby a look that was mostly annoyed. "Let her do what she wants," she said as she lay back down. "If something happens, she'll yell for us."

The wilder didn't respond. Ruby took that as the reluctant acceptance it was and continued past the tree line.

As Serik had said, the stream was just beyond the trees and down a small hill. Ruby made her way gingerly toward it, avoiding rocks and roots. She should have taken a lantern with her, but she was not going back to the camp now, not after admonishing the wilder about her ability to take care of herself. Her feet still hurt, but not nearly as much as they had when she'd woken up in the morning. Serik had changed the bandages before they began their journey again. The wilder had wrapped them well, and the cloth he'd used to bind them served as better shoes than her slippers had.

The stream was about six feet across with a rocky bank on the other side, dotted with dense brush. The side Ruby approached from was mostly small pebbles and sand. Careful not to get her bandages wet, she knelt next to the running water and ran a hand through it. It was cold, but not as icy as she was expecting, which was a relief. Ruby opened the pouch Kai had given her. It contained a washing cloth, a small bar of soap wrapped in wax paper, a brush, and another cloth to use for drying. She silently thanked the gods that her friend had packed these supplies.

The nightdress was roomy enough for her to wash underneath it without removing it, so Ruby spent the next few minutes cleaning herself thoroughly. It wasn't the most comfortable activity with the temperature of the water. If it were in a bucket, she could have warmed it with magic, but it wouldn't have worked well with running water.

Once she was finished, she brushed out her long brown hair, removing the tangles with her fingers and shaking it free of grass and leaves. She wove it into a loose braid again, vowing to clean it properly once they arrived somewhere she could take a warm bath. Lastly, she scrubbed the dirt and grime off her face, feeling almost human again.

Deciding that it was the best she could do, Ruby had started to pack all the items away when she heard crunching leaves. Thinking it was Serik coming to check on her, she frowned in annoyance, but when she looked around, the wilder could not be seen.

"Serik?" she said cautiously. No one answered.

Then she heard the sound again. Ruby stood and whirled around, searching the forest frantically until she thought she saw something moving on the other side of the stream.

Was it wolves?

A clicking noise came from the brush. Ruby froze. That didn't sound like any animal she'd read about.

Leaves rustled again, and the beast that emerged from the brush was big and muscular, with the body of a hound and a disproportionately large head with fangs that were as long as Ruby's forearm. It reminded her of the drawings she'd seen of carnivorous fish that lived in rivers to the south. The dog-like creature was covered in matted black fur and had pointed ears and bulging yellow eyes.

Heart pounding, Ruby took a few slow steps back as the bushes rustled behind the beast, and a moment later, two more identical animals emerged. Thick drool dripped from mouths that couldn't close over those fangs. Three sets of eyes focused on Ruby, and she could hear a low rumble emanating from their broad chests. The clicking that she'd heard before grew in intensity and volume, sounding almost like rocks stuck in the spokes of a wheel.

"Serik! Kai!" Ruby yelled as the one in front crouched like a cat about to pounce. In a panic, she pulled the energy from within her to work her magic.

Power danced at her fingertips, and she raised her hand as the beast leaped at her, its jaws wide. There was a flash of blinding light, and a percussive CRACK echoed through the woods as electricity arced from her outstretched hand and connected with the hound's mass. The force of it threw the beast back, and it hit the ground with a whimper and crum-pled into a heap, but the other two surged forward. Ruby barely had enough time to weave her fingers together and create a barrier between herself and the dog creatures. They hit it hard with their enormous heads, and she felt her magic crack underneath their weight. The spell wouldn't last long.

The one Ruby had electrocuted rose to its feet as the others shook their heads and snarled at her invisible barrier of hardened air and energy. One reared back on its hind legs and, using its massive paws, hit her shield with enough force to send a shivering sensation through her spell. The other two tried to go around it, brushing their shoulders against the barrier, and pacing around to locate its edges. Ruby backed away from them quickly, trying to get as far from the creatures as she could while keeping her spell up. Taking deep breaths, she tried to keep her shaking hands steady. She had to maintain her concentration. As much as she wanted to, turning and running would not only break her focus, but she suspected it could also send the beasts into a hunting frenzy.

But her careful considerations didn't matter. With another slam from the one hound, the barrier cracked and shattered as her magic failed. The backlash sent her stumbling backward, and Ruby tripped over her gown and went tumbling to the forest floor. The beasts let out a howling laugh as they charged her again.

Throwing her arms over her head in a feeble attempt at protecting herself, she screamed.

Gunfire rang out, and the hound that Ruby had injured before jerked and stumbled to the side before it could leap at her. The beast's charge faltered.

Serik raced toward her, a pistol in one hand. He dropped the firearm and drew his short sword, just as he reached Ruby's side, intercepting the hounds before they could get to her.

While the beasts were distracted by their new opponent, Ruby grabbed a handful of dirt and flung it at the face of the hound Serik had shot, murmuring a spell that turned the debris into projectiles as sharp as knives. They cut into its flesh, causing the creature to rear away from her. It pawed at its face, and she scooted back as it turned its maw to snap at her in pain and rage. Its face was bloody, and viscous yellow liquid oozed out of a damaged right eye. It snapped at her again, missing by inches, and Ruby thought frantically for a spell to get it away from her.

Just as she saw one of the other two coming in to attack, there was another thunderous sound of gunfire, and the creature jerked as blood sprayed out of a hole that had appeared in its side. Its roar of pain turned into a screech as the wound burst into angry red flames.

Ruby spotted Kai at the bottom of the hill, holding the rifle that Serik had pointed at her when they'd first met. There was a look of utter astonishment on her face.

"Those bullets cost a fortune!" Serik shouted angrily as he slashed at the beast still snapping at him.

"Tough!" she replied as she dropped the rifle and drew her dagger. The gun's one shot had been spent, and it would be of no use until it could be reloaded. Kai threw the dagger with remarkable force. Her aim was true, and it sank to the hilt into the hound she'd shot. It dropped to the ground, still on fire. A moment later, the dagger disappeared, and Kai was holding it again.

Serik rolled out of the way of the last creature's lunge and thrust his sword up and into its neck. With a grunt of effort, he sliced the hound's head clean off, sending it rolling away from him and toward Ruby. Yellow, fish-like eyes gazed at her, and she stared at it in horror from her place on the ground, unable to look away.

The wilder got to his feet and cleaned his blade on the creature's body, then sheathed his sword. He looked around at the carcasses and shook his head. Rocks and dirt crunched as he approached Ruby.

"Those were riphounds," Serik said as he placed an arm under hers and pulled her to her feet. "Are you all right? Did it hurt you?" He checked her over, looking for injuries, but the beast hadn't touched her. She didn't even have their blood on her clothing.

His words felt like they were far away. Ruby heard them, but their meaning didn't take hold. She couldn't stop staring into the beast's eyes as its blood soaked the forest floor.

Kai prodded one of the hounds with her foot and scoffed, then stepped over to Ruby. Frowning, she watched her friend closely. "Ruby?" she asked when the young noblewoman showed no indication that she had noticed her.

"Serik, I think she's in shock," Kai said as she took Ruby's hand in hers. Kai smiled up at her. "We never had to do anything like that before, right?" The wilder moved to block Ruby's view of the riphounds, and Kai placed a hand on her cheek, gently turning her gaze away. "It's over now, Ruby. There's nothing to be afraid of anymore."

Ruby started. Those words got through to her, and she took a few short breaths. Her knees felt weak, and she started trembling. "It was going to kill me," she whispered. "If you had not come, I would be dead." She didn't think she could stand anymore.

Before Ruby could sink all the way to the ground, Serik caught her with an arm around her waist. He lifted her off her feet like she weighed nothing. Tears welled in her eyes, and she covered her face with her hands. There was no use crying, but they came anyway. She wouldn't let them see.

"You were doing a fair enough job fending them off before we got here," the wilder said, trying to soothe her. "You're alive, and that's all that matters." He carried her back up the hill. The strength and warmth of his arms were comforting, and she only cried harder.

Kai gathered the dropped weapons and her pouch of bathing supplies and followed them back to the camp. "That was a runic bullet, wasn't it?" she asked as she trotted up next to the wilder. "That's why that thing caught fire."

In the part of Ruby's mind that was still able to process information, she recalled that runic bullets were ammunition that was imbued with magic by carving a rune—magical writing used for enchanting otherwise mundane items—into its surface. They had learned about them at Valwen. Once the bullet was fired, the kinetic energy would activate the rune, and the magic would take effect. That must have been why the riphound's wound had burst into flame.

"Yes," Serik said, his voice tight. "And you owe me another one."

"Wait a second. You pointed this rifle at *me*!"

"Good thing you didn't give me a reason to shoot you." They re-entered the camp, and Serik set Ruby down near the supplies and moved her hands away from her face. She tried to resist but didn't put up much of a fight. "Ruby, look at me," he commanded.

She looked up into his eyes. There was a golden ring around his hazel eyes.

"You survived without so much as a scratch on you. Your magic made them hesitate long enough for us to get to you." He smiled, still holding her hands in his. "I was wondering why your feet were healing so quickly. Did you come from Valwen?"

Kai made a strangled sound, but Serik threw her a glare, and she quieted.

Ruby tried to focus on his words. He'd asked her a question.

"Yes," she said quietly. "I am—was—in my last year. I would be graduating in the summer if I had not left." She hesitated, thinking back to the lightning that had jumped from her fingertips. "I have never used magic in a real fight before."

"You did well. You didn't freeze, and you didn't run, which is better than most of the half-baked mages that come out of that place." He brushed a strand of hair out of her face. "Just take a few deep breaths and relax while I pack up." Serik straightened and turned to Kai.

"It's not safe here anymore. We'll have to move our camp," Serik said with a sigh. "The bodies will attract other predators."

Kai groaned but didn't argue. "Do you know of another place to camp close to here?"

"Not one that we can reach before nightfall." He clicked his tongue, and Dream raised her head from where she'd been grazing and trotted over to him. "There's a small cabin where I keep extra food and clothing that's about a day's walk from here. We'll make it there tomorrow." He looked down at Ruby. "If you don't mind wearing my clothes, we can get you into something you can move a little easier in."

Serik placed the saddle back on his mare. "Tonight, we'll just have to get as far as we can."

CHAPTER 5

They traveled for a few more hours before making camp again. Navigating through the dark forest with only a lantern was difficult, so their pace was slower than during the day. Serik let Kai ride on Dream with Ruby, saying that he would be quicker on foot than the petite woman. Once they were a safe distance from their original campsite, they stopped near a large boulder that would give them a little shelter if it started to rain. By the time they had eaten and lay down to rest, all three of them were exhausted.

Ruby still felt numb from the fight with the riphounds. After the initial shock had subsided, she was tired, and every muscle in her body ached. It had been all she could do to stay in the saddle until they found another safe place to sleep.

However, now that she was lying in her blanket on the soft grass, she was unable to relax. She tossed and turned most of the night, and by the time dawn came, she wasn't sure that she'd had much rest at all.

Kai and Serik kept the conversation going as they traveled, but Ruby was too out of it to pay much attention to the words being said. Eventually, she leaned back into the wilder and closed her eyes, the sound of Dream's hooves on the packed earth lulling her into a dreamless half-sleep. Inhaling deeply, Ruby took in the man's scent. He smelled of damp earth, firewood, and cloves. Somehow, it comforted her.

"We're here," Serik's voice roused her from her slumber.

"Already?" Ruby asked as she rubbed her eyes and looked around, blinking rapidly. The sun was low in the western sky, and the trees around them cast long shadows. About thirty feet in front of them was a small building, barely big enough to be labeled as anything more than a shack. It was made of dark, aged wood and had a sloped roof. There was one window, a door, and a fire pit out front. Logs of chopped firewood were neatly stacked high on one side of the shack, and Ruby caught a glimpse of a well behind it.

This must have been the cabin the wilder had mentioned the night before. It seemed to have everything one would need to survive. With the glade of long, swaying grass around them, it was a perfect place for one man and his horse to live.

"You've been sleeping for a while," Kai piped up. "We couldn't even wake you to eat. How are you feeling?"

Ruby stretched her arms over her head as Serik dismounted. A twinge of tightness in her shoulders bordered on pain, and she let out a small gasp. "A little stiff and sore." Serik helped her down from Dream, and Kai laughed as she stumbled around awkwardly, the muscles in her lower back and thighs protesting the movement.

"That's what you get for falling asleep in the saddle," she said. "Come on, I thought I saw a well over there, and I could use some freshening up. No peeking!" she called to their guide as she hooked one arm in Ruby's and pulled her behind the building.

The two women washed while Serik unloaded Dream and set her loose in the little glade next to the cabin. Ruby splashed cold water on her face to wake up, chasing away the remnants of drowsiness. Her muscles still ached, but a warm night of sleep indoors would alleviate that problem. Hopefully. The wilder disappeared inside for a few minutes, then returned with a bundle of cloth.

"Here," he said as he handed it to Ruby. "They'll be a little big, but these clothes should hold you over for a few days. There aren't any shoes, but it'll be fine since you aren't walking much. I'll keep wrapping your feet until we reach the village at the edge of the Wytchwood. We'll get you something better there." He scratched the back of his head with one hand, looking slightly embarrassed, and Ruby wondered why. Serik couldn't have anticipated bringing a scantily dressed young woman back to his cabin. "It's only another day's travel from here. We're deep in the forest now."

She thanked him and went inside to dress. The cabin consisted of one room and was sparsely furnished. No decorations adorned the walls, and everything was set up in a utilitarian way, down to the threadbare blanket covering the mattress. Serik had set a fire going in the hearth, so it was at least warm, and furs of dark brown and gray covered the floor. The small bed rested in the corner, along with a chest of drawers. A table against the wall below the front window sported two chairs and was loaded with cooking utensils, wooden dishes, and a bucket with a folded square of cloth hanging over its side. On the other side of the room from the bed was what looked like a trap door, which she assumed led down to a cellar. Everything was coated with a fine layer of dust. It had been a while since the wilder had been here.

Though it was a far cry from the manors and castles Ruby was used to, the cozy little cabin was much preferable to sleeping outside. If he cleaned and added more colorful decorations, it might even be cute.

Ruby shivered before she stepped closer to the fire. She

pulled her ruined nightgown over her head and began dressing in the clothing Serik had given her: a linen shirt, breeches with a flap that buttoned in the front, and a belt of woven leather. As the wilder had indicated, the garments were a few sizes too large, but Ruby was able to cinch the belt tight enough so the pants wouldn't fall off. The material felt rough on her skin and smelled like the wilder, albeit a bit stale. The cabin had no mirror, but she must have looked comical wearing the man's clothing on her smaller frame.

"Ruby? Are you finished?" Kai's voice came through the door after two sharp raps on the wood. A moment later, she pushed it open and slipped through. Once she caught sight of Ruby, her eyebrows shot up.

"How in the hells do you still look good *in that*?" she scoffed.

"Do not jest, Kai," Ruby mumbled, pulling the pants up again as they threatened to slide down her hips.

"I'm not. This is pure, unbridled jealousy." She covered her mouth and coughed. Ruby's eyes narrowed. That sounded suspiciously like a laugh.

"Serik is making dinner," Kai continued. "There's a fire going outside, but it's so warm in here." She closed her eyes and inhaled deeply, making a pleased sound through her nose. Then she strode across the cabin and sat on the bed, immediately grimacing. "Hard as a rock."

"Were you expecting a feather bed?" Serik's voice drifted through the still-open door. A moment later, the wilder came into view and took a position leaning on the doorframe with his arms crossed, surveying them. A smirk played on his lips as he looked over Ruby from her head to her toes in his over-sized clothing. "You don't look half bad."

Kai mouthed *told you so* from the bed, and Ruby felt her face grow warm.

"Is the food ready yet?" she asked, ignoring Kai's snicker. "I am quite famished."

"In a few more minutes," he said, turning back around and stepping out of view again.

They ate by the fire outside, then retired to the cabin. Serik took the bed—it was his home, after all—while the two women laid their blankets together on the furs. It was lengths more comfortable than sleeping on the ground outdoors.

Ruby stretched out by the fire, groaning softly as her tired muscles throbbed with every move she made. Before this journey, the young woman wouldn't have called herself out of shape. She enjoyed horseback riding and archery, but four days of hard travel had taken a toll on her body that was unlike anything she'd ever experienced. In the past, Ruby had ridden in carriages when crossing the countryside, so she was unfamiliar with this kind of travel. Her entire body felt tight and stiff, and her thighs ached from being in the saddle all day.

"Sleep will help," Kai said sympathetically, lying beside her. "A warm bath would, too, but we'll have to wait until we reach a village.

"Am I really so weak?" Ruby asked with a sigh. The past day had solidified with painful clarity how woefully unprepared she'd been, both mentally and physically. "I do not see you in half as much pain."

"I'm used to this, the traveling around from place to place. Sleeping on the ground or in any nook I can find is the norm. I grew up this way, so it doesn't bother me as much." Kai smiled at her and closed her eyes. Her pale skin was golden in the firelight. "You'll get used to it, eventually."

Ruby pursed her lips. She didn't know much about Kai's life before they'd met at the Academy. They'd talked a lot, but mostly about their lessons or whatever gossip had been floating around the castle. Ruby had been curious as to what Kai had been doing when she'd come in through her window and why she'd had to leave Valwen, but now, she finally had the courage to ask. She *should* know why. They were in this together.

"So, are you finally going to tell me why you were fleeing Valwen in the middle of the night?" she asked her friend. "And do not tell me it was because you wanted to leave. I am not stupid, Kai. Attendance is voluntary, and you have no obligations to run away from." *Unlike me.*

Kai sighed and sat up, leaning closer to Ruby and glancing over to where Serik was wrapped in his blanket. His back was to the women, and they could see his form moving up and down slowly with his steady breathing. That didn't mean he was asleep.

She pulled her travel pack close and dug around until she withdrew a small package wrapped in a linen cloth. "You're right," she whispered so her voice wouldn't carry. "There was a reason that I was trying to get out of the castle that night. I stole this from the inner sanctum." She unwrapped the item.

"Oh, Kai, you did not," Ruby said, unable to believe it. She remembered the architectural drawing they'd found in Professor Morel's desk. Older students were allowed to view the inner sanctum upon request, but none could touch or take the items out of the vault without special permission from the headmage himself. If Kai was in the inner sanctum in the middle of the night after being disciplined by the headmage, it was unlikely she had been there through an official request. Whatever she'd taken was either rare, dangerous, or both. If the mages caught her, she'd be sent to the labor camps at best or, at worst, executed.

Kai held a small item made of polished red sandstone in her palm. It was oval, and on it was carved an eight-point star inside of three interlocking rings. That symbol looked familiar, but Ruby couldn't place where she'd seen it before. She reached out and brushed a finger against it. The stone practically buzzed with magical energy, and she felt drawn into the little object, as if it called to her. "What is it?" she asked in a whisper. It seemed like such a little thing for Kai to risk her life for.

Kai shrugged, speaking just as softly. "To be honest, I'm not sure what it's for. There was some writing about it in one of the books in the library, and it's supposed to have been taken out of some ruins to the east. I stole that book too. My instructions were to infiltrate Valwen and get the item. That's it. Alek thought it would take six months or longer for the professors to trust me enough to show me the way to the inner sanctum and how to get past its wards, but it didn't take that long. The last month, I've been figuring out how to get in without triggering the wards and planning my escape from the castle, but that didn't work out how I wanted it to. I hadn't planned on doing it that night, but when Professor Morel caught us and took us to the headmage's office, it seemed like the perfect opportunity." She flashed Ruby a smile. "I never expected to take someone with me, much less *you*, but here we are."

Ruby thought about that for a minute. "So, you never intended to come to my window, not even to say goodbye?" Just the thought of waking up one morning and having Kai gone made her sad. She was the only close friend that Ruby had. Even if Kai's reasons for enrolling at Valwen hadn't been pure, it was obvious that Ruby cared about her. The fact that Ruby was with her now was evidence enough of that. But that didn't change the fact that Ruby would have been devastated if her friend had stuck to her original plan.

Kai sighed and shook her head as she placed the item back into her bag. Ruby's eyes followed it, and she had the strangest feeling that she should take it from Kai and hold on to it. After it was out of sight, the feeling was gone, and Ruby blinked a few times.

Kai didn't notice Ruby's reaction. "Somewhere deep down, I must have known it was your room I was breaking into. I didn't hesitate, and you think I'd be more careful having just gotten away from the guards." Kai smiled, and her eyes brightened. She nudged Ruby with her shoulder. "Don't worry so much about what might have been. I did ask you to come with me in the end, didn't I?"

"That is true," Ruby admitted. Then she returned the grin. "You have taken me on quite the adventure. You know, it has only been a few days since we left, but I think I am getting used to camping out under the stars."

Kai snorted and lay back down. "Just wait until it rains. You'll be singing a different tune then. You won't be so chipper when you have to walk around in soggy stockings."

"I'm sure it will be better than scrubbing the alchemy lab."

They both giggled.

"Will you two go to sleep?" Serik grumbled and turned over. He opened one eye, staring at them in the flickering firelight.

Ruby smiled at him sheepishly and lay down next to Kai. There would be plenty of time to talk more about Kai's key and this Alek person when they reached their destination.

CHAPTER 6

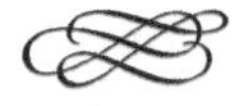

Belleward was exactly what Serik had said it was, a small village that backed up close to the Wytch-wood. Most of the area beyond the village was farmland, with rows and rows of growing crops. A dirt road led north and disappeared in the distance. The sun was low on the horizon, and by the time they had entered the main square, it had dipped behind the mountains. There were no cobbled stones or electric lamps here. The streets were hard earth with wheel tracks dug into them, and the houses they passed looked in a constant state of repair. Stone houses with thatched roofs sat side by side, with the tips of a windmill's blades poking over the tops.

Places like this were scattered throughout the Andrean Empire, quaint little towns and villages that comprised a good part of the citizenry. Ruby didn't know their precise location, and Belleward wasn't on any map she'd seen, so she had no idea who was the lord of these lands. There were maybe two dozen buildings in the village proper, and Serik led Dream to the largest one, which he told them was the inn.

They stopped at the stables, and Serik helped Ruby off Dream, then handed the reins to a young, red-haired boy who ran over to help them. After the wilder was satisfied with the handling of his horse, he led them inside.

Ruby had never been to an establishment such as this. The places she was used to staying in were large and grand, with marble fixtures and elegant wallpaper. This inn was small and weathered, with bare stone walls and shuttered windows. Six tables were scattered around the main room, with additional seating at the small bar. A fire roared in the hearth, and its warmth chased away the chill of the night. A brown-furred bear's head hung on the mantle, its mouth open and full of wicked-looking teeth. It reminded Ruby of the riphounds, and her stomach turned—nothing like the reminder of near death to chase away her appetite. A few villagers sat around the tables, drinking from large mugs. They all looked up when the little group of three entered.

There was only a moment of awkward silence, then—

"Serik!" boomed a loud female voice. A woman of middling years with bright red hair, freckles, and a belly round with child waddled out from behind the bar and placed her hands on her hips. She wore a red dress under an apron with faded stains. Her light eyes were wide, and she looked pleased despite her stern stance. "I haven't seen you in an age! We thought you died in that forest."

"You're not rid of me yet, Johana," the wilder replied with an easy smile, his own posture relaxing.

The woman snorted. Her eyes drifted over to Kai and then finally to Ruby. Her eyebrows shot up as soon as her gaze settled on the young woman in oversized men's clothes. She turned a fierce glare on the wilder, all delight at his arrival evaporating. "What in the hells do you think you're doing dragging this poor girl around in such a state?"

Serik grimaced and gestured to a corner of the room,

back by the staircase. Still with brows furrowed, Johana nodded once and began walking to where he indicated. She was not fast, and the wilder gestured for Ruby to follow him.

"Let's see about getting you something else to wear," Serik said softly.

"I'm going to get a drink," Kai said, eyeing the bar. A large, muscular man with dark hair had taken over for the pregnant woman, wearing a stained apron of his own. It looked almost comical on his physique. "Yell if you need anything."

Ruby followed the wilder to where the red-haired woman —Johana—was waiting. The woman watched her closely, and Ruby tried to look as pleasant and humble as she could.

"Do you have some kind of clothing I could purchase for her?" Serik asked once they were away from prying eyes. "We ran into a few mishaps on the way here. An old dress or two would be appreciated."

Johana's expression softened when Serik said the word "mishap." She looked Ruby up and down and pursed her lips thoughtfully. "I think I have a few gowns that would fit her. I won't be wearing them any time soon," she said, patting her round belly. "And some shoes, of course. Can't have you running around the countryside in men's clothes and bare feet, can we?"

Ruby fiddled with the clasp of her cloak. This woman was kind, but Ruby could not repay her generosity. "I am sorry, but I do not have any money."

"Don't worry about that," Serik cut in before she could say anything else. "Consider it part of the fee for my services."

Johana looked between them, her eyebrows raised. "Very well, then. I'll see what I can dig up. In the meantime, you should have a proper bath, miss. Mattie will get it ready for you. Mattie!" She yelled the name, making Ruby jump.

A girl who looked to be no older than thirteen

approached them. She looked much like a miniature version of Johana, with her hair and freckles. The girl was all gangly limbs and awkward gestures, but she would grow to be just like her mother. Mattie looked first at Serik, then at Ruby, her eyes wide. "Yes, mama?"

"Take this pretty young lady to the room at the end of the hall and help her get washed up, will you? She looks like she's been through an ordeal, and you—" Johana turned her fiery gaze on Serik, putting her hands on her hips again and pushing her belly at him like a battering ram. "We are not finished talking about this."

If the wilder was intimidated, he didn't show it. He smiled and nodded affably at Johana while Mattie took Ruby's hand.

"This way, miss," she said, pulling her along.

The girl took her up the stairs next to the bar and to the second floor. A faded blue carpet stretched a long hallway with four doors, and Mattie took her to the one at the end. Inside was a spacious room with a bed, dresser, and a folding screen, the panels painted with pink and yellow flowers. The windows had wooden shutters, and a little oil lamp on the dresser was the only illumination. This room looked as worn as the rest of the inn, but at least it was tidy. Mattie went behind the screen and dragged out a wooden tub.

"I'll need to boil the water," she said and smiled at Ruby apologetically. "So, it will take a while to fill."

"There's no need for that," Ruby said quickly. The thought of a hot bath and scrubbing herself clean was irresistible. "If you bring the water, I have a spell that I can use to warm it."

The girl's eyes widened again. "Are you a mage?"

"Yes," she said, which wasn't technically true. She hadn't finished her studies at Valwen yet, but she would have completed her training later this year.

Mattie stared at her in awe for a length of time that started to make Ruby uncomfortable.

"Ah, the water?"

The girl started, ducked her head, then left the room in a hurry. Ruby feared she'd scared the girl off, but Mattie returned holding two buckets of sloshing liquid a few minutes later. It took four trips to fill the tub. Once full, the girl stepped back, eagerly waiting for Ruby to cast her spell.

Ruby held out a hand to hover an inch over the water and concentrated. Taking a deep breath, she reached for the energy within her. Power rose inside her like a tide seeking the shore. Focused on the effect she wanted, Ruby touched the water's surface, using her magic to raise the temperature of the liquid as though the tub were over a fire. Steam began to curl up between her fingers.

It took about thirty seconds to get it to her desired temperature, and once she was finished, she slumped forward. A wave of exhaustion threatened to overtake her as the power she'd called up faded. Water dispersed energy quickly, and using her magic like that had been taxing, but it was worth it for the prospect of a hot bath. Ruby stood and began pulling off her cloak and Serik's clothing.

"That was amazing!" Mattie exclaimed, clapping her hands together as Ruby unwrapped her feet.

She inspected them. Whatever damage had been done before, they were fully healed now. The skin was smooth, and Ruby couldn't tell where the cuts had been. Years of training had gone into honing her power, but the benefits of having an aptitude for magic were incredible.

That finished, Ruby gingerly stepped into the now-heated bath. A tingling sensation went up her spine as she sat in the tub, her tired muscles relaxing for the first time in days. She sighed in pleasure.

"There is a wash rag here and some soap." Mattie handed her the items, seeming to have recovered from her awe. "May I ask your name, miss?"

"It's Ruby."

The girl beamed. "That's a pretty name. If you need anything, Miss Ruby, just call for me. My mama will be here soon with something else for you to wear." She gave the pile of men's clothing a disdainful glance, then bent her knees in a clumsy curtsy and left, closing the door behind her.

Ruby scrubbed her skin with the washcloth and washed her hair. She felt warm and clean for the first time since she left the Academy.

A few minutes after she'd finished cleaning herself, there was a knock at the door, and Johana came in with a pile of neatly folded clothes and a towel in her hands. A small, silver-plated hand mirror balanced on top. "Done yet, dear?"

Ruby dried herself off with the towel while Johana placed the rest of the bundle on the bed and unfolded the undergarments. Once Ruby was dry, she donned the linen shift and took a seat on a chair while the woman brushed out her hair and braided it for her. She then helped Ruby with the corset, tying the drawstrings for her at the neckline and waist, then a petticoat and a linen gown in a pale blue. When she was done, Johana stepped back and gazed at her.

"There we are! Now you look like a proper young woman." She picked up the mirror she'd set on the dresser and handed it to her.

Ruby's skin was red from the hot water, but otherwise, she was her old recognizable self, clean and dressed properly. It was not the fine gowns, lace, and silk that marked her as a member of the nobility, but the clothing that Johana had provided was easy to move in.

The older woman sighed. "You are a lovely one. It was hard to tell in those mangy clothes you were wearing." Johana shook her head and frowned in disapproval. "What was that wilder thinking?"

Ruby felt guilty. It wasn't Serik's lapse in judgment that caused the need to wear his clothing but hers.

"Please, it is not his fault. I am afraid what I wore before was ruined, and the only clothes he could provide for me were his own." Looking into the mirror, she stared at the thin chain and the silver and gold pendant resting between the curve of her breasts. Another gift from Mikel. Like her earrings, this too was accented with precious gems. Rubies instead of diamonds were worked into the design of a blooming lily. On the other side of the pendant, the side against her skin, was the seal of house Belmont. At least no one could tell who it belonged to while she still wore the necklace.

"One last thing," Johana said as she stepped up to Ruby and tied a kerchief around her neck. It covered the pendant and chain. "There are a few more items for you here." She gestured to the small pile she'd set on the bed. "Another gown like this one, a short dress, stockings, and a pair of shoes. That should hold you over until you get to wherever you're heading."

"Thank you," Ruby said, and she meant it. "I do not know how I can ever repay you for this kindness."

Johana waved her words away, her cheeks turning pink. "It's nothing, really." She patted her belly. "It's not like I can use them in my state. I was going to save them for Mattie to wear, but, well, it doesn't look like she'll be as tall as I am. Serik is giving me a few coins for the clothing, so I'll use that to get the girl some new dresses that she will actually like."

"Still, this is very kind."

The woman winked at her. "Just make sure you take care of them, all right?"

After dressing, Ruby went back downstairs to the tavern part of the inn. Mattie brought her a plate of toasted bread, cured meats, and pickled olives. Kai had already eaten, which didn't surprise Ruby, but she stayed with Ruby while she ate, chatting softly about how nice it was to be staying indoors. Serik was nowhere to be seen, and Kai told her he'd left to purchase more supplies for their journey.

After their meal, both women went upstairs to sleep. Ruby felt drained, and she hadn't even been the one walking. She couldn't imagine how tired Kai was after being on foot for the past few days. She was thankful Serik had let Kai ride with her yesterday. Kai had the room next to Ruby's, and she bid her friend goodnight with a wide yawn.

Despite her eyes being heavy, Ruby's mind would not quiet, and she tossed and turned for what felt like hours, unable to find a good position to fall asleep. Finally, she gave up and decided that going for a walk would help her sleep. She dressed in the clothes the innkeeper's wife had given her and laced up the new, sturdy shoes. Calling magic to light her way, she slipped out of her room and into the dark corridor.

The inn was closed for the night, and it was dark and quiet when she crept down the stairs. The only sound came from creaking floorboards and her own footsteps. Ruby never even considered waking her companions. Just because she was restless didn't mean they had to suffer with her.

That wouldn't have been an option four years ago. Ruby had been surrounded by servants her entire life and would have needed help getting dressed, but being at Valwen had taught her how to change and wash since she had no lady's maid to help her with those simplest of tasks. Students were not allowed to bring servants with them to the college, and while some bemoaned the inconvenience, Ruby liked being self-sufficient and not having to call for assistance every time she so much as lifted a finger.

It was probably the happiest time in her life, being able to make her own choices and care for herself. But there had always been an expiration date. Once she finished her studies, she would have had to marry Mikel. A duchess wouldn't have been able to attend Valwen. How could she be expected to take orders from the mages when she would have ranked above them? So, the duke had agreed to postpone the wedding, with the agreement that they would marry once she graduated. He hadn't been easy to convince, but in the end, he only asked a few things of her in return.

Breaking her promise to Mikel left a bitter taste in her mouth, but she hadn't wanted to marry him in the first place.

Ruby stepped outside, wanting some fresh air. It was odd. Now that she had her own room, she missed being outdoors. Walking at a leisurely pace around the building, Ruby thought she would go and see how Dream's accommodations were.

Someone had already beaten her there.

Serik's familiar figure was illuminated in the pale moonlight. The wilder was dressed in only a pair of breeches, a light tunic, and boots, less clothing than Ruby usually saw him in. His riding leathers were gone, as was the belt with its many pouches and pistol, though he still carried a sword. He seemed much more relaxed here than at any other time on their journey. Dream stood beside Serik as he brushed her, luminescent in the darkness as her coat reflected the moonlight.

"Can't sleep?" he asked as she approached. His eyes flicked over her before continuing to brush the mare. Dream nickered softly, turning her head in Ruby's direction.

She shrugged and held out her hand for the mare to nuzzle. "Now that I have a warm and comfortable bed to rest in, sleep eludes me."

"A simple 'no' would have sufficed. Common folk don't talk like that." He repeated the words he had said the first day they traveled together. "If you truly want to leave your old life behind, you should try to sound more like the people around you."

"No, I cannot sleep," she said, trying not to sound petulant.

The fine lines around Serik's eyes crinkled. "That's better, but it still sounds a little stiff."

Ruby frowned. What would Kai say? She let out an overly dramatic sigh and placed one hand on her hip. "Obviously not, or I wouldn't be out here."

He grinned at her then. "That's pretty good. Though I don't know if I could stand traveling with two Kais."

She laughed and started scratching the spot between Dream's eyes.

"It's nice to see you in something other than a ruined nightgown or men's clothing," he said with a sidelong glance.

"Yes, Johana was very gracious in what she gave me."

Serik watched her, and he pursed his lips.

Ruby returned the look and waited. When he didn't say anything, she sighed again. "Say whatever it is you have on your mind, Serik. I do not wish to stand out here all night."

He grinned at that. "I overheard the two of you speaking a few nights ago at the cabin. I wasn't trying to eavesdrop, but you should be more careful what you talk about when there are no other sounds to muffle your voice."

It took her a moment to absorb what he'd said. Then panic rose in Ruby's chest. He knew that Kai had stolen from Valwen. "You are not going to turn her in, are you? She did not hurt anyone, but that will not stop the headmage from punishing her severely."

"No. What happens with the mages is none of my business. As far as I'm concerned, they deserve to have their toys taken from them once in a while."

He fell silent, and Ruby thought he was waiting for her to say something, but she didn't have any words for that. She disagreed with him that stealing from the mages was fine, but at the same time, she was relieved that he didn't have any plans to turn Kai over to the authorities. The silence stretched between them until Serik finally spoke again.

"I know why Kai fled the Valwen mages, but why did you go with her?" he asked, continuing his task of brushing Dream. "You're a lady of good breeding. Why go off with someone like Kai?"

"Kai is my friend," Ruby replied but had difficulty thinking of anything else to add. She remained quiet for a minute, thinking of how to answer him. She could make something up. Serik had only been their guide for a few days, and she didn't owe him any answers, but Ruby liked him, and he was easy to talk to. Friend was a word that she would associate with him, too, though she didn't know if he returned the affection. After mulling it over, she decided that the truth was best.

"My father is a baron, and my mother a baroness. Do not ask what house because I will not tell you. They are not bad people, but they are ambitious, and they used me to further that ambition." She laughed a little under her breath. "That makes them sound like they do not care for me, which is untrue. My father has always been more focused on the family reputation and assets than anything else, and my mother… Well, I do not think she ever really wanted children. It was just her duty to have them."

Serik listened to her intently as she spoke. He finished brushing Dream, and once she was not getting attention from him, the mare trotted away from them to find some grass to nibble on. Having nothing else to do with his hands, he crossed his arms and leaned against the fence post, watching Ruby.

Ruby's cheeks felt hot. She'd never needed to explain her situation to anyone before. Most people already knew who she was when she walked into a room. "All that to say, I was engaged at a young age to someone I did not know. It was a little exciting at first. Most women in my position would need to attend gatherings and soirees with other nobility to find a match, but that was taken care of for me." She glanced down at the blades of grass swaying in the evening breeze. "Everything was always taken care of for me. The wedding was scheduled for this summer, after I graduated from Valwen. It will sound ungrateful, but that was not what I wanted. I do not want to marry him."

"Why?" he asked.

"Because I do not love him," Ruby said. "It was a marriage arranged by my parents, and I have realized now that I want more from my life than to be a nobleman's wife. My fiancé—ex-fiancé now, I suppose—he is… he…" Ruby trailed off, trying to put words to her feelings. She remembered the way Mikel touched her, the way he kissed her, and it made her shiver. The gentle and kind face he wore outside was a mask to fool everyone around him, but Ruby knew better now. She wrapped her arms around herself before continuing, suddenly feeling the chill in the air.

"He is not a good match for me, but my parents would never have accepted that reason. He showered them with wealth and notoriety to purchase my hand. Honestly, I did not think it through before leaving. I just did it, idiotic as that may seem to you. When I marry, it will be a man of my own choosing—a man with whom I want to share my life. A man I love."

Serik chuckled, and his expression seemed sad. "You've been reading too many fairytales, my lady. True love is the rarest thing in all the realms. Many do not find it in their lifetime. I'm not saying you should have stayed with the lord who held your marriage bonds, but being free of them does not guarantee happiness in this life."

She glowered at him. It became apparent that he was trying to ignore her look, but eventually, he asked, "Does what I say bother you?"

"No, but I am trying to figure out how long you have been so cynical."

He raised his eyebrows at her. Apparently, that hadn't been the answer he'd been expecting.

Ruby tried to hide her smile. "A man who lives out in the woods, by himself, is trying to give me advice on love."

He scowled at her.

"You must admit," Ruby began, trying to hold down the giggle threatening to bubble up from her chest, "it is quite humorous."

Serik's scowl deepened.

She did laugh then. She couldn't help it. He just looked so upset. "Since I have told you why I left with Kai, tell me why you choose to live alone wandering the woodlands. Please do not take offense. You are a very skilled hunter and tracker, but I am sure you have friends and family elsewhere."

Serik glared at her suspiciously before answering, as if he expected her to make fun of him again. Ruby gave him her most innocent smile.

"Friends, no family," he said. "At least, not any blood relatives. My mother died a few years ago, and my father much longer ago than that. It's been a long time since I've thought of him."

"I am sorry," Ruby said, sobering immediately. "That must have been very difficult for you."

Serik looked away from her, gazing over the small village bathed in a ghostly white glow. "It was, but I've adjusted. Now, I feel more comfortable surrounded by trees than buildings. I spent quite a few years with the nomadic tribes in the north, so being in a large city is uncomfortable for me if I stay too long."

That surprised Ruby. Did that mean that he was a tribesman? His skin was too dark to be from the north. "The northern tribes? You look like you are from Langard."

"I am, but my father was Andrean. When he died, my mother and I needed to leave the empire, and she had some friends in the north. I learned their ways, and it's helped me quite a bit."

Ruby nodded. What he said couldn't be denied. His skills in the wilderness were extraordinary, not that she was an accurate judge, but even Kai couldn't shoot or hunt like that. "Why did you come back to the empire?"

As soon as she asked the question, his expression darkened. It was only for a moment, but it had been clear as day. His features smoothed out as if it had been something he'd practiced a thousand times before. Serik smirked, but it didn't reach his eyes, "I can't tell you all my secrets, can I?"

She had pried too far. "I suppose not. No mystery would be left, and you would be far less interesting."

This time the grin he gave her looked genuine. "Ah, yes. More mystery. That's what I need." He straightened and pocketed the brush, then held his arm out for her to take. "As for you, you need to sleep, Ruby. We have another long day of traveling ahead of us tomorrow, and you don't want to fall out of the saddle. I'm only reasonably sure I can catch you."

Groaning, Ruby placed a hand on his arm, letting him lead her back toward the inn. The prospect of more long days spent riding to Issalden was the last thing she wanted to think about. She'd been wrong. She didn't miss the outdoors. "I was hoping we could stay longer."

"I know," he murmured, patting her hand soothingly. "We'll get to Issalden soon enough."

CHAPTER 7

The three travelers left the village in the morning, saying goodbye to Johana and her family before setting out on the road. Even though Ruby had the proper clothes and shoes she could walk in, Serik insisted she still ride Dream, telling her that even though the shoes were made for working, they should not be used to travel across the country.

Early that morning, Kai purchased a small horse from the farm closest to the inn to help make their journey faster, but the black-coated stallion was not big enough to carry two people. Dream was at least twice the size of the black one, and she could carry both Ruby and Serik with no issues.

From Belleward, it was still another few days of travel to Issalden, but now that they were out of the Wytchwood, they could take the road. The small group camped outside the following two nights, but after that, villages like Belleward spotted the landscape every few hours. The weather was mild, with the days warm and the nights cool. Gentle hills of green greeted them as they traversed the dirt roads, and horse-pulled carts passed occasionally, driven by smiling farmers. Thunderstorms would be coming in the next few weeks, but, hopefully, they would reach the city before that happened. Each day of travel was like the last. They would ride until dark, then find an inn to stay at in one of the villages they passed.

"There are bandits in this area, so it's best to stop at night," Serik had told them.

Ruby wasn't complaining. Boasts of getting used to sleeping in the open air aside, she enjoyed the warm hearths and soft beds provided to her indoors. Excitement filled her as they continued toward Issalden, but as they passed by farmlands and hills, Ruby withdrew into herself more and more. Her future was so uncertain that she dwelled on it for hours during their ride. Even Serik's warm presence at her back could not distract her from worrying about what would become of her after they reached their destination.

The day before they reached Issalden, Ruby's stomach was filled with nerves. She felt as if she would simultaneously throw up and weep. It was even worse than when she'd had a practical exam she hadn't studied for in her second year. The feeling was so strong that she barely touched her lunch. She had no money and no place to go. What would she do when she arrived?

That thought occupied her mind for most of the day, and when they stopped at the last inn they would visit before reaching the city, Ruby waited for Serik to leave her and Kai alone so she could ask her friend the questions that had consumed her thoughts.

"How much is twenty crests worth?" Ruby asked quietly, glancing to where the wilder was leaning against the bar and talking to the tall man behind it. The two women were seated at a small table in the corner of an inn almost twice the size of Johana's. This one was made of wood instead of stone and was decorated in warm, earthy colors. "I know how much it is, but my perceptions might be slightly skewed on the true value. How you spoke before when Serik first stated his fee made it sound like a lot."

"Why does it matter?" she asked, leaning back in her chair and regarding Ruby. "You've already paid him."

Heat crept up Ruby's cheeks. At this moment, she felt woefully inadequate. "It is something I should know if I want to blend in. I cannot count on you to take care of everything for me, can I?"

Kai looked thoughtful at her words. After a moment, she nodded. "Well, to someone like me who didn't grow up wealthy, a crest is a lot of money. But that's not helpful to you." She grunted and waved a dismissive hand in the air. "A common worker could earn between a mark and a mark and a half for a day's wages. Most meals in an inn will cost two or three bits, and an ale would cost another." She blew out a long breath, and Ruby could tell she was adding sums in her head by the way she stared fixedly at the table.

"So," she continued, "if they make only one mark a day, that's already half their wages in food with eight bits in a mark. A night at an inn will cost you about a mark for a decent room, and for a nice lodging house, you'll pay about three and a half crests for a month, which is fourteen marks. Twenty crests could provide four months' lodgings and expenses."

"I see..." She didn't.

Kai snorted at Ruby's expression. "Do you? You look even more confused."

"It is more so that I am still unsure how much a typical guide would have cost." She flicked her braid over her shoulder in a frustrated motion, with more force than was necessary. "Back home, my father would record expenses in hundreds or thousands of crests. It is daunting to imagine how much that money would mean to an average person."

"Let me put it this way," Kai said with a sympathetic nod. "Hiring a guide or a guard would cost you a few crests for a week's worth of service. I wouldn't have paid more than five. Twenty is outrageous." She threw a dirty look in Serik's direction.

"He is useful," Ruby mused, following her friend's gaze, "and he seems to know exactly where to go." She watched as he laughed at something the bartender said.

"Yes," Kai admitted, "but he's still overpriced, and now you have no money to help get you settled."

Ruby's head whipped back around. "I thought I would be traveling with you," she replied, panic creeping into her voice.

Kai placed a hand on Ruby's shoulder. "Calm down. I never said you couldn't, and if that's what you desire, I will gladly take your company." Ruby let out a relieved breath as Kai continued. "Even so, we'll still need supplies for you. I don't think you're cut out to join my guild, but your magic is stronger than mine, so I'm sure Alek can find a use for it."

There was that name again, but while Ruby was curious about this Alek person, she had other more pressing concerns.

"I still have this," she said, pulling her kerchief down to reveal the necklace.

Kai's eyes widened, and she glanced at Serik, who was still busy speaking softly to the innkeeper. She reached over and pulled Ruby's garment up to cover the necklace again. "That necklace has the duke's crest on it, right? You won't be able to sell that to any reputable jeweler. They'll think you stole it."

"Oh," Ruby said, a little disheartened. "Is it worthless then?"

"I didn't say that. You could still get quite a sum for it from the right people, but it's best to save that as a last resort." Kai stopped talking as Serik approached. Seeing her look, he paused.

"Did I interrupt?" he asked, his eyebrows raised.

"We were just talking about money," Ruby said, shifting in her seat. She was glad that the flower pendant was covered again.

"I'm sure you can find guild work in Issalden," Kai cut in as Serik slid into the chair on the other side of Ruby. "They pay well, and I'm sure, if you use your magic in addition to what you learned back at the Academy, you can get a decent job."

"But I..." Ruby trailed off after a quick glance at the wilder. She had been about to say that she had never worked before. While Serik already knew her father was a baron, she didn't want to let him know the depth of her ineptitude. He must have thought she was horribly naive.

There was a tight feeling in her chest. And why should she care what he thought? He was just their guide and nothing more, wasn't he?

Ruby couldn't help thinking about all the times he'd touched her. His gentle hands and his strong grip when he'd cleaned her feet the first night they'd met. His warmth against her back as they rode together. His breath on the back of her neck, and his arms around her, sometimes resting against her hip or thigh. Ruby didn't blame him for the touches. He needed a comfortable place for his hands to rest while holding Dream's reins, and Ruby found that she took comfort in his touch and...

And wanted more of it.

This line of thinking wasn't doing her any good.

Serik stared at her, his eyes bright with amusement, waiting for her to finish her thought.

"Is there something on my face?" she asked, both annoyed and embarrassed. There was no way that he could have guessed what she was thinking, but the man was very perceptive. Maybe he had, which made her blush even harder.

"No, but I like the view," he smirked.

"Ugh! Are you two going to stare at each other like that all night?" Kai cried in exasperation. "If so, I'll find a different table to sit at."

"I do not know what you are talking about. He is not at all pleasing to look at," Ruby said, turning away from him and leaning into Kai conspiratorially. "He is far too rugged and dirty."

"I am not dirty," he said, his tone indignant.

"He also snores," Ruby said, giving him an innocent smile. "Loudly."

Serik narrowed his eyes at her. "I do not."

Kai threw her arms into the air. "Please! I can't take it anymore!"

Ruby laughed, and all her worries seemed to melt away. She exchanged a grin with Serik. "All right, I will stop."

"No more flirting?" Kai asked.

Ruby held up her hand like she was making an oath. "Not that I was, but no more flirting."

Kai eyed her, then looked over to Serik.

"I make no promises," the wilder said solemnly. Kai rolled her eyes.

A few moments later, the innkeeper brought them three steaming plates with roasted quail, rice, and vegetables. After a day of riding, the food was hot and just what was called for. It wasn't as refined as what Ruby was used to eating, but she had a growing respect for food that would never grace a lord's table. The lower-class fare was warm and filling in a way that made her satisfied and sometimes sleepy.

"I need to inform the Guild of my arrival," Kai told her as they ate. "They'll want to set up a meeting right away."

"What guild do you work for?" Serik asked, and the question sounded off, like he was being too casual. Ruby glanced over at him. He was watching Kai closely.

"It's the none-of-your-business guild," Kai replied without missing a beat, mouth full of quail as she chewed on the drumstick. "Heard of it?"

"You know," he started with a glower in her direction, "you would have more friends if you were easier to talk to. Ruby, how do you stand her?" Despite the jab, the sides of his mouth twitched upward.

Kai scoffed and lifted another chunk of meat to her mouth. "And you'd have more if you didn't spend all your time in the woods, *wilder.*"

"He is kind of abrasive, is he not?" Ruby added thoughtfully.

Serik crossed his arms over his chest, turning his feigned displeasure at Ruby. "What did I do to deserve being saddled with the likes of you two?" He couldn't quite suppress the amusement that twinkled in his eyes.

The conversation continued like that until Kai left to find a courier who would carry her message that night. That left Ruby and Serik alone, and while there were a few other people in the inn around them, their closeness made it feel like they were the only two people in the room.

"So, what are your plans when we reach Issalden?" Ruby asked, wondering if Kai would consider the question to be flirting. She did hope he would stay with her and Kai, maybe more than she'd admit. He'd said he didn't like big cities, but Issalden was small compared to those in the south. She hoped he would stay there, at least for a while. The time she had spent traveling with the wilder, day in and out, made her feel like she had known him for much longer. They had spent every waking moment together, and if she was being honest with herself, she didn't want that to end.

He let out a deep breath and scratched at his beard. "I don't know. I wasn't planning to go to Issalden before I met you, but I could head over to the market and get supplies, I guess."

"You won't stay in the city?" Gods, she hoped she wasn't coming off as desperate as it sounded to her ears.

Serik chuckled, seeming to read her thoughts like an open book. "I prefer the wide-open spaces and freedoms of living off the land. As I told you before, cities make me uncomfortable."

Ruby nodded and looked down at her mug. It was still half full of cider. "Then you'll go back to the Wytchwood?"

"Maybe, maybe not. The nice part about having no home is that I can go wherever I please." A smile played at the side of his mouth, and his eyes regained that playful glitter. "Why do you want to know, Ruby? Need to be able to find me later?"

She raised her eyebrows in an exaggerated fashion and propped one elbow on the table, resting her chin on her palm while her other hand fidgeted with her fork. "You mean if I want to be accused of being a thief and have a rifle pointed at me?"

"I didn't point the rifle at *you*." He leaned toward her, and his hand brushed up against hers.

Ruby stopped fidgeting with her fork and looked into his eyes. She felt heat rising up her neck again and was all too aware of the pounding of her heart. *Stop it!* she told herself. *You are not some blushing maiden.* Besides, she had no way of knowing if he was just teasing her or if he was actually interested.

"I believe Kai said no more flirting," she heard her mouth say before checking in with her brain.

His grin widened. "Kai isn't here."

So, he was flirting with her on purpose. There was that

tight feeling in her chest again, and her stomach was in knots. Ruby liked Serik more than she was ready to openly admit, and that made her feel… guilty. It had only been a week since she'd followed Kai out of her window and into the cold night, only a week since she'd decided that she would not marry Mikel, and here she was. Talking, laughing, and—yes—*flirting* with a man she'd just met. What was wrong with her?

She'd never loved Mikel, but still, shouldn't she wait a little longer before she started looking at other men?

"Are you all right?" Serik asked, his smile fading. "You look like you might be ill."

Of course he would notice.

"I'm just tired," she said, pulling her hand away from his and standing from her seat. "I think I'll retire to my room now. There is a lot to do tomorrow."

Ruby turned away from him, taking a few steps toward the staircase that led to the guest rooms before she risked a glance over her shoulder. Serik was watching her, and she could almost feel that gaze burning into her skin. The knot of guilt settled in her stomach again, and she all but fled up the stairs and away from the wilder. Despite the lie she'd told Serik, she doubted she would get much sleep that night.

Issalden was a large city located northeast of the Academy. It wasn't the capital, which was far to the south, but Issalden was still a splendid place of commerce, or so Ruby had heard. Some called it the Gate to the West, as it was the last trade city before crossing the mountains into the surrounding countries. Ruby's parents and the duke resided in the south, so it wasn't a place that she'd traveled to before. She had imagined rows of tightly compacted, whitewashed buildings, cobbled streets painted red, and electric lamps on every corner like the big cities in the south, but Issalden was vastly different from the image Ruby had conjured in her mind.

The Gate to the West was smaller than expected with such a grandiose name. It was still large, being a trade city, but it was not as big as some of the others closer to her home. Many of the structures were made of multiple floors of unpainted wood, giving the place a very natural look. The streets were cobbled, but stalks of grass poked around the stones at the edges of the road, and there was not an electric lamp in sight, just the gas ones that needed to be lit manually and refilled every few weeks.

It was just after noon when the three of them reached the city, Serik and Ruby atop Dream and Kai on her stallion, which she'd named Midnight. Many people were on the streets of Issalden, and as they rode in, more than a few watched them as they passed. Some of the children waved to them, while most of the adults watched Serik warily.

"Is there something wrong with what we are doing?" Ruby asked after passing a group of women who had stopped chatting and scrutinized them as they rode past. "Why do people keep staring at you?"

"Wilders aren't exactly common," Kai answered her. "There aren't many people who choose to live off the land by themselves. A lot of the townsfolk find it suspicious. They think his kind are dangerous."

Ruby glanced back at the wilder. If the stares bothered Serik, it didn't show at all. His eyes flicked around at the buildings, and his expression was unreadable. He hadn't said anything to Kai's comments either. In fact, he hadn't said anything since they'd started approaching the city.

That wasn't like him. For a man who was supposedly living by himself most of the time, he was fairly talkative. She was suddenly aware of his hands resting on her thighs and the feel of him against her back.

Before she could say anything to him, Kai flicked her reins, and Midnight trotted ahead of them to a building with four hitching posts sticking out of the ground. She dismounted and tied the reins of her horse to the post.

"This is where we part, wilder," she said as Dream caught up with her. "You've fulfilled your obligation."

Ruby felt her breath catch. This was it? Was Serik going to leave them now? It seemed so sudden. Surely, before he left, they would stay the night in another inn and figure out what they were doing next. She waited for him to say something, to argue with Kai like he always did, but he said nothing. He moved, dismounting Dream, and walked her over to another hitching post.

Ruby stared at him in disbelief. Was he really going to leave just like that?

After tethering the horse, Serik reached up to help her down. She took his hand and slid off Dream, feeling numb. She was so stupid. It had always been just a job for him. She knew that. Hells, she'd even paid his fee that first night. Why was she surprised?

"It was a pleasure to meet you, Miss Ruby," he said, and she looked up at him. He was watching her with those hazel eyes.

"You have my thanks for your help, sir," she managed to get out, her genteel instincts taking over. Ruby averted her eyes and inclined her head.

He touched her forehead, tucking a loose strand of hair behind her ear. "If you need help again, you can find me if you go to Belleward." When Ruby said nothing, he placed his finger and thumb under her chin. He didn't tug hard, but she looked up at him again all the same. The ring of gold around his eyes seemed to glow in the afternoon sunlight. "I mean it. If you need anything at all, come and find me."

What if I need you now? she thought, but didn't say the words out loud.

Serik released her chin, then reached into his cloak. "Take this with you." He held out a small pouch until she took it. He gave her a brief smile then turned away from them and walked into the tavern, the door swinging closed behind him.

Silence reigned until Kai blew out a long breath. "Damn," she said quietly.

"What?" Ruby asked, and her voice sounded far away. She still clutched the leather pouch he'd given her.

"I thought for sure he was going to insist on accompanying us." Kai gave the knot she'd made with Midnight's reins a sharp tug to ensure it was secure. "He likes you."

That snapped Ruby's gaze from the tavern door to Kai. "Do not be ridiculous. He has not known me for very long. There is no way he would have formed an attachment that soon." She knew she was just making excuses even as she said the words. After all, she'd started to feel… something, and that something made her want to run into that tavern after Serik.

"You should open that pouch. I'm pretty sure I know what's inside it already, but let's see it."

Ruby blinked at her, then untied the drawstring. Whatever was inside was too small to see clearly, so she upended the bag on her palm. Two small objects tumbled out.

Diamonds sparkled in a dazzling array of colors with the help of the warm afternoon light. Her earrings. He'd given back her earrings.

"Idiot," Kai said, shaking her head.

"Excuse me?"

"I said what I said. And I'm talking about him, not you." Kai turned away from the inn. "Come on. Let's go complete this mission."

"But…" Ruby looked back at the tavern, uncertain. "But—"

"He'll still be here!" Kai hissed. She looked around warily. There were a few others on the street around them. A mother holding the hand of a child with curly blonde hair and two men across the street having a quiet conversation. "I don't want anyone else to know what we are doing. Let's get this over with. He just got here. He's not heading out of town any time soon. Now put those away, and let's go."

Ruby deposited the earrings back into the pouch and slipped it into the pocket inside her gown. She vowed to find the wilder again after they finished Kai's task. She didn't know what she would say to him, but she'd figure that out later.

Since the two women could not fit on Midnight without risking injury to the horse, they left him tied to the hitching post outside the tavern next to Dream and continued on foot.

They walked through the city and toward the docks. The Turnwater River ran through Issalden, flowing down from the mountains to the sea. It was the largest river in the area and only fifty miles from the empire's western border. As they approached the waterfront, the small houses and buildings disappeared, replaced by larger buildings that looked like they were for storage and shipping.

A signpost they passed read Brewer Street. Grass and weeds grew freely in the middle of the road here, and no carriages or carts were in sight. The lamp post next to the sign was bent and looked like it had been hit several times. Two of its glass panes were cracked, and the other three were missing entirely. Most of the windows on the dilapidated buildings on this street were boarded up, and one even had a tree growing through its roof. The street looked abandoned.

"Why are we here?" Ruby asked, looking around. Even in

the bright sunlight, the shadowy alleys set her nerves on edge. She walked closer to Kai.

"I just need to give the guild master the item, and then we can head back." Kai glanced at her. She didn't seem bothered by the roughness of the area. "I would have told you to stay with Serik, but I'd rather have you with me, just in case."

"You do not trust him?" Ruby asked, surprised. She had thought that Kai and the wilder were getting along well.

Kai let out a long breath. Despite the ease her body language displayed, her eyes still flicked around constantly. "He doesn't know Issalden like I do, and it's better if you stick with me. It will be quick! I promise," Kai added at Ruby's look. "I know it seems like a shady area, but I'm a guild member, so no one will mess with us."

They passed an alley with a few men down it that leered at them. Ruby wasn't so confident in Kai's words.

A few blocks down Brewer Street, Kai stopped in front of a large building with faded, red double doors. The building had three floors, and like the other warehouses on this street, the front windows had boards nailed across them. Paint peeled from the wood either from age or weather, and there was a sign above the doors, but it was too faded to read.

"Are we really meeting someone here?" Ruby asked, eyeing the building with apprehension.

"Ruby," Kai began patiently, "if you haven't figured it out by now, I'm part of the Thieves Guild. We don't meet in nice places."

Ruby swallowed. Ever since Kai had told her that her mission was to steal from the headmage, she had suspected the Guild that Kai had spoken of would be something like this. "Yes, I did assume."

Kai put a hand on her shoulder. "Don't worry. We'll be fine," she said, pulling on the left door. It creaked open with a groan of rusty hinges.

Sunlight streamed through windows high up on the walls of the large building. Most of the glass was broken, and the building, though rundown on the outside, was mostly clean inside. There would have been plenty of room for machines or workers by the dozens when this warehouse was in operation. The area in the middle of the room was cleared, leaving a wide-open space with furniture stacked against the walls. There was a layer of dust on the workbenches and tables that were pushed to the sides of the room, but the floorboards were free of debris. A staircase on the far wall led up to an office with more broken windows, but the steps didn't look sturdy, and Ruby would not have trusted climbing them.

At the center of the abandoned warehouse stood three men that fit Ruby's definition of a thief perfectly. They all wore hooded cloaks and black clothing. Belts heavy with daggers and other sharp objects were wrapped around their waists. Even from a distance, Ruby could feel the weight of their eyes on her. The feeling made her want to turn around and go back outside. She would rather take her chances on Brewer Street.

Only the man in the middle had his hood back so that his face was fully visible. He was tall and slender, his hair a light brown and cut short, and he wore a neatly trimmed beard. Ruby couldn't see his eye color from where she stood but thought they were dark. His face was all harsh angles, and the heavy shadows made him appear even more menacing.

As the two women entered, the man unfolded the arms across his chest. Kai didn't seem surprised by their presence and continued forward. Looking around nervously, Ruby followed Kai deeper into the warehouse and closer to the men. *This will be quick,* she repeated the words that Kai had said. *Then we can go find Serik.*

The tall man nodded at Kai. "Kai, welcome back." His voice was a soft tenor with a hint of a northern accent.

Kai stared at the man before her as she approached. Her relaxed demeanor changed, and her hand drifted toward her belt. After a quick glance around the room, her frown deepened. "What are you doing here, Joran? I thought this meeting was with Alek. I told him to meet me here, not you."

The man's dark eyes tracked to Ruby. They were a brown so deep that they almost looked black in the shadows of the warehouse. There was no emotion there. His expression was so cold that it sent ice through Ruby's veins. She tried not to shiver.

His eyes only lingered on her for a heartbeat, then flicked back to Kai. "The guild master is occupied." He took three steps forward before continuing. "I've come in his stead."

Ruby backed away as the man named Joran stopped a few feet in front of Kai. She had a bad feeling about this.

"You have my money, then?" Kai demanded. She didn't seem intimidated by the man standing before her, even though he stood more than a foot taller than her. "The thousand crests that Alek promised me?"

There was the sound of boots scuffing the floor, and Ruby looked over her shoulder to see two more men standing by the doors to the warehouse. There was a tight feeling in the pit of her stomach. Something wasn't right. She moved closer to her friend. "Kai..." she said softly.

Kai glanced over her shoulder, then fixed the thief in front of her with a glare. "What's going on, Joran? This is supposed to be just a handoff for the item." Slowly, her hand moved to hover over the hilt of her dagger.

The man smiled, but on him, it looked ominous.

He *tsked* at her. "Kai, stop playing dumb. You don't need to pretend anymore." When Kai didn't answer him, his brows rose. His eyes flicked past her, and he pierced Ruby with his gaze.

"Alek wants *her*."

CHAPTER 8

"Ruby?" Kai asked, unable to hide her shock. She hadn't expected anyone even to take note of Ruby. "What does he want with her?"

"You can drop the act, Kai," Joran said, eyebrows still raised. "We'll take it from here."

"Kai? What is he talking about?" Ruby's eyes were wide as they flicked rapidly from Kai to Joran. Her friend looked ready to bolt, but the two men were still guarding the door.

Growling in frustration, Kai turned back to Joran. "What does Alek want with her?" She moved to put herself between Ruby and the man she was addressing.

What was going on? Why would they want Ruby? The Guild wasn't above ransoming a runaway noble, but Ruby was dressed in plain clothing and didn't look like one of the nobility. There was no way Joran or Alek could have known who she was, unless…

Joran blinked at her slowly, watching her try to ferret out what was happening. Then he grinned. "You have no idea. Alek didn't tell you."

"Tell me what?!" Kai shouted, losing her patience. She was getting tired of his games. Joran was high-ranking in the Thieves Guild, a lieutenant within the inner circle that Alek kept close to him. Kai hadn't worked with him before, but what she did know of the man was that he was vicious, callous, and sadistic. He didn't scare her like he did some of the others working for the Guild, but she tried to avoid him whenever possible. Her fingers itched to feel the cool leather-wrapped grip of her dagger.

"Step aside," Joran said instead of answering her. He motioned to the two men behind them, and Kai knew they would be closing in. "I'm sure Alek will give you a good chunk of the reward."

Kai grabbed Ruby's hand and pushed the taller woman behind her, turning them so that they could see both sets of men. "Not until you tell me what's going on." Kai felt Ruby's grip on her hand tighten but ignored it.

Grabbing her dagger, Kai pulled it free of its sheath. She had intended to throw it at Joran, but his hands blurred before she could even raise it more than a few inches. With a flash of steel, the weapon was knocked out of her hand and clattered to the floor. Kai swore loudly as pain lanced up her arm. Blood dripped from the cut Joran's blade had made in her flesh.

He *tsked* at her again, and it made her want to scream at him. Or punch him in the face. Either would work.

"You're not planning on claiming that reward all by yourself, are you? Alek wouldn't like that." Joran and the men with him stood a few feet from the women. There were four men in addition to the Thieves Guild lieutenant.

Kai needed to buy herself some time to think. Ruby was still behind her. How could she have been so stupid as to lead her here?

"And what reward would you be talking about?" Kai spat.

Flexing her injured hand, she winced. Her dagger was on the ground, but it was enchanted to return to her when desired. She would have to wait for the right time to summon the blade, when the men in front of them least expected it.

"What do we do?" Ruby whispered from over Kai's shoulder. The steadiness of her voice surprised Kai.

"Get your magic ready and prepare to run for it," Kai whispered back. To Joran, she said, "Well?"

"Fifty thousand crests," he said, leering at Ruby. That made Kai draw up short.

"You're kidding. There's no way…" She glanced back at Ruby, whose face had gone pale, her blue eyes wide. She might not have realized the value of twenty measly crests, but tens of thousands was an amount even the richest nobles could not ignore. There was only one person who would offer that kind of reward.

"The duke," Kai groaned, and when she faced Joran again, she was surprised that he was even closer to them than before. She cursed.

"That's right," Joran made a flicking motion with his hands, and the man beside him drew the hand crossbow hanging from his belt. "Alek is fond of you, so I'll give you a choice. Step aside or die trying to keep her from us." He looked like he would have been fine with either option.

Kai pursed her lips. They would have to fight their way out. Schooling her features, she gave Joran a curt nod, and he smiled at her.

In a flash, Kai threw one arm out and summoned her blade back to her. As the weapon disappeared from the warehouse floor and shimmered into existence in her fingers, Kai pulled on her magic, calling forth a blue flame that burst into life around her dagger. Drawing her arm back, she launched the weapon at Joran. "Run!"

The Thieves Guild lieutenant hadn't been expecting the

attack. He tried to dodge it but was a little too slow. Kai's blade sliced into his shoulder then tumbled past him and hit the man behind him, burying into his leg and setting his clothing on fire. The thief screamed in pain and tried to pat out his clothing as Joran snarled, "Get them!"

One of the men surged forward and tried to grab Kai as she dashed past him, but she was too quick, dancing out of his reach. She dashed for the door, but before she could even get halfway, a cry of pain made her whip around.

Ruby had tried to follow her, but the thief that had missed Kai had grabbed her arm. Kai watched as Ruby called upon her magic and sent a shock of electricity through the man, a less powerful version of what she'd used against the riphounds. The young noblewoman ripped her arm free as the attacker convulsed, but another one of the thieves lunged for her.

"Ruby!" Kai called her blade back to her, but she couldn't do anything before he reached her.

Ruby threw up a shield spell, blocking the thief, but a third grabbed her arm from behind, spinning her around and driving a fist into her stomach. She doubled over, coughing.

Kai took a step toward her, but a whistling sound made her jump back as pain sliced through her upper arm, making her fingers go numb. Blood soaked through her shirt, and she felt its warmth trickling down her skin. She looked up to see the man she'd stabbed in the leg holding his crossbow, barrel empty.

The one who'd hit Ruby pinned her face-down on the ground as Joran reached for the hilt of his sword.

"Don't rough her up too much," Joran called to his men. "The duke wants her in one piece." He freed a wicked-looking blade and turned to Kai. "You don't need to make this harder than it has to be, Kai." He slid the sharp edge down his forearm, drawing a long cut on his skin. Blood should have oozed from the wound, but there was the hum of energy in the air, and the steel seemed to absorb it. Joran raised the weapon, pointing it directly at Kai.

"Come with me, and we'll sort out this misunderstanding. I don't want to hurt you, Kai."

Kai felt an oppressive presence press down on her. There was an oily feeling against her skin, and she recognized it as dark magic. The pain in her arm seemed to intensify, and she sucked in a sharp breath as her muscles tensed. She felt the binding being placed on her, but one of the perks of a formal education was that the Academy had taught her how to ward off such a spell.

With a grunt of effort, she pulled on her own power, throwing up her mental defenses before Joran's spell could take hold. The effort caused her to stumble.

"Ruby!" Kai gasped as she steadied herself.

"Go!" Ruby shouted. The much larger thief was still pinning her to the ground. She struggled, but they both knew it was futile. "They won't harm me. Go!"

"Traitor!" Joran snarled. Kai flinched at the word but didn't argue. She had interfered on a guild job. In Joran's eyes, she was a traitor.

Kai didn't want to leave Ruby there but didn't know what else to do. They were outnumbered, and Joran already had Ruby.

"Fuck!" she screamed in frustration. Turning away from her friend, Kai dashed out of the warehouse doors. There were shouts from behind her, but she didn't look back as she turned a corner and, using some of her magic, climbed up the wall of the next building with cat-like grace and speed. Her arm still throbbed, and her fingers didn't work like she wanted them to, but Kai managed to haul herself onto the roof.

She didn't look back as she ran. The Guild would be after

her, and Joran would send his minions to follow, but she had to find help. She had to find Serik to help her get Ruby back.

CHAPTER 9

Serik took a seat at the bar, one that gave him a clear view of the tavern's front window. He watched as the retreating forms of the two women he'd escorted to Issalden faded into the distance. Returning Ruby's payment meant he gained nothing from the trip, but that was all right. She was starting fresh and would need the money. It had not only been the right thing to do. He'd wanted to do it.

Ruby intrigued him, not because of her beauty or status as a member of the nobility, but because she was witty and honest, if a bit naive. She was impulsive, brave, and had the oddest taste in friends. If Serik was being truthful with himself, his interest was in no small part spurred on by how attracted he was to her. Her reasons for leaving seemed simple enough, but he suspected there was more to it than just being discontented with her arranged marriage. She craved something that had been out of reach her entire life.

Freedom.

Running a hand over his face, he tried not to think about the subtle scent of jasmine that lingered in her hair. Every day that Serik held Ruby during their ride through the countryside had been a slow form of torture as he tried to keep his body from reacting to the feel of her against him. He could have made a move on her in earnest one of the many times they had been alone the last few days, but Serik doubted she would appreciate his advances with her broken engagement still fresh on her mind.

Perhaps he should have insisted on staying with them. If he were to judge by their interaction the previous night, Ruby wanted him to stay.

"You look like you could use a drink, wilder," came a gruff voice as the bartender stepped up from the other side of the counter.

The familiar voice made Serik look up.

"Romus, you're still here?" He chuckled as the thin man with graying blond hair gave him an exaggerated bow. "Yes, more than one, I'm afraid."

"Trouble on the roads?" Behind his spectacles, Romus's brown eyes flicked over Serik's face, reading his expression like an open book. The edges of the barkeep's mouth turned down. "Or perhaps, something heavier on your mind?"

The wilder nodded and sighed. "A woman."

Romus blinked. "That's a first."

"And what is *that* supposed to mean?"

"Only that if you've ever had problems with women before, this is the first I've heard of it," the barkeep said as he wiped a spot off the counter.

"You don't know anything about me, Romus."

"I know you never get worked up over women, and I haven't seen you take an interest in the fairer sex before." He adjusted his spectacles. "It makes me think the one that's caught your eye must be special."

Serik grunted. "She is."

He stared out the window again as Romus fetched a mug of a frothing amber liquid. The foam threatened to spill over the sides as he set it down in front of Serik. Midnight was still tethered outside, next to Dream. The younger horse pawed at the dirt impatiently and flicked his tail. That meant that Ruby and Kai were planning to return, didn't it?

He sat there for a while, nursing his drink and watching for any sign of the two women as more patrons entered the tavern. Romus busied himself making food for his customers, though he still came by to exchange Serik's drink for a fresh one when it was low. The smell of rosemary and fresh bread permeated the air. A gentle hum filled the building as people ate lunch and chatted. Some glanced skeptically in his direction.

That was fine by him. He had a reputation for being a suspicious outsider, but that meant they wouldn't bother him.

"Anything new I should know about?" Serik asked when Romus came by with his third drink. Not much changed in this part of the empire, but Serik still asked whenever he came to Issalden to get supplies.

The barkeep frowned thoughtfully. "Well, the Kuchers' farm was raided by imperial soldiers last week, but the mayor is claiming that there isn't a patrol in the area right now." He scoffed at that. "As if that man was organized enough to know who's running amuck on his lands. Oh, and the town's been in an uproar after the notices went up looking for that girl."

"Notices?" Serik asked, picking up the drink Romus had just set down. "I didn't see anything posted when I rode in."

"That's right," Romus said, snapping his fingers. "You wouldn't have seen them." He reached under the bar and pulled out a sheet of parchment.

Serik took a sip of his ale and spluttered when he read the notice the barkeep slid over to him. Ruby's face stared back at him. It was a well-done illustration, capturing the beauty and elegance of the young woman. The notice read *50,000 Crest Reward. Missing. Ruby Valestris.*

Fifty thousand crests was a fortune, an unthinkable amount to pay as a finder's fee. It was almost enough to buy one's way into the nobility.

There was a short description of her beneath the image, but Serik stared at Ruby's surname. Valestris. He knew that name. How did he know that name? Thinking back to their conversation in Belleward, his brows furrowed. She had said her father was a baron. Baron Valestris.

And then it hit him. Mikel Xavier Lucius Belmont II, the Duke of Ayrilon, was engaged to the only daughter of Baron Valestris. That could only mean that Ruby was Mikel's fiancée, and she had left him.

Serik jumped out of his seat so fast that he almost knocked over his drink.

"Watch it!" the barkeep said crossly, then peered at Serik's face. "You look like you've seen a ghost, wilder."

"How long have these notices been up?" he asked Romus hurriedly. "Are they all over the city?"

The barkeep nodded knowingly. He was assuming Serik was interested in the bounty. "As I said, there was quite a fuss over this girl since these were posted." Romus leaned down and plucked up the paper, placing it back under the counter. "No one has seen her, but this is a bloody king's ransom. Everyone's looking for her."

"Why aren't these posted outside?" Serik pressed. "Why didn't I see this before?" He could have missed it, but Serik was certain the notices hadn't been posted on the street when they'd ridden into town.

"The Guilds keep taking them down," Romus replied with a shrug. "Rumor is that one of the guild masters has a lead on the girl, and he doesn't want any competition, but I say that's bullshit. Everyone in town already knows about it. What's the point of tearing them down?"

To set a trap for her, Serik thought. He pulled out a shiny silver mark and set it on the bar. "I have to go." He headed for the door, not waiting for a response.

His head was still trying to wrap itself around the new information. Ruby was engaged to the Duke of Ayrilon, a man whom Serik despised. No wonder she had refused to tell him her surname. She wouldn't know of his animosity toward the duke, but anyone familiar with the nobility would have known who her betrothed was.

If Serik knew Mikel—and he did—he would hunt her to the ends of Asara. The duke didn't like to lose, and his fiancée leaving him would have been a significant loss of face and something that could not be tolerated. He would want to punish her, and offering that much money, he would find her. Bounty hunters and guild enforcers alike would be lining up to drag her back to him. And because the duke wanted Ruby, Serik would never let him have her.

He raced down the steps and over to Dream, untying her from the hitching post, and heaved himself into the saddle. The streets were mostly empty, which was a small blessing. Had anyone recognized her and followed? He should be able to find them quickly. It had been what? An hour since they'd parted ways? They couldn't have gotten far.

Kai had said that she needed to meet with her guild leader. Though the woman had never outright said it, Serik was sure that meant the Kingfishers—the Thieves Guild that was infamous throughout the Andrean empire. She had been contracted to steal from Valwen, and only a guild would have the resources to get her into the school. Serik didn't know the name of the guild master, but he was certain that everyone in the Guild would have seen Ruby's picture. He cursed under his breath and wheeled Dream around.

The women had set off toward the east end of town, in the direction of the river. That would be the first place to look.

Serik urged the mare into a quick trot and then a run as he scanned the streets, looking for any sign of Ruby and Kai. Hopefully, they had not gone straight to meet Kai's contact but had stopped somewhere for food or rest first, though he doubted it. His instincts told him that they had not diverted from Kai's task. Kai seemed in a hurry to get rid of that item she carried. She couldn't have known that a trap waited for them.

Or had she?

Had this been her mission all along? To lure the young noblewoman out of the safe confines of Valwen Castle? Would she hand over Ruby in exchange for part of the reward her betrothed had offered?

Shaking his head, he dismissed the first question. There was no doubt that the women were close, and Ruby trusted Kai, but as for the second…that was a lot of money, and Serik had seen friends turn on each other for less.

Just as that thought crossed his mind, a figure dashed out of an alley and into the street in front of him. Serik had to pull hard on the reins to avoid hitting the person. There was a flash of familiar straw-colored hair, and then he was pulling Dream to a stop. The mare snorted, stamping the ground irritably with her front hoof. Serik turned her around, coming face to face with Kai, who was sitting on the ground looking up at him.

Ruby's friend panted heavily, eyes wide as she stared.

"Where is she?" Serik growled down at her.

His words seemed to finally get through to her. To his surprise, Kai's eyes filled with tears, and she blinked rapidly to keep them from falling. "They have her!" she cried, getting to her feet. "They took Ruby, and I couldn't stop them!"

Fear balled in Serik's stomach, but he pushed it down. There was no time to let his emotions get the better of him. If they wanted to help Ruby, they had to act quickly. "Where?" he asked her as he reached a hand down.

"The old warehouse district, Brewer Street," she gasped. Serik took her hand and pulled her up into the saddle behind him. Flicking the reins, he pressed his heels into Dream's sides, and they lurched forward, quickly gathering speed.

"What happened?" Serik asked as they rode. He was pretty sure "they" meant the Thieves Guild had ambushed them, but any extra information would aid them in trying to free Ruby.

"They knew who she was and were waiting at the meeting spot. There's a reward. Fif—" She stopped talking abruptly.

Serik glanced over his shoulder. She looked at him with wide eyes, and he let out a sharp breath. He knew what she was thinking. Kai didn't know him, not really, and she had been about to tell him about the reward for Ruby's safe return, a fortune that would give anyone pause. But he was not about to hand her over to Mikel, no matter the bounty.

"Fifty thousand crests," he finished for her. "I saw the notice after we parted."

There was a brief moment of silence, then a pressure against his back and a sharp pain as Kai pressed the blade of her dagger into his ribs. He jerked the reins, and Dream reared back, throwing Kai off balance. Serik threw his elbow back, connecting with the woman's chest and knocking her off the horse. She fell to the ground, but instead of landing on her back, she twisted around in mid-air and landed on all fours like a cat, her dagger still gripped tightly in one hand.

She threw the weapon at him, just like the first time they'd met. He ducked to one side, barely avoiding it, and swore loudly.

"Are you serious?!" Serik asked as he brought Dream back around, annoyed. The mare stamped her feet, unhappy with the sudden change of direction. He felt his side. The edge of the blade had cut through his outer leather vest but had not pierced the shirt or skin beneath. He leveled a glare at the woman. "Would I have told you I knew about the reward if I'd planned on taking her to the duke myself?" he asked hotly.

"Or you could be lying to try and get to her," Kai said as she rose. "That's a lot of money for a wilder who would take jewelry from a half-dressed woman he came across in the woods."

Serik clenched his jaw as he slid off Dream, never taking his eyes off Kai. He wanted to be ready in case she threw that blasted knife again. "In case you don't know, I gave her the earrings back," he growled, stalking toward her. "I gained nothing from our little trip. I want nothing from her."

Kai scoffed. "Everyone wants something, Serik. I've seen the way you look at her."

He was tired of this. "Who else is going to help you? You can't save her on your own, can you? If you want her back, you'll have to trust me."

Kai pursed her lips. After a few seconds, her dagger appeared in her hand again. Serik eyed it warily, but she put it back in its sheath. "Fine, but if I even *think* you will betray us, I'll kill you." Her voice was deadly flat.

Serik turned away from her with a scoff and swung up onto Dream. This little altercation had cost them precious time, time that Ruby simply did not have. "Let's go," he said, pulling her up behind him again.

Kai talked as they road, describing in detail the ambush the two women had walked into. Serik didn't say it, but he thought Kai shouldn't have taken her there in the first place. If she had left Ruby with him, they wouldn't be in this mess.

When they approached the warehouse district, Serik pulled on the reins, slowing Dream's pace.

"What are you doing?" Kai hissed.

"If we barge in there, we'll just get caught. We'll be outnumbered, and I'm betting those men are waiting for you to return. It would just be another trap." He pulled Dream into an alley, then slid off the saddle.

Kai followed him in short order. She stared at Serik as he unstrapped his rifle. "I *know* that," she muttered. "I know where they are for now, so we can hit them when they move her from the warehouse."

"Do you know where they're taking her?"

"I would think they would take her to headquarters, but I can't be sure. The warehouse was just to make the exchange. Joran said Alek wanted her specifically, so he'll want to ensure it's her. He wouldn't risk turning in the wrong person with that many crests on the line." She grimaced. "If they make it there, we won't be able to get her out. There will be too many people for us to even get close."

"How did you get away from them?" Serik asked, looking around. "You're quick, but not quicker than an arrow." Or a bullet.

"I used magic to climb the building. They didn't follow me onto the rooftops."

Serik nodded, understanding. Up there, Kai's nimble and light frame would have the advantage. She could have gotten away before they'd even scaled the wall.

"Let's go that way then," he said. "Even if they are watching for you, we can come from a different angle." He scratched the spot between Dream's eyes, and his voice quieted as he spoke to the horse. "We'll be gone for a little bit, girl," he told her. "You know what to do."

Kai eyed him. "What are you doing? Shouldn't you tie her up so she doesn't wander off?"

"Dream is well trained. She knows to wait here for us. But if someone comes by and tries to take her, she'll run off and circle the area until I return." He checked the barrel of the rifle to make sure it was loaded and shouldered it.

Kai looked doubtful, but nodded.

"All right," she said, reaching into the pouch at her belt and pulling out a snow-white feather. Her brows furrowed in concentration. As Serik watched, the feather dissolved into motes of blue light. The little lights swirled above her palm like dandelion fluff in the breeze. Kai held out the same hand to him, palm up.

Serik had seen plenty of spells cast in his life. He had no skill with the art and hadn't had many enchantments cast on him, but there was no time to be hesitant about what effects the magic would have. Serik took Kai's hand.

Nothing happened at first. Just as he was about to ask her what the spell did, a tingling feeling went up his arm and spread throughout his body. Kai grinned at him, then let go of his hand and backed up a few steps. Dashing at the alley wall, she used her momentum to scale it. She grabbed onto the edge of the tiled roof and hauled herself up with as much effort as Serik took climbing into the saddle.

He had to admit that he was a little impressed.

Kai leaned over the edge, one hand reaching down to him. Serik's eyebrows climbed his forehead. He had to weigh at least twice what the small woman did. Did she expect to be able to lift him on her own?

Then he thought of the little blue motes that had floated above her palm. Could she have made him lighter?

He ensured he had a good grip on his rifle, then reached up and took her hand. To his amazement, she pulled him up after her as if he weighed no more than the snowy white feather she'd used to fuel her spell.

"That's a neat trick," Serik said once he was firmly on the

rooftop. The tingling feeling was quickly fading from his limbs.

"Yeah, well, it's a one-time deal, at least for the next few hours. My magic isn't as strong as Ruby's. I was only in my first year at Valwen, but it was never very developed to begin with." Kai looked up at Serik, and he swore her cheeks had turned pink. The admission to her lack of skill embarrassed her.

"Once is enough," he said and walked over to the other side of the roof, looking out over the tops of the buildings on Brewer Street. "How much farther to the place she was taken?"

"The end of the street," Kai said, shaking out her right hand and wincing.

Looking closer, Serik noticed a deep cut that went from her thumb to a few inches below her wrist, but before he could ask about it, she moved.

She dashed forward like she had in the alley, then leaped to the next roof over. The gap had to be at least six feet wide, but the petite woman cleared it easily.

Serik was athletic, but his expertise was living in the forest, not jumping from building to building in the city. He backed up, giving himself plenty of room, then ran and leapt across. He barely reached the other side, rolling forward and hugging the rifle close to him so he didn't lose it.

By the time he got to his feet, Kai was already running toward the next building. Serik swore under his breath. He could barely keep up with her as they moved, and gained a new appreciation for the woman's skills. There hadn't been a chance for Kai to show off what she could do while traveling through the Wytchwood, but, now, he could see why she was a guild member.

They reached the last building and slowly crept across the roof to the other side, watching for any sign of movement.

"No one seems to be up here," Kai said in a low voice as she looked around. She got on her stomach, crawling up to the edge.

"Thank the gods for that," Serik muttered as he tried to catch his breath. He didn't crawl like Kai, but crouched low as he approached the edge of the roof, looking down at the large warehouse on Brewer Street.

A couple of men were at the entrance, standing next to a horse-drawn wagon that held an iron cage. They wore all black, and the sunlight glinted off their weapons. Sitting inside the cage with her back to the door was Ruby.

Serik let out the breath he'd been holding. Her dress was stained with dirt, and her hair was mussed, but she looked unharmed. He didn't think they would have hurt her since the duke would want her back in one piece, but there was always a chance that the wrong man could have gotten his hands on her. She looked all right, and the tenseness in his shoulders that had been there since he'd first seen the notice eased away.

Ruby was talking to someone who was sitting in the wagon but was outside the cage, a man with auburn hair and wearing a bright red jacket. Unlike Ruby, this man looked like he'd been through hell. Even from this distance, Serik could see that the red jacket was torn, and his face was dark with bruises. The man's arms were positioned behind his back, making it obvious that his hands were tied.

Serik doubted this man was one of the thieves, but if he wasn't, then who *was* he?

Kai spoke before Serik could ask the question himself. "Who in the hells is that?"

CHAPTER 10

Gav was minding his own business, taking a stroll down the mostly empty streets of Issalden. It was still early in the afternoon, so the townsfolk were most likely in the city's center, visiting the market or finding meals at the various array of taverns and eateries the city offered. He was on the outskirts of Issalden, taking in the "view," if one could call it that. Despite its size, this place was a rare destination for a man like Gav, who had attended court in the emperor's palace only a few months ago, but sometimes one needed to go to drastic measures not to be chased by one's enemies.

His steps took him toward the warehouse district, which was not a place he frequented. Issalden had a few guilds that operated out of the city, being the "Gate to the West" or some such nonsense, and where coin flowed, guilds prospered. The Kingfishers Guild was rumored to be headquartered here, and Gav had had a few run-ins with them before, so he preferred to stay in the more densely populated areas. But he'd needed to stretch his legs today after weeks of his new, sedentary lifestyle in hiding, so here he was, in the shady part of town.

He loosened the collar of his shirt as he peered down Brewer Street. It was turning out to be another fine, sunny day in the west, and his jacket was definitely too heavy. The clothing he wore was a little too fine for this area, but the lute strung over his back marked him as a *loresinger*—an entertainer who made his living playing songs and telling stories—and he refused to wear the fashions of the farmers here. The embarrassment would kill him. He had a reputation to uphold, lying low or not.

He could see the river behind a few warehouses and was just thinking about heading to the water's edge for a refreshing swim when voices reached his ears.

"Get your hands off me!" shouted a woman's refined lilt. She sounded both angry and scared.

"Now, now," came a gruff voice that made Gav imagine some big, burly mountain of muscle. "If you struggle, you'll just get yourself hurt. Be quiet and be a good girl. We'll get you back to where you belong as soon as we get paid."

Slinking forward on quiet feet, Gav peered around the corner of a rundown building to see two men, one holding the arms of a young woman with dark hair behind her back while the other watched. The men were much larger than the slender lady and dressed in black clothing and cloaks that seemed to absorb the afternoon sunlight. Gav's eyes narrowed.

The man shoved the young woman into a cage secured to the back of a wagon, like the ones that toted around prisoners. The difference on this one, however, was that there was a ring of iron around the bottom. Little crystal shards were tied to the iron band with copper wire every few feet, and the gems glowed with a faint blue light.

Gav's eyebrows climbed his forehead. He hadn't seen an

abrogation prison since he'd left the southern cities. The device neutralized magic within its confines, allowing authorities to transport prisoners who could use the art. It was unflatteringly nicknamed a "mage cage," but the moniker described it accurately enough. Mage cages were supposed to be carefully regulated, but it seems this one had slipped out of the hands of the government. Just by looking at them, he highly doubted that these men worked for the empire.

"Mind your own business, Gav," he muttered to himself. "Don't get yourself into trouble. *Again*." The loresinger tended to stick his nose where it didn't belong, and it had landed him in hot water on multiple occasions. It was partly why he was stuck all the way out here in this gods-forsaken city.

The young woman yelped in pain as she stumbled and fell to her knees. The one looming over her laughed as he secured the door of her prison, and Gav walked toward them before his brain caught up with what the rest of his body was doing.

"Excuse me!" he called to the men. "I may be misreading this situation, but I don't think she likes that."

The men whipped around, their hands a blur as they drew weapons from belts where they had previously been sheathed.

"Come now! Let's not be hasty," Gav said as he threw up his hands, palms out to show that he wasn't holding any weapons. That wasn't to say that he was unarmed. There was a very well-hidden knife up his sleeve. Then there were the two pistols and a rapier at his belt. "Surely, we can talk about this."

Eyes roving over this newest distraction, the thug who had stood there watching his comrade manhandle the young woman scowled. He focused on the lute strapped to Gav's back and gave a dismissive shake of his head. "Piss off, loresinger, before you get your throat cut," he said.

"That would be a shame, as it's how I make my living." Gav lowered his hands, keeping them away from the weapons at his belt. "And it would be a shame for the two of you to be arrested for kidnapping a young woman. Do you feel like being hanged, hmm?" Gav thought he saw a worried look cross the slightly less burly man's face.

Pressing his advantage, Gav took a few steps closer to them. The young woman stared at him from within the cage, her captivating blue eyes wide as she gripped the iron bars. The light blue gown was covered in dirt stains and dust, and her hair was messy in its over-the-shoulder braid, but she appeared to be unharmed. "I'm sure if you let the young lady go now, she would agree not to run to the constabulary. Yes?" he directed at her with a wink.

"There are mo—"

The one closest to the cage hit the metal bars with his sword, silencing the young woman and causing her to flinch.

Gav clenched his jaw but forced himself back into a relaxed smile. "Be reasonable, gentlemen. You won't get far with her, not in broad daylight. Someone will see her and report you. Release her, and we can all go our separate ways." There were only two of them, but neither had any firearms he could see. Gav thought he could take out the bigger one with a pistol, and then fend off the smaller one long enough for the gunfire to draw more attention. Hells, there was a reward for slavers in the empire. He was betting he could convince them to give up whatever scheme they had planned.

It was a risk, but not a large one. If it came to a fight, Gav was quite skilled with his blade and an excellent shot. It was how he'd survived for so long, traveling alone.

Instead of complying with Gav's request, one of the men

did something decidedly odd. He turned to the warehouse and hit his fist on the door twice. The loresinger blinked, and he felt he was missing something crucial. Intuition nagged at him, and he started to back away. What had the girl been about to say?

Gav swallowed hard. *More.* She had been trying to tell him that there were more of them.

The door to the warehouse creaked open as another two dangerous-looking men stepped out into the sunny afternoon.

"You know," the big man said as he crossed his arms, his lips spreading in a wicked grin. "I thought you looked familiar. There's a reward for a loresinger by the name of Gavin Ilias. Heard of him?"

A chill went down Gav's spine. "N-no! I'm afraid I don't know the man of whom you speak," he spouted nervously. It didn't sound very convincing, even to him. Dammit. He wouldn't even be in this mess if he hadn't gotten so drunk that night two months ago.

"There's a rumor he's in Issalden," the man glanced over at his comrades. "And a large bounty on his head. One thousand crests."

"I heard he poked some nobleman's wife," one of the others who'd exited the warehouse said with a chuckle.

"Word is that he's wanted alive so the earl can rip his cock off."

It was time to go. Gav had no intention of being caught.

His eyes met the young woman's, and he felt a pang in his chest. As much as he didn't want to leave her with these men, he couldn't do anything if he, too, was captured. Gav could leave and report these men to the authorities, and with any luck, the constabulary would catch them before they got very far with her.

One of the thugs who had stepped out of the warehouse pointed a crossbow at Gav, and he froze mid-step.

"Don't move, loresinger."

A fifth man eased out of the warehouse. This one was tall and lean with light brown hair and a beard. The man eyed Gav, his stare cooler than the northern snowmelt.

Great, Gav thought, *me and my big mouth*. He was sorely outnumbered now. One or two men he could have taken, but five? There was no way he was getting out of this unscathed. He could have just kept walking, but he'd had to play the hero. His eyes slid over to the young woman watching him from the cage. Wide eyes in a face that was as terrified as it was beautiful.

No, he couldn't have left her to this fate and lived with himself.

Since going for his weapons would surely result in his death, especially with that crossbow pointed at him, he remained still as the closest of the men approached him. Gav's mind raced frantically, going through options. He couldn't allow these men to take him. There was no doubt that the earl would cut off his cock like they'd suggested and torture him before he was hanged. Noblemen were always so prickly about their honor. Gav would have to be quick to get out of this with all his appendages still intact.

The smaller man reached for the weapons on Gav's belt, his eyes flicking away from the loresinger's hands.

That was when Gav made his move. Grabbing the man's arm, he yanked him to the side, putting the thug between himself and the crossbow.

"What the fuck?!"

There was the click of the trigger, and the man jerked, crying out in pain.

The one with the crossbow would need to reload. Gav released the thug, letting him writhe on the ground as he pulled a pistol, pointing it at the bowman. "I would drop that if I were you."

To his surprise, the man complied. Gav had been expecting the man to refuse or argue with him. He allowed himself a small smile. Perhaps things were finally starting to go his way.

Just as that thought crossed his mind, the lean man who had exited the warehouse last dashed forward so quickly that the loresinger barely had a chance to adjust his aim. Between one breath and the next, the man had dodged under his outstretched arm, coming up behind Gav in a low crouch.

As Gav began to turn, this new attacker lashed out, smashing the pommel of his dagger into the back of Gav's knees. A loud crack of gunfire echoed off the buildings, but the bullet went wide, completely missing his assailant. The next thing he knew, Gav was tumbling forward. He threw out his arms to break his fall, cracking his elbows on the stone and hitting the ground hard as pain shot up his legs. Who the hell was that? He was so fast!

Once the firearm was discharged, the other men moved. Shot spent, Gav dropped the pistol and tried to scramble away as they closed in on him. One laughed as he stepped on Gav's hand, drawing a pained gasp from him. Gav drew the knife from his sleeve and slashed at the thug's calf, freeing himself as the man yelped in pain and surprise.

Regaining his footing, he tried to put some distance between himself and the others, but the large man he'd taunted before stepped into his path and swung a giant fist. Stars exploded in Gav's vision, and agony lanced through his jaw. The sharp taste of iron filled his mouth as he stumbled back.

The large man wasn't finished with Gav yet. He grabbed a fist full of his shirt and rammed his other hand into his stomach, releasing him as he doubled over with a groan. Gav clutched his stomach, trying not to retch.

More pain erupted on the left side of Gav's face as another one of the thugs landed a blow. His legs gave out, and he crumpled, curling in on himself to shield his vital areas from the blows raining down. Wood crunched and splintered as the lute broke, and discordant notes sounded when the strings snapped.

Just as suddenly as they'd come, the impacts let up, and, a few moments later, something sharp prodded the arm covering his head.

"Don't kill him," said a voice he didn't recognize. It must have been the man with the light brown hair. It was obvious that he was their leader. "The bounty is for him *alive*. He's worthless dead."

Gav risked a peek. The man looming over him lowered his sword, but the relief was short-lived. Drawing his leg back, the thug kicked Gav in the stomach again for good measure, then lowered the blade to his throat.

"If you try anything else, loresinger," the tall man said, while another one of his ruffians knelt beside Gav with a length of rope in his hands, "I *will* have my man kill you, regardless of the bounty. We can't risk a fortune for pennies."

That last comment wasn't directed at him, but it made Gav look up all the same. One of his eyes was swollen shut, but the good one tracked to the young woman in the cage, taking a good look at her for the first time. Under the disheveled appearance that he was sure was due to the men around him, he saw she was younger than him by a few years. The plain gown she wore looked a little off on her. The perfect posture and bearing did not match the simple clothes. There wasn't a flaw on her skin that he could see, which was rare for a commoner. That was *if* she were of low birth, which he was beginning to think she wasn't. She looked familiar, though he was sure they had never crossed paths. He would have remembered.

Gav had assumed they were taking her to sell her off as a slave, but now, his mind upgraded her situation to kidnapping and ransom. There was a falling feeling in his stomach. Only one group in this area was bold enough to follow through with such a dangerous plan. These men were Kingfishers and worked for Alek. No wonder that man had been so fast.

Of course, it was just his luck that he would run into the very people he was trying to avoid.

Gav rolled onto his back. "Oh, you don't need to worry about that. I'm certain I couldn't draw my blade if I tried." There was a pang in his chest as he felt the broken pieces of his lute under him, but he clenched his jaw shut—no need to mouth off to this thief and get his throat slit.

"Tie him up and throw him in the wagon," the leader said. "Alek is expecting us."

CHAPTER 11

The man in the red jacket was in bad shape, the one the thieves had called Gavin Ilias. One eye was swollen shut, and his face was covered in angry red marks that would eventually fade into garish purple bruises. His clothing was ripped and torn where the thieves had beaten him, and he was covered in dirt. his shiny auburn hair was sticking up at odd ends. Blood stained his lips, and a cut above his right eyebrow slowly oozed as well. Ruby didn't doubt that he would be sporting many more injuries under his clothing. The lute he'd been wearing was smashed to pieces on the cobblestones. The thugs had bound his hands behind his back, and the loresinger sat in the wagon, leaning against the cage Ruby was trapped in, between two of the little glowing crystals.

Looking over at him, she felt the hot swell of guilt in her chest. The man had only been trying to help her, and this had been his reward.

As if the loresinger could sense her attention, he opened his good eye. It was blue like hers but darker in color.

"Are you all right?" he asked, and his voice sounded much

better than the rest of him looked. It was comical that he would be asking after her when he himself looked like he'd been through hell.

"Yes." Ruby leaned down next to him. She didn't dare reach through the bars of her cage. "Thank you for trying to help me."

He let out a chuckle that turned into a cough. "That didn't go very well for me. Perhaps playing the hero was not the smartest idea, but I've had worse." He breathed deeply and winced. "Not much worse, mind you."

Ruby rested her head on her knees and sighed. "I am sorry."

"What do you have to be sorry about? You didn't kick me while I was on the ground and destroy my instrument."

"But I am the reason you are bound. You would not be here if you had not tried to help me."

"My dear, *I* am the reason that I have been beaten and bound. My choice, my consequences. Though you should take my advice and never let a countess pour your drinks." He looked her up and down. "Or an earl. Or anyone for that matter."

Her lips turned up at the corners. "I will try to remember that."

"See that you do." He glanced over at the thief standing at the door to the warehouse. It was the big one who had done the most damage to the loresinger. After a moment, his eye tracked back to Ruby. "I am Gavin Ilias, though you may call me Gav." He tried to incline his head politely but grimaced in pain. "As those men said, I am a loresinger. One that is quite well known within the empire, if I do say so myself. I would bow or demonstrate my abilities with my lute, but, well," he shrugged one shoulder, "I'll need to replace it first. What is your name?"

"Ruby." She was going to leave out her surname, but it seemed useless since she was already in a cage. "Valestris."

His blue eye widened. "Ruby Valestris? You're the girl that everyone has been looking for. The one with the outrageous reward."

Heat rose to her cheeks. "Yes, that appears to be so. Though, I did not know of it until today."

"I assume you are related to the Baron Valestris. Your parents must really care for you to put out such a reward."

Her jaw clenched, and there was a tight feeling in her stomach. "I doubt that it was my parents."

Gav blinked his one good eye at her. "Who else would be willing to pay so much?"

Ruby just stared back at him.

"I do not mean to pry. It's just surprising, is all." He considered her, tongue flashing out to lick the dried blood on his lips. "A fiancée, then? You look about the right age for marriage, and the nobility do so love their matchmaking."

Before she could answer, the door to the warehouse opened. Two of their captors exited the building, one being the man Kai had called as Joran, who waved at the others sitting on crates across the street.

"We'll be leaving in a minute," he told them. "I can't wait for Kai any longer." The men started getting to their feet as he approached the wagon.

Ruby and Gav stared as Joran pulled himself into the back of the wagon. Thin eyebrows raised as he looked at the two of them huddled close together. "Please, don't let me interrupt."

Neither of them responded. Ruby got to her feet and backed up as far as the cage would allow her. The man stepped over Gav to get to the cage, ignoring the loresinger completely.

Pulling a large iron key out of his pocket, Joran unlocked

the door of the mage cage and slipped inside, closing it behind him again. Ruby pressed herself back into the bars. The cage wasn't overly large, and she and Joran stood only a few feet apart. The way he leered at her made her uncomfortable. She had seen that look before from men, but with the duke's aegis at her back, no one would dare touch her. Not only that, but the professors at Valwen had taught her how to defend herself, and she had grown more confident in her capabilities than she'd been in her entire life.

But, thanks to this cage, Ruby's magic was out of reach. Now, nothing protected her from men like him. She averted her gaze as he stepped in front of her, their bodies almost touching.

"It appears your 'friend' has abandoned you after all," Joran whispered with a sneer curling his lips.

Ruby turned her face away from him. She wanted to scream at him that Kai would come for her, but she held her tongue.

He grabbed her chin, forcing her to look up at him. She tried to turn away again, but Joran held her there, fingers digging into her skin. His eyes roved over her face, inspecting her features.

"Lovely. It's almost a shame to hand you over to the duke." The sneer was still in place. "When I first saw your image, I thought your beauty was exaggerated, but I see now that I was wrong." He released her chin. Eyes never leaving her face, he picked out a lock of her hair that had fallen out of her braid and twirled it around his fingers. He brought it to his nose and inhaled deeply. "We could have some fun before you have to go back to him."

"Touch me again, and when you hand me over to the duke, he will make sure that you will never be able to take pleasure in the embrace of a woman again," she hissed. "He will present your manhood to me on a platter." Her eyes flicked down and up again dismissively. "Little gift though it may be."

Joran stared at her, his eyes wide in surprise.

The blow landed before Ruby even realized it was coming. Pain exploded on the right side of her face as she fell back against the bars of her cage. Joran grabbed her arm and yanked her to her feet, pinning her. He *tsked*, forcing her head to the side and examining her cheek. Hot tears stung Ruby's eyes, and she averted her gaze as he checked the damage he'd wrought. She would not let this man see her cry.

"You shouldn't say things that might get you hurt, Ruby." Hearing her name on his lips made her grit her teeth. His fingers brushed her skin, and she winced. "As long as nothing blemishes that flawless skin of yours, the duke won't care if I have to use a heavy hand to obtain your cooperation." His eyes meandered down her body, and his fingers moved to her neck. Joran untied the kerchief and pulled it off.

"Much better," he murmured with a growl in his voice that made Ruby's skin crawl. Joran tugged at the silver chain, pulling the flower pendant from between her breasts. He turned it over and ran a thumb over the duke's crest.

"I wonder why he wants you back so badly. A man like him could have any woman he wants, but he spends so many resources on the one who ran away from him."

It was something that had crossed Ruby's mind as she'd sat in her cage. Even without Kai explaining the value of money for commoners, she knew that fifty thousand crests was a fortune. She had assumed Mikel would move on once he heard she was gone, but then again, she hadn't left so much as a note. As far as the duke was concerned, she could have been kidnapped, and she knew Mikel well enough to know that he wouldn't stand for anyone else touching what he viewed as his.

Perhaps it was all a misunderstanding. There was no

doubt Mikel would be angry with her, but he would be better off finding a new bride than suffering through the scandal of taking an unwilling one. Once she was out of this mess, she would have to find a way to formally dissolve their betrothal.

Joran was still speaking as she mulled over the duke's intentions.

"Not that it matters to me," he was saying. "If he wants to throw his money away, he can do whatever he wishes. Still…" Joran's thumb caressed her skin, making her stomach clench as she fought against the urge to push him away. It would only serve to earn her another slap. "It is such a waste."

"Get your hands off of me," she said, unable to keep the contempt out of her voice.

He *tsked* again, and now, she really wanted to hit him. "You're not in a position to be making demands, miss. If I wanted to hurt you, no one would stop me." The man gestured toward the men around the wagon. Their heads were turned away from them, waiting for their leader to finish his conversation. All except for the large one, who watched her intently. Joran grinned at her, and the look made her stomach turn. "There's no one here to help you."

Joran leaned into her. Ruby pressed her back into the bars and turned her face away from him. She felt his hot breath, then his lips, and finally his tongue on her neck, and she gripped the iron bars as hard as she could, clenching her jaw against the scream that wanted to tear from her. One of his hands ran down her side, and the other squeezed her breast. Ruby gasped and tried to wiggle out of his grasp.

Joran laughed and pressed himself against her, pinning her against the wall of her prison. "Yes, I do love it when they fight."

"Stop!" She pushed against his shoulders, trying to find

leverage, but he was heavy, and Ruby was not physically strong. "Let go of me!"

Joran seemed to be enjoying her struggle. "You're going to have to try harder than that if—"

"Leave her alone!"

Gav's voice cut off Joran's. Eyebrows raised in surprise, he stopped attempting to fondle Ruby and looked over at the man who was tied up next to her cage.

His eyes narrowed dangerously. "What did you say, loresinger?"

"You heard me. She clearly doesn't want you to touch her." The loresinger straightened, and he made a show of looking Joran up and down. Gav grimaced. "Honestly, I don't blame her. You're not much of a looker, are you? Oh, I don't mean to insult you, sir. I'm sure these country maids think you're a fine catch." He rolled his eyes dramatically. "You also smell like you haven't bathed in days, though the blood on your shoulder is a nice touch. I'd like to thank the man—or woman—who gave it to you."

Joran released Ruby as Gav spoke, and she scrambled away from him, hugging the opposite corner. He glanced at her for a long moment, then slowly turned away and opened the cage door, stepped out, and shut it. He took his time locking it again, not acknowledging Gav the entire time. Gav breathed heavily, glaring up at Joran.

Pocketing the key to the cage, he stepped in front of the other man and crouched so that they were at eye level. Gav swallowed hard, the calm facade he'd displayed cracked under Joran's level gaze.

"Why don't you say that again?" His voice was deadly flat.

Gav's face paled, but his jaw set in a stubborn line. "Leave. Her. Alone."

Joran's hand blurred, and a fist hit Gav in the side of the head, knocking him over. Stunned, Gav shook his head as if trying to get his bearings. Joran straightened and placed one boot on the loresinger's side, pushing him out of the wagon and onto the ground. A groan of pain rose from where Gav landed.

"I don't think a thousand crests is worth the hassle," Joran said loudly enough for all his men to hear. "Gentlemen?"

The large man who had done most of the beating on Gav stepped up, a sick grin stretching across his face. He let the loresinger get to his knees before he struck, hitting him in the face with his huge fist. Then he drew his foot back and snapped it forward, kicking Gav in the side as he hit the ground. Kneeling, the thug grabbed a fistful of the loresinger's hair and pulled his head up, making his back bow. He brought his other fist down on Gav's face repeatedly, cries of pain muffled by the sickening wet sound of the large thief's blows.

"Stop!" Ruby yelled, leaning against the bars. Reaching a hand through, she grabbed the sleeve of Joran's shirt to get his attention. "Stop it! You'll kill him!" She didn't know this man, but he had tried to help her. Gav had put himself in danger to try to stop these men from taking her. She couldn't just let him die.

Joran looked over at her. There was no sympathy in that expression. Ruby met his stare. She wouldn't let her fear of this man stop her from doing whatever she could to stop them from killing. Joran held out a hand as his man was pulling back for another blow, and the thug paused, Gav's blood staining his knuckles.

"Why?" he asked, expression unreadable.

"Please, I will cooperate," she said through clenched teeth.

"I don't need you to cooperate."

"But it will make the transaction easier, will it not?" Ruby grasped at any thought that came to her. "I... assume the duke is not in Issalden, and if he is to part with that much coin, he will want to verify that it is truly his betrothed that is waiting for him." As she spoke, her argument gained momentum. "That means it could be weeks until he arrives, or if you plan to take me elsewhere, transporting me in this device will draw unwanted attention and questions that you cannot afford to reach the ears of the authorities. I doubt any decent person would allow you to convey me thus."

Joran watched her, the suspicion evident on his face. Her logic was reasonable, and Ruby thought that he was giving her words serious consideration. After a few moments, he nodded. "Your word on it, Miss Valestris?"

She took a deep, steadying breath. "Yes, you have my word."

The man smirked. "I'm not sure I believe you." He reached through the bars, and Ruby had to stop herself from cringing away from his touch as he cupped her cheek. "Why don't you show me how sincere you are?"

Ruby gripped the bars hard, her knuckles turning white as he leaned toward her.

The sharp CRACK of gunfire reverberated off the walls of the battered buildings, and the large man looming over Gav jerked to one side, blood spraying from one leg. With a cry of pain, the man stumbled and fell to the ground.

While the men looked around wildly for the source of the attack, Ruby caught a glimpse of Gav, legs propelling himself away. The large man clutched his injured leg with one hand and grabbed at Gav with the other. The loresinger kicked the man's wounded leg and scooted away from him as the thief cried out in pain.

One of the other thieves dashed across the empty street and over to the next structure, another warehouse, and took cover behind a stack of crates. Joran hopped to the ground, using the wagon as a shield. The horse attached to it stamped its hooves and neighed loudly, startled by the sudden noise and movement. Ruby was surprised it didn't take off running, dragging her with it. At least then she would be away from Joran and his men.

A second shot rang out, this one less robust than the first but still just as loud. The spark of metal hitting stone flashed a few feet from the wagon, and the cobblestone there shattered.

The two remaining thugs still on their feet followed their comrade and took cover beside the building across from the wagon. Recovered from the surprise attack, they moved along the wall and back toward the main road, in the direction that the shots came from. The horse reared, and Joran had to grab its reins to keep the animal from bolting. Watching the street ahead of him, his eyes narrowed. Ruby followed his gaze. Something moved a few buildings down.

"In that alley!" he yelled to his men, pointing at the narrow space between the warehouses.

Ruby leaned against the bars, hoping to catch another glimpse of movement. Could it be Kai? Or Serik? Kai had a pistol, Ruby had seen it strapped to her belt, but that first shot sounded more like a rifle, which could only mean that she had found Serik.

There was a rustling behind her, and Ruby glanced over her shoulder. Gav was trying to boost himself into the wagon. The way he moved, with his hands still tied behind his back, reminded her of a worm wiggling in the dirt. She didn't think he would be able to make it over the lip, but he jumped and used the momentum to roll over the edge, stopping next to her cage. He was out of breath from the exertion and, by the look on his face, also in a lot of pain. His injuries looked worse than before. Blood stained his nose and upper lip, and most of the skin that was not covered by clothing, was dark with bruising. Ruby watched as he tried to catch his breath, but didn't dare move toward him. Joran was still preoccupied with trying to keep the horse calm, and she didn't want to draw his attention to Gav.

"Friends of yours?" he asked once he could finally speak.

She smiled. "Hopefully."

"Gods, I hope it's not someone else coming for the bounty," he groaned. "If so, we're fucked."

"I believe that is called an understatement."

He grinned at her, and his teeth were stained pink with blood.

Movement caught Ruby's eye, and what she saw when she looked up almost made her burst into tears.

Crouching and moving slowly so as not to draw attention to herself, Kai moved like a shadow against the warehouse. Catching Ruby's eye, she pressed a finger to her lips, signaling for her to stay quiet as she moved toward the wagon, now unguarded thanks to the gunfire.

"What…" Gav's words trailed off as Ruby threw him a frightened look. He clamped his lips shut, seeming to understand the situation in an instant.

Another thunderous blast echoed down the street. One of the thieves shouted.

Ruby tried not to stare at Kai, but watched her from the corner of her eye. Joran had the steed under control again and put one foot on the wagon tongue, presumably to boost himself into the driver's seat.

"What about your men?" Ruby blurted. She needed to buy time for Kai to reach them. "You're going to leave them to die?"

Joran paused and glanced back at her, mouth open to respond, but Kai had broken into a full run and bore down on him.

Her dagger flashed, but Joran moved faster, whirling around and catching her arm. "I knew you would be back!" He grinned at her as he pushed her back. "That bounty is too good to leave behind, and you want it for yourself." As Kai leaped out of his reach, Joran drew the same wicked-looking sword that he'd used before. "How dare you betray the Guild?!"

Kai scoffed, unphased by his hostility. "The deal was for the item, not for Ruby."

"Alek was wrong about you." Joran scowled. "He thought you'd understand and do what was best for the Guild. He's always favored you. How could you do this to Alek? To us?"

"Don't try to use him against me!" Kai shouted back, her face twisted in rage. "Alek was the one who was supposed to be here, not you! He would never have done this to me!" Her anguish was almost palpable, and Ruby thought that her eyes glinted in the sunlight.

Joran laughed, a sound that grated on Ruby's nerves. "You don't know him at all if you believe that! I always thought you were a bit green, but I never thought you were stupid. How do you think he became the leader of the Guild? Alek is ruthless." He took a step toward Kai and held out his blade. She took a few quick steps away, clearing the back of the wagon. "He would have killed you and whoever was helping you, then collected the bounty on that girl without a second thought. It would have been better if you'd cooperated."

With startling speed, Joran lunged at Kai, swinging his blade down at her. Swearing, Kai turned away from the weapon, trying to dodge the strike. The sword bit into her forearm, slicing through her clothing and drawing a large gash across her skin. Blood spattered to the ground as she jumped back, getting out of the range of another swing.

"Kai!" Ruby shouted. She tried to grasp her power, but she couldn't reach it. It was like hitting a wall, a wall that kept her magic just beyond her touch. Growling in frustration, she looked down at Gav. "Can you help me? I cannot cast any spells from inside."

The loresinger examined the cage intently, blue eyes roving over the iron bars and settling on the glowing crystals. He wiggled, turning himself so that his legs were closest to the cage. He hooked one foot under the iron ring that held the housing for the crystals in place, then pulled his other leg back and kicked out, hitting the luminous stones with his heel. He repeated the motion, but it didn't budge. "Dammit!" He scowled at the glowing stones. "This might take some time. If I can disrupt the current, you should be able to use your magic."

"She doesn't have *time*," Ruby said desperately as she watched Kai dodge another swing from Joran by ducking beneath his arm. His sword passed inches above her head. She was quickly losing control of the fight as Joran pressed her.

There were more sounds of fighting, yelling, and something large crashing to the ground behind them. Ruby glanced over her shoulder to see a barrel toppling onto one of the thieves as Serik kicked it at the man. Her heart leaped. He *was* here. He held the rifle in his hands and was in the process of reloading it while fending off Joran's men. The sword swing aimed at his neck went wide as the assailant stumbled out of the way of the tumbling barrel. Tossing the ramrod aside, Serik raised the rifle and pulled the trigger, hitting the thief squarely in the chest. The man fell backward, crumpling to the ground.

"Watch out!" Ruby cried as another one of Joran's men charged Serik, steel flashing in the afternoon sun.

He blocked the strike with the barrel of the rifle. Pushing forward, Serik shoved the thief's blade to the side and smashed the heavy butt of his firearm into the man's face.

The last man looked back and forth between the two fights. He took a step toward Kai and Joran.

"Get the gunman!" Joran snarled as he deflected a swing

of Kai's dagger. He countered, but she rolled to the side and out of his reach again.

Ruby tore her eyes off Serik, focusing her attention back on the battle between Kai and Joran. The Thieves Guild lieutenant had the much smaller woman in retreat, forced to block and parry as he rained blows on her. With a few quick steps, she gave herself a moment of reprieve. Her lips moved with a cadence that Ruby recognized as an incantation even though she couldn't feel its power from within her confinement. The dagger came alive with the same blue flame she had used in the warehouse. Kai lunged forward, slicing at Joran with a ferocity brought about by desperation and rage. Her blade connected, and she drew a long cut on his arm. At the contact, the fire jumped from her blade to his clothing, setting it aflame.

Joran screamed as he stumbled back. He tried patting out the flame, but Kai's magic would not be quelled so easily. His lips moved in a silent chant as he waved the opposite hand over the quickly burning clothing. The air rippled around him, and the fire died back, leaving the remaining cloth smoking and the skin beneath red with burns. While he was distracted, Kai rushed him, dagger going for his ribs.

She would have connected, but Joran turned with the strike. He drove an elbow into her back, sending her stumbling forward, then whirled back around, smashing the pommel of his blade into her side.

Kai stumbled to the ground, clutching at her side as she curled in on herself, face contorted in pain. A wicked grin stretched across Joran's face as he raised his sword, black blade seeming to pull at the shadows around them.

There was a sharp sound as the loresinger's boot finally cracked through the crystal, breaking it out of its housing. The blue lights flickered and died as Ruby threw her arm out, gathering her magic and focusing it.

"Fractus!"

Joran's blade shattered under the pressure of her spell. Shards of metal exploded out from where it had been, a long piece embedding itself in his shoulder. Letting out a cry of pain, he clutched at the shard, gritting his teeth as he pulled the bloody piece of metal out of his skin. He turned murderous eyes on Ruby.

"You," he growled, in that same deadly flat voice, "said you would cooperate."

Ruby felt a chill go down her spine, but set her jaw. He would not cow her. "The circumstances have changed, Mister Thief," she said with all the dignity she could muster.

Joran held her gaze a moment longer, then glanced at Serik, who was walking toward them, the dirt crunching under his boots. His rifle rested against his shoulder, and he looked unharmed. Behind him, two men lay on the ground, unmoving. The others who'd gone after Serik were nowhere to be seen. They must have run while Joran had been fighting Kai.

Serik said nothing as he approached but shifted to holding the rifle in both hands. Kai pushed herself off the ground, gripping her dagger and glaring at Joran, one hand still pressed against her side.

"It's over, Joran." Her voice was surprisingly steady.

The Kingfisher lieutenant scowled at her, but without his weapon and outnumbered three to one, the look wasn't as intimidating as it had been earlier. He seemed to realize this and took a few steps back, then turned and fled down an alley.

Swearing, Serik raised the rifle, but Joran was too fast. He was out of sight before Serik was able to aim. Kai's dagger flashed again but sailed through empty air as its target turned a corner and was gone.

She glared after Joran, then turned and walked over to

where the large man who had been shot in the leg still lay, grunting in pain. Ruby couldn't see him well from where she was but could hear his heavy breathing.

"Traitor!" he snapped. "Alek will have your head." Ruby heard him spit.

Kai scoffed. "He'll have to catch me first," she said, crouching beyond Ruby's line of sight. There was a meaty thump and a pained grunt, and then he fell silent.

"What an idiot," she said, moving over to the wagon. "You'd think he would keep his mouth shut and not antagonize the person looming over him with a bloody dagger." Kai pulled herself onto the wagon and looked down at Gav, raising one eyebrow.

"Oh, don't mind me," the loresinger said as she stepped over him. "I'll just lie here, bleeding."

A smile tugged at the corner of Kai's mouth as she knelt in front of the door to Ruby's cage.

Ruby wanted nothing more than to throw her arms around Kai. "Thank you for coming back."

Kai glanced at her, a wry smile on her lips. "What should I have done? Leave you here? When I went to all the trouble of 'kidnapping' you in the first place." She sounded annoyed and rolled her eyes at the word "kidnapping."

Ruby laughed, but it sounded more like sobs.

Kai pulled a small, rolled bundle of leather that Ruby recognized from a pouch on her belt and unfurled it to reveal little metal instruments. Selecting two, she inserted them into the lock. Clicking noises came from it as she worked.

After another dozen seconds of working on the lock, the catch released.

Ruby sighed in relief, and, now that she was free, she did throw her arms around Kai. The reality of everything that had happened in the past few minutes hit her all at once, and she clung to her friend, barely holding back tears.

"Whoa!" Kai staggered backward under Ruby's weight. "Let's get out of here before we start with the emotions."

"Pardon me, but if you would be so kind as to cut me free, I would be very grateful," came Gav's voice from behind them.

Kai glared down at the auburn-haired man. She released Ruby and crouched next to him. "Who in the hells are you, and what are you doing here? Are you part of the Guild?"

"Gavin Ilias, but you may call me Gav. Pleased to make your acquaintance." The smile he gave her was ghastly with the condition his face was in. "I happened to stumble upon your friend here while those brigands were accosting her."

"And then you decided to stop them by pounding your face into their fists?" The corner of Kai's mouth twitched.

"It seemed to be the best way to get their attention."

"It was very gallant," Ruby told Kai seriously, trying not to smile. She stepped out of the cage and put one hand on her friend's shoulder.

"If you're done fooling around, we should get out of here before the ones who ran can bring reinforcements."

Serik's voice made Ruby's breath catch as all the emotions she'd been feeling when they last parted welled up in her chest. He still held his rifle and glared down the alley Joran escaped through. He looked uninjured. In fact, he barely looked roughed up at all.

"You are no fun, sir. Where is your sense of adventure?" Ruby teased, this time unable to keep the grin off her face.

"I'll be more fun once we get you somewhere safe." Holding a hand out to Ruby, he smirked back at her. "My lady."

Ruby took his hand and hopped off the wagon while Kai cut Gav free. When she reached the ground, she shuffled from one foot to the other, then, throwing caution to the wind, threw her arms around Serik. Eyes stinging with tears, she held on to him tightly as his arms wrapped around her.

"You're safe now," he whispered into her hair, low enough that only she could hear his words.

"You came for me." Ruby breathed in the scent of firewood and cloves. It calmed her as her tears stained his jacket.

His chest rumbled with a low chuckle. "Did you think I would just let them take you after all the work I put in getting you here?" He pulled back, looking down at her face, and wiped a tear off her cheek with his thumb. "Are you hurt?"

She shook her head. "No, just a bit… I think 'manhandled' is the term."

Serik leaned close, examining her face. "Your cheek is red."

"Is it?" She reached up and touched where Joran had slapped her. It was tender, and there was a dull ache as she prodded at it. "I told Joran he had a small manhood, and he hit me, but I will be fine," Ruby added quickly as Serik's expression darkened. "Really, Serik, it barely hurts at all."

If he was going to respond, it was cut short by Kai jumping off the wagon and landing lightly on the cobblestones. "We'd better get out of here before Joran returns with more people, yes?" She repeated Serik's suggestion. Kai surveyed the damage she and Serik had done, then sighed. "Well, I guess I'm out of the Guild and a thousand crests."

She looked disappointed, and Ruby reached out to her friend. She had been the cause of Kai's misfortune. If Ruby hadn't been with her, she would have been able to turn in the key and collect her money without issue. "I am sorry I derailed your plans, Kai. I will find a way to pay you back."

Kai took her hand and shook her head. "This is not your fault Ruby. It's that damned du—" She cut herself off as she glanced at Serik. "—that damned reward. Let's get out of here so we can figure out what to do."

Having been freed from his bonds, Gav rubbed his wrists as he got to his feet. He looked first to Kai, then Serik, then Ruby. His one good eye was still a little wide at the edges as he slid off the wagon, surveying the unconscious and possibly dead Kingfishers guild members.

Ruby glanced back at him as Serik began to lead her away. Gav was dabbing at the blood under his nose with the sleeve of his jacket. Kai followed them, leaving the injured man behind.

"Wait! You can't just leave me here," he called, snatching up the items from the wagon that the thieves had taken from him and putting his weapons back on his belt. He looked down at the splintered lute and grimaced.

"We can," Kai said with a glare. "And we will."

"But you can't! I have a place you can stay!" he said in a hurry, trotting to catch up to them. The limp in his right leg made Ruby's heart ache for him. As the loresinger had said before, it was not her fault they beat him, but she still felt a little guilty.

"He did try to help me," Ruby said, putting a hand on Serik's forearm to slow him, "and if he does have a place where we can stay safely for the night, it would be worth going with him for the time being, would it not?"

Serik didn't look happy with that. "We could leave Issalden and stay off the road," he suggested, "and travel through the country as we have been."

"The young woman looks like she needs a break, and I have a room at a very comfortable inn—not that I'm inviting her to share it with me!" Gav added quickly when both Serik and Kai glared at him. "I'm certain there are rooms available. But if not, she would be welcome to use my bed. I will sleep on the floor, like a gentleman. There's a tub as well if you want to clean up." He looked at Ruby, eyes imploring. She had the feeling he really didn't want to be left on his own.

In a way, she did owe him for trying to help her. While whatever he had been planning went poorly initially, he did end up slowing the thieves down and ultimately disrupting the mage cage so that Ruby could work her magic.

She looked at Kai first, then Serik. "I think we should go with him. He did not have to help me as he did and only found out my identity once he had already been taken captive. It is only a small risk, and I am sure Joran will tell the others that I escaped. Perhaps we should get off the road as soon as we are able?"

Kai sighed at her words, which Ruby knew meant that she agreed. Then she scowled and fixed the loresinger with a glare that could have soured milk. "This better not be another trap, or you won't have to worry about the Kingfishers anymore."

Gav swallowed, but attempted to remain upbeat and winked at her. "Of course. Follow me, ladies. And gentleman."

CHAPTER 12

Kai gave her friend her cloak to wear as they traveled through the town, the hood pulled low to obscure her features. Ruby had introduced the man who had been tied up with her as Gav and informed them that he was a loresinger. Kai wasn't sure if they could trust him, but he had stopped Joran when he'd accosted Ruby, so maybe he wasn't all bad.

Gav had tried to clean up his face, but that alone couldn't improve his overall appearance. His jacket and cravat were beyond hope, so he'd thrown them—and his broken lute—into a bush before they'd left the warehouse district. The dark blue vest and linen shirt he wore beneath had fared much better than his coat had. While his eye and the bruises on his face still looked ghastly, the loresinger looked more like he'd been in a tavern brawl than been beaten in an alley.

To Kai's surprise, they found Dream chewing a stubborn tuft of weeds right off Brewer Street, where the turn-off to the main road was. That damn horse was something else.

Serik clicked his tongue, and the mare raised her head, flicking one ear in his direction. She watched them walk toward her, then trotted over to nuzzle the wilder's outstretched hand. With a glance at the loresinger, Serik let out a long sigh, then helped the man onto his horse. They stopped at the tavern they had parted ways at earlier to retrieve Midnight, then followed Gav's directions to his lodgings.

The inn the loresinger took them to was on the other side of Issalden, a place in the market district called *The Fancy Duck*. Naturally, a wooden sign was hanging above the front door with just such a waterfowl painted on it.

Their little incident had only taken a few hours, so it was still well before sundown. The market district was still buzzing with activity at this time of day. Stalls of men and women selling food and other goods crowded the market square, but the four travelers skirted around the crowd and hurried into the inn.

Serik and Gav spoke quietly to the innkeeper, and Kai thought he saw Serik hand the man a few crests—which was much more than the cost of a room—then the wilder ushered them upstairs. They entered a large suite at the end of the hall. There was a double bed, a table, and a comfortable-looking armchair in front of a roaring fireplace. It was decorated with plush red carpets, flowers, and other fineries they hadn't seen since leaving Valwen. This was much nicer than the inn they'd stopped at in Belleward and was probably similar to what Ruby was accustomed to as a lady of high birth. Kai turned to comment on it to Ruby, some quip to lighten the mood, but paused. Her friend seemed uneasy. Perhaps the reminder of the life she left behind was distressing.

Kai decided what Ruby needed was a hot bath and a drink. Or five.

Kai was about to ask the loresinger where that tub he'd promised was when the wilder turned to them, his expression grim. He snatched Gav's arm, making the loresinger jump.

"Stay here. We'll be back in a few minutes," Serik said to the women, then hauled Gav out of the room. The door shut behind them before Kai could ask him what he was doing.

Which was probably for the best. She was in a foul mood. Her deal had fallen through—a thousand crests was a lot of fucking money—and she was definitely out of the Guild. She would be lucky if they didn't put a price on her head as well. It had not been a good day for her.

But at least Ruby was okay. She wasn't on her way back to the duke.

The young noblewoman was a mess. Her gown was filthy from when she'd been pinned on the warehouse floor, and her long braid hung askew, large locks having fallen out of it. There was a mark on her cheek that was certainly going to bruise—Joran or one of the other men must have struck her —but otherwise, she looked unharmed. Scared and disheveled, but whole.

"You're okay now," Kai said, gently resting a hand on her arm. Ruby flinched. "The duke can't get to you now, and we'll leave the city soon."

Giving Kai a watery smile, Ruby stepped over to the fire, then sank to the floor in front of it. "I did not know that Mikel would do that," she said, looking up at Kai. "I put you in danger because I did not think. Of course, he would have assumed I was kidnapped. What woman engaged to a duke just disappears without a word? I should have left a letter or something to explain what I had done."

Kai felt her lips turn up in a bitter grin. "I don't think a letter would suffice to explain why you left."

"I should at least tell him I'm all right," Ruby insisted. "If he knows that I am not in danger and have decided to break off the engagement, he will retract the reward."

Kneeling next to her friend, Kai pursed her lips. "Ruby," she began, "no matter what you say, the duke will not relent. If the rumors about him are true, I don't think he will ever let you go." There was little gossip about the Duke of Ayrilon floating around Valwen, but most of the nobles agreed he was possessive, and that his charming and handsome face was merely a facade.

Ruby looked like she wanted to argue, but Kai saw the realization dawn on her face. She knew the duke better than anyone, and the look of hopelessness that spread across Ruby's features made Kai clench her fists. She didn't want to ask her next question, but she'd wondered about it since they'd been together at the Academy.

She chewed on her bottom lip. "Can I ask you something, Ruby?"

"After what happened over the last week, you've earned the right to ask whatever you want. What is it, Kai? What do you wish to know?"

Kai was silent for a moment, thinking over her words carefully, but she didn't know how else to say it. "What did the duke do to you that made you not want to marry him?"

Ruby's eyebrows lifted in surprise. Then her expression closed off. "I'm not sure what you mean," she said evasively.

"Come on, Ruby. Even back at the Academy, I could tell. You never wanted to talk about him. You still don't." Kai waved a hand before Ruby could argue. "You can deny it all you want, and if you don't want to tell me, that's fine, but I know there's more to it."

They fell into silence. Ruby looked away from her and glanced into the fire crackling in the hearth. Kai waited, unsure if she would answer.

After a minute, she spoke.

"Mikel didn't want me to go to Valwen at first. We had plans to get married once I turned twenty, and attending would mean postponing the wedding by three years. He didn't want to wait, but I was persistent." Her voice was even as she spoke, but she still didn't meet Kai's eyes. "In the end, we made a bargain. I could attend, and we would postpone the wedding until I graduated. In exchange, I would immediately move into his residence and spend every term break with him, unchaperoned."

Kai's mouth fell open. "Unchaperoned? Does that mean he…"

Ruby brought her knees to her chest, resting her chin on them. "We acted like husband and wife while I was in residence. I took care of the household and did whatever he wished. 'Training for my role as duchess,' he said."

Kai felt heat rising up her neck as anger and disgust made her scowl. "He wanted control over you and used your desire to enter the Academy to secure it." It was despicable, making a young woman trade her life away just to get a tiny taste of freedom.

Well, the joke was on him, wasn't it? Behind her roaring emotions, Kai felt smug for having yanked her friend out of the duke's clutches.

Ruby nodded and finally turned her eyes to Kai. She'd expected tears, but there was no glisten there. And why should there be? Ruby had been suffering for years. "I think he wanted to isolate me. Some of the nobility still have the notion that if a woman is unwed and not a virgin, she is somehow worth less than if she is pure and untouched." She snorted derisively. "It is an antiquated way. If they only knew what went on at the Academy."

Kai scoffed. "You mean the way students were engaging in 'intimate relations' all over the grounds."

Ruby blushed. "Well, yes. So that part was less damaging than he expected. Or maybe he just wanted me and did not want to wait three extra years." She shivered and hugged her knees a little closer, turning back to the fire.

"Living with Mikel, I got to see what he was like away from the rest of society." Ruby bit her lower lip and closed her eyes before continuing. "I did not like what I saw. Mikel has a cruel streak and can be rough with his desires. If I disobeyed or fought him, he threatened to pull me out of the Academy and marry me immediately. When I was stuck in that gods-forsaken cage, I wondered, 'What would he do to me if I was brought back to him?' There's no doubt that he would punish me severely, but, honestly"—Ruby smiled before continuing—"being here with you and meeting Serik, it is worth any punishment he could dole out. I like being able to choose my own destiny."

Kai had never met the duke, but as Ruby spoke, her hatred of him deepened. Red-hot anger coursed through her veins, and there was a bitter taste in her mouth. It was difficult to keep her hands from shaking. If she and the duke were ever in the same room, she would do everything in her power to make sure her blade was the last thing he ever saw.

"He'll never let you go," Kai said, her voice somber. "Not willingly, at least. We'll have to convince him that the two of you are done or leave the country."

Ruby pursed her lips, seeming to doubt that they could convince the duke of anything, but she nodded. She knew the man better than Kai, but this sheltered woman had no idea how dangerous a nobleman could be if he didn't get what he wanted. They were like children throwing tantrums, except they had the money and the means to *take* anything they desired. The bounty for her return was proof of that.

There was a knock, followed by a soft click, and the door opened. Serik reentered the room, Gav behind him. Whatever the wilder had said to the loresinger, he did not look pleased. Kai pressed her lips together to keep from grinning.

The look of outrage on his battered and bruised face was comical.

As he entered, he puffed his chest out like some colorful bird, as though trying to flaunt his manliness. "Your man threatened me!" he all but shouted, sounding highly offended. Gav looked first at Kai, then at Ruby, seeking sympathy. "Normally, I wouldn't mind being menaced by a man of such fine stature and bone structure, but I've had a very long day."

"Can't you take anything seriously?" Serik growled. He kept his scowl focused on Gav as he positioned himself by the door.

"Maybe you need to show the tiniest modicum of gratitude since my face supplied the distraction for you to rescue your young lady? Gav shot back.

Kai glanced at Ruby, who blinked in bemusement. If nothing else, the loresinger was entertaining.

"I didn't hear you complaining when *I* threatened you," Kai said, schooling her face to appear serious.

"Forgive me for saying so, but you are far less intimidating than this"—he flicked a hand at Serik before scrutinizing him from head to toe—"brutish mass of hair and muscle."

Ruby had to cover her mouth. Kai was able to keep her composure, barely.

Gav approached where they were seated in front of the hearth and made himself comfortable in the armchair a few paces away. He sighed. "I've asked the innkeeper to bring up bath water, but it may take a while. I, for one, could do with a soak."

"How are you feeling?" Ruby asked, wincing a little as she eyed his face.

"Like shit. Everything hurts, and I think something might be broken or at least cracked." His blue eyes tracked over to

Ruby. One of them could barely open through the swelling. "I don't suppose you're a healer?" Ruby shook her head, and he sighed. "Of course not. I'll need to get a potion or two on the way out of town, then."

That's what he gets for running into this headfirst, Kai thought, but she didn't say it. She was grateful that he'd tried to help Ruby, ill-advised as that was. She suspected he was why the thieves had still been at the warehouse. Oh, it was obvious that Joran had been waiting to see if she would come back, but they would have gotten bored and impatient much more quickly without the loresinger to focus their attention on.

Gav watched Ruby, while Serik stood his silent vigil by the door.

"What are you staring at?" Kai asked, narrowing her eyes at the loresinger. He was too focused on Ruby.

"That thief we encountered mentioned a duke," he said after a few more moments. "I'm just wondering which one is looking for you, Miss Ruby?"

Kai scoffed before Ruby could answer. "That isn't any of your business, is it?" There was no way in all the hells that they would tell him the Duke of Ayrilon was Ruby's fiancé. Even if he didn't want the reward, which seemed unlikely, he might want to curry favor with the duke. "I think a better question is, why were you tied up in that wagon? There must be a reason. If you were worthless, Joran would have just killed you."

"There is a bounty on him," Ruby jumped on the question, and Kai knew she was trying to change the subject from the duke. "Those men said an earl wanted to…" she trailed off, her cheeks turning pink.

"Rip my cock off?" Gav finished sourly. "Really, his wife supplies me with drink and seduces me, and it's *my* fault? Is there no justice in the world?"

Kai sighed and ran a hand over her face. Great, another problem to add to their ever-growing list of difficulties. "Which earl was that?"

"The Earl of Stalen," Gav replied with a dignified sniff. "Beast of a man."

"Oh yes," Ruby chimed in. "Rumor has it that the countess is quite promiscuous. She had a scandalous affair with one of her footmen last summer."

"See!" The loresinger gestured at Ruby. "Where is the justice in that?"

"Maybe you shouldn't put yourself into questionable situations with countesses of ill repute?" Kai suggested.

Gav looked at her askance. "And deprive the world of my handsome face? Never!" He framed his face with his hands.

Unable to hold it in, Kai let out a sharp laugh. "Says the one who looks more akin to a bloody steak than a man."

Ruby covered her mouth to keep from laughing.

He put a hand to his chest. "You wound me."

"Can't be any worse than the beating you already received."

"If I am not allowed to flirt, you two most certainly are not," Ruby giggled, her voice upbeat for the first time since they'd rescued her.

Kai raised an eyebrow. "This isn't flirting. It's bickering."

"If that is what you choose to believe, Kai," she answered with a sideways look at Gav.

"If you three are finished," Serik muttered from where he now leaned against the wall, arms folded over his chest. "Perhaps we should discuss what we plan to do about those men who are after Miss Valestris. With the reward in place, I doubt this will be the last we see of them."

Anger flared in Kai's chest. They were having fun. Why would he remind Ruby of that?

"After everything Ruby's been through today, the least

you can do is give her one night of peace," she snapped, getting to her feet.

"We aren't going to be able to stay in one place long with the Kingfishers looking for her," the wilder countered, pushing away from the wall. "She doesn't have a night of peace to take from her troubles. The Guild certainly won't take time off from looking for her." Serik's posture was no longer relaxed as he faced off against Kai.

She scoffed. "Even so, she doesn't need you hovering over her every second of every day. She left Valwen to be free, not to have another man controlling her every move."

"Kai—"

Ruby's voice was lost in Kai's next words. Kai tried to temper her emotions, but it was difficult in the face of what had happened today. "Why are you still here anyway? I thought you weren't after the reward. You've already given back her initial payment. There is no profit in this for you. So, *why* are you here?" she repeated the question. After everything they had been through, Kai wasn't convinced that the wilder's intentions were benign. He had helped them, yes, but he wouldn't be doing this if there was no gain for him. At least, that was what Alek had taught her. Even her own guild had turned on her, and that left her heart aching and her thoughts suspicious.

As she spoke, the wilder's face grew redder and redder. His eyes tracked from her to Ruby, and there was something in them that hadn't been there before he'd seen the notices.

Seeming to realize he was staring at Ruby, Serik swore under his breath, then whirled around, his cloak snapping out behind him. Throwing open the door, he strode out of the room, slamming it shut again.

"Kai, why would you do that?" Ruby stared after the wilder. She looked like she wanted to run after him.

"It had to be asked," she replied, but there was an uncomfortable feeling in her stomach. Maybe she shouldn't have pushed him so hard. Serik had helped her rescue Ruby after all. It had been necessary, hadn't it? The question could have been asked later when emotions weren't so high. Kai had just been so annoyed that he'd brought Ruby's situation back into the forefront when her friend had finally started to relax. They all needed rest, not more anxiety.

Kai looked from Ruby, who frowned in concern, to Gav, who was pointedly looking at the fire, then to the door through which Serik had made his exit.

"Fuck," she breathed and went after him.

CHAPTER 13

How was it that Kai found herself striding toward the stables of an inn called *The Fancy Duck*, an establishment that was far too reputable to host someone like her? The stables were a quick walk from the inn proper, and she covered the distance with expediency, afraid of being identified by a passerby. Night was quickly gaining on the late afternoon light, and the western sky was painted in rich reds as she slid open the heavy oak door. A boy a few years younger than her, with mousy brown hair and a light jacket, was sitting on a stool and jumped up when he saw her.

"Can I help you, miss?" he asked, sounding startled.

"Is the gray mare that was brought in a little while ago still here?"

He looked puzzled at her question. "Yes, of course. Her owner only rode in about an hour ago."

"Good," was all she could think to say as she slid the door shut again on his bewildered face. That meant Serik had not left but was lurking around close by. Kai chewed on her thumbnail as she strode back to the inn, thinking.

If Dream was still in the stables, Serik was still here. Kai hadn't meant to make him so angry, but she needed to know what he planned to do. She was increasingly certain that her friend was developing strong feelings for the wilder, but Kai worried Ruby was too trusting. The young noblewoman didn't know what life was like outside of the high society that she'd been raised in.

That had changed today. She had caught a glimpse of how cruel others could be, and the poor girl seemed shaken by it. Kai wasn't going to let another man she cared for betray her. If the wilder had an ulterior motive, they would just have to leave him behind.

Out the corner of her eye, Kai caught the flash of movement toward the back of the inn. Pausing her trek to the front door, she tried to look around the corner, but in the fading light, it was difficult to tell if it had been an animal or a person. Drawing her dagger, she crept along the wall. It could have been one of Joran or Alek's men. If they had found this place already, she would need to deal with them before they could report back, and then move Ruby to another inn.

Before she'd taken more than ten steps, she heard a soft scoff.

"Put away your weapon before you draw attention to yourself," Serik's voice drifted from around the corner. "You're not half as stealthy as you think you are."

Kai scowled but did as he suggested. He was right. Anyone from the road could see her. How in the hells had he heard her? Perhaps he'd seen her checking the stables and assumed she would circle the building to look for him. That made her scowl deepen. Was she that predictable?

Serik leaned against the wall near the inn's back door. The sweet, earthy scent of tobacco reached Kai's nose before she saw the pipe sticking out of his mouth. The ember within it lit up his face in a golden red glow as he pulled on it, breathing out the smoke through his nose. She hadn't seen the pipe before, but she also hadn't seen the wilder this upset all the time they'd known each other. In her experience, most men smoked either out of habit or to calm their nerves.

Serik let her watch him without saying anything for a full minute as they stood in awkward silence. Finally, he took the pipe out of his mouth and asked, "What do you want, Kai?"

"To talk," she said and cringed at the obviousness of her words.

The wilder snorted and took another drag on the pipe. "Where's Ruby?"

"In the room, where else?"

"You left her alone with that loresinger?" he asked, straightening.

Good gods, was he about to go charging in to "rescue" her like some knight?

"That man can barely stand. He's too injured to try anything, and if he did, Ruby could push him over without much effort. A little zap of electricity, and he'd be out for the rest of the night."

He threw her a level look before leaning back again. "Even so, he could alert someone to her location or send a message to the Kingfishers."

Her eyebrows rose. "You mean alert the very people who tried to kill him? He may be daft, but I don't think he's that big of a fool." She crossed her arms and leaned one shoulder against the wall, mimicking the wilder's position. "You seemed very concerned about Ruby's well-being for someone whose contract with her is finished."

Serik sighed. "Are you here to question my intentions again? Accuse me of trying to *control* her in some way?"

Kai took a deep breath and counted to five before answering. "I may have been a bit aggressive before—"

"A bit?" he interrupted with another scoff.

"Yes," Kai said, trying to be patient. "A bit. But you have to admit, it's odd that we stumbled upon you back in the Wytchwood right when we needed a guide. And I appreciate that you helped save Ruby from the Guild, but how can I believe that you're not interested in the reward for yourself? Have you so much wealth that you can ignore fifty thousand crests?"

The wilder glared at her.

"Look," Kai began again. "I've learned the hard way not to trust people so easily. Meeting you in the Wytchwood seemed fated by the gods, which makes me even more suspicious. Maybe you were sent by the Academy, or by someone else who knew what I was doing at Valwen. It was best to keep an eye on you and see if you were really guiding us to Issalden and not into a trap." She took a deep breath before continuing. Serik seemed to be listening. "Once we got to Belleward, I knew how to get to the city, but I wanted to know who you worked for, so I didn't say anything.

"But I don't believe that's the case anymore, not after traveling together for so long. I don't think you want to hurt her or turn her in, but I saw that look you gave her earlier. You didn't use to look at her like that. Not until today, after seeing the notices. What is your motive, wilder? And why did it change?" Kai tried to keep her voice even but couldn't stop the last two questions from sounding accusatory.

A muscle in Serik's jaw twitched. He glanced at the ground. Kai had the impression he didn't want to look her in the eye. Was he ashamed? What secret could he be hiding that involved Ruby?

She remained silent, waiting for him to speak.

When he did, his voice was soft, as if he was afraid of being overheard. "I have a history with the Duke of Ayrilon."

Kai felt a cold chill settle into her bones. "Was the duke's name on the notice?" she asked quietly looking over her shoulder. They were alone in the fading twilight. She needed to get a copy of that damned flyer.

"No, but I've kept up with his comings and goings enough to know that he is betrothed to the daughter of Baron Valestris. I didn't make the connection until I saw her name." Serik leaned his head back to thump softly on the wall. His eyes flicked over to her, but his expression was unreadable. "You have nothing to fear from me. I hate that man with every fiber of my soul. Ruby will never see him again if I can help it."

"Fifty thousand crests is a lot of money," she reminded him. "Hearts have been swayed for less." It was cynical, but Kai couldn't take any chances, not with everything Ruby had confided in her. She couldn't let her go back to that. "What is it that the duke has on you?"

He didn't answer at first. "I cannot tell you why I want to see the duke suffer, but you have my word that I will keep Ruby out of his grasp. I do care for her, and I don't need the duke's money."

It was Kai's turn to snort. "I can believe that you hate the duke and would help Ruby to spite him, but everyone needs money, wilder. Are you telling me that you will take no payment? Do you not need supplies of your own?"

"I have what I need for now."

She watched him closely and started chewing on her thumbnail, thinking. A cricket hopped onto Serik's boot and chirped at them. He flicked his foot, forcing it to jump back into the grass.

"Fine," Kai finally said. She opened her mouth to say more, but found that she didn't have anything to add. As much as she didn't want to admit it, Serik had come through for them twice now—even if she had suspected him before of being after the reward in the heat of the moment. Kai was reluctant to trust anyone after what Joran had done, but she could try to trust the wilder.

They should have ended the conversation there, but Kai's mouth kept moving. "She likes you."

"I know."

"And you like her."

He didn't respond to the statement.

"I see the way you watch her. Anyone could." She continued staring at him. His fingers had started fidgeting with the pipe, and she wondered what he was thinking. Kai frowned. "I don't like it, but Ruby is becoming attached to you. What are you planning to do about it?"

The wilder was quiet for a few moments. "Nothing."

"Nothing?"

"That's what I said," he growled, voice laced with annoyance. "We've only just met. And even if I did have those kinds of feelings, I can't give her what she needs. She deserves so much more than what I can offer her."

Kai resisted the urge to roll her eyes. When had she become close enough with this man to give him relationship advice? It wasn't as if she wanted this man and Ruby to court, but Ruby had never been able to choose anything for herself. Who was Kai to take another choice away from her?

She placed one hand on the hilt of her dagger. Better end this with a threat. "Just know that if you toy with her feelings, I'll stab you."

A surprised laugh burst from his lips. "I'll keep that in mind." He placed the pipe in an inner jacket pocket. "What are you going to do now? I'm guessing your guild didn't pay you."

Kai's expression darkened. "No, they did not." She reached into a pouch on her belt and pulled out the sandstone key she'd shown Ruby. "I guess the only thing to do is find out what this goes to. It has to have some value. Otherwise, why would Alek have wanted it? From what I'd found out before stealing it, this thing was taken out of some ruins far to the east. Maybe there's treasure there that I can use to set us up until Ruby can join a guild or find some other work."

Serik reached out and plucked the trinket out of her fingers, examining it. "It doesn't look like much."

"The headmage called it a key. I stole it from him," Kai added as an afterthought. She didn't think Serik would care but wanted to gauge his reaction.

If he was surprised, he didn't show it.

When she continued to watch him, he clarified. "I knew that already."

"The cabin?" She inwardly cursed her carelessness.

He nodded. "Are you sure there is something at these ruins?"

"No, but I have the mages' books on them with me." Kai blew out a long breath. "I know it's not much, but it's the only lead I have right now, and we need to get out of Issalden." She took the little stone back from him. "If it's a key, that means it opens something and that it's important enough that someone paid my guild a lot of money to get it."

"That doesn't mean it's valuable," Serik said, but scratched his beard, sounding intrigued.

"If there is no risk, then the reward would hardly be worth it," she said cheerily and put the stone back in her pouch. "But if there is something valuable at those ruins, it could be profitable for all of us, especially you, since you seem to be in the habit of refunding your fees."

"Is that an invitation to join you in whatever scheme you're concocting?"

Kai grinned. "If you can keep up with us. There's sure to be some sort of payout at the end of this."

"And if there isn't?"

She threw her hands up in exasperation. "Then we'll figure something else out! I don't have all the answers right now, but it's not as if I'd let her starve!" Kai glared at the wilder. "Are you in or not?"

His eyes crinkled in amusement. "Do you even know how to get to these supposed ruins?"

"Why do you think I took the books?" she said as she rubbed her arms. The sun had set, and the night was quickly becoming cold. "You can stay out here and sulk if you want, but I'm going back inside. You're not going to ride off back to the Wytchwood, are you? I would have to hunt you down and..." She made a stabbing motion and blood spurting out of a chest wound with much exaggeration.

"I'd like to see you try," he said, but the wilder was finally smiling. Serik followed her back inside to join the others.

When Kai opened the door, Ruby and Gav were in the same places she'd left them, Ruby sitting by the fire and Gav in the armchair nearby. The loresinger's eyes were closed, even the good one, and while he appeared to be sleeping, Kai doubted he was. Ruby stared into the fire, her gaze seeming to look beyond it. Whatever she was thinking about, it was heavy on her mind. Serik closed the door quietly behind them and put his back to it.

The noise startled Ruby out of her thoughts. "The innkeeper said another room is ready for us," she said as she looked up at Kai. Her gaze drifted over to Serik, and her lips pushed together. Kai knew she was keeping back the flood of questions about what had happened with the wilder. Serik, for his part, was looking at a spot on the floor, avoiding her eyes.

"I hope there's a bath waiting." Kai looked down at the hand that Joran had cut earlier that day. It didn't hurt anymore, but all the blood around it had dried, and the wound looked a mess. It would need to be cleaned and bandaged.

Ruby didn't seem to hear the comment. "What are we going to do now, Kai?" she asked. "That guild is still looking for me."

"The only thing we can do is get out of town for now. Do you remember that—" Kai glanced at Gav. "—thing I showed you before, at the cabin?"

Frowning, Ruby nodded.

"I think we should check out the ruins where it came from. There could be something valuable there since Alek was after it. He's the guild master," she said as an afterthought, in case Ruby hadn't figured that out yet. "It will give us something to do while the hunt for us cools off. In a month or two, everyone will have forgotten about you." *Unlikely*, she thought, but didn't say it. "Or at least what you look like. And if there is treasure to be had, it would compensate me for the money I lost and give us funds to get you started on your new life."

Ruby made a contemplative sound. "Exploring old ruins does sound interesting. Do you know where they are located?"

"The books I..."—Kai gave Gav another look—"*borrowed* have some maps of the area it came from. I'm sure the exact location is marked on one of those." Kai rubbed one arm and sighed, suddenly self-conscious. "I know it's not much of a plan, but it could have a big payoff if I'm right, and since it's so far east, it's unlikely that anyone is looking for you there."

"I never said it was a bad idea," Ruby said with a smile at her friend. "It sounds like quite an adventure."

"More than the one we've had the last few weeks?"

She laughed, and Kai felt relieved. Ruby been so quiet and somber since they'd rescued her.

"We should hide our true identities, at least while we are

around other people," Serik said from his spot by the door. He was still looking at the floor, the coward. "All three of you are wanted now, and many people already know what Ruby looks like due to those notices."

Ruby frowned, but not like she thought the idea was bad. It was a thoughtful frown. "Shall I go by Violet, then?" she suggested. "It was my grandmother's name, so it would be easy to remember."

Kai nodded. "That's not bad, but you can't go by Valestris either…" she trailed off, having a wicked idea. She had to say it just right so as not to draw the ire of everyone in the room, most especially the wilder's.

"It would be odd if two *unwed* women and men were traveling together," she said, trying to make her words sound offhanded. "Perhaps we should claim to be related in some way, but, ah, we look nothing alike."

Gav stirred from his place on the armchair. He gazed at Ruby. "Miss Ruby and I could pass as cousins," he suggested, looking up at Kai. "Our eyes and hair are similar enough."

"I don't remember inviting you to join our group, loresinger," Kai said, but she gave him a brief smile. She didn't fully trust him yet. "But I guess we can't leave you here to tell the Guild where we've gone."

"I want to get as far from Issalden and the Kingfishers as possible," he said, his eyes practically glittering, "and the prospect of treasure is enticing."

Kai nodded and turned to Serik. "Well? Any ideas on how the two of us are related to these *cousins*?"

Serik threw her a flat I-know-what-you-are-doing glower, but the expression softened when his eyes tracked to Ruby. "Violet Belin. You can use that name."

Meddling. That's what she was doing.

"What?" Ruby squeaked, a pretty blush spreading across her cheeks.

"Married," Gav mused. He wouldn't know the wilder's last name but had guessed at the intention. "If you pose as the wilder's wife and Kai as mine, there would be no question as to why two young women are traveling with two men of no relation. It's a simple enough idea, but can you sell it if questioned?"

"As long as you don't expect me to kiss you," Kai said, one eyebrow raised. The loresinger gave her a deceptively innocent look.

Ruby glanced at Serik. "Kai, I'm not sure about this."

Kai knelt next to her. "He's the only one of us no one is looking for," she explained. "It might be a little awkward, but you posing as his wife is the safest option." Despite her reasons for pushing them toward this ruse, it was the obvious choice, and deciding on their cover story would have to have been done sooner or later. Best to get the conversation out of the way now.

Serik's hazel eyes met Ruby's blue ones, and they stared at each other for a few long moments. The gaze was intense, as if they were alone in the room, which they weren't.

Kai cleared her throat loudly, and Gav mouthed, "Thank you." She flashed him a grin.

"Is that agreeable?" she asked, looking between Ruby and Serik.

Looking down at her hands, Ruby nodded, her cheeks pink again.

"We've missed our chance to leave without the Thieves Guild watching for us," Serik said, obviously trying to change the subject. "With four of us, it will be difficult to escape Issalden unnoticed."

Kai grinned and winked at Ruby. "Leave that part to me. I have an idea."

CHAPTER 14

What Kai considered a "plan" was for her, Ruby, and Gav to hide in the back of one of the many wagons leaving town the next day while Serik rode in front with the driver, dressed as a farmer. The man driving the wagon was a shepherd by the name of Halis, who had come in to sell his wares at the market a few days ago and had stayed in town long enough for Kai to find him again. Ruby hadn't been certain that this plan of Kai's would work, but her friend apparently knew the shepherd personally and seemed confident that he would help them, so she didn't voice her concerns. Hopefully, no one would be checking the wagons leaving town.

The aroma in the back of the wagon stung Ruby's nose. The scent of musk and manure permeated both the wooden slats that made up the bed of their conveyance and the canvas tarpaulin laid over them. So, this was what sheep smelled like. Ruby had never actually seen one in person before, but she'd viewed paintings at galleries that featured the animals. They looked like white fluffy clouds under an artist's brush, but up close, they weren't as pleasant as she imagined.

Thankfully, Halis had offloaded all the sheep he'd brought, leaving them in an animal-free wagon, lying on blankets and hidden from prying eyes.

Serik had loaded the wagon full of their supplies, leaving room to hide his three companions who were wanted by the Kingfishers. Dream joined the shepherd's brown mare while Midnight was tied to the back. Kai had argued that their horses would stick out, but there was nothing for it. Serik had flat-out refused to leave Dream in Issalden with the Guild sniffing after them.

Ruby was relieved that he'd fought so hard to keep Dream. She was growing quite fond of her, and it would have been a shame to leave the mare behind.

Being the only one that the Guild wasn't looking for, Serik had snuck out of the inn just before dawn. Kai had given him a list of who to talk to and what to purchase since it was too dangerous for the rest of them to show their faces in the market. He had come back three hours later with their provisions and a time to meet the shepherd.

"He owes me a favor," Kai said in explanation as to why Halis would help them. "I got him out of some trouble with a debt collector. He used to have a problem with gambling, but as you can imagine, a shepherd doesn't have a lot of coin to begin with."

The healing potion Serik had procured for Gav made his cuts and bruises look weeks old and had helped immensely with the swelling on his face. Healing potions were made by practitioners of magic who focused their skills on repairing the human body. As Ruby understood it, the potions perfected and accelerated the body's natural healing abilities, much like how those who could use magic healed faster than those who could not. The loresinger still moved with some pain, but Serik had examined Gav and assured him nothing was broken.

Once out of Issalden and away from prying eyes, they pulled back the tarpaulin to get some fresh air. Ruby sat at the back of the wagon, her legs hanging off the end, and gazing at the countryside as they rolled along. Now that they were on their way east, she could see the hills for miles around them and the snow-topped mountains in the distance, with little farms dotting the landscape.

The sun was warm on her face, and Ruby closed her eyes, disturbed only by the occasional jostling as the wagon ran over a rock or other debris on the road. It was peaceful out here without the bustle of the city. It had felt like this in the forest, but the hard travel and fear of what could find them had dampened the effect. She was being pursued by the Thieves Guild now, but that weight seemed to lighten the farther they moved from Issalden.

Gav took the lull in conversation to nap while Kai pulled a heavy tome out of her pack and became deeply engrossed in its pages. Ruby thought about sleeping herself, but she wanted to enjoy the quiet and the beauty of the countryside while she could.

Around midday, they stopped by a stream, and while Halis untethered the horses and let the animals drink, the rest of them congregated at the back of the wagon.

"So," Gav began cheerily, "what's the plan? Do we know where these 'old ruins' are supposed to be, or will we just be wandering around the countryside aimlessly?" He sat with his back against one of the traveling packs. Without his lute, he now held a slender wooden flute. Even though he hadn't played a single note yet, his fingers danced idly down its polished surface.

Kai scoffed. "What is this 'we' that you keep referring to?" She sat beside Ruby at the edge of the wagon, resting her back against the sideboard. Serik was the only one standing on the ground. He leaned against the corner closest to Ruby with his arms crossed.

Ruby stole a glance at him while the others talked. He seemed to be paying attention to what was being said, but his eyes flicked to her, and one side of his mouth tilted up in a smirk. Heat blossomed across her cheeks, and she turned away from him, concentrating on what was being said and not at all *embarrassed* that he'd caught her staring.

"My traveling companions, of course!" Gav pointed the flute at Kai. "You can't get rid of me now. I'm your beloved husband! Besides, I distinctly heard a mention of treasure."

Kai scowled when he'd said the words "beloved husband" but didn't correct Gav. "There might be nothing there," she reminded him.

That didn't seem to faze the loresinger. "Well, money isn't the only reason to travel with you lot."

"Why *are* you still tagging along with us then?" Kai growled. Her furrowed brows were a sign that she was quickly losing her patience. Ruby had to pinch her lips together not to smile.

"Because," he started, not taking umbrage at Kai's tone, "the three of you seem capable, which is more than I can say for most people traveling these roads. There is safety in numbers, you know."

Kai snorted. "You just don't want to be caught alone by some headhunter after your bounty. Afraid they are going to cut off your cock for the earl?"

"I prefer my extremities right where they are, thank you," he replied with a dignified sniff. "And I can tell that you are trying to divert my attention from the task at hand. Tell us, did you find these ruins that you spoke of last night?"

Kai rolled her eyes dramatically but reached for the book she'd been perusing. Opening it to a section about halfway through, she thumbed through a few pages before setting the open book on the wagon floor so they could all see it.

"To answer your question, yes. The place we are heading is as far as we can go to the east before we hit the Frore Peaks. To get there, we'll have to travel to Lanevin and then take the train to Calsith."

"Calsith?" Serik asked, his brows raised. "That's on the other edge of the empire. Does the train even go that far?"

Kai pointed at Calsith on the map. "It's the last stop on the line. I remember when the project was announced in the capital. There was a lot of talk of it being a waste of money, but the emperor went through with extending the rail system. That was almost six years ago, so the line should be finished now."

Ruby stared at the spot marked "Calsith" on the map. She had never heard of the place, but Serik was right. It was at the very eastern edge of the empire, between the coast and the mountains that marked the beginning of the hinterlands, the Frore Peaks. Since that area of the country was so far from the capital and the surrounding southlands, not many people lived there. It was the domain of Duchess Zetris. Fortunately, she'd never met the woman, so there was little chance of her recognizing Ruby if they crossed paths.

Serik made a pensive sound while Gav scratched at the day-old stubble on his chin. "It would take us weeks to get there on horseback, but the train only goes beyond Lanevin every few days. If we run into trouble in Calsith, we won't be able to escape easily," the loresinger said.

Kai tapped the map again. "Look more closely. The entire area is surrounded by dense forest. If we run into trouble, we can hide out until the next train or travel west to the next stop." Her eyes slid to Serik. "We have the perfect person for that. What good is having a wilder around if we don't use him?"

"Have you been able to find anything about the ruins themselves?" Ruby asked as Serik scoffed at Kai's comment.

"Yes, actually," Kai said as she reached for another stolen text, a large leatherbound volume whose pages crinkled as she turned them. The parchment looked to be old. It was the kind of book the headmage would have had in his study and never let out of his sight. Ruby grimaced as she considered the lengths to which Kai must have gone to steal it.

A devious grin crossed her friend's face. "I know what you're thinking, Ruby, and yes, I did steal this from that bird-witted old mage. Now, there are a few pages about the ruins here, along with a drawing of the key."

"Key?" Gav asked. "What key?"

"The one I stole. Do try to keep up," Kai said as she threw a glare at the loresinger. In response, Gav played a few high-pitched notes on the flute. "Anyway, we are looking for the remains of an old temple called Ta'Dormus Deva, which translates to the Temple of the Slumbering God in ancient Andrean. The book says the exact location is unknown, and traversing the forest surrounding the mountains is danger-ous, so it's unlikely that any of the villagers from Calsith have stumbled upon it."

"Unexplored ruins," Ruby said breathily, her lips curling up. "It is exciting to think about. Imagine the history we could uncover."

"And the traps," Serik said, voice somber.

"And the treasure!" Kai and Gav said at the same time. They looked at each other in surprise.

Gav grinned at her and said, "A woman after my own heart."

Kai rolled her eyes again, but her cheeks had a distinct pink tinge. "Well, we can only hope this is profitable enough to keep the Guild off our backs for a while. If not, we'll have to think of something else."

"I should write to my fiancé—and my parents, I suppose—to see if they will retract the bounty. If I tell them I do not wish to return, perhaps they will consider the matter settled and just… disown me." Ruby grimaced. She hadn't thought about that, but it seemed the logical response to her actions. They would be ashamed of her, their only daughter, running off to spend time with thieves and commoners.

Kai gave her a look that told Ruby that she saw through her lies. Gav may have had heard Joran mention that a duke was looking for her, but thankfully he had never mentioned Mikel's name or the dutchy he governed. Ruby did intend to write Mikel when they reached their next destination and formally break the engagement. Perhaps then he would stop looking for her.

"Maybe that will work," Kai hedged, but we'd best assume it won't, and you need to lie low for a while. Either way, the Thieves Guild will want the rest of us dead. Well, they don't know who *you* are," she said to Serik, "so even if they want you dead, there won't be anyone looking for you specifically."

Serik shrugged, seemingly unbothered by the fact that a guild wanted to murder him. "It's not the first time someone has tried to kill me, and judging by how much trouble the two of you are, it won't be the last."

"Trouble?" Ruby asked, her eyebrows flying up. "I believe 'exciting' is the word choice you seek."

"My apologies," Serik said, catching her tone and bowing his head to her. The corners of his eyes crinkled in mirth. "How could I have been so inconsiderate? Being in your presence is anything but dull."

She sniffed. "That is a much more accurate statement. Best you remember that."

"Do they do this often?" Gav directed his question at Kai.

"I am just pointing out that calling us trouble is rude,"

Ruby insisted, but she couldn't keep her smile concealed any longer.

"I thought we had an agreement on flirting?" Kai said as she closed the books with a snap.

"I agreed to no such thing," Serik shot back. "We're supposed to be married, remember? Why wouldn't I flirt with my wife?"

"He's got a point," Gav interjected. He leaned in close to Kai. "Maybe we should practice too?"

"Get lost, loresinger."

Serik winked at Ruby, and she had to fight to keep a giggle down, but before they could continue with the banter, Halis returned with the horses. Serik left their little gathering to help the shepherd re-tether them to the wagon so that they could continue on their way.

As the wagon continued, Gav played a slow melody on the flute, and Kai went back to reading. Ruby regretted that he'd lost his lute in the fight. Even so, he seemed skilled in more than one instrument, and she found herself humming along with the familiar melody. She couldn't recall what the song was called, but it had been popular a few years ago.

About an hour after they had stopped at midday, a bitter scent filled Ruby's nose. Looking over her shoulder, she scanned the landscape. Burning grass and smoke. A lot of it. She recognized the aroma from the campfires they'd sat around on their journey to Issalden.

"Do you smell that?" Ruby asked as she got to her feet in the back of the wagon, holding on to the sideboard to keep her balance. Moving forward and into the front of the wagon, she gazed over Serik's and Halis's heads.

The field ahead of them was black. All the plants were burned to ashes. Wisps of smoke rose in dark tendrils against the midday sun, and as they approached, she could see figures in the distance. A few men held shovels and were covered head to toe in soot, making them look like chimney sweeps. They weren't close enough to hail but appeared to be watching their wagon as it passed. There was some greenery behind the men, so some crops hadn't burned, but it was a small fraction compared to what had been lost.

"What happened here?" Ruby asked, looking around at the burnt remains of acres of farmland. The skeleton of a structure stood off in the distance, as black as the fields around it.

Halis scowled, not taking his eyes off the men digging in the ashes. "The emperor's knights came through, that's what."

"I beg your pardon?" Ruby asked in surprise. He couldn't have been implying what she thought he was. When he didn't speak, she continued. "You cannot mean that the emperor's men did this on *purpose*?"

His scowl deepened. "I do. They've been plaguing the countryside for months, extorting the poor farmers who live in these lands and razing their fields when they have nothing to give them." He spat on the ground.

Ruby glanced at Kai, who just shrugged. She didn't know what he was talking about either. It seemed ludicrous to Ruby that anyone under the employ of the emperor, especially his knights, would do something as detrimental to his people's livelihoods as this. She'd seen knights before, and they were exactly what she would have envisioned from the books she had read. Tall, uniformed, and honorable. She couldn't imagine the men she'd seen before burning the countryside or harassing innocent farmers.

"That is the rumor that is going around," Gav said from his seat at the back of the wagon. "Don't look so shocked, Miss… Miss Violet. This far north, the emperor's men are far from the capital. Outside of the watchful eyes of their superiors, some revert to their darker instincts."

"This is the second farm burned this month. Looks like

Sorin Cole and his sons escaped with their lives, but now, they'll have to rebuild their home." He nodded toward the men digging.

Ruby shook her head, unable to pair the destruction she saw with Gav's and Halis's words. "Surely, this has been reported to the capital."

Serik and Halis exchanged a look.

"What is it?" Ruby insisted. "What was that look for?"

Halis glanced back at her. "Pardon me saying so, miss, but you seem oblivious to our struggles here. The government doesn't care what happens to us poor hardworking folk. They only care about lining their own pockets."

"It makes the emperor very unpopular in these parts," Gav said as he leaned back again. "And the lord of these lands even less so."

Halis gave Gav a sidelong look. "I'm as loyal to the emperor as the next man, but he's far away, and the men he chose to watch over these lands are hurting his citizens."

"If they are truly knights, I cannot imagine the emperor condones their actions," Ruby said stubbornly. "It should be reported immediately."

Halis looked like he wanted to argue, but Serik placed a hand on the man's shoulder and shook his head.

"She doesn't understand," he said to the shepherd, then turned around in his seat. "Violet, I doubt the emperor knows what is happening here, and even if he does, it's none of our concern. We need to focus on getting to Lanevin."

Ruby glowered but didn't argue the point further. Serik was right, but she still felt the need to defend the emperor. She was a member of the nobility, people who had sworn their loyalty to their sovereign and had promised to help him rule. It rankled her to think that those same people were taking advantage of the citizens they were charged with caring for.

Serik chuckled at her expression and propped his elbow on the back of the bench, resting his chin on his hand as he watched her. "You look like you want to argue more."

She must not have been hiding her thoughts well. "There is no use arguing when the other party will not listen," Ruby replied loftily.

Serik reached out a hand and brushed her cheek, tucking a lock of hair behind her ear. "No need to pout."

Her eyebrows shot up, and she knocked his hand away. "I am *not* pouting!" Ruby had never been prone to violence, but at that moment, she seriously considered hitting him. "You are just being an ass."

Halis smiled at the exchange and leaned back in his seat, more relaxed than he had been a moment before. Belatedly, Ruby realized that Serik had done that on purpose, making fun of her to direct the conversation away from the burned landscape around them and put the shepherd at ease.

Still, Serik didn't have to cheer him up at her expense.

Ruby turned her back on him with a huff and carefully picked her way back around the blankets and bunched up tarpaulin to the rear of the wagon. He laughed under his breath, and she had the sudden urge to grab him by the collar of his shirt and shake him, but refrained from doing so. It was beneath her.

"We'll be there soon," Halis called over his shoulder as Ruby retook her seat. "Once we get to my farm, it'll still be almost another fortnight of travel to Lanevin. There's a road that leads to the east and will take you most of the way there. Along it will be a few villages for you all to stay in, but you should sleep at the farm tonight. If you need an extra horse or two, I have a few that I can sell you."

"Thanks, Halis," Kai said as she stretched out in the back of the wagon, massaging her backside. Sitting on the hard wagon bed had left them all a little sore. "Any chance your wife will make us dinner? If memory serves, she's a good cook."

Halis chuckled. "She'd be happy to make something for you. With all the help you gave us last year, we'll still be in your debt when we have grandchildren."

Kai snorted. "All I did was scare a few people off. You're the one who kicked the habit." She must have been referring to his gambling.

He shook his head, a wry smile on his lips. "That's not how Aethra sees it. We'll make sure you're all well-fed and rested before we send you on your way. We've got room in the house for all of you."

It was near dusk when Halis pulled the wagon off the road and onto a farm track that ran up to a small, white-washed structure next to a larger barn with double doors. As they pulled to a stop, Kai and Serik hopped off the wagon and grabbed the reins of Dream and Midnight. Gav helped Halis lift the supplies off the wagon and take them into the large barn. With the doors open, the sound of bleating reached Ruby's ears. More sheep.

Climbing out of the wagon, Ruby was the only person who didn't have a task to complete and stood watching the others, fidgeting with a tie on her dress. She wanted to offer her assistance, but she felt out of place on the small farm and feared anything she attempted would be more of a hindrance.

The door of the farmhouse banged open, and a woman looking to be in her third decade, with tawny-colored hair and wearing a washed-out green dress, stepped outside into the fading sunlight.

"About time! I was beginning to think you weren't coming back to—" The woman stopped midsentence as she spotted the strangers standing in front of her home. Her brows furrowed, and she looked as if she was about to ask who in the hells all these people were when her eyes settled on Kai as she and Serik ambled back from stowing the horses in the barn with the raucous sheep.

"Kai! It's been an age since I've seen you." The shepherd's wife looked Kai up and down as she approached, a grin blossoming across her features and making her look years younger. Kai bounded forward, and they embraced. The tawny-haired woman was all smiles as she pulled back, still clasping Kai's forearms. "Still as skinny as ever, I see! I'll cook something up to put some meat on those bones so that you can find yourself a good husband," she said happily, then looked over Kai's head at the rest of them. "Though, maybe you already found one. Who might these folk be?"

"Aethra, this is my friend, Violet," Kai said as she turned away from the other woman, gesturing at Ruby. "Her husband Serik"—she pointed at the wilder—"and Gav, my… something," she finished with a level look in the loresinger's direction.

"Also husband, as you so astutely guessed," Gav said as he strode forward, taking one of Aethra's hands in both of his. "I'm pleased to meet such a beautiful woman."

Aethra blinked as Halis scoffed in amusement.

When the woman glanced at Kai, there was a knowing look that was a bit ruined by the flush on her cheeks. "And who are they really?"

"That's need-to-know, Aethra. Sorry," Kai apologized. "We just need to stay the night. Then we'll be out of your hair. Oh, and before I forget—"

"I know, I know," Aethra cut her off with a sigh and wiggled her hand out of Gav's grip. "You and your companions were never here. Honestly, whatever you're involved in, I don't want to know." The older woman placed her fists on her hips. "Well, let's get you all settled before dinner. Lucky for you, we have enough space for you four." She raised one eyebrow. "Are the 'married' ones sharing rooms?"

The way she said the word "married" made it clear that she didn't believe that for a second.

"No," Kai said before Gav could open his mouth. "Violet and I will share a room, and the men can do the same."

Aethra chuckled before turning away. "Very well, follow me."

Leaving Halis to finish storing the supplies he'd brought back from Issalden, they followed the shepherd's wife inside. She took them on a short tour of the farmhouse. It was much more spacious inside than Ruby had assumed, with a cozy parlor with white-washed benches, a large living and dining area, a kitchen, and two spare bedrooms aside from the master suite. Aethra fussed over the women, insisting that they wash up before eating while the men brought in their effects.

After the long day riding in the wagon, Ruby was thankful for a hot bath. The two women washed up quickly, and by the time they were dressed again, dinner was ready.

"I didn't know we were having company," Aethra said by way of apology as she served them portions of roasted chicken with cabbage and potatoes, pea soup, and mulled wine. "It's a bit simple, but a full stomach will help you sleep and plump you up a bit." She directed that last comment at Kai.

"Why does everyone think I'm too skinny?" Kai grumbled.

"*I* don't, dear," Gav said as he leaned toward her. "You're perfect to me."

She pushed his face away with a chicken leg.

"It is exquisite," Ruby cut in before they could start bickering. "Thank you, Aethra, both for hosting us on such short notice and for your hospitality," Ruby said with a gracious bow of her head.

Aethra's lips quivered, and Ruby had the impression that the woman was trying not to smile. "I haven't heard anyone talk like that for a while. Not from around these parts, Miss Violet?"

"Missus," Serik said with a wink and a smirk. He was seated next to Ruby at the edge of the table. He touched Ruby's shoulder and leaned over to kiss her cheek.

Ruby choked on her wine, making Aethra smirk. "Of course, my mistake. So, where is it that you are headed?" she asked as she sat next to her husband.

"Far east of here, toward Lanevin," Kai supplied, having successfully fought off Gav with chicken parts. There was a telling smear of grease on the loresinger's chin. "We'll need another horse. Halis said you could spare one?"

"Ah, Kevin," she mused.

"Pardon?" Gav interjected. "Kevin?"

"She's an older horse, but she's sturdy and strong," Halis said.

"A female horse named *Kevin?*" the loresinger asked, incredulous.

"She'll be perfect for you, *dear*." Kai was grinning as she nudged Gav's shoulder with her own.

Though Gav looked unhappy about the prospect of riding a horse named "Kevin," he didn't say anything else on the matter.

Kai talked happily with the couple about what she had been doing the past few months. Apparently, her time at Valwen was not a secret from Halis and his wife, and she regaled them with stories about learning magic and mingling with the nobility. "I kept my nose clean, mostly. And if I couldn't, Violet was there to keep me out of trouble."

Aethra seemed impressed while Halis commented about

"stuffy mages" and "entitled nobles" as Kai talked. By the time they had finished eating, all of them were laughing over a particularly vivid tale of how Kai had switched out Professor Morel's two lemurs with exceptionally bad-tempered tabby cats.

"His face was so red, I thought he was on the verge of exploding," Ruby said with a laugh into her cup. "I had never seen him lose his temper like that before, stomping around the classroom and threatening to hang the guilty person outside the window by their ankles."

"You and me both. Luckily one of the lemurs learned how to open the latch on the wardrobe I stuck them in and escaped at the peak of his tirade, causing just enough distraction to make him forget about sniffing out the culprit, at least not at that moment." Kai sat back in her chair, grinning. "Valwen was fun at times, but it's nice to be free again."

Aethra rose and collected the dishes, still chuckling. She smiled at Ruby. "I'm glad Kai has someone to keep her out of too much trouble."

"Hey! I never get myself into anything I can't get out of," Kai said waspishly.

Everyone laughed at that.

After dinner, Halis enlisted Gav and Serik to help him with a few repairs around the house while Kai and Ruby retired to their room, exhausted from the events of the past few days. The space was furnished with a double bed, clean white sheets, an old wardrobe that had seen better days, and a square mirror propped up on a short bookshelf filled with faded leather-covered novels. Ruby changed into the linen nightdress that Johanna had given her and brushed out her hair while Kai donned a light shirt and breeches.

Now that they were out of immediate danger and far from Issalden, Ruby's mind had wandered back to her decision to leave Valwen.

"Kai, I have been considering my situation and have some concerns."

"Here we go," Kai sighed as she kicked off her boots.

Ruby bristled at her friend's tone but pushed forward. This was too important to let Kai's comment throw her off. "What is going to happen after we explore the ruins? It is not as though this problem will just go away." Ruby looked down at her hands. She was wringing the end of the sheet. "You and Gav have already been hurt trying to help me."

"I made my choice, and as for that idiotic loresinger, that was his own damn fault. Ruby, look at me," Kai said seriously, waiting for her to look up before continuing. "It's okay for you to want a different life from what you had, and it's okay to try to change your fate." Her expression softened a degree. "Don't blame yourself for the actions of other people. You did not put that bounty out, and you did not hurt Gav. Those were the choices of others. You did not ask to be engaged when you were a child, and I certainly can't blame you for wanting to get away from the duke." She sat on the bed next to Ruby and took her hands in her own. "You deserve to be happy. Remember that. Don't let anyone try to tell you otherwise."

Eyes swimming with tears, Ruby nodded, letting out a sharp laugh. Why was her body's reaction in situations like these to cry? "You are right, Kai. It is just so hard not to feel responsible for what happens to those I care about. You are all trying to help me, and I do not want that to be the cause of your misery."

Kai barked out a laugh. "That loresinger has a bounty on his head as well, remember? And as for the Thieves Guild, well…" A troubled look flickered across her face, but she shook her head like she was warding off an irksome fly. "I don't want to be part of an organization that would force me to betray my best friend, so it's really not a loss."

The look Ruby was giving Kai must have conveyed her skepticism because Kai clicked her tongue in annoyance and said, "I'm serious! I can make more money on my own anyway."

"Mmm."

Kai rolled her eyes. "To answer your earlier question, once we get whatever treasure there's to be had at Ta'Dormus Deva, we can use that money to buy you new identification papers or perhaps even pay a mage to change how you look. With any luck, it will be enough funds to get us started in a new country. The duke's reach doesn't extend beyond the empire. I can find work for us, so there's no need to worry about how we'll make a living. You'll just have to get accustomed to a simpler life."

"I doubt it gets 'simpler' than sleeping wrapped in a blanket on the ground in the middle of a forest." Ruby managed a small smile.

"*Ha!* I guess that's true." Kai yawned and stretched her arms over her head. "We should get some rest. Lots of riding tomorrow, but I guess you'll be nestled up to Serik all day," she said with a mischievous grin.

It was Ruby's turn to roll her eyes. "After over a week of near-constant 'nestling,' it is not nearly as intimate as you insinuate."

"Uh-huh. Sure, it's not." Kai laughed at Ruby's expression as they both slipped under the sheets.

After blowing out the candle, Ruby heard Kai murmur, "Everything will be okay, I promise," before she drifted off to sleep.

CHAPTER 15

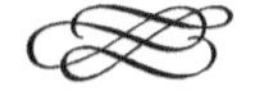

A loud crash from the front room roused Ruby from the dream she'd been having about Professor Morel's lemures. Groaning, she rolled over, determined to go back to sleep. She wasn't ready to get up for lessons yet. If someone came to check on her, she would feign a stomachache and skip classes.

The next thing Ruby knew, she was being shaken awake.

"Kai?" she asked as she blinked her eyes open and yawned. The memories of Valwen faded, and she remembered that she had left the school and was on a farm a day's ride outside Issalden. "What is happening?"

"There are some soldiers here threatening Halis," Kai replied, her voice deadly low. The door was ajar, and a thin line of lamplight shone into the room. Kai leaned across the bed, one arm on Ruby's shoulder.

"What?" Ruby asked, sitting up. She'd heard Kai's words but could hardly believe them. "Where?" She rubbed at her eyes. Was this another dream?

"They're outside. Serik and Gav are already awake." Kai

stood, handing Ruby a shawl to cover her nightdress. She had already put on a jacket over her sleeping shirt.

"Why are there soldiers here?" Ruby asked as she accepted the knitted wool fabric, panic creeping into her voice. Had they been sent by Mikel—or her parents—to drag her back home?

"I'm not sure. I couldn't hear much from the window, but they accused Halis of not paying enough taxes." She snorted disdainfully. "As if soldiers would be coming here to collect if that were the case. It sounds like extortion. We should prepare for trouble." Grabbing her dagger and sword off the bedside table, she secured the weapons to her belt as Ruby laced up her shoes. If she was going to be caught outside in nothing but a nightgown again, at least she would have proper shoes this time.

Once armed, Kai pressed a finger to her lips to signal silence and crept into the parlor, crouching low. Ruby waited for her signal, then followed, mimicking Kai's movement, albeit less gracefully. Broken glass littered the floor, fallen from the parlor windows. A few large rocks lay scattered in the mess, the source of the damage. Ruby was careful to skirt around the debris.

Kai gestured for Ruby to come closer, and the two of them peered out the parlor's broken window.

There were people outside, a few holding torches. Serik and Gav stood close to the farmhouse and blocked Aethra. Halis was a little farther out on the farm road, speaking to the men there. From what Ruby could see in the flickering torchlight, she counted ten men dressed in the blue uniform and leather armor she recognized as the outfits worn by the emperor's knights. Most of the men stood even farther back while Halis and a blond man spoke. He must have been the leader, but it was hard to make out anyone's features in the dim light.

They argued loudly, and their voices carried in the otherwise still night.

"We already gave you everything we could spare! As I said, the lambs won't be ready until next season," Halis was saying. "We always pay the emperor's taxes on time and—"

"I don't care about your excuses," the man cut Halis off. "If you can't pay, then you forfeit the protection of the empire." The man raised a hand, and the soldiers began moving toward the barn and the field where the sheep were.

"What are you doing?!" Halis moved to stop them, but the blond man put a hand on his shoulder. "Let go of me! Stay away from my sheep!"

"Halis!" Aethra shrieked as Serik stepped forward. Gav put an arm out to prevent the woman from running to her husband.

"We don't want any trouble," the wilder said. Despite his words, he placed a hand on the hilt of his sword. "As he told you, they have already paid their taxes. Why don't you end this peacefully and go on your way so we can all go back to sleep? I'm sure Halis will visit the tax office the next time he's in Issalden to ensure everything is paid and in order."

The blond man stared at Serik, scrutinizing him. "I don't think you know how this works, stranger." He gestured to his men again, and two of them drew pistols and approached. "Either I collect what's due, or they lose their farm."

"I'm going to throw my dagger at the one on the left," Kai whispered to Ruby. "Can you take out the other one's pistol? Can you shatter it like you did Joran's sword?"

Ruby thought about what had happened before with the blade. It had been long and thin, so she'd only had to target one area to break it, but with a pistol, the steel would be thicker than the blade Joran had used. "Perhaps. I'll think of something."

Kai gave her a grim smile and nodded. "Wait for me to

make my move, then cast your spell while they're distracted." Keeping low, she crept over to the front door, reached up to turn the nob, and pushed on it slowly with her shoulder. It opened an inch. Her eyes met Ruby's, and she waved her over.

Ruby tried her best to imitate Kai's careful movements again and thought she did a passable job. She didn't trip over anything, at least. Once she reached Kai's side, she peered over her head and out the crack in the door. She could see Serik's and Halis's backs and the blond soldier still talking, though her heart was pounding in her ears too loudly to hear what they were saying.

The leader gestured one hand to his men, and they started moving toward the field again. Serik's hand twitched as if he wanted to draw his weapon. The wilder was quick, but there were so many knights.

"He doesn't want to get shot," Kai said as if reading her mind. She was still staring intently at the gunner to the left of the leader. The other wasn't visible from their position, but Ruby doubted he would have moved if this one hadn't.

"Are you ready?" Kai asked.

Ruby drew in a deep breath, stilling her mind and drawing on the power within her. She said a quick prayer to the gods that the spell she had in mind would work as she intended. The incantation wasn't one she'd practiced often, but if she combined it with a shield spell, it should work. Concentrating on the effect she wanted, she nodded.

"On three, then. One. Two." Kai held her dagger up and flashed Ruby a cocky grin, then pulled her hand back to throw the blade as she slammed the door open with her other hand. "Three!"

At the word, she flung her arm forward, releasing her dagger. Her aim was true. The projectile hit the barrel of the gun, sparking against the metal, and knocking it off target, firing harmlessly into the air. The gunman fumbled with the weapon, and every eye fell on Kai, giving Ruby her opening.

Ruby exited the farmhouse behind Kai and held out one hand, releasing the energy she had gathered.

"Obstructum!" she hissed under her breath, making a tiny version of her shield of hardened air and energy right at the tip of the other gunman's barrel, plugging it as if she'd put a finger into the opening. It wasn't a second too soon. As her spell locked in place, he pulled the trigger. With her magic obstructing the barrel, the gun backfired in a small explosion of fire and metal as the chamber burst back on its wielder. The soldier cried out in pain and flung the now-useless weapon away, blood dripping down his hand.

While the rest of the knights seemed momentarily stunned by the turn of events, Gav burst into motion, dashing forward and pulling his rapier. "Get inside!" he called over his shoulder to Aethra as he lunged, the tip of the weapon piercing through the leather armor of the closest soldier. The man couldn't react in time to block Gav's strike, and more dark blood splattered across the ground as the fighter stumbled back from him with a cry.

"Kill them!" the blond man yelled as he drew his sword. At his command, the other men seemed to snap out of their stupor and charged forward.

Kai's blade returned to her hand, and the taste of magic was in the air as a blue flame enveloped the weapon. She dashed away from the farmhouse and hurled the blade at the blond man, but seeing the projectile coming, the leader ducked, and the dagger flew over his head.

The soldier closest to Halis drew a short sword and swung the weapon at the shepherd, but Serik grabbed Halis's tunic and jerked him back and out of reach of its edge. The blade missed him by inches as the farmer stumbled. Serik pushed the man behind him. "Get Aethra and get inside!" the wilder bellowed as he whipped out his own sword and parried another blow.

Halis nodded and turned from the fight. He dashed toward Aethra, who had not moved from where she'd been standing, and grabbed her arm.

She seemed to come back to her senses as he reached her. "Halis! Are you all right?" she asked, looking him over. Her voice was strained.

"I'm fine! Come on!" He pulled her toward the house, and, after a few steps, Aethra ran alongside him.

Ruby's eyes flicked from the shepherd and his wife back to the battle at hand. Gav was fighting two soldiers simultaneously, dodging their attacks and lunging with his rapier. He was quick, but the soldiers were well-trained and worked together to bypass his defenses. Ruby held up her hands, drawing on her magic to help Gav, when movement behind him caught her eye.

The gunman Kai targeted had finished reloading and pointed his pistol at the retreating Halis and Aethra.

Thinking quickly, Ruby's hands wove over her chest, her magic forming a shield between the couple and the barrel of the firearm. She was fairly certain a bullet would punch through her shield if she tried to block the projectile with blunt force, so she angled the plane of her spell forty-five degrees, hoping it would divert its trajectory.

The crack of gunfire echoed through the night, and Ruby felt her shield fracture, but it had the effect she'd intended. The bullet ricocheted off the shield, up and over their heads. The impact against her spell created a flash of blue light, and the gunman looked from the retreating forms of the couple to Ruby, his expression darkening as he met her eyes. If the soldiers hadn't known that she had caused the other weapon's backfire, they did now. Halis and Aethra rushed past Ruby with a nod of thanks, and, a moment later, the door to the farmhouse slammed shut.

A pained cry from Gav drew her attention.

"Gah!" Gav had been moving out of the way of one sword strike when another hit him in the shoulder. Breathing hard, the loresinger retreated a few steps and switched his rapier to his other hand. Steeling his resolve, he lunged forward again, striking his opponent and proving that he was just as good at wielding a sword with his offhand. The soldier went down, holding his side as he crawled away from the loresinger.

Two more men charged at Kai. She danced out of the way of their blades, their strikes wild. Ruby guessed that the soldiers had not been expecting a fight this night, and if they had, they'd be against farmers, not people skilled at defending themselves. Slashing her dagger at one of the soldiers, Kai feinted right, then jumped back and flung her fiery weapon at the other man, the blade burying deep into his arm and setting his clothing on fire. The man screamed and dropped to the ground, rolling around and trying to extinguish the blue flame that was devouring his sleeve.

Serik held a dagger in his offhand, using it and his sword to attack the soldier before him. Ruby hadn't seen him fight with two weapons before, and the wilder moved so quickly that his hands were almost a blur. A worried expression crossed the face of the knight he was opposing, and the soldier took a few quick steps back as he desperately blocked Serik's strikes.

He proved to be less skilled of a swordsman than the wilder. Two jabs in succession from Serik's blade sent the man sprawling, clutching at his lower abdomen as blood seeped through the fabric.

Gav dodged two more attacks and scrambled back,

putting himself shoulder-to-shoulder with Serik. Three of their assailants were down, but there were still many more.

"Come now, gentlemen!" the loresinger said, his voice ringing out as the other soldiers quickly closed in on them. "Surely, we can still work this out!"

"I think we are past that, Gav!" Kai called as she stepped out of the way of a lunge from another short sword. The tip of the soldier's blade scored her upper arm, and she sucked in a sharp breath. She held out her hand, and her dagger appeared back in it again. She pounced forward, slashing at the soldier's face. He screamed and staggered back, clutching at his eyes.

Ruby held her hands before her, eyes flicking over the fight, unsure what to cast to aid her friends. They seemed to be faring well without her help thus far, but she couldn't just stand there doing nothing. The gunman whose shot she'd blocked had dashed behind the fight, and with all the knights dressed the same way, she'd lost track of him.

Serik evaded another jab, then sprang forward, putting himself close to the man he was facing off with. He brought his forearm down hard on his attacker's wrist, causing the soldier to lose his grip on his sword, then elbowed him in the neck with the other arm and sent the man sprawling on his back. Kicking the downed weapon behind him, Serik retreated out of grabbing range while the man on the ground gagged and clutched his throat.

As the wilder stepped back, the leader rushed him, and Serik could barely get his sword up in time to block the attack.

"Who are you?!" the man shouted at the wilder as he struck with his sword again. Serik blocked, but the blond man placed his other hand on the flat of Serik's blade and pushed, causing the wilder to stagger. Swinging a third time, his blade pierced through Serik's clothing, and blood coated the edge of the enemy's blade.

"Serik!" Ruby screamed. Reaching deep within herself, she called forth fire to aid her. Her teachers at Valwen warned that while easy to draw on, fire was a dangerous manifestation of energy and emotion due to its difficulty to control. Those lectures seemed unimportant as she watched Serik raise his sword to block another blow, his movements slower than before. A lance of white-hot flame burst forth from her outstretched hand and flew at the blond man.

Eyes wide, he held up his short sword to block the fire and ducked his head. The metal quickly grew red hot. With a curse, the blond man dropped the weapon and dove to the side, out of the way of her spell.

As the fire died away, she started the incantation to break his weapon. "*Fra—*"

The thunderous clap of gunfire cut off her spell, and the force of impact jerked Ruby's body to one side. Pain exploded right below her ribs, and she cried out at the intensity of it. Looking out at the soldiers, her eyes found the remaining gunman. The barrel of the pistol was pointed at her, and he wore a satisfied smirk on his face. The thought *why is it so hard to breathe?* crossed her mind as she looked down at herself. Crimson-red liquid blossomed across her nightgown, originating from where the pain pulsed. It was hard for her to focus on what was happening, but one thing was certain. She had been shot.

"No!" Kai screamed, breaking into Ruby's thoughts. A moment later, her friend was at her side, catching Ruby as her knees buckled and helping her to the ground. "Ruby!"

Ruby tried to think, but it was hard to string together thoughts over the pain from her wound. Kai held her as the fight continued around them, but Ruby couldn't focus on what was happening and squeezed her eyes shut. Her breathing shallow and pained, she winced as another crack of gunfire echoed through the night. Had someone else been shot?

There was the sound of running footsteps and then Gav's melodious voice.

"Hold this against the wound!"

Ruby gasped as pressure was applied to her side, then clenched her teeth together to keep herself from crying out.

"I have her," Gav said as he lifted her from the ground and Kai's grip.

Laying her head against Gav's chest, Ruby opened her eyes and glanced around Halis's farm. Five men were down with various injuries, and the man who had shot her was holding a cloth stained with blood to his other shoulder, his gun nowhere to be seen. The blond man had regained his feet and had drawn a knife.

Serik and the blond man stared each other down, both poised to continue the fight.

"Orders, Sargent?" one of the knights asked as he dragged back one of his companions. The man's eyes were wide as he waited for direction, flicking to the other wounded soldiers.

After a few tense moments, the leader grimaced, then said, "Torben, we're done here. Gather the injured." He glared at Serik. "Watch your back, stranger. I won't forget this."

Without waiting to see how the rest of the exchange played out, Gav turned his back on the men and rushed Ruby into the house. "Clear the table!" he ordered to a confused and scared-looking Halis and Aethra. At his words, they rushed into action and moved the piles of clean dishes and candles off the table.

"We need to get that bullet out," he said as he set Ruby gently on the tabletop. "Do you have pliers? Clean bandages would be good, too," he asked them.

"Yes!" Aethra said and hurried out of the room to get the supplies.

Ruby focused on the sound of her own breath as Gav set her on the hard surface as gently as he could, but jostled the injury. She gripped the sleeves of his shirt in her fists as a new surge of agony raced up her spine. Her vision darkened, and it took her a few minutes to catch her breath. If she didn't move too much, the pain was manageable.

There was the bang of the front door opening and closing.

"They're leaving," Kai's voice floated in from the parlor. Her boots scuffed the floorboards. Then her face appeared over Ruby, cheeks flush and eyes wide. "Have you done this before?" she asked, looking at the loresinger suspiciously. Her expression was drawn.

Gav grimaced. "Well, no, but I've seen it done. So it shouldn't be that hard, right?"

At that moment, Serik came through the doorway, pushing the loresinger out of the way as he moved to Ruby's side. "I'll do it," he said as Aethra returned with the pliers and a pile of clean white cloths that Gav had requested, along with a shallow bowl of water and a bottle filled with amber liquid. No one argued with the wilder as he took the supplies from the shepherd's wife.

"Are those men gone?" Aethra asked, her voice sounding far away through the pain.

"Yes." There was the sound of splashing water, then, "Kai, can I get some light?"

A whisper of power filled the air, and a magical ball of bright-white light floated over the table. Gav held Ruby's hand as Serik examined her wound. He ripped away part of her nightgown and dabbed at the wound with the cloth, making her suck in a sharp breath.

"I think I see the bullet." He met the shepherd's eyes. "She needs something to bite down on." Halis left and returned a few moments later. "I need you to open your mouth, Ruby. There we are," Serik said as he placed a thick leather strap between her teeth. His warm hand cupped her cheek, and he stared into her eyes. "This isn't going to be pleasant, but you'll be fine, I promise."

Ruby closed her eyes. It still hurt to breathe, but she nodded.

"That's my girl," he said soothingly, then he pressed one hand to her stomach, and her whole world was nothing but pain.

The agony was all-encompassing, and the seconds felt like hours. There was no frame of reference to compare it to because she had never felt such suffering. As she tried to scream, Ruby was only dimly aware of voices other than her own. Serik yelled, "Hold her!" Someone was crying. Aethra, she thought, or maybe it was herself.

"I have it. One more push, Ruby," the wilder said, and then there was another ripping pain, and she jerked, but firm hands held down her arms and legs.

The pressure eased a little, and there was a different feeling, a sting as the wound was cleaned by strong-smelling alcohol and bandaged by Serik's steady hands. She knew it was him without looking. His touch was warm against her skin. It felt similar to when he'd tended to her feet. Gentle but firm, with a confidence as if he had done it a hundred times.

The leather was removed from her mouth, and she sobbed. She wanted to cover her face and hide her tears, but someone took her head in their hands and leaned over her, pressing a cheek to hers.

"It's all right. You're okay," Kai whispered in her hair as she held her.

"She'll heal quickly, and her magic will prevent the

wound from getting infected," Serik was saying to the shepherd. Ruby barely heard over the sound of her own weeping. "But she will need to rest a few days. Do you think we can stay here for that time?"

"Yes, of course," Aethra said immediately. "Anything you need, you'll have. We're alive thanks to you four."

Kai left her side, and the next thing Ruby knew, her tears had quieted, and she was being lifted off the table. The scent of firewood and cloves filled her nose, and she opened her eyes to see Serik gazing down at her. She reached up and touched his face, his beard course under her fingertips.

"You're brave. Helping me when you should have been protecting yourself," he said.

Her lips moved, but they felt slow. "Are you hurt?"

"Only a little. The loresinger is in much worse shape than I am, but we still have a few potions left to help with that. I have one for you too." He carried her into the bedroom.

Ruby grimaced. Potions for healing wounds tasted bitter. She'd had to drink one a few years back when she'd fallen off her horse during riding lessons.

Serik chuckled and set her on the bed, seeming to read her mind. Kai slipped in behind the wilder, carrying a white bundle in one arm and holding a small vial in the other.

"A new nightgown and potion," she explained. "Courtesy of Aethra."

Ruby glanced down at herself. Her current nightgown was ripped almost in two and stained red with her blood. Her navel and hips were showing. She blushed. Serik might as well have seen her naked.

Kai shooed the wilder out, but before he left, he leaned down to press his lips to Ruby's forehead. Kai helped Ruby change and dabbed at her face with a damp cloth to wipe away the sweat that slicked her skin. The pain was a dull ache now, but she drank the potion readily enough. There was a tingling sensation in her stomach, and after a few seconds, it felt like something hot was being held against her skin where the bullet hole was. The potion would accelerate the healing process, and that, combined with her own natural healing abilities, would mean that she would be ready to ride in a day or two. In a week, there would be no sign that she had ever been injured.

By the time the potion had worked its magic, Ruby was exhausted.

"Sleep," Kai instructed as she stepped toward the door. "I'll be back soon."

Ruby didn't need to be told twice. She lay on the soft mattress, letting out a long sigh. Her eyes fluttered closed, and the aches of her injury soon faded into blackness.

CHAPTER 16

They left the farm early in the morning three days later, after ensuring Halis and Aethra had all the supplies they needed in case those men came back. Ruby's wound was mostly healed, thanks to the potion Kai had given her that first night. It still ached when she prodded at it or twisted her torso at the dinner table, but she was alive and able to ride. That was all that mattered.

Much to her discomfort, Serik had checked her bandages every morning and night. She undressed for these visits, covering her breasts and hips, and leaving her midsection exposed for him to examine, but it was necessary. Neither of them thought there would be an issue or risk of infection, thanks to her magic, but it was beneficial to keep the wound clean. She couldn't wear a corset with the bandages, and that left her feeling even more vulnerable.

Kai was hesitant about leaving, thinking those men could return any day, but Aethra nearly shoved her out the door into the cloudy gray morning.

"Get going! I've already written to my brother to have him come and stay with us for a while, and Halis will talk to the neighboring farmers and try to get a militia together. Hopefully, that will keep those ruffians from coming back, knights or not."

"But—"

"Don't worry about us! You needed to get away from Issalden and that gods-damned guild. You can't stick around here and help us, or the farm will be crawling with guildies." Ruby had learned over the past few days that "guildies" meant anyone who was a member or worked for the guilds.

Glancing at Ruby, Kai let out a frustrated grunt. "Fine! But if they do return, promise me you two won't try anything risky. Those men are trained to kill, and you, Halis, or whoever else you can round up aren't."

Aethra laughed. "Tell you what, I won't take any more risks than *you* would."

Kai didn't seem happy with that answer but only nodded.

The shepherd gave Kevin the horse to Gav without asking for any coin in return. When the loresinger tried to protest, Halis said, "Just take her. Because of you four, I still have a farm to tend to."

It was hard to argue with that.

Serik helped Ruby climb onto Dream, and by noon, their little procession left the farm behind them, Halis and Aethra waving goodbye.

The first day of riding was miserable. It started raining shortly after they left the farm and continued throughout the day. The group had to stop multiple times to clear their horses' hooves of grass and mud so that they could continue. After their midday stop to eat and rest, Serik took out a heavy wool blanket from his supplies and wrapped it around himself and Ruby when they reseated themselves atop Dream. The closeness made her blush, but she only gave a half-hearted protest.

"You were shivering so hard it was making my teeth rattle," he said by way of explanation, quelling her objections.

Ruby didn't argue further. Serik was right. She was so cold that it brought her sore muscles and aching injuries into sharper focus. With the blanket wrapped around them, the chill faded as the wilder's body heat warmed her. Sighing, she leaned back into him, letting her eyes flutter closed.

She flitted in and out of consciousness, and, before she knew it, the gray and cloudy day had grown darker, and they were stopping to rest for the night.

Gav was particularly useless when they set up camp. During their travels, Ruby had learned to gather firewood while Serik saw to the sleeping arrangements and Kai helped to unload the supplies. But being injured, she couldn't be of any help for now. The loresinger sat atop his horse, looking at the others' actions with confusion.

"Isn't there an inn close to here?"

"No," Serik said as he inspected a few low-hanging branches of a pine tree. They'd chosen to camp inside a copse of trees twenty feet from the road. "The closest inn is at least another day out in this weather. We could have reached it tonight if it had been sunny, but the rain makes travel slow."

Looking like he'd eaten something bitter, Gav dismounted. He looked around their small campsite, then approached Serik, rubbing his arms for warmth. His auburn hair was plastered to his forehead in the damp. "What are you doing?"

"Looking for material to make a lean-to. I need branches like this to help keep the rain out."

"But everything's soaked! How is that supposed to keep the rain off us if it's dripping?"

Serik didn't respond to the loresinger's comment, instead taking his axe and getting to work on removing the branches he'd selected from the tree. Once the wilder had a large pile of the limbs, he built a shelter by leaning the branches up against another two trees and securing a brown spotted animal hide over it, creating an area underneath that was sheltered from the rain.

Kai used her magic to dry the wood and ground in the shelter, creating a place where they could rest comfortably. After a few more minutes of the loresinger's complaints, an annoyed-looking Serik shoved a pile of blankets in the other man's arms.

"If you can talk, you can work."

Kai snickered, earning a glare from Gav. Stalking over to the fire she'd started, Serik set up the supplies for their meal.

While Kai tied up another animal-skin hide for the horses to shelter under, Ruby sat on the blankets that Gav had spread out under the lean-to. The rain was lighter than it had been earlier, and she found the pattering sound against their roof soothing. Like Gav, she would have preferred an inn, but sleeping outside wasn't so bad.

"We're going to freeze tonight," Gav said as he pulled his soaked shirt off and settled a few feet from Ruby, in as foul a mood as the wilder.

"We will not," Ruby said, trying to hide her amusement. "Serik is an excellent outdoorsman, and not a drop has come through since he erected this shelter."

Gav mumbled something under his breath that she couldn't make out, but she distinctly heard the word "brute." It made her smile.

"Have you really never slept outside?" Ruby asked him. She went to hug her knees to her chest to ward off some of the cold, but a twinge of pain from her injury stopped her. Instead, she sat with her back straight and legs bent in front of her. It was how she would have sat during a picnic at home. Not the most comfortable position, but it kept the pain away.

"I have," Gav admitted, "but when I sleep outside, I just roll myself in a blanket. Staying at an inn is far better. In weather such as this, *I* wouldn't have left the farm until it stopped."

"I too am not fond of the cold," Ruby admitted. "But necessity dictated our departure. I am certain it would not have taken much longer for those soldiers to figure out who we were and come for the bounty on our heads."

He pressed his lips together, one eyebrow twitching up. "What happened to the emperor's knights being honorable men?"

"Those ruffians were anything but honorable," she sniffed indignantly. "The emperor must not know of their actions here. It is the only possible reason they have yet to meet his justice."

The loresinger chuckled. "I'm guessing you've never met the emperor." Crossing his ankles, he clasped his arms behind his head and leaned back. Gav closed his eyes and sighed. "I have. He's too busy keeping the other nobles around him in check to care about what happens to a couple of farms out in the middle of nowhere."

"He *should* care," Ruby snapped, incensed by Gav's casual tone. "Farms like Halis and Aethra's provide food not just to the surrounding area, but to the larger cities in the south. A few small farms may not be an issue, but if this is allowed to continue, it could create scarcity and famine, as well as unrest in his people and distrust in the crown."

One of the loresinger's eyes opened, giving her a sidelong glance. "You're more perceptive than you seem."

"It is simple cause and effect. Inaction will create larger, less manageable issues in the future."

"Well, you are already more knowledgeable than most of the lords and ladies in the emperor's court." He smirked. "Half of them just flit around balls and parties, while the other half can't comprehend anyone outside of their own social status."

Ruby frowned at that. It had been many years since she had taken a trip to the capital with her parents. They had a few friends there, but being a child, she had been sectioned off with the others her age. Was high society truly as Gav described it?

The bobbing lantern light that marked Serik's approach drew her attention. He wore a heavy cloak with the hood covering most of his face, and the thick mud sucked at his boots. Before entering the shelter, he removed his boots and hung the cloak over a branch. Serik knelt next to her. The small bag in his hands was the one that carried his medical supplies.

"I need to check your bandages," he said softly.

Ruby felt her face heat. "Here? *Now?*"

"I'm afraid so." He smiled apologetically. Then he plucked up the thick wool blanket they'd been wrapped in together when riding Dream and handed it to her. "Just lift your dress and cover yourself with this. That will suffice."

She glanced over at Gav. He'd turned onto his side with his back to them, and she was thankful that he, at least, was an honorable man. Serik averted his gaze and busied himself with cleaning off his boots with a dry cloth as she did what he asked. Laying the blanket across her hips and pulling her gown and shift up to her ribs, Ruby exposed her midsection to the chill night air.

With delicate hands, Serik unwrapped her bandages and held up the lamp to examine her. "It's healing well. You'll only need bandages for another day or two." He made a pensive sound, and his cool fingers brushed her skin, making her draw in a sharp breath. Serik tilted his head to one side as he applied gentle pressure to the area around the wound. It ached, but Ruby was more aware of the feel of his calloused fingers on her stomach. "But you still should leave the corset off. The cloth will rub against the wound and irritate the skin."

All she could do was nod. It was awkward enough having him look at and touch her like this, but to have him tell her not to wear her undergarments was too much. Ruby tried to keep her breathing steady as Serik replaced her bandages with fresh ones. His fingers brushed the skin below her navel, and she shivered.

"Almost done," he said. "Then you can sit closer to the fire." He must have assumed her shiver had been from the cold.

"Thank you." Her voice sounded steady. Good. "You seem very knowledgeable about medicine," she said, trying to change the subject.

"Well, when you live out by yourself far from any towns, it's a requirement. I mentioned spending time with the northern tribes, yes? I stayed with the *Talgari* for ten years. Most of what I know is from them." He chuckled, and his eyes took on the glint of someone recalling a fond memory. "I only have myself to rely on, so I became very good at tending my own wounds."

"Sounds lonely," Ruby mused.

"It can be," he agreed, "but sometimes, I have young noblewomen and thieves to guide. At those times, I find myself with too many people around."

"You can go back to the forest and leave the treasure to us," she replied with false irritation. "I would be happy to keep your share."

Serik smirked, and she could see the mirth crinkle the skin at the edges of his eyes. "And waste all my efforts to keep you alive? I think not."

"Has it been such a chore?" she mocked.

"You'd be surprised how much work it truly is."

They both laughed as Serik finished with his ministrations. Ruby righted her clothing as he left to check on the pot hanging over the fire.

The four of them slept side by side that night, Ruby and Kai in the middle with Serik and Gav on either end. It should have been awkward, but the chill in the air banished any thoughts of impropriety. On the contrary, Ruby found it comforting and warm to have both Serik and Kai beside her. When she awoke in the morning, she felt refreshed. Even more so since the sun was out and the clouds had disappeared, leaving the crisp morning clear and blue.

The little group was in high spirits with the change of weather, and the ride that day was pleasant, with them talking and laughing as they traveled.

Gav regaled them with stories of his escapades and adventures. From his stories, he had stayed mostly in the large cities in the south, which were only a day or two's ride from each other. Many of his tales began with a beautiful woman seeking his affection and ending with a slew of jealous husbands and suitors. It was a wonder that he only had one earl seeking his head.

According to the loresinger, he had played for most of the high court in the Andrean Empire and was friends with not only the Archduke of Athoen and the high priest of Finrur—the god of art and beauty—but the emperor's court magician as well.

"Bullshit," Kai had said more than once, but Gav repeatedly swore that his stories held nothing but fact.

Serik had scoffed at that. "I'm sure you think that's the truth, but loresingers have a habit of exaggerating their own significance in their fish stories."

Ruby and Kai laughed while Gav gaped in indignation.

By the time twilight approached, they had reached a village called Rochdale and were settling in for the night at the small inn. They purchased two rooms and walked up to them in pairs to keep up the appearance that they were couples, but once out of sight of prying eyes, Ruby and Kai went to one room and the men to another. The bed was cramped, and hay from the mattress poked through Ruby's night dress, but it was warm inside and offered the women privacy to bathe.

After another surprisingly restful night's sleep, the group continued on their way. Farms dotted the countryside, and they passed little village after little village. It seemed their days of riding between towns was now behind them.

The next ten days continued in much the same manner, riding most of the day and stopping at an inn once the sun went down. There was only one night that the group had to spend outdoors again, but the weather was nice, and Gav only complained a little.

Ruby's gunshot wound was fully healed by the time they reached Lanevin, a tiny pink blemish on her skin the only sign that anything had marked her. In time, that too would disappear completely. The magic in her blood left no scars behind.

Lanevin was a large city, one of the largest in the north, due to the fact that the Imperial Rail Line came through the center of the city, making it easy to travel to and from the south. Most of the area's agricultural goods came to Lanevin to be shipped to other parts of the empire.

There was some farmland as they approached the city, but it quickly gave way to rows of neat houses and small gardens. Brass lampposts dotted the street, and people hurried past large shop windows displaying various women's dresses, ribbons, and jewelry. Most were dressed in styles that Ruby recognized as being popular in the south. Women wore long skirts and heeled boots, their dresses adorned with high collars and ruffles. Men wore form-fitting breeches with light jackets and wool top hats. The residents seemed too busy to notice the small group riding into town, but like in Issalden, a few stared at Serik with shock and apprehension, the wilder ominous-looking in his leather gear and hooded cloak.

Serik found them an inn near the train station on the east end of town. It was a tall building with four floors and made of dark red-brown bricks. It reminded Ruby of structures she'd seen in the Valkea, the capital and the home of the Imperial Seat. Despite the familiarity, she found herself uncomfortable here, looking down every alley and street they passed, alert for any sign of danger. Lanevin was a far cry from the tiny hamlets and sleepy villages they had ridden through thus far. It was surprising, as the city outside her own home had looked similar to this place, but she had been away from it for so long she supposed she had gotten used to the farmland and forests surrounding Valwen.

"We should stock up on supplies tonight," Kai said as they dismounted and handed their reins over to a pair of scrawny-looking teenagers. "There's no guarantee that we'll be able to find what we need in Calsith. Lanevin is a big city, so no one should pay attention to us. Oh!" Her face brightened. "We should get some dinner while we are at it. The food here is pretty good, and no offense, wilder, but I'm sick of your cooking."

Serik gave her a sidelong look but didn't offer a response to her words.

"I, for one, adored your cooking," Gav piped in. "It's so quaint."

"I am not sure that is a compliment," Ruby added, smiling as Serik handed her the small satchel that contained the clothing from Johana, along with the few belongings she'd collected thus far on their journey.

"Let's meet by the stables in an hour," Kai said, cutting off Gav's flippant response. "I could use a bath."

"That sounds heavenly," Ruby mused with a sigh.

Once they had stored their belongings and washed up from the day's travel, Ruby and Kai waited for the others on a bench in front of the inn. The sun was low in the sky, painting it a deep red near the horizon, and tall buildings cast long shadows over the cobblestone streets. It wasn't long before twilight. Young men dressed in rough spun clothing walked the streets, turning levers on the bottoms of the streetlamps and activating the device within that allowed electricity to flow into the bulbs above. The soft yellow glow of the lights winked on one by one as the two women watched.

"I forgot how amazing it was to be in a larger city," Kai said, leaning back and threading her fingers together behind her head. "All the convenience of modern technology and the money to upkeep it."

"Issalden is a bit rural," Ruby agreed. "That is where you were living, yes?"

Kai nodded. "For the past few years, anyway. I'm originally from the capital. That part wasn't made up."

Ruby stared at one lamplighter who was having trouble turning the lever. It appeared to be stuck. "Can you tell me about yourself, Kai? I realize that the information you gave me before may have been a cover for your true identity."

Kai let out a long breath. "Yeah, well, you're not wrong. I wasn't an apprentice scribe as the mages at Valwen were told." She lowered her hands to her lap and closed her eyes. "I grew up on the streets in Valkea. My mother died in childbirth, and my father a few years later. He worked in one of the factories by the river. He left me with his sister while he was at work. One day when I was five, he never came home. There was an accident, and that was it. I was an orphan."

"I am so sorry, Kai. That is awful." Ruby had no idea that she'd lost her parents so young.

Kai shrugged. "It was, but I was too young to really know him. I don't even remember what he looked like, only that he wore a rough, scratchy beard and had green eyes like mine." She opened her eyes and looked over at Ruby. "My aunt didn't want to take care of me. She couldn't, really. She already had three children of her own, and none of my family was well off." Her expression hardened. "She tried to sell me, but I ran away before the man who had paid her could come and collect me."

"Sell you? You mean—"

"Slavery," Kai answered. "Or worse, but like I said, I left before he could collect. There was a group of kids around my age living as urchins in the area, and I was small and skinny, so I was useful. We stole scraps and lived under bridges or wherever we could find shelter. I was eight when Alek found me." She smiled then, gaze distant. "I'd pickpocketed him, and he didn't notice until I was down the street. Then he chased me through half the city before finally catching me. I almost got away, but he was faster than I'd expected. Even then, he'd been the leader of the Kingfishers. He told me that if I was going to steal, I needed to learn to be more discreet, and he took me under his wing. I thought he would be like the man my aunt had sold me to and fought him at first, but it wasn't long before I realized that I was lucky that he was the one I'd tried to steal from."

Ruby smiled. "It sounds like the two of you are very close."

Kai stood and slipped her hands in her pockets. She was frowning, and her brows were furrowed as if she was carefully considering her words. "We were, which is why it's odd that he didn't come to that warehouse back in Issalden himself. If he had, I could have convinced him that you could be more useful to the Guild than that reward, and we wouldn't be here. Joran has never come in his stead before, at least not with me." She turned to look at Ruby, her eyes full of worry. "What if something happened to Alek while I was away at Valwen?"

Ruby wanted to tell her that it was all okay, and that she was sure Alek was all right, but they would have been empty words. She had no idea who Alek was, and she was certain that Joran was capable of killing anyone who got in his way. Perhaps the Thieves Guild lieutenant had removed its master.

But that wasn't what Kai *needed* to hear right now.

"Alek sounds like a competent man to have been leading the Guild for so long." Ruby patted Kai's shoulder, trying to comfort her. "Joran used his name when talking with you, remember? I doubt he would have done so if he had overthrown your friend." She remembered what Joran had said.

Alek wants her.

It sounded to Ruby like the guild leader was alive and well, though she suspected he was not as trustworthy a man as Kai thought he was.

Kai blinked at her, then realization filled her eyes. "He did, didn't he?"

The door to the inn opened, drawing both women's gazes. It was about time for the men to show up, but the person who stepped out of the building was almost unrecognizable.

Serik wore cream-colored breeches and a fashionable dark-green coat that brought out the color in his eyes. He'd trimmed his beard in a sharp edge that accentuated his strong jawline, and his dark hair was pulled back into a loose tail that barely brushed his collar. Under the outerwear was a gold-threaded waistcoat and a white frilled shirt. The look was such a drastic change from the leather-clad wilder she was used to that if Ruby didn't know it was Serik, she could have mistaken the gentleman in front of her for a man of high society.

There was a twinge of discomfort in her stomach. The way Serik held himself reminded her of Mikel. Perhaps it was the clothes. Ruby found that she preferred him in his woodland attire, but it was hard to deny that he cut a handsome figure. His eyes met hers, and all thoughts of the duke were banished from her mind. If she'd had a fan, she would have used it to help her catch her breath.

Gav poked his head out from behind Serik and smiled knowingly at the women. "I told you," he began, "no one will even think the word 'wilder' now."

As the men approached, Gav was grinning from ear to ear. He was also dressed well in a red jacket like the one he'd lost in Issalden and blue breeches, but it wasn't as striking as Serik's dramatic change. Ruby was used to the loresinger dressing along society's standards.

"Where did you get those clothes?" Kai's voice was laced with surprise, even if her face didn't betray that emotion.

"If you can believe it," Gav began before Serik could answer. "The coat and the breeches were among his possessions. The other items are mine."

Both Ruby's and Kai's heads snapped to Serik. There was the slightest tinge of pink to the wilder's cheeks.

"You look very handsome, but now I feel a bit underdressed," Ruby said with a giggle. She wore another of Johana's dresses, and while it wasn't unbecoming on her, it wasn't up to the capital's fashion standards.

"You and me both," Kai muttered. She looked down at herself. "I prefer pants anyway. Easier to get away in pants than skirts."

"They can be cumbersome, though it would feel strange to have myself so exposed," Ruby said thoughtfully. Glancing at Serik, she added, "Perhaps we should attend a ball? I am certain we could find one before the night is up."

Kai laughed while Serik rolled his eyes.

"I could ask around if that's how you ladies wish to spend your evening. Though, it would be difficult to keep our identities unknown if we were to do so," Gav said, examining his fingernails.

"Tempting," Kai snorted. "Think of all the expensive jewelry that could be, er, lost." Ruby was sure she was going to say "stolen" but changed her mind at the last minute. "Or the tableware. Most nobles use silver for their forks and knives, and that can fetch some coin. I know some shops that wouldn't ask too many questions."

"I thought we wanted to keep ourselves out of trouble," Ruby said. "I fear that will be near impossible if we are arrested for thievery."

"You mean if *you* were arrested. They won't be able to catch me."

"Terrible," the loresinger said, askance. "Honestly, I can't take you anywhere."

The women chortled at that, and even Serik was smirking. The wilder tugged at the collar of the fancy shirt, and Gav reached over and swatted his hand. "Stop that. You'll ruin it."

Serik glared at him, then turned toward Ruby. "I would rather throw these clothes into the canal if that means we can skip the ball." Gav looked highly offended by his words, but Serik ignored him and held his arm out to Ruby. "Shall we?"

Ruby glanced at Kai and winked as she placed her hand in the crook of his arm.

Lanevin was bustling with activity, even at night. Men and women strolled the streets in the early evening, arm and arm and chatting quietly. Young children dashed from place to place, followed by harried-looking parents.

No one gave Serik a second look. A few men even tipped their hats to them in greeting as they passed. The wilder had looked uncomfortable in the dignified garb as they left the vicinity of the inn, but after a few minutes, he seemed to be getting used to the clothing and the anonymity it granted him. Ruby smiled to herself. Now, the only thing that could appear odd about them would be the stylish gentleman strolling with a country maiden.

"Is something amusing?" he asked as they passed a particularly lively restaurant with outdoor seating. The smell of coriander and nutmeg permeated the air.

"Only that it is *I* being stared at now that I have a dashing man beside me. Johana's clothes are comfortable and sturdy, but they are hardly fashionable. Not that I am complaining!" she added hastily. "It is only that we appear to be an odd pair."

"I told the loresinger this was too much," Serik grumbled, the blush returning to his cheeks. "Though I would argue that you are radiant in anything, even a nightdress and ruined slippers."

"And you, sir, must think yourself quite humorous."

They slowed as they approached a large square. There was a fountain with a sculpture in the form of a fish in the middle of it, and people sat around the water, some eating pastries out of paper sacks while others talked or read books. Several cafes and restaurants lined the square, and four streets branched off from it in different directions. Glowing electric lamps encircled the fountain and illuminated the area with their soft yellow light.

"Here we are! Central Plaza," Gav said as he looked around excitedly. "All the finest shops and restaurants are located right here."

Kai's eyes narrowed as she looked around. "It looks expensive, but I guess we can wander about." She inhaled deeply. "At least it smells good."

They wandered around the plaza for a while, looking at the shops. It was the first time that Ruby had felt relaxed since leaving Valwen. Issalden and the Thieves Guild were far behind them now, and it wasn't likely she would be recognized in a city with so many people. Once she cleared everything up with the reward, she would be happy to find a place like this to settle.

Along with the restaurants, there were clothing and other specialty stores, though most of them were closed at this time of day. Serik slowed to a stop in front of the glass windows of one of the open stores.

It was a jeweler's shop. Gold and precious stones glittered in the display, reflecting the orange glow of the lamplight within the shop. Stunning necklaces, jeweled broaches, and rings of every different color and size adorned the red-velvet lining the case, from sparkling diamonds to glistening topaz.

"What are you looking for?" she asked curiously, watching his eyes flick over the display.

There was a long pause, and he glanced at her before answering. "If we are pretending to be married, you should have a ring."

Ruby drew in a sharp breath. She had not expected *that* answer. "I do not believe that is necessary."

It was a few moments before he spoke again. Ruby had the impression that he was choosing his words carefully before speaking. "On the contrary, if we are to keep this charade up until we reach Calsith, we will need to play our parts well. If we don't make every possible effort, the towns-folk may grow suspicious."

Ruby felt her eyebrows lift. "I do not think the townsfolk

care about one random gentleman and lady's relationship, both of whom are unknown to them."

"A fair point," he admitted, and Ruby could see the corners of his mouth lifting. "But are you willing to risk it?"

Laughing, she replied, "Very well! But know that just a simple band will not do. You will need to express your love for your 'wife' in the piece you pick." Ruby reached into the pocket inside her dress and handed him a small pouch, the one that contained the earrings Serik had given back to her.

"Use this to pay for it," she implored, her tone turning serious. "You should not waste any more resources on helping me hide my identity."

"It's not a waste," he argued but took the pouch. "If you wait with the others, I should only be a few minutes."

Ruby, Kai, and Gav continued wandering Central Plaza, perusing the eateries, while the wilder entered the jewelry shop. It was close to thirty minutes before he returned, a fact stated repeatedly by Gav, who took to glancing at a pocket watch on a gold chain every so often. Kai had also started to grumble about obtaining refreshments.

"We were about ready to find something to eat without you," the loresinger complained. "My lovely wife is in a foul mood." He leaned in conspiratorially. "Apparently, she is quite murderous when hungry."

"Keep talking, and you'll be my first victim," Kai growled.

"One more moment," Serik said and pulled Ruby aside.

He took her hand, sliding a delicate gold band on her finger. The ring was simple compared to some of the jewelry she'd seen women like her mother wear, but it was exquisite. A ruby was inlaid in the center of the band, while four smaller rubies were set at each corner of the larger gem. In between the red stones were diamonds, giving the setting a floral look. Filigree in the shape of leaves ran around the top of the band, further adding to the flowery design. It fit on her finger perfectly.

"It is beautiful!" she exclaimed. "The earrings were enough to cover an item such as this?"

"The stones aren't as high a quality as what you gave me, so I was able to get a good deal on it." Serik handed the pouch back to her, and Ruby heard the distinct clinking of coins. "Five crests," he clarified. "That's what was left over from the trade."

There was excitement bubbling in her chest as she looked at the ring, moving her hand back and forth to watch the lamplight reflected in the cut of the stones. Ruby reminded herself that she had technically purchased the item, not the wilder. Still, it had the feeling of a gift.

"Thank you," she said, feeling the grin on her face. Her cheeks felt hot, but it accompanied a pleasant flutter of her heart, and she welcomed it. Taking the coins from him, she placed the pouch in her pocket once more.

Serik inclined his head, returning her look.

Kai made a frustrated sound, bouncing on one foot and then the other. "Yes, yes, It's very pretty. Now can we please get some food?"

CHAPTER 17

Ruby hadn't had a chance to ride on the train yet. The city that her parents lived in did not have a rail line since it was only a few days' carriage ride outside of Valkea, and the roads to the capital were all well-maintained. There was also the fact that her mother did not like the idea of taking the same mode of transportation that the "peasants" frequented and declared that a carriage was far more comfortable anyway, even though she, too, had never ridden on the train.

It occurred to Ruby that most of the nobility she'd known did not favor the newest and quickest means of transportation for the same reasons as her mother, but Ruby was excited. Not only were they taking the train to Calsith, a two-day journey, but she would be riding it as a commoner and would get to experience it as the common folk did.

She still could scarcely believe it. A distance that would have taken weeks by coach would be completed in two days. They would be stopping overnight in Easthollow, a place that Gav informed her was not as big as Lanevin, but held a great many inns and boarding houses for those passing through.

Once they reached Calsith, their plan was to stay overnight and purchase any last-minute supplies, then make their way to the ruins. Kai and Serik had determined that it would take only a day and a half to reach the area they believed the ruins to be in, so long as the weather held.

The wilder didn't seem happy to leave Dream behind, but there was no choice. They could not take their mounts on the train, so the horses would need to be boarded in Lanevin and retrieved once they had completed their task. Gav gave them a few suggestions of places to board them, and the group had taken the horses there right after leaving the inn.

Ruby gave Dream's muzzle one last scratch as Serik told the stable hand, "You'd better take good care of her," in a menacing voice.

The black-haired man was unfazed. "Of course, sir. She will be ready for you when you return."

Serik and Gav carried most of the supplies as they walked along the thoroughfare leading to the train station. It was on the east side of town and close to the inn. The wilder condensed everything into four travel packs, one for each of them. There were quite a few items he had to leave behind with the horses, but he assured them that they would have everything they needed. The feeling of having something strapped to her back was unfamiliar to Ruby, and she kept scratching at the place where the rough canvas rubbed the back of her neck.

There were even more people about than the previous day, many in more threadbare clothing than what Ruby had witnessed around town, and several of them moving toward the train station along with her group.

The station was bustling with people. Ruby had never seen so many common folk in one place before. Mothers pulled along children or carried crying babies in their arms. People dashed out the doors in the back to sunbathed platforms, and men in blue uniforms checked tickets before allowing them onto the trains. There was only one railroad line in the empire, but there were multiple trains going in both directions each day.

Lanevin Station itself was a large building with an arched glass ceiling attesting to the marvels of modern architecture, hosting multiple shops and cafes. The trains themselves were on outdoor platforms. Benches were situated at the back of the station, near the tracks, so that those waiting for their trains could see when they arrived. The aroma of coffee and freshly baked bread permeated the air, making Ruby's stomach rumble. As soon as they entered, Kai pulled her into one of the shops that sold ice cream and other sweets. Gav followed while Serik went to buy their tickets.

Ruby purchased a small, powdered-sugar-dusted pastry, and Kai was handed some sort of chocolate-dipped confection on a stick. Gav followed Kai around the shop, making suggestions and pointing out food that he found particularly decadent. Instead of getting annoyed, Kai seemed to take what he said about the food seriously, nodding at his words and examining each dessert with close scrutiny. While they were leaning over a particularly enticing raspberry mille-feuille, Ruby bought another flakey baked good for Serik.

Their train was set to leave at twelve-thirty. It was only half past eleven, so there was some time before they needed to board the train. Serik picked up a few news pamphlets from a stand near the doors leading outside to the tracks while the others found a bench inside by the windows. It was warm in the station with the sunlight shining in through the glass above, and Ruby wished for a fan. Perhaps there would be time to purchase one before they left.

"Anything interesting?" Kai asked the wilder as he sat on the bench across from the women.

Slowly chewing one end of the croissant Ruby had given

him moments earlier, Serik turned the news pamphlet over and showed them the back. He tapped one finger on the bottom left corner. There was a notice that they all knew well. Ruby's face with the reward amount of fifty-thousand crests stared back at them. Ruby sank down in her seat, glancing around. There wasn't anyone seated near them, and she didn't see any travelers looking in her direction, but even so, she felt exposed.

"At least it's not on the front page," the wilder sighed and took another bite. "I suppose the fervor to find you has died down a bit. It's been the better part of a month now since you went missing."

Ruby started. Had it really been that long? Ten days to Issalden and then four days at Halis's farm… She glanced at the date on the paper, realizing that the wilder was correct.

That reminded Ruby that she still needed to write to Mikel and let him know she was alive and well, and inform him that she would not be returning. In all the excitement of getting shot and traveling to Lanevin, she had completely forgotten about it.

Kai placed a hand on her shoulder, and Ruby turned to face her. Worry creased her brow. "Give it another month, and they won't be printing your image anymore."

"I don't know about that," Gav said. "Not only is that reward outrageous, but she's highborn. I'd be more surprised if they ever stopped looking."

Kai glared at him. "Not helping."

He shrugged. "It's the truth."

"It is all right, Kai," Ruby cut in before her friend could snap back at Gav. "I will just have to keep a low profile until they *do* stop." She managed a small smile. "No one has noticed me yet. Perhaps they will not."

Kai looked doubtful, but she only nodded. She leaned

back in her seat, staring out at the train. "How long will we be riding today?"

"About eight hours," Serik responded, glancing at the tickets. He'd finished the croissant and wiped his hands on a napkin.

Kai made a face like she'd eaten something that didn't agree with her and jumped to her feet. "I'm going to buy some snacks for the road then."

"They are going to feed us. It's included in the ticket." Serik said. He didn't mention that Kai had already purchased a bag full of pastries.

She scoffed but otherwise ignored his comment. "Come on, Ruby." Kai held out her hand.

Glancing at Serik and Gav, Ruby took it and allowed Kai to pull her to her feet.

There were many food vendors set up in little stalls in the station, more than Ruby had noticed before. They purchased steamed buns of fluffy dough filled with sweetly spiced pork. Kai called it "street food", a term Ruby had only heard spoken with sneers and tones of disgust from other nobles. She didn't know why, as the steamed pastry she tried was delicious, though it would have been awkward to eat with a knife and fork.

Kai bought a half dozen, and the merchant put them in a box for her. When they returned to the benches, the others were rising from their seats and gathering their belongings.

"I reserved a private compartment, so we can board early," Serik said by way of explanation. He tapped the newspaper lying across Ruby's pack. "It would be good to keep you out of sight for now. It will probably be safer in Easthollow."

No one argued with that, so the group of four made their way over to the platform. Warm air and the smell of burning coal blasted Ruby in the face as she stepped outside. There was a short balding man in a tidy blue uniform checking tickets before people could board the train. Serik handed theirs to the man, and he examined them closely, then narrowed his eyes at the wilder. Serik was dressed well today, as sharply as he'd been the night before, so the man made no comment. Ruby and Gav also seemed to pass his inspection, but when his eyes fell on Kai, the man glowered.

"Is she with you?" he asked Serik in a condescending tone after scrutinizing her from head to toe. Kai was dressed in a light shirt, vest, and breeches. Her clothing was neat and clean, but clearly *not* made for a woman.

"There are four tickets, aren't there?" Kai cut in crossly.

The uniformed man seemed unperturbed by her outburst, still focusing on Serik.

"She is," he answered, giving Kai a sideways glance that even Ruby could tell meant "shut up."

Continuing to glare at the ticket inspector, Kai visibly bristled, but she didn't say anything else.

After a moment, the uniformed man gave him a curt nod and turned from them, waving to another employee. He came trotting over.

"Please assist the young women with their luggage and show Mr. Belin's party to their seats," the ticket inspector said, handing Serik back the tickets.

The wilder inclined his head in thanks as the other man took Ruby's and Kai's luggage from them.

The compartment that Serik had purchased for the trip was near the front of the train, in the second car. It was a comfortable cabin with two plush benches that faced inward, and a small table bolted to the wall beneath the window. Racks above their heads provided room for storage, and the door of the compartment could close and lock, so they could have privacy as they traveled. According to the slip of paper placed on the table under a bottle of wine and four glasses, there was dinner service at six o'clock, and in car three, a bar where food could be purchased outside of the meal schedule.

Kai and Gav sat across from each other next to the window. Ruby and Serik took the seats closest to the door.

"Can you believe that guy?!" Kai growled once the station employee had strapped their bags to the shelves above their seats and left. "Questioning if I was with our party? *Ha!*" She leaned back in her seat with a huff, folding her arms across her chest.

"It's because you're wearing pants. No respectable woman of station wears pants." Gav said, sitting across from her.

She stuck her tongue out at him.

"Very mature." Amusement coated the loresinger's words.

"Apparently, I'm not good enough to be with you all anyway. Why not lean into it?"

Ruby smiled as she sat next to her friend. "Shall we jinx the ticket inspector? We still have some time before we leave."

Gav started, staring at Ruby while Kai seemed to mull it over. Ruby realized this was the first time he'd heard her suggest cursing someone. After all, they'd not known each other for very long. Gav clearly still thought her prim and proper, but she and Kai used to get into all kinds of trouble at Valwen. It would not be the first time she'd used magic to play a prank on someone.

The methods she employed were harmless, but annoying, with possible embarrassment sprinkled in. Ruby had once jinxed another student's books to fly across the room every time he reached for them, but not do it if anyone else tried. Another time, she and Kai combined their power to stick the desks in the history classroom to the ceiling. The enchantment had only lasted an hour, but that was long enough for the professor to find it and nearly pull all his hair out attempting to figure out who had ruined his lesson.

"It hardly seems worth it, does it?" Kai finally answered, pulling Ruby out of the fond memory of Professor Rodan raging at their class before having to dodge a falling chair.

"It would be riotously funny," Ruby countered.

"You're a bad influence," Serik said to her, a grin threatening to spread across his face.

Gav seemed to be the only one who was taking her seriously. "What if you are caught?"

Ruby laughed. She couldn't help it. The look of utter disbelief and shock on his face was priceless. It felt good to laugh. She had been so scared and strained the past few weeks that she had almost forgotten what it felt like to have fun.

They didn't jinx the ticket inspector, though Ruby and Kai went through an extensive list of what they *could* do to him. Various embarrassing events ranged from tying his laces together to ripping a hole in the bottom of his breeches. Gav seemed to lighten up the more scandalous their suggestions became, and by the time the train's whistle sounded, even Serik was chuckling at their antics.

With a lurch, the train finally started to move, and they were on their way to Easthollow.

They passed miles of tenable farmland, hills and fields green with growth bursting to life after the cold of winter. This being the first time Ruby had ridden on a train, she wanted to soak up the entire experience and kept her eyes on the view outside. She'd never seen the countryside pass at such a pace.

The novelty faded quickly.

As enamored with rail travel as she was, two hours into the journey, Ruby found herself wishing it was over. Her bottom was sore, and shifting in her seat every few minutes did nothing to alleviate the pain. There were still six hours left. She didn't know if she could make it that long.

Ruby stood, steadying herself by grabbing onto the shelf above her seat. Serik didn't stir. His eyes were closed, and he appeared to be sleeping, though how anyone could sleep with the bumping of the tracks, she didn't know. Gav also appeared to be dozing off, but Kai looked up at her, blinking her eyes blurrily.

"I am going to stretch my legs," Ruby whispered loudly to be heard over the noise of the train. "I will be back soon."

Kai nodded and turned back to the window, staring out. She too looked tired. They had all been through a lot to get this far.

Ruby opened the door to their compartment and stepped out into the little corridor beyond. Windows lined one side of the hallway while doors like the one she had just exited stood on the other. The floor was covered with a maroon-dyed carpet, and the fixtures appeared to be made of brass on polished mahogany walls. If she remembered correctly, the next car down had a bar and eating area. There were still plenty of coins in her pouch. Dinner wouldn't be served for another four hours, and Ruby wasn't hungry yet, but it would give her something to do other than sit in that compartment. Placing one hand on the wall to keep herself from tripping when the train rattled and bumped, she made her way to the back of the car.

She passed a man sitting by the door to the dining car, hands folded in his lap with his head bowed and eyes closed as if he were resting. There was something familiar about him, and she looked back him as she passed. He looked gangly, with brown hair and a narrow face. She was sure that she had never met him before, and yet…

She shook her head, continuing forward.

Air blasted her as she opened the door to the car. Ruby looked down at the little platform over the coupler that connected the train car she was currently on with the one next to it. Tracks flashed between the gap, and the wind whipped the loose strands of hair that had escaped her braid around her face. There were chains on either side of the platform, serving as a guard against falling, but it all looked rather flimsy to her. If one were to be thrown against them, they would not keep the person from falling under those wheels and being cut in half. Ruby swallowed hard. She would just need to be quick.

Ruby took a running step onto the platform, nearly jumping to the other side. Opening the door to the next car, she hurried inside.

* * *

KAI YAWNED AND STRETCHED, continuing to look out the window as the train passed more of the same landscape, miles and miles of green fields and trees. She had been on this line once before, when she had moved from the capital to Issalden but had gotten off the train in Lanevin. This was the furthest east she had ever been, and so far, it was not very impressive. Kai preferred the city to the open country. To her, every farm looked like the last.

Gav sat across from her, resting his head on the arm that was propped up on the table, eyes closed. His breathing was deep and steady. Asleep.

She glanced over at Serik. The wilder was in a similar state, his arms crossed over his chest and his head leaning against the velvet-lined compartment wall, eyes also closed. Kai didn't blame them. It had been over a week's journey to get here from the shepherd's farm, and it wasn't even half over. There was still one more day's train ride, followed by a trek through the heavily forested eastern mountains—where they didn't know the way and there would be no trail. Then they'd have to locate and explore an abandoned temple, all in the hope that there was some reward on the other side.

If all had gone according to plan, she would have never considered doing this, but being betrayed by the man who'd raised her had made her desperate.

Maybe. She still wasn't sure if Joran had been acting under the guild master's orders or not. It was hard to believe that Alek had agreed to let Joran take Ruby without consulting her first. Alek was a practical man. He had always been, if not kind, at least compassionate toward Kai. Over the years, she'd come to think of him as an older brother of sorts, but now, she was questioning if he had ever felt any real affection toward her.

Kai sighed heavily. She had been dwelling on that thought for days. It was no good. She had to talk to Alek, but it could wait until after they finished with Ta'Dormus Deva, hopefully with their pockets laden with riches.

Getting to her feet, she checked her pocket watch. Ruby had been gone for over twenty minutes, and it had been a few hours since they'd left. Perhaps she would get something to eat, but maybe she should wait for her friend to return. Either way, Kai wanted to get up and move around. At least when they had been riding across the country, there had been the horses to direct and terrain to weave around. Kai wasn't used to being as idle as this. She looked out the window again with a sigh and considered digging into the last of her pastries.

"Will you just go?" Serik growled, his eyes still closed. "Some of us are trying to sleep."

Kai scowled at him but stepped toward the door. It was decided. She would go find Ruby and see what her traveling companion was up to.

Kai exited the compartment, closing the door softly behind her. Looking up and down the little corridor that marked the other first-class compartments, she considered where her friend might have gone.

There was a water closet in every car and a place to purchase food in car three. They were in car two, so that was only one car over. There wasn't anything else to see or do on this train. It seemed unlikely that she would have been gone this long just for the toilet, so Kai made her way over to the door leading to car three.

She hopped over the coupler and went into the next car. The man behind the bar looked up as she entered, and waved to her, smiling. The dining car was set up to look like a tiny restaurant, with a dozen little tables and plush armchairs next to the windows. Surveying the people sitting at the little tables around the car, eating sandwiches and cakes, Kai frowned. She didn't see any sign of Ruby.

"Did you see a young woman come through?" she asked as she slid into one of the stools at the bar. "Tall with dark brown hair in a braid. Pretty."

The bartender nodded. "I did, but she didn't order anything. She passed through the car, and the man she came in with followed her."

Her stomach clenched. "The man she came in with? What man?"

"Skinny fellow, dark hair and a long jacket." The bartender gave a dignified sniff. "He didn't look like a first-class passenger, but he'd come from the front cars, so who am I to judge." His eyes scanned the car as he thought. "Though, I'm not sure why they went to the next car. This is the only dining car on the train. There's nothing else for them in the back of the train. The attendants will come around with a cart to the lower-class passengers, but they should be able to purchase whatever they want here."

"Are you sure he came in with her? That he wasn't *following* her?"

An uncertain look crossed the bartender's face. "I… don't know."

Shit. Kai jumped off the stool, hurrying over to the door connecting cars three and four. The next car would be the middle-class seats. Could it be the Kingfishers? How had they known where they were headed? Or perhaps it was some other party after the reward money? Why in all the hells had she let Ruby wander around the train alone?

They had assumed that they were safe in the moving transport. No one had known where they'd been planning to go, but perhaps lookouts had been placed in all the northern cities. The fight at Halis's farm had delayed them a few days. Had that been enough time for Alek to get his people into position in Lanevin?

Kai hopped over the next coupler and threw the door to car four open. Men and women looked up at her, rows and rows of people sitting shoulder to shoulder on padded seats facing the front of the train. She moved forward, uncaring what these people thought of her. Her only concern was finding her friend. She scanned the faces of the people sitting there, though most had adverted their eyes. One little girl with hair the same color as hers was sitting in a row by herself, watching as Kai made her way down the aisle.

"Hello," Kai said as she knelt next to the girl. "I'm looking for my friend. She's tall with dark hair and very pretty. Did you see her come through here?"

The little girl nodded, then glanced over her shoulder toward the back of the car. "That man grabbed her. She didn't look like she liked it very much."

"He's a bad man," Kai replied, inwardly cursing. Springing to her feet, she ran, ignoring the cries of surprise and alarm from either side of her.

Cars five and six were much the same as the ones before it. When Kai reached car seven, she knew she'd reached the lower-class cars. Instead of the plush seating of the middle- and first-class compartments, bare wooden benches were bolted to the floor in tight rows. The people here were dressed in simple, rough-spun clothing and held small rucksacks on their laps, tucking in their elbows so as not to crowd the person next to them. These were travelers riding the train out of necessity and had paid the bare minimum to board.

Eyes searching the rows of people for any sign of Ruby, Kai continued forward, walking with purpose down the aisle.

She traversed two more cars in a similar fashion, stopping twice to ask about Ruby. The first person ignored her, and the second was a young mother with her two children. The woman shook her head, but the little boy pointed to the back of the train. Nodding her thanks to the boy, Kai dashed down the length of the car and threw open the door. This coupler didn't have a walking platform installed over it, so she concentrated and brought forth her power, using it to maintain her balance and reflexes as she jumped over the gap between the cars. As she straightened from her landing, she heard a scream from beyond the door in front of her—a feminine scream.

"Ruby!" she yelled, throwing the door open and pulling her dagger, prepared for a fight on the other side.

It took a few seconds for Kai's eyes to adjust to the darkness. Crates and leather trunks were stacked in neat rows in this rail car. Hay was strewn on the floor to keep it clean, and Kai swore she heard clucking from a few of the crates toward the back. This part of the train was reserved for cargo.

Standing in the center of it was Ruby. The woman's eyes were wide, and there was a man on the ground before her, but she appeared to be unhurt.

Ruby whipped around, hands raised, but dropped them when she saw who had entered. "Kai!" she cried in relief.

Kai ran toward her, and the two women embraced. "What happened?" she asked, looking down at the unconscious man. He looked so familiar. She was sure that he was in the Guild.

Ruby let out a shaky breath. "I saw this man in our car and noticed that he was following me. So, I tried to get away from him, and when that didn't work…" she mimed hitting him on the head with something. That was when Kai spotted the lamp on the floor near him, looking as if it had been torn off the wall.

"Levitation spell?" Kai asked, and Ruby nodded. "That was some good, quick thinking, but we should get out of here and back to the others. There could be more of them."

Just as those words left her mouth, Ruby's eyes widened, and Kai whirled. A shadow darkened the doorway behind her.

The large man they had seen with Joran's thugs back at the warehouse back in Issalden stepped into the train car, blocking their exit. He walked with a limp, and there was a large purple and green bruise on the side of his face, faded as if it was a few weeks old, which it was. He was the one Serik had shot, and Kai had knocked out with the hilt of her blade.

Eyes widening as he caught sight of Ruby and Kai, he went for the pistol strapped to his waist.

Kai was faster.

With lightning-fast reflexes born from years of training and desperation, she threw her dagger before his hand could close on the handle of the firearm.

The Thieves Guild thug had been expecting the attack, and he rolled to the side as the blade flew toward him, grunting in pain as he hit the floor of the train car, pistol skittering out of his reach as Kai's dagger sank into the wall.

Kai took a defensive stance, placing herself between Ruby and their new assailant, and summoned blue fire to her hand.

Getting to his feet, the large man looked at the pistol that was just out of arm's reach and then Kai. Some emotion that she couldn't read crossed his face, and, without another word, he turned and fled back out of the rail car.

"Dammit!" Kai swore and leaped forward, snatching up the pistol. She couldn't let him get away. There could be more Kingfishers on the train, and even if there weren't, he could get off at Easthollow and tell the others where they were. There were only so many stops on the rail line, and, given the size and reach of the Guild, there could be members living at any one of them.

Glancing back at Ruby, Kai paused before she rushed out of the car. "Tie that one up."

Ruby stared at her like she was speaking a foreign language. After a long second, she managed, "With what?"

"Figure it out!" Kai barked and whirled around, following their second would-be assailant into the next car.

When she threw the door open, there were men and women on their feet, looking anxiously toward the front of the car where the large man was trying to shove people out of the way to get to the door. Most had moved rather than be trampled, but a few were not quick enough to keep him from knocking them over.

"Get down!" Kai screamed out to the people around her, holding out the pistol she'd picked up.

Seeing the firearm, the passengers either ducked or ran from her, pulling their children close to them. Kai took a few precious seconds to aim, then pulled the trigger.

Thunder roared in the tiny train car, and the man jerked as the bullet caught him in the left shoulder. He stumbled forward, but a shot like that wouldn't take him down.

Calling her dagger to her, she launched her other arm

forward as the blade materialized in her hand and flew true, burying itself in the man's right thigh.

With a scream of pain, he fell forward, clutching at his injuries. There was the slightest twinge of guilt as she strode forward, summoning the dagger again. He'd already been shot in that leg by Serik, and without serious healing, he would be lucky if he could use it at all after this. No one moved as they watched her advance down the aisle with slow, measured steps.

The large man rolled over onto his back, scooting away from Kai with his good arm as she approached.

"Did Alek send you to find her? Does he know where we are heading?" Kai asked while staring down her nose at the man, voice full of cold fury. Alek would know that she still had the key in her possession. Would he have guessed that she was heading to Ta'Dormus Deva?

He glowered up at her, his mouth staying shut.

Perhaps she should use a different approach. Kai let out a short breath through her nose and squatted back on her heels. "If you answer me, we'll get you some healing. There may be time to save that leg."

That seemed to get through to him. He grimaced, then said something she didn't quite catch, but she thought she heard him say Alek's name.

"What?" Kai asked, leaning forward to hear him better over the noise of the train.

That was when he struck. The large man tried to punch her, and when she wobbled back to avoid the strike, he snatched her wrist, twisting it hard. Pain shot up her arm, and she was sure that he would break it when she felt the rush of magic flowing past her. His grip slackened, and a moment later, he slumped to the ground, fast asleep.

Kai blinked once, then looked over her shoulder.

Ruby stood in the doorway at the back of the rail car, one

arm extended toward Kai and the unconscious attacker. The wind whipped her hair around her face and tugged at her dress, and a few people backed away from her. She was breathing heavily, and her eyes were wide, but she stared intently at the man on the ground.

Kai understood. The man would only lie unconscious for as long as Ruby could concentrate on her spell. She hadn't knocked him out completely, as she had the other man who'd tried to take her. The pain from his injuries and the rumbling train would wake him as soon as Ruby released her spell, so Kai had to work quickly.

She used his belt to bind his hands behind his back and tied his feet together with a strip of cloth ripped from his shirt. She tore off another and gagged him for good measure. Satisfied that he could not get out of his bindings, Kai gave Ruby a nod.

Her friend sighed, sagging a little and placing one hand against the car wall as she released her spell.

His eyes immediately flew open, and he flexed his arms, trying to break free, but his bonds held.

"Get the conductor," Kai ordered a middle-aged man dressed in a dirt-stained jacket and pants. She didn't wait for him to comply. Turning away from the man on the floor, she strode back toward Ruby, inwardly cursing herself. She knew better than to allow an injured opponent to get the better of her. All this running around had dulled her senses.

"Where are you going?" Ruby asked as she made to move past her.

"Checking that the other one is properly secured. Wait for me to explain this to the conductor," she said, then exited the rail car.

CHAPTER 18

Once they arrived in Easthollow, an attendant came by their compartment, asking them to remain on the train.

"The local authorities will want to talk to you about those men. We have someone alerting them as we speak."

"We'd really like to rest," Gav argued. "Can't they meet us at the inn?"

"I'm sorry, sir," the young man said, ducking his head, "but they will want to speak to you before you get off the train. I apologize for the inconvenience."

"Well, I tried," Gav said softly after the attendant closed the door. "We'd best have our stories straight before the constabulary arrives."

"Would we not just tell the authorities what we told the conductor? That I was attacked by these men? Surely, we do not need to lie to them about that."

"It's not that we need to lie to them per se," Kai answered. "But they will want to know why they went after you, and we can't very well tell them that you have a fifty-thousand crest reward for your return. Even if you insist you don't want to go back, that's enough money that they just might bend a few rules and take you into custody anyway."

Ruby hadn't thought of that. It was difficult to accept that men employed by the empire to serve justice would be swayed by money, but those knights had done the same thing, hadn't they? "Then what should I tell them?"

"Well, you can tell them you don't know why they grabbed you," Gav continued for Kai. "I mean, you're a pretty young woman. The inspector will make his own assumptions." He scratched at his chin. "I could fan the flames a little in that regard."

"Shall I tell them that I used magic to stop him?" she asked, looking between him and Kai.

"No, that would make you more suspicious. Besides, there are laws about using magic without a license, though they vary from city to city, and, well, we weren't in one when he attacked you. They might just detain you while they figure out who has jurisdiction over the case. Best to leave it out." The loresinger straightened his clothes, and, a few minutes later, a knock sounded on their compartment door.

The man was tall and dark-skinned, with coarse black hair and a mustache. The dark-gray officer's overcoat he wore appeared to be well-used, but impeccably clean and pressed. His shirt was tucked in and had the sharp creases of a garment recently ironed. His entire appearance was meticulously neat, from his hair to his polished black boots.

"I'm Inspector Leonte." The man introduced himself with a handshake for Serik and Gav and inclined his head to the women. "I've been informed that there was trouble on the trip from Lanevin. Can you tell me what happened?"

"Those men accosted my cousin!" Gav jumped right in, gesturing toward Ruby. "She had gotten up to stretch her legs, and they followed her into the next car." There was a tinge of red to his cheeks as he spoke fast and heated. He huffed and placed one hand on his hip. "And where was train security? To think that they would allow this to happen on the Imperial Train Line," he finished with a scowl, his acting abilities on full display.

"Do you know why they attacked her?" the inspector asked mildly, taking out a notepad and pen, nodding along with Gav's words as if he was listening intently.

"Why else would men like that attack a young woman?!" The tone he used would have anyone who didn't know him assuming that he thought the inspector was daft. "You are arresting them, are you not? You're not going to let them get away with this!"

"Sir, please calm down, I just need to take your statements," Leonte said placatingly, then turned to Serik, and Ruby thought she saw the inspector glance at her, his brown eyes calculating. She hoped she looked sufficiently scared. "Are you the young woman's husband?"

"I am," Serik said gruffly, tightening his grip around Ruby's waist.

"And what are your names?"

"Serik and Violet Belin."

"And the other two?"

"Kaiya and Gavin Harper," Kai supplied. They had chosen to use a completely fictitious surname since both were wanted. She grabbed Gav's arm and pulled him close, glowering up at the inspector. It might have been better if she'd looked scared as well, but Kai's version of fear was so close to anger that it was hard to tell the difference.

The only sound was the scratching of the inspector's pen on paper. When he looked up again, his gaze finally fell on Ruby. She would have thought that, being the victim, she would be the first one the inspector would question. "Ma'am, can you tell me everything you remember?"

"It is as my cousin told you," Ruby said, trying not to let

her nervousness show. "I left our compartment to stretch my legs and walked to the dining car. Noticing that there was a man following me, I continued on, through the other cars. I wanted to believe he could have been a passenger making his way back to his seat, but something told me otherwise. He caught up to me, grabbed my arm, and dragged me back into the cargo car." Her eyes flicked over to Kai. This was the part where she'd used magic to dislodge one of the lamps and bash the man over the head with it.

"That's when I found them and threw a lamp at his head," Kai finished for her.

"You… ripped a lamp off the wall and knocked him out?" the inspector asked, doubt heavy in his voice. His eyes flicked down to her toes and back to her face. Kai stood a good foot shorter than him.

"I'm stronger than I look," Kai said, setting her chin. "Or maybe it is he who has a weak constitution. Either way, he was knocked out, and we were going to head back to tell the conductor but his friend decided to join in."

Leonte narrowed his eyes at Kai. "Yes, I've seen his wounds. Gunshot to the shoulder and a stab wound in the leg."

"I carry a very sharp dagger for occasions just like this," Kai said simply, a smile tugging at her lips. "A woman needs to be able to defend herself. Surely, you would agree, Inspector?"

The inspector seemed suspect. Kai's question was a trap. If he said no, then he left himself open for another tirade and complaints from both Gav and Kai, and if he agreed, he would be condoning her use of violence on the man who tried to accost her husband's cousin. Leonte knew he was backed into a corner and cleared his throat. "Well, it's good you can protect yourself, but the police should really handle this next time."

"I'll be sure to let you know the next time someone tries to rape our cousin," Kai shot back. She and the inspector glared at each other for a moment, then the man's eyes flicked to Ruby and softened marginally.

"I'm sorry this happened to you, Mrs. Belin. We've taken these men into custody and will make sure they are punished to the full extent of the law." He glanced around at them. "Are you staying in town?"

"Yes," it was Serik who answered him. "But we are leaving for Calsith in the morning."

His eyebrows shot up. "Calsith? Why, in the name of all the gods, are you going out *there*?"

"I have a friend by the name of Stefan Barrett who lives there. He owns a small bookshop and needs some help." Serik turned to Ruby and smiled. "My wife is an avid reader and will be able to assist him with ordering the latest titles from across the empire."

Ruby smiled back at him, having no idea if this Stefan Barrett actually existed.

"And that takes four of you?" Leonte asked, eyes narrowing.

"I just like to travel," Gav interjected, "and I've never been to Calsith before."

The inspector let out a long breath. "Do you know yet where you will be staying? In case I need to reach you?"

"Not yet," Serik answered. "It has been a very long time since I was last here. Though, if you have a suggestion for reasonable and clean accommodations, we would be most appreciative."

"Speak to Jona over at the *Drunken Lion*," Leonte said, flipping his notepad closed. "He runs a good place and won't gouge you like some of the other inns near the station that caters to travelers. It's down Terrace Street. Big blue building."

Serik thanked the inspector as he left, and the group made their way off the train.

"We should stay somewhere else," Kai said as they left the platform, looking over her shoulder for any sign of the inspector.

"If he comes looking for us and we aren't there, he knows we have tickets for the train tomorrow and will just catch us as we board," Serik responded as they entered the covered part of the station. "Best to seem as innocent as possible. I doubt the men you two knocked out will talk. They'd have to admit to attempted kidnapping in addition to the assault."

Kai looked like she wanted to argue, but she held her tongue. Serik had a point. They had done nothing wrong, and unless the two men confessed to their reason for trying to take Ruby, the only crime the police could convict them of would be assault.

The *Drunken Lion* was housed in a three-story residence painted blue with white trim. Located on Terrace Street, as the inspector had indicated, it was a lovely establishment from the outside, much different from the other inns and taverns lining the road by the station. The buildings near Easthollow Station were large and square with a utilitarian look to them. For travelers seeking respite for the night before their next journey, those were perfectly adequate, but Terrace Street was lined with small gardens and two-story townhomes, and this place gave off the aura of being for those less desperate for a place to lay their heads.

"Are you Jona?" Serik asked the man who greeted them as they entered. "Inspector Leonte recommended your establishment."

"He did, did he?" The dark-skinned man responded with a grin. "Good man. Known him for years." He scratched the back of his head as his gaze settled onto each of them in turn.

"You're not from around here, by the looks of you. Get into some trouble with the law?"

Serik smiled. "No, but with men determined to break it."

"Ahhh. I suppose the inspector wants to know where you are if he has more questions."

"Something like that."

"Very well then, a room for you and the lovely lady, Mr. …"

"Serik Belin, and my wife, Violet," the wilder said, putting an arm around Ruby's shoulders. Smiling at the innkeeper, she leaned into him. She was getting used to this charade.

"Two rooms then? Another for the couple traveling with you?" Jona nodded toward Gav and Kai.

"Gavin Harper," the loresinger said as he shook hands with the innkeeper. "Mrs. Belin's cousin."

Jona smiled pleasantly and nodded, writing down their names in a large book lying open on the back counter. "Very well, very well. That will be two marks a piece, then."

Serik paid the man, who handed him two keys.

"Feel free to get settled," the innkeeper continued. We've already served supper, but if you're still hungry, I can bring something up. Or perhaps draw a bath for the ladies to wash in? I can at least set up the kettle for you if you want some privacy."

"A bath would be divine," Ruby murmured.

That made Jona's smile widen. "Of course, mistress. Please make yourself comfortable, and I will be up soon with the water and some nourishment."

The four of them made their way to the second floor of the little inn, Serik and Gav carrying their belongings. Their rooms were adjoined, which was convenient for the purposes of their ruse.

"Should we be worried about the inspector?" Kai asked as she sat on the bed that she and Ruby would be sharing, the door to the identical adjoining room standing wide open. "Do you think he will stop us from leaving?"

"I doubt it." Gav was the one who answered. "I think I made enough of a scene so as to ensure that the authorities will avoid having to talk to us again." He sounded very pleased with himself.

"I'm not so sure he bought that," Ruby said, remembering the inspector's eyes. "He was much more intelligent than he was letting on. Perhaps he saw through your act."

Kai shrugged. "If the men talk—which, as Serik said, I doubt they will—there are lots of witnesses who saw what happened. A man dragged you to the back of the train, I came looking for you, and we defended ourselves."

"Did you not say the promise of my reward could prompt the upstanding lawmen to seek, ah, alternative solutions?" Ruby's first impression of Inspector Leonte told her he wouldn't do something like that, but she'd only met the man for a few minutes.

"We could always leave town tonight if you're worried," Kai said with a frown.

"How?" Gav asked. "We have no horses, and there is no train departing tonight."

"You have feet, don't you?" she retorted.

Serik cleared his throat before they could bicker more. "We agreed to come here not to rouse suspicion, remember? If we are suddenly gone by morning, that would draw even more attention."

Kai let out a long sigh and lay back with a muffled thump. "Right, right. We are just travelers on our way to Calsith to—what? Help your friend with his bookstore?"

Ruby thought she saw the wilder blush. "It was the first thing I thought of in the moment."

"So, what will we actually be doing when we arrive in

Calsith?" Ruby added quickly, trying to save Serik from embarrassment.

"Get a room, then look for the ruins?" Gav supplied. "Do we know where even to start?"

"We'll need to see what the villagers know. Otherwise, we'll never find it," Serik said as he took off his jacket and hung it on the back of a chair by the small table. Next, he unbuttoned the top of the frilly shirt.

"If you're going to undress, do it in your own room," Kai said, still lying on the bed. She glanced over at Ruby, who had taken a seat next to her.

"This collar is itchy." He unbuttoned another two buttons and attempted to roll the fabric away from his skin.

"Stop that!" Gav gasped and rushed over to him. "This shirt is worth more money than someone like you sees in a year!"

Before he could do anything further, there was a knock on the door. The innkeeper and a pair of women who must work for him brought in hot water for baths and a small platter of food.

"Let's get some rest," Kai said as she closed the adjoining door to Serik and Gav's room. "It's going to be another long day tomorrow. We'll have plenty of time to discuss our plans on the train."

CHAPTER 19

The train arrived in Calsith the following afternoon. The ride had been uneventful, for which Ruby gave a prayer of thanks to the gods. If there had been another abduction attempt on the train, Serik and Gav probably would have shot the would-be kidnapper and thrown the body off. They had kept their pistols ready and insisted on accompanying Ruby every time she stood up, even going so far as waiting for her outside of the water closet.

She was relieved to finally be off the train. After the events of the first leg of their journey, Ruby found that she preferred the feeling of Dream's muscles moving beneath her and being able to fully take in the countryside as they rode. The train had been noisy, and, if she were honest, claustrophobic.

Stretching her arms over her head and taking a deep breath of the crisp, mountain air, Ruby smiled at the feeling of the sun on her skin. Two days on the train was far too long.

The Calsith Station was comprised of a single platform

and a building that only looked big enough for one attendant, with a window cut into it to sell tickets. Unlike the other stations in Lanevin and Easthollow, there were no shops or stalls selling food near the little platform. In fact, it appeared that there were only five others exiting the train, a man and a woman holding the hands of a young child and two men in heavy wool coats and hats.

That didn't surprise Ruby. This was the last stop on the line. She supposed that not many people traveled this far out.

The town of Calsith itself would barely be classified as a village. There were only about two dozen or so buildings clustered around the small dirt-covered square. Ruby could see farms dotting the hillsides in the distance, but it seemed that not many people actually lived within the village itself. The edge of Calsith backed up to a dense forest, much like Belleward did with the Wytchwood.

There was one inn, so after getting directions from the attendant at the ticketing station, that was where they headed. It was small, just two floors. The tavern area had half a dozen men sitting at small tables around the fire, talking and drinking among themselves. The man at the bar gave them a warm smile as they entered, set down the towel he'd been using to clean a glass, and came out from behind the heavy oak slab to greet them.

"We don't see many strangers in these parts. Two rooms? I'm afraid I don't have four."

"Two is fine," Kai answered, and he nodded.

"Very well, mistress. My name is Tavian. Please let me know if there is anything you need. Are you here for business or pleasure?" The innkeeper asked conversationally as he reached behind the counter and retrieved a small pouch.

"That depends," Serik said. "Have you heard of a place called Ta'Dormus Deva? It's the ruins of an old temple that is supposed to be near here."

Tavian shook his head. "Can't say I've heard that name, but most of us don't venture out into the woods much. Are you archeologists? Historians? It's been a while since we've had scholarly folk in town."

Serik nodded. "Something like that. Is there anyone who might know? We are hoping to find something there and update the records for the mages at Valwen."

Tavian straightened a little when Serik mentioned Valwen. Along with training the future mages of Andrea, Valwen kept the most vast and complete library in the empire and received large sums of money from the emperor. "Ah, official business then. You should talk to Raul Stoka. He's in the corner over there." The innkeeper pointed to a man with salt and pepper hair sitting near the fire with the other villagers. "He used to be a hunter before he injured his leg. If anyone knows where these ruins are, it'll be him."

Serik thanked Tavian for the information and paid a mark a piece for the rooms. Meanwhile, Kai took Ruby's arm and tugged her along, toward the man the innkeeper had pointed to, with Gav following behind them.

The villagers looked up as they approached, their expressions not unfriendly, but not welcoming either.

"Are you Raul Stoka?" Kai asked, undeterred.

"Might be," the man said, looking her up and down. His eyes drifted to Ruby and did the same. "Who is asking?"

"Kai Harper. We are looking for the ruins of Ta'Dormus Deva, and Tavian said you could help us."

Raul made a soft sound through his nose. "Possibly." He glanced around at the other villagers, then leaned in closer to Kai. "What would that information be worth to you."

Ruby saw Kai's mouth twitch up at the corners before her features fell into a stern expression. "It depends on how helpful your information is."

The man barked out a laugh, startling Ruby.

"You've got guts, I'll give that to you, girl." he said to Kai as he stood and moved from his seat by the fire and chose a larger table a few feet away, motioning for them to sit with him. Kai, Ruby, and Gav took seats around the table, with Kai sitting closest to the villager. There was an empty chair between Ruby and Gav for Serik.

"Do you have a map of the area?" he asked as Kai took out the book she'd been referencing about the ruin's location.

"I have one for the empire, but not for this far east."

"Well, you'll need to stop by my place before you head out then. I have the most accurate map of the area. I was a hunter up until a few years ago, you see. I spent so much time in the forest, I was almost like one of those wilders, though I like having a house in the village."

"Then you must know the area very well," Serik said as he joined them, flashing a quick grin at Ruby. He set four mugs filled with a frothing amber liquid on the table and passed them out to his companions.

Raul nodded in agreement. "If you are looking for the place I think you are, it's about a day and a half's walk northeast through the Caligo Forest. You could probably get there in a day, but it's been so long since anyone has been to that area, I'm not even sure of the temple's exact location. The mages who came through twenty years ago couldn't find it, but I remember the valley they were looking in. It's not a pleasant place, mind you, and it's right dangerous at times. There aren't many villages besides ours out here, so the forest and its creatures have run wild." He looked at each one of them in turn, and his eyes settled on Serik. "*You* at least look like you know what you're doing."

Serik gave the older man a nod, but Kai bristled.

"Just tell us where we need to go, old man," Kai snapped. "Whether or not *all* of us can handle ourselves is not up to your judgment."

"All right, all right, keep your breeches on," Raul grumbled. "I meant no offense. You just need to know what you're getting into. The mages had four times as many people as you brought." He tapped a finger to his lips in thought. "It's a little valley created by two arms of the mountain range on either side. The area isn't terribly hard to get to on foot, but what's more dangerous is staying overnight in the forest. There are—"

"No!" another villager shouted over his words, making Ruby start. He was older than Raul, looking to be in the later years of his life, with a shock of white hair and deep lines on his face. "Raul! Do you want to send these people to their deaths?!" He'd jumped up from his chair by the fire and stood over the other man.

"We'll be fine," Kai said, looking annoyed at the interruption. "You don't have to worry about us. We can handle ourselves."

"You can't be out at night!" the old man implored, grabbing at Kai's sleeve. "There are monsters in the forest! You won't come back!"

"What kind of monsters?" Serik asked as Kai tried to wiggle out of the old man's grip. "Are you speaking of beasts? Or are their brigands living in these woods?"

"Creatures that don't walk around in the light of day!" the man all but shouted at him. He released Kai's sleeve, then dropped his voice to a whisper. "My cousin Marcel was attacked by one of them. He died less than a month later, ranting and raving about a dark shadow with claws and fangs."

"Your cousin died of influenza!" one of the other villagers jeered.

"No! That thing cursed him!" he insisted, dropping any semblance of secrecy. "When he returned, his face was white as a sheet, and he was all weak, like all the life had been sucked out of him."

"That's because he slept outside in the rain, you daft man!" another laughed.

"I am not daft!" the old man cried indignantly.

"Who is that?" Kai asked one of the serving women as she passed, hands laden with drinks. Raul seemed to be wrapped up in the conversation with the old man now, sneering and insisting that he'd never seen anything like that in the forest.

The woman clicked her tongue in disapproval. "Oh, that's Dorin Eune. He owns a farm about half a day's ride from here. Lives on his land with his wife and extended family. Strange things happen out here, but don't believe a word that man says." The woman gave Kai a nod, then continued on her way.

"The thing that attacked him had large fangs and eyes red as blood," Dorin was shouting for anyone who would listen. "A giant beast!"

"But you weren't there?" Kai asked loudly, skepticism lacing her voice. "How would you know what this supposed beast looked like?"

"I know!" he shouted to the entire room. "Because Marcel told me before he died!"

"Sure, he did!" another scoffed. "Known for being sober, that one was," the villager's tone made it clear that Dorin's relative was never sober.

"You dare speak ill of the dead?!" Dorin roared back.

"What do you think?" Ruby asked under her breath. Raul had gotten up to get another drink. It didn't seem like they were going to get any more information from him tonight.

"I think he's full of shit," Kai said with a scowl at Dorin as she took a sip from her mug. "There might be something in those woods, but the riphounds we encountered before were also dangerous and could have easily killed one of us, so I'm guessing it's probably something like that."

"It is fascinating, though," Gav said, staring at the mad villager who was still trying to convince his peers that his cousin really was cursed by a monster. "What people will believe. Perhaps I should write a song about it."

"Gods no," Kai groaned.

"I take offense to that comment," Gav sniffed, indignation heavy in his voice.

"Good," she said, taking another pull on her ale.

"No one here appreciates my talent," Gav muttered, sinking low into his seat. "I'm famous in the empire, but here I am, roaming around these gods-forsaken backwaters with you three. I haven't even been able to replace my lute yet since we haven't been anywhere for more than a day." The loresinger was pouting. Kai looked like she felt a little guilty about her comment, gazing at him like she wanted to offer words of comfort. Ruby covered her mouth to hide her smile, feigning a cough.

"Instruments are memorable, as are songs," Serik said as he glanced over at Ruby. "We don't want anyone to take note of us."

"My good man, we are in the wrong place if that is your goal," Gav countered. "We are probably the only visitors this imperial reject of a town will see all year."

"More note than necessary," Serik amended with a scowl. "With any luck, they will have forgotten our names by the time we leave."

"Do you really think anyone would come here looking for us?" Ruby asked. "We're at the very edge of the empire.

Serik turned those hazel eyes on her. A lock of dark hair had fallen over his face. She wanted to reach out and brush it back.

"I don't think there is a limit to how far those pursuing you would travel."

Ruby licked her bottom lip nervously. Serik watched the motion.

"Are you certain you want *separate* rooms tonight?" Gav asked with an air of nonchalance. "If the two of you need a more private situation…" He trailed off, letting his words hang in the air.

The wilder turned a glare on him while Ruby blushed and looked down at her mug. She knew he was teasing them, but she still felt embarrassed.

"They've been like that," Kai interjected, "ever since that first night. Did you know he pointed that rifle at me?"

"Surely, that was uncalled for!" Gav gasped in outrage.

"It was! All I did was throw a knife at him because he startled me, and that was what he decided was necessary? It was too much if you ask me. Trigger happy wilder."

Gav nodded along, while Serik's frown deepened. "Turning a firearm on a young woman. Shame on you."

"He was under the impression that I kidnapped R— I mean, Violet. He wouldn't take the barrel of his weapon off me until she told him she'd come with me willingly. I mean, really! Does he think I would just let someone I'd taken prisoner run around with no restraints? What kind of criminal do you think I am?"

"A foolish one, apparently," Gav said as she took a sip of ale.

"And it was loaded with a runic bullet! Can you believe that?"

Gav's expression was scandalized. "He really would have killed you had he shot."

"I know!"

Ruby met Serik's gaze, grinning. The wilder rolled his eyes, but she saw the smile tugging at the sides of his lips.

While the other two were distracted with disparaging their woodland companion, he reached over, tucking a lock of hair behind Ruby's left ear, doing the exact thing she'd wanted to do moments before. His fingers brushed against her cheek as he pulled away.

"Would you like to join me outside?" he asked. "I think I need some fresh air."

"It *is* rather hot in here," she said, glancing at Kai. Her friend and the loresinger didn't seem to be paying attention to them at all anymore. Kai was in the middle of telling Gav about the riphounds they'd encountered in the Wytchwood.

When they slipped outside, the night air was cool against Ruby's skin, a stark contrast to the warm—almost stiflingly so—air inside the tavern. She shivered as a breeze drifted through the village.

"Here," Serik said, noticing the shiver and shrugging his jacket off his shoulders. "Use this." He took a pouch out of one of the inner pockets, then placed the jacket over her shoulders and arms. It was a few sizes too big for her, but very warm and smelled like firewood and cloves.

Ruby wrapped it around herself. "Thank you."

Smiling at her, he led the way to the back of the building. It faced the trees, and though it was hard to see in the darkening night, they were able to find a stump used for cutting wood and a stool that they could sit on. Ruby and Serik sat across from one another, their knees almost touching. Crickets chirped as the light faded around them, late afternoon becoming evening as stars became visible in the sky.

"How do you feel about your first train ride now that it's over?" he asked as he opened the drawstring on the pouch and pulling a lacquered rosewood pipe and a small tin from within.

"The first day was eventful, to say the least." Ruby watched him fill and light the pipe, the scent of sweet tobacco drifting through the air between them. "I will admit, I never thought I would miss long days of horseback riding, even though the train is much faster."

"I, too, prefer the open road," he agreed, placing the pipe between his lips. The ember within glowed bright orange as he inhaled, the light reflecting in his eyes. He turned his head as he exhaled, blowing the smoke away from Ruby. "I'll be only too glad to get this over with so I can go back to Lanevin to retrieve Dream."

"I am sure they will take good care of her," Ruby reassured him. "She is a very special horse. What breed is she?"

Serik shrugged. "I don't know. Whatever it is, they don't breed them in the empire. Dream was a gift from my stepmother before I left home. According to *Ama*, my mother selected her for me before she died."

Remembering that Serik had told her that his father had died before he and his mother moved north, sympathy welled in her, and Ruby took his free hand in hers. She traced the tendons with her thumbs. He didn't pull away. Ruby didn't know what it was like to lose a parent, let alone both, but it must have taken its toll on him. "She will be all right. I am sorry that your mother did not get to see how beautiful she is."

He pulled the pipe out of his mouth and smiled at Ruby, his eyes looking distant. "I have a feeling she knew how perfect Dream would be." He held out the pipe.

She stared at it for a few moments before realizing he was offering her a smoke. "I cannot. My mother taught me that proper ladies do not partake in such things," she added when he raised an eyebrow.

"But you are no longer a proper lady," he said with a twitch of his eyebrow. "Proper ladies do not flee their betrothed and traipse around the countryside, pretending to be married to dangerous wilders."

Eyes narrowing, she felt herself grin as she took the pipe from him. "I suppose you are correct." Ruby ran her fingers over the smooth object. Her father smoked occasionally, so she had seen one before, but he had never let her hold it. It was warm to the touch, but not hot enough to burn her, even with the smoldering ashes within. What could it hurt?

Opening her mouth, she placed the bit between her lips and inhaled.

Immediately her throat and chest felt like they were on fire. Ruby's eyes watered, and she coughed, choking on the smoke and burning sensation, nearly dropping the pipe.

Taking the pipe out of her loose grip, Serik placed a hand on her upper arm to steady her as her coughing fit subsided.

"That," she said, clearing her throat and using the back of her wrist to wipe at her eyes, "is horrible. Why do people do that?"

The wilder tried to keep a straight face, but he couldn't hide his grin fast enough. "You get used to it after a while. I find it helps me relax at times."

"It is vile." Ruby scowled at the pipe. She wondered how anyone could relax when their throat burned.

Serik chuckled. His hand was still on her arm, and he placed the pipe on a rock next to the stool. Reaching out, he brushed back a strand of hair that had been knocked out of place during her coughing fit. He tucked it behind her ear, just as he had done inside, but his touch lingered. Without the prying eyes of others, he didn't remove his hand, and Ruby's heart sped up, thumping loudly in her chest. It was difficult to see his expression in the gathering darkness, but the look in his eyes was unmistakable.

"I can think of more pleasant ways to relax," he all but growled.

Perhaps she should have excused herself or pulled away like a proper young lady, but as the wilder had pointed out, that was no longer who she was. Ruby wanted him just as much as Serik wanted her. She tilted her head back as he leaned into her. There was a moment's hesitation, as if he was unsure what her reaction would be, then his lips pressed against hers, and they were warmer and softer than she could have imagined. The hand touching her cheek slid to the back of her neck, tangling itself in her hair, his thumb brushing her skin. Ruby's eyes fluttered closed as his tongue ran over her bottom lip, and she arched into him.

Serik's other hand reached into the jacket, fingers gripping her waist as he pulled her closer. Her lips parted, and she tasted tobacco smoke and bitter ale as he deepened the kiss, the hand at her waist becoming more insistent.

Before they could go any further, there was the sound of rocks crunching under booted feet, and a moment later, a familiar male voice said, "Ruby, are you back here? The innkeeper says—"

Gav stopped in his tracks as Serik and Ruby pulled away from each other. The loresinger stared at them, seeming at a loss for words. Ruby hugged Serik's jacket tightly around her, face burning. She was sure that if there had been enough light to see the color of her skin, she would be bright red.

"—the baths are prepared," Gav finished lamely, a sheepish grin spreading across his face as he eyed them. "But I can see that you are busy."

"No! I'm ready now!" she said jumping up, heart still racing. Throwing a glance at Serik, she inwardly cringed. The wilder's mouth was set in a hard line. Whether from the interruption or her reaction, she wasn't sure. Ruby wanted to reach out and touch him, to put him at ease or perhaps to continue where they left off, but she resisted. Shrugging off the jacket, she folded it in half and handed it back to him. Ruby opened her mouth to say something, maybe thank him for lending her the garment, but when their eyes met, the words died in her throat.

That burning desire was still there as he gazed back at her, even more intense than before, and it scared her. It made her feel like a rabbit that had caught the attention of a fox, and it wasn't a sensation that was unfamiliar. The duke's gaze would sometimes leave her feeling like a trapped animal. But what disturbed her the most now was how *her* body reacted to Serik's look, the longing for the wilder that she could feel through every inch of her redoubling.

Managing a watery smile, Ruby inclined her head to him, then turned to the loresinger. "Thank you, Gav," she said with all the confidence she could muster. With one last glance back at Serik, Ruby hurried past Gav, fleeing toward the safety of the inn.

CHAPTER 20

The sun had barely crested the horizon when Ruby, Kai, Gav, and Serik set off to begin their search. The plan was to leave Calsith and head northeast through the forest and toward the mountains. The books Kai had taken from Valwen had described the general area where Ta'Dormus Deva was supposedly located, and Raul had confirmed it, but they couldn't be sure that the text or the old hunter was accurate.

Raul had said it was in a little valley created in the middle of two towering mountains—"arms" he'd called them— that formed a "V" shape. The wilder compared the map in the text to one he purchased from Raul and thought he knew which mountains the book referred to. Thus, with their packs laden with more than a week's worth of supplies, they left the small village, traversing through the dense pine trees of the Caligo Forest.

The trees here were some of the tallest that Ruby had ever seen, reaching heights of more than a hundred feet. Their branches blocked out the sun, casting the entire forest floor in shadow. Fallen pine needles crunched under their feet, and there was a quiet feeling that permeated the air. Birds did not sing, and they spotted little movement beneath the canopy. The entire place had an ethereal feeling about it, something that grated at Ruby's nerves in a way that she couldn't explain.

There was no trail for them to follow and no marked path to take. Serik was in the lead, directing them through the underbrush and navigating what looked to Ruby like the easiest-to-traverse path. He would stop every few minutes and examine something, a broken branch or an impression in the dirt, take out his compass, then continue forward without a word. Ruby and Gav shared a few confused looks, but Kai seemed unperturbed by his actions. The wilder hadn't done this while they had been traveling through the Wytchwood, but Ruby supposed that was because he knew those woods well.

They walked for an hour or two, then rested and repeated that pattern throughout the day. Ruby was not used to walking so much or climbing over rocks and tree roots. She tired quickly, and the muscles of her lower back and calves protested. Kai seemed to be doing better, but Gav was in the same condition Ruby was. The loresinger muttered dark thoughts under his breath. It was clear that he did not enjoy this. She couldn't blame him. Ruby was feeling just as discontented as he was, though she didn't voice this opinion. She longed to be sitting atop Dream, letting the mare navigate the tricky forest floor while she contemplated the man in the saddle behind her. It really was the preferable way to travel.

By the time it was getting dark, the forest was almost unnavigable. The high canopy of trees cast them in twilight hours early, and it was difficult to tell where Ruby was placing her feet. Serik called a stop to the search and got to work building a lean-to, much like the one he'd built for them the night it had rained. Gav and Ruby collected firewood and tinder while Kai unloaded their supplies.

Finished with her task, Ruby sat on a rock next to where Kai had directed her to place the firewood. She shivered, and her breath fogged before her. The air here was colder and thinner than it had been in Easthollow. She watched as Kai worked on building the fire, Gav handing her fresh logs and sticks.

Once the fire had caught and no longer needed tending, Gav went to collect water from a nearby stream and Kai wrapped herself in a blanket, holding out her hands to the flames for warmth. Serik finished setting up their sleeping arrangements, then pulled out the map and sat down on the rock next to Ruby.

"I think we are more than halfway there," he murmured quietly as Ruby leaned over to get a glimpse of what he was looking at.

He leaned toward her, showing her the map. "We're about here," he said, pointing at a spot in between the mountains, about an inch under the little circle that indicated the suspected placement of the ruins nestled in the valley.

"How can you tell?" she asked. It was amazing that he could tell anything at all with all the branches over their heads. She would have been baffled.

"Do you see that?" Serik pointed at a gap through the trees. The sunlight was fading fast, but a large, jagged silhouette with a white tip loomed in the distance. "That's this mountain," he indicated the spot on the map, "and over there," he pointed to where another silhouette could barely be seen through the trees, "is its twin. So, we are going right between them."

It was amazing that he had been able to keep them on track all day as they wandered around the forest in a way that had felt aimless to her, and she turned to tell him so.

Realizing the closeness of their bodies, the words would not come. Their shoulders were almost touching. Kai had retreated to their shelter to huddle under her blanket, face hidden, and Gav was still gone, so they were alone for the moment. Serik shifted, placing his hand on the rock right behind Ruby's bottom, allowing him to face her better. His eyes roved over her face, lingering on her lips before flicking back up to meet her gaze.

"How are you feeling? Are your feet sore?"

It took Ruby a second to process what he'd said. "What? Oh, no. I am fine."

He raised an eyebrow at her.

"Well, yes, actually." She could feel her face getting hot. "I am not used to all the walking, and I doubt these shoes were designed with such activity in mind."

A grin played at the sides of his mouth. "It's much easier when Dream is doing all the hard work."

He was so close to her now that she could feel the heat radiating off his body. Her eyes met his. "Serik, I—"

"What are you looking at?" Gav said, sitting on Ruby's other side. "Is that the area? How much farther do we need to travel?" Ruby glanced back at him, and the loresinger gave her a wink. Then she got it. Back in Calsith, Gav had stumbled upon their intimate moment by accident but had seen the way she'd panicked. He had purposefully interrupted them this time to save her from any further embarrassment.

The immense relief and affection she felt toward the loresinger made her smile.

"How many more days must we sleep outdoors?" Gav continued.

"It's hard to say," Serik said, seemingly unbothered by the interruption, but he removed his hand from behind Ruby and held out the map so that both Ruby and Gav could see it. His arm brushed up against hers, but with Gav there, it felt less awkward. "The ruins should be located somewhere in this valley, but without knowing the exact location, we could be searching for days before we find them."

"Can't you just climb a tree when we get there and see the whole valley?" Gav suggested. "Surely, you'll be able to see it from a height."

"It's not that simple," Kai approached sans blanket and sat cross-legged on the ground a few feet away from them with her back to the fire. "If the place has been abandoned for a century or two, there's a good chance that nature has overtaken it. We don't know what condition it was left in. It might be indistinguishable from the rest of the landscape."

"Then how are we supposed to find it?" Gav asked with dismay in his voice.

"The old-fashioned way, by looking for it," she replied with a roll of her eyes. "There would have been some kind of road or courtyard leading up to it, even a hundred years ago, so we should start by looking for evidence of that." She glanced at Serik, and he gave her a curt nod in agreement.

"So, we are looking for cut stones, something that would be manmade?" Ruby clarified.

"Exactly," Serik answered. "Or anything that looks like it would not have occurred naturally."

There was the sound of snapping twigs in the trees beyond the little clearing they had made their camp in. All four of them looked up, gazing into the trees and the darkness beyond. The sun was below the tree line to the west, and the dark reds and blues of twilight made it so they could not see much beyond their little fire.

"It's likely an elk or perhaps a wolf, and our fire will deter the latter," Serik said as he stood. Taking a few steps back, he leaned down and picked up his rifle, which had been resting against his travel pack near the lean-to.

There was another sound of rustling leaves to their left,

and Ruby flinched. An almost feline whine reached her ears, and she thought she saw the reflective flash of eyes in the darkness.

"Did you hear that?" Gav asked nervously as he scrambled to his feet. "Please tell me that is a normal forest sound."

"It's not," Serik said, his voice low. He raised the rifle and stared out into the trees. "Wolves don't make that sound. Stay by the fire so that if it tries to attack us, we'll see it coming."

There was the flash of something moving out in the darkness. A twig snapped to Ruby's left, and she jumped to her feet, whirling around, but she couldn't find the source of the noise. "There is something there," she said, backing up until Serik placed his hand on her shoulder. She'd almost backed into him.

The wilder pointed the rifle to where she indicated, and the young woman hid behind him, eyes scanning the trees.

"There!" Gav shouted as he drew a pistol from his belt, firing at a dark form in the trees. The bullet ricocheted off a trunk, sending splinters flying, and missed its target. The creature growled loudly from the darkness, and two more feline growls answered it from the other side of their camp.

"Shit," Kai mumbled as she turned in a slow circle. "They're surrounding us." She took a few measured steps around the fire, looking as if she would just continue scanning the tree line, but with a blur of her hands, she snatched her dagger from her side and launched it into the woods.

Though the weapon disappeared into the darkness, the screech that followed it told them the blade had found its mark.

Ruby raised one hand over her head, calling power to her fingertips. A ball of light as large as her fist formed above her, illuminating the clearing with white light far brighter than what their meager campfire produced.

There were three of them. Large, muscular creatures with

sleek, black fur. It was difficult to tell in the shadowy darkness, but Ruby thought she saw the flash of blood-red eyes. The beasts were nearly the size of Dream, but looked more like panthers, and she could see the ripple of muscle as their coats absorbed her light. Kai's silver dagger had sunk to the hilt in the shoulder of the closest monster. Dark, purple-ish blood oozed from the wound.

The thunderous clap of gunfire drew Ruby's attention away from the beasts to her left just in time to see the third animal that Serik had been aiming at jerk back, yowling in pain as that dark blood sprayed the ground. The creature had been preparing to pounce but now retreated from the wilder, seeking the safety of the trees again. Serik quickly began to reload.

"What, no fire?! No burst of flames?" Kai called back to him, keeping her eyes on the other two creatures. "I'd say *this* situation calls for those runic bullets!" Ruby was reminded of their first meeting when Serik had fired a runic bullet at a riphound, its wound erupting in flames.

"I wasn't expecting to get attacked by giant cats!" Serik snapped back.

"Here they come!" Gav squealed as the ones nearest Kai dashed forward.

A blur of fangs and fur rushed at them. Kai ducked as one flew over her head, heading straight at Ruby. Before she could react, Serik pushed her out of the way, blocking the thing's fangs with the barrel of his rifle. Its claws swiped out, tearing a large gash in the wilder's side. He grunted in pain as he shoved the beast back, then dropped the rifle and snatched up his sword belt, unsheathing his blade.

The second beast had pounced at Kai, but she'd been waiting for it and rolled to the side, coming up in a crouching position as it sailed passed. The creature was light on its feet, and before it touched the ground, it turned in midair and landed facing Kai. A low growl rumbled in its chest as it stalked its prey.

There was no sign of the last creature, which had melted back into the darkness outside the range of Ruby's light.

Gav drew another pistol, firing at the one that had tried to take Kai's head off, but his aim was too far to the right. He swore, tossing the spent firearm to the ground, then drew his own blade and stepped up beside Serik to block Ruby from the monster.

"Are you all right?" he asked the wilder.

"I'll live," Serik replied, keeping his eyes on the beast as it prowled around them.

Kai drew the sword at her belt and lunged at the creature that stalked her. Before she connected, the dagger shimmered out of existence and appeared in her off-hand, both weapons plunging toward the black mass of fur and muscle. She feinted right with the sword, then as the beast moved to avoid her attack, she brought the dagger down and into its rib cage, its fur quickly erupting in blue flames.

The roar of pain the wounded animal emitted was loud enough to make Ruby's ears ring. It flung itself away from Kai and landed on the beast menacing Serik and Gav. The second creature cried in surprised agony, its fur singed by the other, and it danced away from the burning threat.

Ruby watched as both cats carefully padded around the ground that was singed from Kai's spell. Neither would touch the blackened grass, and they even gave the campfire a wide berth. Realization stole her breath. The creatures seemed to fear the fire! That gave her an idea.

Calling on her power once again, she shouted the incantation *"Exus!"* and reached through the small gap between Gav's and Serik's shoulders, slashing her hand through the air.

A line of red-hot flame burst to life in the brush between

her companions and the two black creatures in front of them. The beasts jumped back in surprise, snarling, but turned from the flames and bolted into the trees again. Their own heavy breathing and the crackle of the fire were loud to Ruby's ears as the sounds of snapping twigs and rustling foliage faded. She slowly let out a sigh of relief as Serik sheathed his sword and retrieved his rifle. Gav picked up his pistols and began reloading one.

Ruby was about to grab one of their wool blankets to put out the grass fire she had started when there was a rustling behind her.

"Ruby, watch out!" Kai screamed.

She looked up, meeting a pair of blood-red eyes staring at her from the bushes less than ten feet away. There was an instant of stillness. Then everything happened at once. Gunfire rang through the night as both Serik and Gav raised their weapons and fired. Kai grabbed Ruby's wrist and yanked her back, as the beast that Gav's first shot had missed flew through the trees at her, claws extended and mouth open in a snarl.

Both the wilder and the loresinger aimed true. Purple blood splattered the grass as the two bullets hit their mark, and fire burst forth from one of the wounds as Serik's runic bullet activated. The impact threw the creature to the side, and it let out a cry before it slumped to the ground.

There was a tense silence as they watched its fur burn away.

"Is it dead?" Gav asked the question they were all wondering. Serik set his rifle down on the rock they had been sitting on earlier and drew his sword again, then approached the smoldering beast cautiously. The others watched tensely as he slit the large cat's throat with his blade and then moved in to examine it.

"Your bullet pierced its eye and went through its brain. It was dead a few seconds after it hit the ground."

"Good gods," Kai breathed. "What a lucky shot."

"That's what we call *skill*, my dear," Gav said with a smug grin.

"Right. Skill," Kai responded with a roll of her eyes.

Serik staggered back over to them, his left hand clutching his right side. He looked around the campsite at the damage that their magic and the creatures had done. "We won't be able to move camp like we did in the Wytchwood," he grumbled. "I don't know these woods and can't be certain we'll find another safe spot close by." He glanced over his shoulder back at the lifeless mound of black fur. "We should try to get that as far from our camp as possible, though. We don't want to attract any other predators. Do you think the others will return?"

"Maybe," Kai said, answering his question. "We'll have to keep a watch."

Ruby stepped forward, taking the wilder's arm and moving him over to the rock so that he could sit. He gave her a grateful smile as he settled down.

"Gav and I will move the body," Kai nodded at the loresinger. "I have a spell that will make it easier."

"We will?" Gav asked. Kai glared at him as she stamped out what remained of Ruby's fire. "Right, we will. Ruby, I trust you can assist our woodland guide with his injuries." She nodded. "Be right back," he said with a wink, striding over to the carcass of the large cat. "How on Asara are we going to lift this?"

Kai was already pulling a feather out of a pouch on her belt. "With magic, duh."

Ruby turned from them, focusing on the wilder. He was still sitting on the rock. His features were set in a grimace with his lips pursed, his brows furrowed, obviously in pain.

"Let me take a look at that." She indicated the bloody scratches on his side and moved over to their bags. "Where are the healing potions?"

Serik tried to get up but sucked in a pained breath and settled back down. "I don't think the wound is deep, but it's hard to tell. If we can, I want to save the last two potions for when we need them."

"It looks to me like you need them now," she countered.

He shook his head, and Ruby thought what an incredibly stubborn man he was. Would he rather bleed out than take the medicine? Perhaps he was right, and the wound was not as bad as it looked to her, but the right side of his shirt was soaked through with blood.

"At least let me see to it," Ruby insisted. Serik looked like he was going to protest and say that he could do it himself, so she continued with, "You have treated my wounds multiple times. Allow me to do this for you."

He let out a long breath through his nose, then finally nodded. "Very well. There is a small pouch in my pack with medical supplies." While Ruby looked through his pack, the wilder took off his jacket and the shirt underneath.

Once she'd located the little pouch that he had used to bandage her feet on the first night they met, she returned to him. Serik leaned back, giving her a good look at his bare chest and arms. He was muscular, and the firelight high-lighted every dip and curve of his skin, casting his tanned complexion in a golden glow. She noticed thin scars on his arms, like cuts made with a tiny blade over and over again, seemingly without pattern. Another larger scar started at the bottom of his ribs and continued down toward his navel.

Feeling her face heat up as her eyes traveled south, Ruby tore her eyes from him. What was wrong with her? He was injured, and here she was, ogling. Kneeling next to Serik, she scolded herself for such inappropriate behavior.

"Do you know what you are doing?" Serik's voice brought her out of her head.

"I am afraid you will need to walk me through it," Ruby admitted with a sheepish shrug. "I have seen a wound tended but do not have the practical knowledge."

He chuckled. "I figured as much. There should be a bottle of vodka in there. It's a clear liquid. Use that to wipe off your hands on one of the clean cloths."

Ruby easily found the bottle and did as he instructed. "Now what?"

"Take another one of those cloths and press it gently against the wound. If blood soaks through, you'll have to get another and apply pressure until the bleeding stops."

She took another one of the clean white strips of cloth and folded it into quarters, then pressed it against the three jagged marks the creature had left on Serik. "Is that hard enough?"

"A little more." He winced. "Yes, that is good."

She kept the pressure on the cloth while he took a few deep breaths, letting his head fall back and closing his eyes. "Are you in a lot of pain?"

"Not as much as I'm about to be. Is the blood soaking through?"

Ruby checked under her hands. "No."

"That's good. Now you want to wash the wound off with water, and then you'll use the tweezers in that bag to pick out dirt or anything that shouldn't be there."

Ruby grimaced at the thought of picking debris out of his flesh, but she wasn't the one sitting there with the slashes in her side. Grabbing one of the canteens from his pack, she dribbled the water over the wound and got to work. It was hard to see if there was anything stuck in his bloody flesh with only the campfire's illumination, so Ruby called another little ball of light and let it float next to her shoulder as she worked. She picked a few blades of grass and small rocks out of the wound, having to rinse it off with water one more time to make sure she got all the dirt.

Serik's breath stayed at an even, measured pace that was artificially calm. She could tell he was in pain by how his muscles twitched when she touched him, so Ruby tried to be quick about it. She placed a hand on his abdomen, leaning closer to the wound as she inspected it from every angle.

"There," she said, sitting back on her heels. "I think I got it all."

He nodded, inhaling deeply through his nose and letting out a shaky sigh. There was a thin sheen of sweat across his forehead. It was almost a minute before he spoke. "Take the vodka and pour a little over the wound. Then you can bandage it.

This was the most painful part, she knew that much. Ruby didn't want to hurt him further, but it had to be done. She carefully dribbled some of the vodka over the wound, which made him grunt in discomfort, then took the last clean cloth and the rolled-up bandages from the pouch, using them to cover the wound and secure the dressing around his torso, much like he had done to her after she'd been shot. Ruby cleaned her hands again as Serik caught his breath.

When she looked back at him, the wilder was watching her, the intense look reminding her of the night that he'd kissed her. "You did well," he said, with little hint of pain in his voice anymore.

She smiled at that. "Your instructions were very clear." Ruby placed the bottle of vodka back in the bag and then frowned down at the bloody strips of once-white cloth. Perhaps she should wash them. They might need them again. She let her light spell fade as she set the medical supplies aside.

He reached for his travel pack, and Ruby handed it to him

before he could undo her handiwork. Digging around in it for a few moments, he pulled out a silver-plated flask and unscrewed the top.

"What is that?" Ruby asked as she watched him take a long drink.

"Whisky. It'll dull the pain for a little while." He held out the flask to her and quirked an eyebrow.

She took it from him and drank. It tasted of smoke and chocolate and burned pleasantly as it went down her throat. It wasn't the first time she'd tasted the drink—it was one of Mikel's favorites—but this type was different from what she'd had before. It was sweeter than the kind most nobles preferred, and she liked it. Liquid fire pooled in her stomach and heated her body from within, which felt good in the chill night. Serik watched her through half-lidded eyes as Ruby returned the flask.

"You should rest," she said, standing and brushing dead leaves and grass off her dress. Helping him stand, she walked the wilder over to the shelter.

He lay down on a blanket, and Ruby sat on his left side, opposite the wound. The wilder hadn't donned his ripped and bloody clothing again, choosing to stay bare from the waist up. He lay back, eyes closed and his right arm lying across his forehead. Ruby thought he must have been cold, but she didn't dare look at him. Sitting this close to Serik with half his clothing removed was enough to speed up her heart, wounded or not.

As she stared at the fire, encased in her own thoughts, Serik's arm snaked around her waist and tugged, throwing her off balance. Ruby fell backward as he pulled her right up against him.

"You are injured!" she protested, placing a hand on his chest and pushing back. He held her firmly. "Serik!"

"If you don't squirm about, it won't hurt, will it?" He

opened one eye, looking at her while a smile tugged at his lips. "It's not as if I could ravish you in my current state. I'm just cold."

"I can get you another blanket."

"You're no fun," he said with a huff, his arm still holding her firmly in place.

"And *you're* injured," she reiterated.

"I've been injured before. I'll be fine." He pouted.

Ruby laughed. He was being such a child about her rejecting him. "Does whisky always make you so petulant?" she asked as she leaned down and pressed her lips to his forehead. Serik reached up and ran one finger down her cheek and neck as she pulled back. His gaze made her body feel warm. It could have been an aftereffect of the whisky, but she suspected that was not the cause. Despite his injury, she desired nothing more than to lean into him and place her lips elsewhere.

The sound of rustling bushes and crunching leaves brought Ruby back to her senses.

"Do you think we could get a reward for killing the monster that the old man was talking about?" Kai's voice drifted over to them from the trees.

"I wouldn't get your hopes up. I doubt those villagers have two crests to rub together," Gav said as he entered the clearing, holding a branch back for Kai. "Besides, we didn't really get rid of their problem. There are still the two others that got away, and who knows how many more."

"That's reassuring," Kai grumbled.

"It's the truth. We know little about these woods and even less about what we can expect throughout the night." His eyes drifted to the lean-to, and the loresinger's steps slowed to a stop. He placed his hands on his hips like a mother who'd just caught her children doing something naughty. "Are we disturbing you? Should we go on another serene yet terrifying walk through the woods for, what, thirty minutes?"

Finally able to extract herself from Serik's grip, Ruby scooted back from him and cleared her throat, cheeks warm. "There is no need to jest, Gav."

"I'm certain we could find somewhere else to be," he continued like she hadn't spoken. "Have you ever tried your hand at hunting?" Gav asked Kai. "With our efforts combined, we could bring back a rabbit or two."

"I'm not sure you could find your way out of a sack, let alone track down a rabbit," she replied, but she grinned at Ruby and Serik. "You're more likely to stumble onto something untoward."

Ruby rolled her eyes and pushed herself to her feet. "Very funny." She picked up one of their blankets and handed it to Serik as he propped himself up on his elbows.

Kai was already digging through their supplies. "It's going to be cold food tonight," she said. "We have some salted fish and bread. That will have to do."

Gav grimaced but accepted the bundle of wax paper she handed him without complaint. She handed another portion to Ruby and one to Serik. "We can have hot food in the morning, but I'd rather not be distracted with trying to cook tonight." As soon as she sat on the rock next to the fire, she devoured her meal within seconds.

"We'll need to have someone on alert all night," Gav said. After a few bites, a sour expression took over his face, and he handed the rest of his fish to Kai, who shrugged and took it from him, downing it in two bites.

"We can take turns," Serik said. "Let Ruby and Kai rest."

"If anyone is resting, it should be you," Ruby countered. "I can stay up."

"You two get some sleep," Serik insisted as he finished his paltry dinner and pushed himself to his feet. He didn't so much as wince as he pulled out a fresh shirt from his bag and retrieved his jacket. The wilder moved slowly, being careful not to move his right arm too much. "The pain will keep me awake for a while still. Gav and I will keep watch."

Ruby wanted to argue more, but Kai caught her eye and gave her a slight shake of her head. Frowning in acknowledgment, she said nothing further on the subject.

"Rest well," Serik said as he settled by the fire. "We still have a long way to go in the morning."

CHAPTER 21

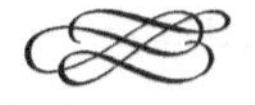

Sunrise came too soon, waking Ruby from her dreamless slumber. It had been difficult to get to sleep after being attacked by those monsters, but having Kai next to her the entire night helped. Serik and Gav had slept in shifts, and both looked tired, their eyes red-rimmed, as she and Kai packed away their blankets and stoked the fire.

Kai took over the cooking for the morning, a job that usually belonged to the wilder, so that he and Gav could get a little more rest before they left in search of the ruins. Neither man complained. Ruby helped where she could, but having never tried her hand at preparing food, she followed Kai's instructions, cutting vegetables into irregular chunks and stirring the pot when needed.

Serik and Gav retreated into the lean-to and slept for two more hours before Kai sent Ruby to shake them awake. The men packed their belongings with a slowness that only came from a lack of sleep. Kai boiled water to make coffee, using a cheesecloth to strain the grinds.

"Marry me," Gav said as she handed him a tin cup filled with the dark liquid, and Kai rolled her eyes.

Ruby had not tried coffee before—tea was the drink of choice for her parents and her ex-fiancé—and she frowned down at the bitter drink.

"It's not so bad if you have sugar and cream," Serik said as he settled next to her. "Of which we have neither."

"I think I will pass," she said, handing the wilder her cup. He took it from her and poured the contents into his own, then took a big swig. He closed his eyes and sighed like it was the most divine thing he had ever partaken in. "How are you feeling?"

"Good, all things considered. It still hurts when I move around too much, but not as bad as last night. I fear I may need that healing potion after all." He sighed again, this time without any pleasure. "Do you mind changing the dressings after I eat? I have extra bandages in the bottom of my pack. Somehow, I knew we'd need them."

"Of course."

Kai dished out their breakfast, a porridge heavy with rice, the vegetables Ruby had cut, and little bits of meat that looked like it could have been chicken. The food was bland, but it warmed Ruby and sat heavy in her stomach.

Gav and Serik weren't as talkative as they normally were, which Ruby attributed to exhaustion. She and Kai discussed what they might find in the ruins while the other two fully woke up.

Kai pored over the map again. "This was a religious site, and places like that tend to be built where they will look prominent."

"If that is true, it could also be at the north end of the valley since that would look bold on a map," Ruby suggested, and Kai nodded, tapping the map with her finger.

"We should probably start in the middle and work our way out."

After they were finished eating, Kai smothered the

remaining coals of the fire while Ruby tended to Serik's wounds. He drank half of one of their remaining potions, waving off Ruby's insistence that its potency would be greatly affected by not taking the full dose, and they packed up their little campsite before continuing on their way.

Once they were well within the valley between the two mountains, they began their search for Ta'Dormus Deva. It was past midday when they arrived, having left their campsite about three hours after dawn. The four of them scoured the forest for anything that looked manmade, any stone or structure that was not a natural part of the landscape.

Despite what they had been through thus far, Ruby was excited. All her life, those who watched over her were concerned with her being brought up as a proper young lady who would marry a duke. The idea of Ruby exploring dark and decrepit temples on the other side of the empire would have made her mother faint. She knew she was woefully unprepared for the task at hand, but that didn't stop her from joining the search with enthusiasm.

By dusk, her excitement had faded. She and the others had been searching all day with no luck.

"Perhaps we should stop for the night," she said as she watched Kai climb over a large boulder, navigating carefully through the dense underbrush. "It is going to get dark soon, and my feet are sore."

Standing atop the rock, Kai looked out over the trees of the Caligo Forest. The forest was thinner here. Shaking her head, she let out a long breath and placed her hands on her hips. "I would have thought we'd find *something* by now. A road, a statue, anything!" Letting out a groan of frustration, Kai hopped down the other side of the boulder, but Ruby could still hear her talking, even if she couldn't see her. "Maybe I was wrong. Maybe it's in a different valley in this stupid mountain range."

"It's a large area," Serik's voice carried from somewhere off to Ruby's left. She glanced over her shoulder to see the wilder a ways off, traipsing through the tall grass and brush. This forest was even more difficult to navigate than the Wytchwood. The ground was rocky, and there were large outcroppings of rock, hills, and bends that made it treacherous to traverse. "It could take us days to find anything."

"I don't know about you, but I don't want to spend another night being attacked by those monsters from before," Gav's voice came from behind her.

"It's not like we can find an inn," Kai snapped as Ruby walked around the boulder Kai had climbed over. A little ahead of her, Kai was about to take a step, then stopped suddenly, her head tilting to one side.

"What's wrong, Kai?" Ruby asked, pausing as well and listening. She didn't hear anything besides the sound of her own breath.

"I hear running water beyond that bend just ahead." Kai bounded forward, walking more quickly than Ruby could manage.

Beyond the rocky hill was a small tarn with a waterfall fed by mountain runoff. Trees hid much of the sky from view, but it was a peaceful little sanctuary in the otherwise foreboding forest. Ruby could see all the way to the bottom of the little lake, the water clear as glass. It didn't look deep, and there were silvery glints every so often, evidence of the fish that swam below. The tarn emptied into a brook that flowed farther down into the valley.

Kai walked around the waterline, looking at the rocky section below the waterfall. Portions of it seemed almost dug out of the hill.

"This would be the perfect place to hide something," Kai spoke almost to herself. "But there's nothing here."

"It's a good place to stop for the night," Serik said as he

rounded the bend, putting his pack down next to the jagged stump of a fallen tree. He was moving much more easily than he had that morning. Even at half potency, that potion worked wonders. Maybe one day, Ruby could seek out training in healing magics.

"Thank the gods! I feel as though my feet are about to fall off." Gav let out a weary sigh. "Much more of this, and they'll just be one big blister."

"That would prove difficult for you to continue our search," Ruby said as she leaned down and ran her fingers through the water. It was cold, just above the point of freezing. Cupping her hands, she splashed some of the liquid on her face. It was refreshing, but the temperature made her shiver. "That is brisk."

They began unpacking their belongings, and before long, the gathering dusk gave way to night. This was beginning to feel normal to Ruby, eating dinner outside under the stars, chatting softly with her friends, and then curling up together to sleep. It was cold in the mountains but, huddled together as they were, she barely felt it. Thankfully, the sky had been clear for most of their journey. Stars twinkled above them, and the moon even came out of her hiding place behind the towering peaks. Ruby did miss the comforts of city life at times, but she enjoyed the company she was with and found herself content where she never thought she would be.

Ruby caught Serik giving her a few sidelong glances when he thought no one was looking. He must have been feeling better.

Catching another look from the wilder after they'd eaten their fill of a dish consisting of chopped meat and vegetables he had called a "hash," Ruby asked, "Is there something on my face?"

He gave her a look that could have rivaled that of a child

caught with his finger in a pie. "No. Forgive me. Am I making you uncomfortable?"

Ruby shook her head. She was wrapped in a blanket. It was even chillier in this valley than when they'd left the village. Why was she always so cold? It was spring. Wasn't it supposed to be getting warm? Ruby gave him an appraising look. He didn't look bothered by the temperature. "We could share my blanket," she said, thinking about how warm his skin would be, then immediately cringed at the boldness of her statement. "Only if you're cold, of course," Ruby added, trying to sound nonchalant. Kai and Gav were both looking up at the stars, pointing out constellations, so they didn't notice Ruby and Serik's conversation.

He gave her that knowing smile, the one that made her heart race. Scooting closer to her, Serik placed an arm around her shoulders.

It wasn't quite what she'd proposed, but she leaned her head against the curve between his neck and shoulders and inhaled deeply. Firewood and cloves.

Serik and Gav took turns keeping watch again that night, and once Ruby and Kai awoke near sunrise, the men both slept for a few hours as they'd done the previous day. Kai reasoned it wouldn't hurt to get a later start since they had been moving through the forest from sunup to sundown for two days, and all of them were weary. It wasn't as if they knew what they were looking for anyway.

Ruby went to wash up while Kai cooked something simple over the fire, toasting bread and cheese. The one thing she missed the most was hot running water, but she would have to make do. She filled her canteen with water from the tarn, then used her magic to heat it so that she could wash under her shift, much like she had done in the Wytchwood before she had been attacked by riphounds.

The memory made her shiver and look around at her

surroundings. She didn't want to be surprised like that ever again.

Out of the corner of her eye, Ruby thought she saw one of the vines overhanging the hillside to the left of the waterfall twitch. She turned her attention to it, but it hung there, unmoving. Perhaps it was a trick of the light. They had been looking for anything out of the ordinary, and now she was seeing things that weren't there. Ruby squinted at the vines, leaning forward.

There *was* something underneath them, carved into the rock. She got up and approached the waterfall, choosing her steps carefully so as not to slip and fall into the tarn. Ruby bent forward, just short of sticking her head under the running water and pushed some of the overgrowth out of the way. To her surprise, there were carvings under the foliage and dirt, and they looked suspiciously like runes.

"Kai! I think I found something!" Ruby shouted as she tugged at the vines obscuring the symbols. It struck her how familiar the designs were, and she was certain it was the same carving that was on Kai's key, an eight-pointed star inside of three interlocking rings. When she ran her fingers over the grooves, energy buzzed under her skin. It felt identical to when she'd touched the sandstone object in Kai's possession.

Kai jumped up at her words, leaving the bread on the fire and rushing over to the waterfall, footing more certain than Ruby's had been.

"What is it?!" she asked excitedly.

"There is something here!" Ruby stepped to the side so that Kai could get a good look at what was hidden beneath the vines. The growth and dirt still covered the runes, and Ruby filled her canteen again so that she could pour water over the stone, cleaning away the muck.

Kai dashed away, returning a minute later with her pack.

She fished around inside until she withdrew the little bundle she'd unwrapped that night in the cabin. With shaking hands, Kai held up the key. Ruby had been right. The symbol in the rock face was the same as the item in Kai's possession, and she felt another rush of excitement. Even if these weren't the ruins, this was proof that Ta'Dormus Deva existed. Both women pulled at the debris, cleaning the rock wall of dirt and detritus until the area was clear.

"This has to be it!" Kai's face was flush, and her breath came in short bursts after their exertion. "Look! There's a seam here." She pointed to a long line running the length of the rock face.

Ruby examined it more closely. It was a perfect seam, nothing that nature could have made on its own. It was almost as if there was a way to open the rock.

"What are you two looking at?" came Gav's sleepy voice from behind them.

Ruby glanced over her shoulder, realizing their commotion probably roused the men from their sleep. She took note that Serik had his sword in hand and a look of concern on his face as he rushed to where she and Kai were huddled under the waterfall, mistaking their excitement as possible danger.

After a nod of apology, she explained, "I found this while I was washing." Brushing her hand over the symbols again, she went on, "We think—"

A surge of power went up Ruby's arm, and she pulled back so quickly that she almost lost her balance. Gav caught her shoulders, steadying her. As they watched, the rockface shimmered. What had been uneven but naturally formed stone a moment ago faded away, leaving smooth blocks that had been precisely cut and arranged in its place. Water still fell from above, but now it was not splashing down the rocky outcropping, but off a stone roof built into the hillside.

The structure was not what Ruby had been expecting when she imagined the ruins. She had been envisioning a stone building in the middle of a clearing, with pillars covered in moss and a tiled courtyard. This looked like little more than a dwelling dug out of the earth, overgrown and crumbling. The only homage to her fantasies was the large stone doors that now stood before them.

There was a long silence. Then Gav cleared his throat. Ruby looked back at him.

"Perhaps we should prepare before we try to get inside." Gav coughed into his hand, glancing down at her and averting his gaze, the tops of his cheeks red.

Ruby looked down at herself, her face feeling like it was on fire as she realized she was still only in her shift.

"Excuse me!" she squeaked and hurried back to their camp, to where she'd left the rest of her clothing. *What is wrong with me? How embarrassing!* she thought as she dressed. She had been so engrossed in her discovery that she hadn't even noticed her state of undress until it was pointed out to her. It hadn't been *that* long since she'd left Valwen. Had she forgotten a lifetime's worth of propriety in such a short amount of time?

She dressed while the rest of them packed up the camp. The bread Kai had been cooking had a black crust on the bottom, burning while they'd been preoccupied with the suddenly appearing Ta'Dormus Deva, but it still satisfied their empty stomachs.

Ruby found herself standing in front of the doors again ten minutes later. She couldn't believe their luck at choosing this place to camp and that none of them had noticed it the night before. If she hadn't gone over to the waterfall to bathe, they might have missed it completely.

Kai echoed her thoughts. "I don't understand how you found that. I'd already looked there last night," she said as she stopped beside Ruby, inspecting the door. "It was just a stone wall last night."

"Did you feel that pulse of energy before?" Kai shook her head as Ruby ran her fingers over the symbol. There were little runes around the rings in the symbol carved into the door, so small that they would be unnoticeable at a distance. "Look here. I think this is the rune for 'hidden.' I am guessing it was under a veil enchantment."

"Then how did *you* notice it?" Kai asked.

That was a good question. "I… I do not know. I could see it just fine."

Kai looked skeptical. "How would you see through a millennia old veil when *I* couldn't?"

All Ruby could do was shrug. "I cannot answer that, Kai."

"Well, we're just lucky you found it!" Gav said, placing a hand on Ruby's shoulder. "Who cares about what spell failed when? Now, how do we get in?"

"Those doors look heavy. I doubt the hinges are still intact." Serik said and scratched at his beard in thought. "Maybe they are on a track. There could be a lever or pulley device nearby."

"Perhaps we can pry them open," Ruby suggested, reaching out and placing her hands on the stone again.

Pushing on the doors to see if they would move at all—which she knew was impossible, given their age and weight—Ruby jumped back in surprise, almost tripping again. When she'd leaned on the entry, the heavy slabs immediately began to slide open, almost as if they had responded to her touch. The stone groaned as it parted, moving by some mechanism that had not been activated in what she guessed had been centuries.

Sunlight poured into the darkness before them, revealing a crumbling stone staircase covered in a thick layer of dust.

Ruby stared into the dark depths in front of her, letting

her eyes adjust to the lack of light. It was about twenty steps down to the floor below. From what she could see with the shadowed sunlight, the area inside was damp and overgrown with vines and roots. Leaves littered the ground, slowly rotting and turning to mulch.

"Because that isn't creepy at all," Gav murmured under his breath.

Kai shrugged her shoulders. "The doors might be responding to the key I have in my possession, or"—she gave Ruby a quick glance out of the corner of her eye—"maybe it's Ruby's magic. The temple only showed itself when she touched the runes. They could have been set up to respond to a mage's power, and mine just wasn't strong enough." She said that last part with a grumble.

Ruby opened her mouth to tell Kai that her magic was not insignificant—she had been accepted to Valwen after all —but her friend just shook her head.

"I don't need the flattery, Ruby. Let's focus on getting the treasure. That's why we are here."

CHAPTER 22

Ruby, Kai, Gav, and Serik descended into the depths of Ta'Dormus Deva. Kai led the way, pulling out her lantern and holding it before her. In the time that they had been traveling together, Ruby had learned the device was called a bullseye lantern, focusing the light in a single direction instead of allowing illumination for a wide area as a normal lantern would. Kai examined the floor as they walked, looking for anything out of the ordinary.

"Sometimes, these old places are set with traps," she explained when Ruby had asked what she was doing. "But it's been so long since anyone has been here, I doubt anything that was set is still active." She peered into the gloom. "There are no tracks, animal or otherwise. No one has stepped foot in this place in years."

They arrived at a large receiving hall. If Ruby didn't know better, she would have thought they were entering a grand castle, one in sore need of refurbishment, but something that could have rivaled Castle Belmont, Mikel's home and where she'd lived when she was not at Valwen. To think that something like this would be carved into a rocky valley was beyond comprehension. It would have been difficult for even the emperor's greatest trackers to find.

The stone beneath their feet was uneven and, as she had guessed, covered in decaying roots and leaves turned to mulch. Sunlight shone through the ceiling in uneven patches where parts of the roof had caved in. None of the holes looked like they would be big enough for them to have entered through, so it was a good thing they had found the doors.

There were a few images painted on the walls, faded to the point that all the faces and symbols looked muddled in the near darkness. On the other side of the giant room was a stone arch, an entryway deeper into the temple.

The chamber that followed was a circular amphitheater. Stone steps that could have once served as seats lined the walls and descended to a flat stone floor with a raised dais in the center. A walkway from the dais led to another archway in the back of the room, no doubt the area where the person who would have addressed the audience entered from. Ruby could almost imagine the crowd of people that would have gathered here, listening intently to a speaker dressed in ancient robes on the dais.

Here, too, there were cracks in the ceiling, giving them just enough illumination to see where they were stepping.

Kai looked around, then began descending the stairs, using her lantern to inspect each row as she passed.

"This place is amazing," Gav said in wonder as he stared down at the room below him. "If only I still had my lute."

"So you could make an ungodly amount of racket?" Kai said over her shoulder. "No thanks."

"You wound me, *dear wife*." He sprinted down the steps to catch up to her. "It's almost as if you don't like my music."

"Call me 'dear wife' one more time, and see where I shove that lute of yours."

Ruby smiled at them.

Serik lingered behind with her as Kai and Gav made their way down the steps, bickering as usual. Ruby studied the wilder out of the corner of her eye in the dim light. He moved carefully, picking every step so that the motion was not wasted, and she reminded herself that he'd been injured less than two days ago.

"I forgot to ask this morning with all the excitement, but how is your wound today?" she asked as she stepped up next to him. "You did not ask me to assist you with your bandages this morning."

"It's scabbed over and doesn't hurt much unless I bend too quickly. I doubt I need the dressings anymore as the wound wasn't that deep to begin with."

"You really should take the rest of the healing potion. You never know what we will come up against in here."

He shook his head. "Kai was right. There are no tracks here, animal or human. I don't think we have anything to fear, other than maybe falling stone."

"Yes, falling stone. What danger could a ton of falling rock possibly be?" She glared at him, her tone flat.

His lips tugged up in a smirk. "I think you underestimate my abilities."

"I believe I correctly estimate your abilities, Serik," she said with a huff. "What if we do run into trouble, despite your insistence otherwise?"

"Then I will be in a little pain but still able to function normally otherwise. Are you worried about me, Ruby?"

"I worry that if more stone falls from the ceiling, it will break against that hard head of yours." She gave a lofty sniff.

Serik's smirk grew more pronounced, and he held a hand

out to her. Ruby glared at him but took it, using his hold to maintain her balance as they descended the steps after Kai.

"What are your plans after this?" she asked. "After we find this supposed treasure and liquidate it, I mean."

The wilder made a pensive sound. Ruby risked a glance over at him. He was watching Kai and Gav, who were still arguing while she searched the room. After a few long seconds, he finally spoke. "I haven't decided yet."

She didn't know what to say to that. What was she hoping for? That he would pledge to follow her wherever she went? He couldn't be expected to abandon whatever reason he had for staying out in the wilderness to be with her, but she remembered their shared moment behind the inn and the feeling of his lips against her skin. A not insignificant part of her hoped that what they had shared was real. She liked him, that much was obvious, and she wanted him to stay with her. To stay *for* her.

But that was selfish, and she felt guilt squeezing at her stomach. Ruby had to admit to herself that, though they had been traveling together for a while now, she barely knew anything about his past and his reasons for living by himself. The few tidbits he'd shared made her even more curious, but she had yet to get any specifics out of him. Perhaps when they were finished here, Ruby would find a way to wheedle the information out of him. She wanted to know everything she could about him.

As they descended to the dais below them, she hoped that he felt the same attraction to her. If so, how could he leave her? *He wouldn't*, Ruby told herself, *he won't leave me*.

A chill went up her spine, distracting her from her thoughts of the man beside her. Ruby looked around, expecting to see someone else, but they were the only people in the amphitheater. She could have sworn she'd felt the heaviness of eyes gazing upon her.

"There's nothing here," Kai's disappointed voice floated up to them. "Damn," she stared into the darkness of the stone pathway leading from the dais. "I guess we should move on. Who knows how big this temple is? It could take days to explore it thoroughly."

"Did you feel that?" Ruby asked as they made their way out of the chamber.

Kai glanced back over her shoulder to face Ruby. "Feel what?"

Ruby bunched up her shoulders, an itch forming between them. It was almost as if there was a presence at her back, but nothing appeared behind her. "It feels like someone is watching me. Watching *us*. Can you not sense it?" She glanced at Serik, and he shook his head.

"This place is pretty creepy. It's probably just your mind playing tricks on you." Kai paused, holding up her lantern to illuminate an ancient mural. The paint that once must have been vibrant reds and yellows was now brown and faded to the point that it was difficult to discern what the artist wanted to portray.

"I've never seen this goddess before," Kai said, leaning in close to the surface of the painting. "There's some writing here, but I can't make it out. It's in Ancient Andrean."

"It could depict any one of the gods," Serik said as he stepped up next to Kai. "The appearance of the deities in historical text has changed over the centuries. We could be looking at an interpretation of any of them from hundreds of years ago." The wilder frowned as he bent close to examine what remained of the composition. He reached out a hand to brush away some of the grime. "Does she...?"

"She looks a little like Ruby," Gav finished for him as he peeked over the wilder's shoulder.

"What?" Ruby asked in surprise, then squeezed between the men to get a better look at the image. The woman who stared back at her was tall, with delicately beautiful features, dark hair, and blue eyes. Maybe there was a little bit of similarity in the shape of the woman's nose or mouth, but the image was not in sharp focus due to its condition, and patches of the elaborate painting were missing. Still, that face was a little eerie.

Ruby let out a nervous laugh. "I believe you are seeing things. Just because we share the same hair and eye color does not mean this goddess looks like me. Besides, the image is too faded to be seen in much detail."

Serik and Gav both gave her an unreadable glance.

Kai snorted. "They're just seeing things. We should keep going. I'm not sure I want to stay in this place overnight, so we should get as far as we can before we have to turn back."

"It's probably safer than staying outside with more of those monsters," Serik pointed out. "We'll have to camp somewhere before going back to the village."

With a shiver, Gav peered around them, then up at the crack-riddled ceiling. "I'm not convinced that this place will provide ample shelter from the elements. What if it rains?"

"Then we will find somewhere dry to sleep," Serik growled as they moved forward.

The group of four walked down the narrow hallway beyond the amphitheater. The walls were covered in vines growing out of deep crevices in the stone. Late afternoon sunlight filtered down through the gaps in the ceiling, and the floor here was also covered in moldering brown leaves. Ruby wondered briefly how stable this structure was. It would be just their luck to be caught in an earthquake and have the entire place come down on them.

Continuing, Kai led the group, followed by Gav. Serik hung back to walk with Ruby, holding out a hand to her when she needed to climb over a large stone or when the footing was precarious.

The hall they traversed split into three. Kai told them to wait for her signal, then went off down the corridor on the right. It was a nerve-wracking few minutes before she returned, but when she did, she reported that the hallway was a dead end, then crept down the left corridor.

"That way is blocked," she told them a few minutes later. "There is something down there, but there is too much rubble in the way to get through. Hopefully, the treasure isn't that way, but if we can't find anything down the middle corridor and want to pursue it, it will take days to move all that stone."

"What exactly is it that we are looking for again?" Gav asked. "I'm beginning to think that there is nothing of value here."

"We are looking for anything that we can make a profit from, loresinger. I refuse to believe that this trip was for nothing but moldy stone. If so, why was the item so important? I'm sure we will know it when we see it."

Gav looked as if he wanted to say more but kept quiet. He gave Kai a flourishing bow, inviting her to continue leading the way. She snorted, moving past him and down the only remaining path forward.

Ruby appreciated Kai's confidence, but even *she* was beginning to think that the ruin's value rested in the historical and not the material. Why had the Kingfishers been willing to pay Kai a thousand crests to retrieve the key?

Approaching another chamber, Kai held out her hand to stop them, but when she stuck her head in, she reported that it had been caved in. As they passed, Ruby caught a glimpse of a large room with a hole in the ceiling. Rubble covered the floor, and a large tree had grown in the room's center, its branches reaching up toward the sunlight filtering through the destroyed portion of the building. Flashes of color on the walls caught her eye, and she guessed that this chamber was lined with murals much like the one they had seen before.

The sense of eyes following her intensified, and Ruby got a strange feeling of déjà vu, as if she had been here before. But that was insane. She had never been to this temple. She had never even been this far east in her entire life, but for a reason she could not explain, Ruby could almost smell the incense that once burned in these halls and feel the silk robe on her skin, cloth whispering as she walked forward with purpose, to the altar room at the end of this hall and the heart of the temple.

She expected a crowd to be there, men and women lying prostrate on the floor, waiting for their goddess to grace them with her presence. Wine and riches waited for her, she needed only to take them.

Reaching out, she brushed her fingers along the wall, over the colorful tiles that were set in tribute to her and her sisters, who were worshiped alongside her. They were a part of her, but she was the only one who walked Asara at this time.

A sound ahead caught her attention and she slowed. She had a terrible feeling in her stomach that something was wrong.

Ruby shivered and stumbled as her mind snapped back to reality. The wilder caught her arm before she could topple forward.

"Ruby? Are you all right?" he asked, concern and alarm in his voice.

She could only manage a nod, head still spinning from the foreign memories. It had been so vivid. One moment, she was walking the decrepit corridors with her friends, and the next, she had been striding through the temple in its prime, a woman of power going to greet her followers.

"There is a large chamber ahead," she said when she

finally found her voice, "with an altar. If there is a treasure to be had, it will be here. Don't ask me how I know, but I am sure of it."

Ruby saw the look that Gav and Kai exchanged and felt her face grow hot. A wave of nausea fluttered through her stomach, and she had to take a few deep breaths to stay on her feet. They must have been thinking that she had taken leave of her senses. She couldn't blame them. It sounded to her as if she was not in her right mind. How could she know the layout of a temple that had fallen into ruin long before she was born? What was happening to her?

Before anyone could question further, a loud scraping sound echoed down the corridor from beyond the illumination of Kai's lantern, followed by a low chittering. Stone wouldn't make that sound. A feline yowl followed, and Ruby thought it oddly similar to those creatures they had seen two nights ago.

"That's not a good sound, right?" Gav said, looking around nervously. He seemed to have the same thought that Ruby had. "Maybe we should go back."

"And leave here with nothing?" Kai's voice was sharp. "We have to find *something*, Gav, or did you forget why we are here?"

"Quiet!" Serik hissed. Both Kai and Gav glared at him, but neither voiced their ire. As they fell silent, the wilder drew the pistol from his belt and held it ready before him. He looked at Kai, indicating with a nod of his head for her to keep going.

Kai crouched low to the ground and stepped forward, carefully placing her feet where they would avoid the crunch of leaves and loose stone. She pulled her dagger from its sheath, holding it as if ready to launch it forward in an instant.

Ruby stayed rooted to the spot. She could not move as

silently as Serik or Kai, who were almost shadows as they advanced down the corridor. Gav stayed back with her, no doubt realizing the same thing she had. Neither of them was suited for the skillset that their companions possessed.

That chittering sounded again, echoing off the stone around them. From the volume of it, whatever was making the noise was just ahead, in the altar room that Ruby had somehow known was there. Kai set down the lantern and continued forward without the aid of her light. For a brief second, Ruby felt the pull of magic from her friend, but she couldn't identify the spell because Kai murmured no incantation. Kai crouched low and clung to the walls, but otherwise strode confidently forward, as if the darkness was no longer an issue.

After what felt like an eternity, Kai reappeared and beckoned them forward. Serik picked up Kai's lantern as he passed, and they entered a large chamber, the altar room. Ruby stared around as the wilder held the lantern up high, running the focused light along the walls. It felt so familiar to her, though that was ridiculous. Perhaps she had eaten something that didn't agree with her.

The room was large, smaller than the amphitheater, but larger than most of the taverns they had visited on their journey here. Instead of steps leading down, a short incline led up to a large altar sitting atop a circular platform. Kai climbed the stairs as Ruby watched, walking over to the altar.

"This has to be the place," Kai said, examining the stone. "We should spread out and search. I haven't seen any traps yet, but be careful anyway. Hopefully, whatever was making that sound left."

"I don't see any tracks," Serik said as he approached the stairs. The lantern illuminated the floor as he searched. Then he shone the light at the ceiling, where a single beam of sunlight poured through a hole a foot wide. "It could have come from outside."

"If this place is veiled, perhaps the creatures do not know the temple is here," Ruby supplied. "We could be safe from them."

"Perhaps," the wilder said slowly before directing the lamplight back to the floor.

Serik and Gav searched to the right of the altar while Ruby searched the left, gazing up at the murals on the walls as she walked around the perimeter. Colorful tiles of glazed stone had faded over the centuries, much like the paint in the rooms before. There was another image of the dark-haired woman, the one who the others said looked like her, and she got a little closer, leaning forward to examine it.

While she was focused on the image before her, a dark form moved in her peripheral vision. Ruby turned her head, blinking into the shadows. Something in the corner was reflecting the lamplight, and she leaned a little closer.

The reflection blinked.

"Kai…" she said, then much higher and louder yelled. "Kai!" Her voice was threaded through with panic, and she scrambled back from the *thing* that rose out of the shadows.

It was a large cat-like beast, similar to the ones that had attacked them two nights ago, its feline form covered in black and purple fur and four times the size of the others. Yellow eyes instead of blood red peered at her through the gloom, its muscular body reminding Ruby of illustrations she'd seen of the lions that lived to the south beyond the borders of Langard, except without a fluffy mane and much, much bigger. Standing taller than two men, its reflective yellow eyes were the size of dinner plates, and claws as long as daggers dug into the stone. The creature's pupils contracted, lips pulling back to reveal sharp fangs the size of her leg.

Before Ruby could get more than a few feet back, the beast opened its large jaws and let out a high-pitched shriek. Ruby stumbled back, wincing at the noise. The creature crouched, ready to pounce.

Ruby tried to call forth a shield spell, though she doubted it would do anything against the massive creature's bulk. The spell flickered to life, but the beast sprung forward with its back legs and soared over her head, going for her companions instead.

Gav was on the ground, holding his ears and momentarily stunned by the shriek. The large cat landed atop him. Fangs flashed, and Gav screamed as teeth met flesh.

The loresinger kicked out in vain, trying to get out from under the gigantic form, but his arm was between its teeth. Blood splattered the stone floor as it shook its head, and Gav let out another cry of pain.

Blue-white flame flashed as Kai's dagger flew from her hands and buried itself in the creature's neck. Letting out a screech of pain, it released Gav as Kai bounded forward, leaping into the air. She called her blade back to her hand and brought it down on the thing's right flank.

Steel connected with muscle, accompanied by the stench of burning fur, and it screeched again, turning to snap at Kai. She danced out of the way as the wilder shot his pistol.

The bullet should have connected. Ruby didn't know if her eyes were playing tricks on her, but the feline creature seemed to melt into the shadows. With a flicker of darkness temporarily blocking out the sunlight from above, the creature reappeared behind the wilder.

"Look out!" Ruby cried as she held out her hand, reaching for her magic. Static sparked at her fingertips as lightning arced from her outstretched hand to where the form was coalescing. The beast tried to dodge, and Ruby didn't think her spell would hit it in its immaterial form, but even though it wasn't quite solid, it howled as her magic touched it. Its eyes turned to her, and the yellow orbs looked… betrayed?

A colossal paw swiped at the wilder, throwing him ten feet and into the wall. Then the creature seemed to melt into the shadows again. This time, it didn't reappear right away. Ruby and Kai looked around frantically while Serik struggled to pick himself up, and Gav whimpered in pain.

There were a few more seconds of silence, then Ruby lowered her hands.

"What was that thing?" she asked of no one in particular. Despite the similarities to what they faced before, it was different, much bigger, with yellow eyes instead of red, and a supernatural affinity with shadows.

"Whatever it was, it seems to be gone now," Kai said as she put her dagger away, eyes still darting around the chamber. "How is your arm?" she asked Gav, who was still on the ground.

"Hurts like hell," he said. "But my fingers still move."

"Small mercies," Kai muttered as she took a step toward him.

The shadows behind her stirred.

"Kai!" Ruby and Serik yelled together, but they weren't quick enough.

Before their friend could even turn around, the beast reappeared, rising from the darkness cast by the altar. It pounced on Kai and slammed her to the ground. As she hit the rough stone, it placed one of its paws on her right leg, pinning it there.

Its lips pulled back from razor-sharp fangs, bearing down on Kai, whose leg was still stuck. Realizing that trying to escape was futile, she shielded her face with her arms and shut her eyes tight.

"No!" Ruby screamed. Kai couldn't die. Not here, not now. "Stop!"

As her words echoed off the stone, the creature froze a second before it would have torn into Kai. It slowly closed its mouth, turning to peer at Ruby. Head tilting to one side, its tail flicked like a thick snake behind it as it turned to face her and padded forward.

Ruby took a few quick steps back as the beast stalked toward her. Her back hit the altar, and she turned her head away. Tears rolled down her cheeks as her legs shook. It was too close to run from. The creature leaned in, whiskers twitching as it sniffed her like a curious house cat. Its nose nudged her stomach, and she whimpered, waiting for it to open its massive jaws and tear at her delicate flesh.

The sound of thunder echoed throughout the chamber, and the beast jerked away from Ruby, letting out a feral scream. A heartbeat later, flame burst into life, covering one of its shoulders in angry red fire. Black ichor splashed the ground and sizzled on the stone as it whirled away from them, sprinting down the corridor at the far end of the room.

Serik lowered the barrel of his rifle. They waited for the thing to reappear, but the only sound that could be heard was their own heavy breathing.

Rifle still in hand, Serik ran to Ruby. His hands ran over her stomach, and she realized he was searching for any sign of damage.

"I- I am okay," she stammered out. Her legs felt weak, and she slid down the wall, placing a hand over her chest. Her heart raced. "It didn't hurt me."

"Well, it hurt *me!*" Gav called, voice sounding pained and irritable. "A little help, please?"

Serik placed one hand at the back of her neck and touched his forehead to hers in relief, then left her to tend to their friend.

"Is anyone else hurt?" Ruby asked into the silence as Serik

started dressing Gav's wounds and administered the other half of the healing potion he'd taken the previous day.

"I've got a few scratches, but nothing serious," Serik said. Kai murmured in agreement.

"That one was *not* like the others. Did anyone else see how it turned into shadows?" Gav asked, his voice higher pitched than normal.

"It seems that the villagers were right to fear this place," the wilder mumbled as he picked up his rifle and strapped it to his back. "That creature has probably been here for years, and the way it moves might explain why there were no tracks." His eyes flicked to Ruby, but he did not say the words she knew he wanted to utter.

It had only stopped because she had gotten its attention. The creature had been drawn to her. As afraid as she was, Ruby didn't think it would have hurt her. It didn't make sense. What connection could she have to it?

"Should we move forward? I don't think that thing is coming back," Serik said after adjusting the straps on his travel pack. "It was injured, so it will go somewhere where it can rest, that is unless the creature has supernatural healing abilities as well." He scratched at his beard. "If we don't stay much longer, hopefully, it won't bother us again."

"Always the optimist," Gav quipped.

Kai gazed around the room, frowning. "I didn't see anything of value," she said, her voice laced with disappointment.

"We were just attacked by a giant shadow cat creature, and that's what you're concerned about?" Gav snapped waspishly back. "That thing nearly took my arm off!"

"You're fine now!" she said defensively. "We're here for the money. I, for one, would like to find it and get out of here before that thing decides it wants a snack."

Gav glanced nervously at the archway at the end of the

room, the one that led to the corridor where the beast had fled. "Is there another way out of this room?"

"There might be," Kai mused as she craned her neck to look around. "Some of these old ruins have hidden doors that will open if you find the right mechanism, assuming it hasn't crumbled to dust by now."

"Let's find another path. I don't want to follow that thing deeper into the ruins," Serik said, and they all nodded in agreement. Continuing their search of the room, the four of them made sure to check every corner for another passageway.

Ruby examined another mural behind the altar while Kai searched the walls for any sign of a concealed exit. There was something there that Ruby couldn't quite make out, a scratch or a drawing on the wall apart from the colored tiles. She concentrated and pulled power to cast a light spell, letting the little ball of illumination float a few inches above her right shoulder. In the bottom corner of the mosaic tiles, there was something carved into the wall.

"There is an indentation here," Ruby said loudly enough for her companions to hear as she attempted to brush away the dirt and moss covering this section of the mural. "I think it's the same symbol as that key you have." As she cleared away the last of the grime, her fingertips brushed the stone beneath. A jolt of tingling energy made Ruby jerk her hand back. The stone had been hot where she'd touched it.

Kai knelt next to her and examined the markings. Digging around in her back, she pulled out the red sandstone artifact—the reason for their entire journey from Valwen. Holding it out as if to press it against the symbol, Kai paused. She stared down at the trinket in her hand, then looked back up at Ruby. "I have a feeling that *you* should do it."

"What? Why?" Ruby replied, eyeing the object warily. With the creatures and the vision she'd had, Ruby wanted nothing more than to leave this place and never look back. She longed to get this over with quickly, but that didn't mean she was willing to use some ancient artifact that might react to her strangely, as everything else in Ta'Dormus Deva had.

"My instincts are telling me that this will not work unless you do it. You're connected to this somehow. Don't ask me why." Kai held up a hand to silence any objection her friend might have. "It could just be because you look like the goddess this temple was devoted to, or your magic is stronger, like I suggested before, but whatever the reason is, it will probably be safer for all of us if you are the one to do it."

Ruby pursed her lips, realizing her friend was right. If they could avoid getting attacked by whatever else was living in this gods-forsaken temple, she would do whatever she needed to. That was a risk she was willing to take. Reaching her hand out, Kai set the key in her open palm. Ruby couldn't help shivering as the object warmed at her touch.

Running her finger over the symbol carved into the little key, Ruby said a silent prayer to the gods that this worked so that they could leave. She swallowed hard, then set the key into the socket on the wall, symbol-side in.

The sound of something heavy thumping into place echoed throughout the chamber. The mosaic shook, and Ruby jumped back as the wall began to move upward, revealing another chamber adjacent to the altar room. This one was much smaller, shelves with ancient, dust-covered pottery lining the walls and another corridor adjacent to them.

"I knew it would work for you!" Kai said excitedly as she sprang forward and clapped Ruby on the shoulder. "Good job, Ruby!"

Her face felt hot. "All I did was place it on the wall. It would have worked for anyone," she grumbled.

"Just take the credit!" Kai said as she glanced around, carefully placing her feet on the stone as if she were testing her weight. "It seems okay to walk on."

Serik joined them in the room, examining the shelves. "A secret passage would be a likely place to hide valuables."

"Excellent," Gav said as he pushed past them and headed straight for the adjacent corridor. "Let's get out of here!"

"Wait, loresinger!" Serik reached out to grab him and—

The place where he'd stepped sank into the stone around it, and the walls began to tremble.

CHAPTER 23

As the stone shifted under his feet, Serik stumbled into Gav, and the two men went tumbling forward.

"Get back!" Kai shouted and grabbed Ruby, pulling her away from the others as a heavy stone slab came crashing down with a deafening roar. Ruby coughed as dust and dirt filled her lungs. Kai muttered an incantation under her breath, and another ball of white light appeared, floating above her palm. She swore, waving dust out of her face.

The trap had sealed off the corridor, with Serik and Gav on the other side.

"Serik! Gav!" Ruby shouted, jumping to her feet and trying in vain to find purchase on the stone. *"Levarius!"* Power imbued the air, but aside from moving some of the dust around, nothing else happened.

"It's no use," Kai choked out. "That has to weigh at least a ton."

"What good is my magic if I can't use it to help them?!" Looking down at her hands, Ruby clenched her fists in frustration. "The power to control reality, and I can't even lift a rock. What if they're hurt? Or…" She couldn't bring herself to finish the sentence.

Kai leaned close to the stone covering the corridor and cocked her head to listen. "Can you hear us?!" she called.

"We're okay!" Gav's voice drifted through the stone. It was muffled, but he didn't sound like he was hurt. "There has to be another way back. We'll meet you in the entrance room!"

"I can try to disable the mechanism that dropped the stone," Kai muttered, touching the walls around the now-sealed exit. "But I have a suspicion it's on the other side of this." She glanced around the room, searching for any evidence of a release, and her eyes settled on Ruby. "Don't look so anxious. Let's go wait for them at the entrance. If they take more than an hour, we can come back and look for them ourselves."

"How can you be so calm?" Ruby asked. She was about ready to try to blast her way through that wall, though, deep down, she knew that would be a stupid idea. She had already questioned the integrity of the ceiling. "What if they run into that cat thing again? What if they get *hurt*?"

Kai let out a long breath through her nose. "I *am* worried, Ruby, but there's nothing we can do for them right now. We're not that far off from the entrance, and who knows. This could have been an escape route for the priests if they were ever under attack." She chewed on her bottom lip in thought. "Only someone with the key could get into this room, right? It would be stupid if it just led them to their deaths. We could go back to the room with the altar and take the other corridor to look for them, but…" she trailed off.

"But we could run into that monster ourselves or get lost trying to find them," Ruby finished for her. Looking closely, she could see Kai's anxiety in the set of her mouth and brows. Sinking to her knees, Ruby covered her face with her hands. She couldn't lose her friends now. "Are we really that helpless?"

Kai knelt and hugged her. When she pulled back, her eyes were wet. "We've come this far. There's no sense in giving up now," she said. Her smile was weak, but Ruby found comfort in it. Kai sniffed and then stood. "Serik knows what he's doing, and Gav… well, he's survived so far." She held out her hand to help Ruby up. "Come on. We still have to find that treasure."

Taking Kai's hand, Ruby pulled herself to her feet. Her friend was right. She needed to pull herself together.

"Here." Kai handed her a canteen. "We'll rest for a few minutes before going back. I want to examine this room and the last one a little more closely."

Nodding her thanks, Ruby took the canteen and drank. The liquid was soothing on her throat, which was raw from choking on dust. Kai left the light spell she had cast going and picked up the clay containers on the shelves one at a time, peering inside each.

Letting out a frustrated grunt, she headed back out into the room with the altar. Ruby followed her, considerably calmer than she had been, but still worrying about their companions. Gav had claimed that he and Serik were all right, but what if he'd been lying so they wouldn't worry? Or what if they ran into that *creature* again, having to battle it without Ruby and Kai's magical aid?

Kai walked around the perimeter of the room while Ruby stood by the altar. She was no longer interested in the murals on the walls. The only thoughts she had were for Serik and Gav's safety and getting out of the temple as soon as they could. She didn't know what she would do if Serik—

No, she couldn't think like that.

Taking a few deep breaths to calm herself, she stared at the altar. Ruby hadn't been able to get a good look at it before, but now that she was up close, she could see hundreds of little symbols carved into the stone, spilling over the top and continuing down the sides. As with everything else here, these looked like runes, but if they were, she had never seen their like. A glint of light caught her eye, and Ruby knelt for closer inspection.

Near the altar and beside the gouges in the floor that were evidence of their fight with the giant cat beast, one of the stones had shifted, and there was something shiny beneath it.

"I found something!" Ruby called to her friend.

Kai trotted over, a spring in her step. She inspected the area and pulled out her magical dagger. Prying more of the stone away revealed a shiny square buried beneath. "A lockbox!" she exclaimed. "There's a lockbox here!"

Ruby knelt to help her pull the metal object out of the rubble. The box was heavy, taking both women to wiggle it out of the stone. The rectangular object was silver-plated and about as big as a watermelon. It was heavy, and Kai grinned as they set it on the floor in front of them, panting.

"Those two are going to be upset they missed this," she said breathily. "Should we wait to open it? No? My thoughts exactly." Kai hadn't waited for Ruby's answer.

Kai brushed the dirt away, which revealed symbols etched into the lid of the box, ancient Andrean if Ruby were to guess. None of them had memorized the dead language, and it could take them a while to translate. Kai stared at the writing hard, then shrugged.

"Nothing for it then," she said, holding out her dagger to hover over the lockbox. Tapping the lid three times with the blade, she closed her eyes, brows furrowing in concentration. Ruby felt the pull of Kai's magic.

"*Revelare*," Kai murmured as she opened her eyes, irises glowing with a faint ethereal light.

A larger symbol materialized on the lid, appearing to be drawn in blood—a curse.

Ruby gasped, scooting back from the box. Curses were a dangerous perversion of magic, magic that the mages at Valwen did not teach. At one time, mages were hunted close to extinction in the empire because people feared what a wizard could do to those less powerful than they. Most would never use dark magic to curse a person, but it only took a few malicious mages to paint them all with the same bold brush. Mage hunting was outlawed decades ago, but most of the older wizards still remembered and forbade the area of study at Valwen.

Kai extended her blade again, placing the tip in the middle of the symbol. Her power flared as the energy gathered—it was like putting a hand close to a copper electrical wire—and the cursed symbol began to boil and sizzle. The ball of white light flickered and faded from existence as she concentrated, plunging them into heavy shadows, illuminated only by the single beam of sunlight from the ceiling above them. After a minute, the symbol faded away to nothing, leaving no evidence of its presence behind.

Kai grinned and put the dagger away. The light in her eyes also faded, and they returned to their normal green, grassy color.

Her friend may have thought her magic was weak, but even if that were true, the spells she did cast had the skill of a master.

"That was amazing!" Ruby jumped up. "Did you learn that at Valwen? I've never seen a curse dispelled like that!"

Kai snorted. "I doubt those old geezers at the Academy would know anything about blood magic," she said as she took out a smaller spare lantern and lit the wick. Serik still had her bullseye lantern. "Not that it's practiced much anymore, but in my line of work, you still run into cursed items. It's rare, but Alek taught me how to neutralize the magic." Kai frowned. It was the same look she had whenever she spoke of the master of the Thieves Guild.

After a few moments, her smile returned, though it seemed forced. "But anyway, time to open it up!"

Placing her pack on the ground, she took out the same roll of tools that she had used to free Ruby from the mage cage back in Issalden.

She inserted the little metal hooks inside the lock, and after a few minutes, there was a loud *click*, and the top of the lockbox popped open half an inch.

Ruby leaned in close as Kai opened it, a wide grin on her friend's face.

Gold and blue glittered in the lamplight. Old coins with the stamp of an unrecognizable visage stared back at them, with chunks of the blue stones mixed in. Kai picked up one of the stones, examining it closely.

"I think these are uncut sapphires," Kai said, looking up at Ruby. The expression on her face was nothing short of elation. "We found it! I knew there was something here!"

Ruby picked up one of the coins. Around the image of a woman, there was writing, but like the inscription on the outside of the lockbox, it looked like Ancient Andrean. How long had this box been hidden? *Probably since the temple was abandoned*, she thought, answering her own question. A few hundred years, then? Perhaps this was one of the old empresses.

Kai shifted the coins around with one of her lockpicks. "There's got to be a few thousand crests worth of gold and gems here." She pursed her lips, then looked at the entryway at the end of the room and shut the lid. "As much as I want to go through it here, we should get back to the entrance room and wait for Serik and Gav."

She stood, and a look as though she'd just realized something important crossed her face. Kai set the box on the altar and opened it again, scooping out a large handful of coins and gems and holding them out to Ruby.

"Put these in your pack. If something happens to this box, I don't want to leave here empty-handed."

Ruby took the coins and gems with a nod and placed the treasures in the main compartment of her travel pack, wrapping them in the short dress that Johana had given her. Kai handed her another handful, then closed the box again and slipped it into her own travel pack. Wobbling as she shouldered the bag, Kai waved off Ruby's offer of assistance.

Laden with the valuables they'd found, and in considerably higher spirits, the two women put the altar room behind them and picked their way back through the ruins of Ta'Dormus Deva. Ruby was still anxious about the safety of their companions, but at least now they could leave as soon as they were reunited. The temple could house other treasures, but with the dangers that lived in its depths, she hoped what they'd found would be more than sufficient to convince the others to leave.

Ruby ran her fingertips over the mural of the mysterious woman that resembled her as they passed. This place would remain a mystery. She wished she still had access to the library at Valwen to research it further, but that couldn't be helped now. Maybe some mysteries were never meant to be solved.

When they reached the antechamber, the doors they'd come through were still open, and sunlight poured through. Now that Ruby's eyes were adjusted to the dim light of Kai's lamp, the room seemed much brighter than it had before. The darkness didn't seem as oppressive, but she still felt uneasy here. The feeling of eyes on her had never left, and Ruby felt like there was a string attached to her chest, pulling her back toward the heart of the temple.

"Let's wait outside," Kai suggested. "We'll still be able to hear them with the door open, and I really don't like this place."

"Agreed," Ruby said with a sigh of relief.

The sun was still high in the sky when they exited the temple. Ruby had to shield her eyes, wincing at the brightness. It had only been a couple of hours since they'd awoken that morning. Nothing outside had changed. The lean-to that Serik had built was still there, as were the ashes of their campfire and what was left of the burned bread they'd had for their meager breakfast.

"Now we wait," Kai said, sitting next to the little pool created by the waterfall, dipping her hands into its cool depths. She let out a moan of pure pleasure and splashed her face with the cold mountain water.

Ruby knelt next to her and did the same. The water was crisp and clean. She shivered, but as chill as the water was, washing off the grime of Ta'Dormus Deva held more appeal than being warm at the moment.

The sound of creaking branches caught Ruby's attention. She looked up and inspected the trees. It could have been a bird or some other harmless animal making that noise, but they had been attacked by one too many strange beasts as of late. She caught the glint of something through the leaves, and her body reacted before her brain caught up.

"Kai!" Ruby grabbed her friend's arm and yanked her to the side just as there was a whistling sound and a crack as a crossbow bolt ricocheted off the stone where Kai had been kneeling.

Both women sprawled on the ground by the tarn, but Kai was quicker than Ruby, rolling to the side and jumping to her feet. Kai whirled around, seeking their attackers in the shadows of the forest.

A familiar face stepped around a large tree trunk, and Ruby felt the bottom drop out of her stomach.

"Well, well," Joran began, a sharp grin spreading across his face. "Just the two of you? Where are your friends?"

"They'll be here soon," Kai said, exuding confidence, and she reached down to help Ruby to her feet. Ruby saw more movement in the trees. There were others here, not just the Kingfishers lieutenant. She tried to count how many, but it was difficult to pinpoint them in the shifting shadows of the Caligo Forest.

"You know what I think?" he drawled.

"No one cares what you think," Kai muttered, but Joran continued over her.

"I think you left your companions to die in those old ruins. Why else would you emerge by yourselves?" His gaze shifted to Ruby, and one eyebrow quirked up. "You know she's using you, right? Once she gets what she wants from you, she'll hand you over to the duke and collect the reward."

"Shut up!" Kai snarled, drawing her dagger.

Joran flicked his wrist, and there was the sound of shifting rock as a rope was pulled taught. Kai suddenly darted away, and a net fell over Ruby's head, throwing her off her feet as she was jerked back. She put her hands out to break her fall, scraping one on a jagged rock. From her position on the ground, she spotted two men standing above the waterfall, holding the end of a rope that connected to the net. They started pulling, and Ruby was dragged backward as she flailed trying to free herself.

There was a glint of steel in the sunlight, and Kai's dagger flashed, slicing through the rope.

"Now!" Joran shouted. Whistling air reached Ruby's ears, and Kai dodged another crossbow bolt, the shaft with its black fletching sticking out of the ground.

Kai called her blade back to her and flung it away again

into the trees where the bolt had come from. "Same old trick —ugh!"

Kai lurched forward as another bolt hit her in the back, just below her shoulder. She slumped forward as blood soaked through her clothes.

"Kai!" Ruby screamed as she struggled. Concentrating on a spell, she slashed at the netting with her hand and cut through it as if her skin were as sharp as a blade.

As she untangled herself, more men emerged from the forest, holding crossbows and swords. They were surrounded.

With a grunt of pain, Kai ripped the bolt out of her shoulder and summoned her dagger back to her. The silver blade was stained red with blood.

"Run, Ruby!" she yelled, facing off against Joran. "Find the others!"

"I cannot leave y—"

"GO!"

Ruby looked around as the men closed in on them. Joran stared, a sadistic grin stretching his lips. There was another man standing next to him, someone who looked out of place to her. He had an expressionless face that was all sharp angles and midnight-black hair. Their eyes met, and Ruby thought she saw the ghost of a smile. Before she could linger on this new enemy, Ruby choked down a scream of frustration and dashed back into the ruins.

* * *

KAI LET OUT A LONG BREATH. Now, she was the only one between Joran and her retreating friend. It would be easier if she didn't have to worry about protecting anyone else. With any luck, Ruby would find the others quickly and bring them back to help. Serik and Gav had to be close. At least, she hoped they were. As good as Kai was, she wouldn't be able to take all these men by herself, but she could hold them off for a little while.

The wound in her back throbbed. She was pretty sure the bolt had glanced off bone, and judging by how she was still breathing fine, it hadn't punctured a lung. She glared at Joran. This guy just didn't know when to give up.

Kai backed up toward Ta'Dormus Deva as Joran's men closed in on her. None of them were guild members that she knew personally, but she thought a few of the faces were familiar. She counted eight thieves in addition to Joran and a man that she knew she had never seen before, the one with black hair. Kai didn't know what it was about him, but there was a glint in his eyes that told her he was dangerous. There could have been more people still hiding in the brush.

A little overkill, Joran, Kai thought to herself as she surveyed the others.

"So, what is your plan now?" she asked, trying to distract them from Ruby. "Attack us in the middle of nowhere, and then what? Drag us back to the village and wait for the train? That would be pretty suspicious. The villagers might not take it very well." Kai focused on her dagger, which was buried in the trunk of a tree after it had grazed one of the men who'd fired at her. It would only take her a second to retrieve it and throw.

Joran sneered at her. "Do you think I would tell you what we were planning? I thought you were smarter—"

As the smooth leather hilt reappeared in her fingers, Kai launched the dagger at Joran's smug face, but his sword flashed and knocked it out of the air.

He *tsked.* "Really, Kai? Now that I know what you can do, that little stunt won't work again." Joran waved one hand, gesturing to the others.

Kai tensed, listening for all she was worth. There was the

click and snap that came with a projectile being released, and she danced to her left, dodging, then immediately taking another step back as a second bolt came at her.

She swore under her breath. At this rate, they would eventually hit their mark, and it would be over for her. Not to mention that her shoulder still throbbed painfully, distracting her. Joran would drag her and Ruby back to Issalden, and she would have to face the wrath of the Guild. Kai doubted she would survive for long, even if Alek defended her. She would rather face her death than be at the mercy of the madman before her.

What she needed to do was buy herself some time.

"How much of the reward did Alek promise you? It must be a lot to come out to this remote backwater." She laughed, hoping it would throw him off. "Or maybe he didn't, and you're just as stupid as you look. There are things in those ruins that will gleefully feast on your entrails if you step foot in there. Are you sure you want to send your men in for that?"

If anything, Joran's smile became sharper. There was something he knew that Kai didn't. She wanted to wipe that smug smile off his face.

Kai glanced around. She counted no fewer than four crossbows pointed at her. It would be hard to dodge all the shots, but what choice did she have? Now, her only decision was to either run back into the ruins and join her friends or stay here and fight to give them time to charge in like the cavalry.

If she went back inside, there was no guarantee that Joran would follow her. They could just wait for them out here. She and the others would have to leave the ruins eventually, and when they did, they would be walking right into an ambush.

No, it was better to keep them busy for as long as she

could. The others would come soon. She had to have faith in them.

"You'll never have her," Kai taunted Joran. "If you get through me, the others will keep her safe. The duke will just have to find himself another bride to torment."

Joran laughed then, making Kai feel like she was really missing something.

"You still don't get it, do you?" the Thieves Guild lieutenant asked, mirth still in his tone. "I'm not here for Miss Valestris, though she will be an entertaining prize. I'm here for the one who betrayed the Guild. I'm here to kill *you*."

CHAPTER 24

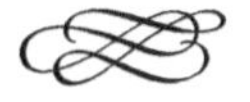

Joran was here to kill her. On Alek's orders. Kai stared at the lean Thieves Guild lieutenant, unable to believe the words he was saying. She felt numb. Rationally, Kai knew that anyone who turned their back on the Guild as she'd done would have a death mark placed on them—a bounty that any in the Guild could collect—but she never thought that Alek would have approved one on *her*. Alek cared for her, didn't he? Why would he have authorized her assassination?

"You're lying," her voice sounded uncertain, even to her ears.

Joran grinned, and the smug look on his face made Kai want to stab him. "Why would I lie about that? You know what happens to those who betray the Guild. Only death awaits those foolish enough to oppose us."

He took a step toward her, and Kai backed up, keeping the same distance between them.

"I would have never acted against the Guild if you hadn't attacked us first," she reasoned. "Alek was supposed to meet with me."

"You put that girl above the welfare of your comrades," Joran growled, mirth disappearing from his features. "Alek is convinced you are under her spell, but I think she paid you off, and you're just another filthy traitor."

Kai screamed in frustration, summoning her dagger and hurling it at the nearest man pointing a crossbow at her. Dodging out of the way of two more crossbow bolts, she pulled the pistol she rarely used from her belt. She'd loaded it this morning before heading into the ruins and prayed that the lead ball was still properly in place. She aimed and fired, not at Joran, but at the last crossbowman. The pistol barked, and the man jerked, dropping his weapon and buying her precious time.

Letting the firearm tumble from her fingers, Kai dashed forward, pulling her rapier from its sheath and slashing at Joran.

Surprising him with the sudden ferocity of her attack, the Kingfisher raised his own sword to block, but he was a second too late. If she could take Joran out, the others might leave with their commander dead.

There was a blur of movement, steel crashed on steel, and her sword connected with another. She met the dark amber eyes of the man with black hair. They struggled against each other, but he was much bigger than she was. The man shifted his weight suddenly, throwing Kai off balance, and hit her in the shoulder with his elbow, the one she'd been shot in.

Kai screamed in fresh agony as hands grabbed her from behind, hauling her away from Joran and the mysterious man who protected him. Someone kicked the back of her knees, and she crumpled forward, kneeling before the Thieves Guild lieutenant as her arms were held out to her sides by two men.

"Go after the girl!" Joran shouted to those closest to the ruins entrance. Kai couldn't see them from where she was being held, but the retreating sound of their footsteps told her that his subordinates had obeyed without a word.

"Stop playing with your food and kill her," the strange man with the amber eyes said, staring down at Kai. The expression sent a chill down her spine. It was so cold and emotionless, she wondered if this man was even human. "We didn't agree on drawing this out."

"You'll still get paid," Joran said, throwing him an irritated look. "It doesn't matter if she dies right away or later."

The other man sighed as if he was indulging the antics of a petulant child. "If this goes wrong, it is on you."

Joran scowled at him but didn't contradict the mysterious man.

Again, Kai wondered who he was. He couldn't possibly be a new recruit, not with the way he was talking to one of Alek's inner circle. Joran was calling the shots, but the mystery man was obviously displeased with the lieutenant's methods. This man was dangerous and moved faster than Kai had expected when he blocked her attack. His dark clothes were form-fitting under his leather armor, and Kai could see the tightly corded muscles in his arms and legs that only came with dedicated exercise. There was a bluish sheen to his weapon. Poison. Her people didn't use poison. Leaving a trail of bodies was a good way to get the emperor's knights after you.

Joran said that he would "still get paid," so that ruled him out as someone deferential to both Joran and Alek. She didn't doubt that all of the men here would get a cut of the reward money, but the man with the black hair did not seem interested in Ruby at all.

That only left one option—a guild assassin.

Guild assassins were a special ranking. While the various guilds took outside jobs and contracts from anyone in the empire, guild assassins only worked for the Guild masters.

They did not accept outside assignments. This ensured that the assassins would never be used against the Guilds, though there had been rumors of some of the assassins breaking the rules recently. This man had to be one of them.

That could only mean that Alek hired him. The truth of it was like a punch to Kai's gut. She'd denied that Alek would do this to her, but here was the proof, standing right in front of her.

She didn't know whether to scream or cry.

Instead, she taunted Joran.

"You needed to hire an assassin just to take me out? One young thief who was never worth your notice?" She flashed him a grim smile. "You're slipping, old man. How long will it be until you are the one on the other end of this assassin's sword?"

Joran stared at her for a few moments, then struck without warning. He hit her across the face hard enough that she bit her tongue. The taste of iron flooded her mouth, and she had to spit out blood. Then he grabbed the front of her shirt in his fist.

Leaning in close, his breath hot on her face, he snarled, "Fuck the duke's gold. After I kill you, I'll kill the other so-called protectors and take the girl for myself. Her screams will be music to my ears." The gleam in his eyes made Kai's insides writhe. "When I'm finished with her, I'll give her to Alek to do with as he pleases. You can die knowing that her future agony is entirely because of you."

He shoved her back as he released her. "String up this traitor," he instructed the two holding her arms. "There is only one punishment for betraying the Guild. Let the 'friend' she risked her life for see what becomes of those who aid her."

The black-haired man frowned as though he didn't like what Joran was doing, but didn't challenge his orders. Kai didn't think the expression was out of sympathy for her but more for a lack of efficiency.

She kicked and struggled as a noose was forced around her neck, but as nimble as she was, she couldn't outmaneuver men twice her size. Kai had spent her life either avoiding fights or ending them quickly. That was how she'd survived all these years.

The past few months flashed through her mind. Her first day at Valwen, when Professor Morel sneered at her as he looked down at Kai's schedule. Ruby's voice, quiet and defiant as she told Kai the reason she'd helped her with Lord Sarlus as they cleaned the alchemy lab. Ruby, Gav, and Serik as they sat around Halis and Aethra's table, eating and laughing.

Kai's hands were bound behind her back, and she was dragged over to the nearest tree, kicking and screaming. One of the men drove his fist into her stomach, cutting off her shouts, and she curled in on herself, retching. He laughed at her pain and gripped her arm, pulling her as her body scraped the dirt.

Intrusive thoughts assaulted her. This was all her fault. If she'd turned Ruby over to Joran in the first place, she'd be on a well-deserved vacation in Langard. If she had never taken Ruby with her, she could have avoided this fate altogether. Ruby would be safely tucked away at Valwen, getting ready to marry the duke, and Kai would be lying low for a few months while the mages searched for her. She stared over at Joran. Her vision blurred with tears. Don't get attached. It was the first rule Alek had taught her.

But she was an idiot. She loved Ruby. Kai would never abandon her to the Duke of Ayrilon or anyone else.

Kai didn't regret her decision, even as the noose tightened around her neck, and she was hauled off her feet.

She still struggled, but there wasn't much she could do to

stop them. Her arms were tied behind her back, and kicking with her feet would just cause her death to come faster. The rope scratched and burned her neck. Kai tried to gasp for air, but she couldn't get in a breath. Tears ran down her face as she looked at Joran. The bastard was smiling.

Kai prayed to the gods that, if nothing else, her friends would avenge her and kill this smug asshole.

One of the men said something. The words didn't register with the sound of her heart pounding in her ears and her body's desperate struggle for air. Her eyes felt heavy, even as she struggled. Maybe closing them for a while wouldn't be so bad.

A piercing scream cut through Kai's darkening thoughts.

"Kai!"

She thought she recognized that feminine voice, but it was becoming difficult to think. Her lips moved, but no sound escaped them.

A tremor that shook her entire world jolted Kai's eyes open again. She hadn't known she'd closed them. Glancing around wildly, she watched as the earth beneath her dangling feet fractured. A few seconds later, the tree Kai hung from split in half with a deafening *CRACK*. There was the snap of breaking wood, and the next thing she knew, she was falling to the ground. She landed on her feet, then sank to her knees, struggling to free herself from her bonds. With forced calm, she brought her bound hands around her bottom and legs, then clawed at the rope around her neck, loosening the noose.

Kai gasped in a deep breath of air, and it was the sweetest thing she'd ever tasted.

There was another thunderous noise, and the thug closest to her fell to the ground, screaming in pain. He held one hand to his gut, where blood gushed from a wound.

With a jolt, Kai's brain started working again. Gunfire.

That sound had been gunfire. But then, what had done that to the tree?

She rolled onto her side, staring at Ta'Dormus Deva.

Serik and Gav stood by the entrance to the ruins, the wilder still holding the smoking rifle in his hands. Gav had a pistol and sword out, pointing it at the nearest opponent, a guildie near the tree line. Ruby was kneeling, her hands touching the ground where the deep crack in the earth started. Their eyes met, and Ruby's were alight from within, glowing an eerie molten gold.

There was a moment when no one moved, shocked by what had just happened. Even Joran and the black-haired man stared. Kai herself blinked her eyes and looked over her shoulder at the tree, unable to believe what she was seeing. The trunk was split in two as though a giant had ripped it apart with bare hands. Had that immense power come from Ruby?

As Ruby straightened, the thieves closest to her flinched, taking a quick step away from her as she turned those eyes on them.

Kai had a second's warning as rocks crunched under booted feet, and then a blade came straight for her head.

She rolled to the side, hands still bound together, and called her dagger to her. The steel from the black-haired assassin's sword sparked as it hit the ground where she'd been just a second before. With reflexes that she could barely track, the blade arced toward her as he brought it up.

Kai tried to roll out of the way again, but he changed direction mid-swing, stabbing down into her abdomen.

Pain shot through every inch of her body as she screamed.

"No!" Gav cried.

Another gunshot rang out, coming from the loresinger's pistol, and the Guild assassin ducked. With a jerk, he pulled his blade from Kai, creating another jolt of searing agony in her gut, and turned his attention to his new enemy.

With a yell of frustration and rage, Gav charged at the assassin, who backed away but maintained an attack stance. Gritting her teeth against the pain, Kai kicked out with her feet, connecting with the assassin's leg, and he stumbled.

It was just the opening Gav needed.

The loresinger sidestepped the assassin's blade and, with a lunge, stabbed into the area between the man's shoulder and chest, where his armor wouldn't protect him.

The black-haired man grunted in pain, then took a few quick steps to get beyond the reach of Gav's weapon.

Serik's rifle clattered when he dropped it and drew his sword.

Ruby strode forward, her steps confident and unhurried. It was almost like she was a different person. The stunned Thieves Guild members seemed to come back to their senses, and action exploded in the little clearing at the entrance to Ta'Dormus Deva.

Serik's blade flashed in the sunlight, knocking a crossbow bolt out of the air that had been aimed at Ruby.

Kai watched her friend raise a hand, palm out, and felt magic fill the air. The water from the little tarn surged forward, washing over Joran and his assassin, pushing them back. The flow circled quickly around Kai, creating a barrier of fast-moving water. Ruby moved her hand like she was batting away an irksome fly, and a jet of water lashed out at the remaining thug who had assisted with Kai's hanging, throwing him back into the trunk of another tree.

Joran stared at Ruby, the shocked expression on his face giving way to seething anger. He stepped around the assassin, pulled his sword, and pointed it at Ruby.

"Kill her!" he commanded his men as he drove his own blade at Gav.

Ruby moved her other hand, and Joran's attack met resistance in the air in front of the loresinger. He swung again, and there was a spark of gold light.

A shield, Kai thought, watching the display with amazement, *and a strong one!* Ruby was holding multiple spells at once. Normally, enchantments like that were weak. A spellcaster's mind could only be focused on so many things, but she seemed to be having no issue maintaining concentration. A real mage. Is that what Ruby had become? How?

Another crossbow bolt flew at her friend, but Serik had been waiting for it, striking the feathered shaft out of the air again. Another man drew his weapon, charging at Ruby. Now, it was apparent why the wilder had stayed behind while Gav had surged forward.

Serik guarded Ruby, moving between her and the thug trying to attack her. He parried the blow intended for her head, using his strength and leverage to push it back.

The man swung at Serik, and the wilder jumped out of the way. Steel clanged on rock as he missed, and the wilder stepped on his opponent's blade as he hit the thief in the jaw with the hilt of his sword and sent the man reeling backward.

A second thief rushed them out of the trees, but before he could get within ten feet of Ruby, a whip made of water lashed out from the liquid surrounding Kai. The tendril wrapped around him and flung the man over to the other side of the tarn. He landed badly and fell into a groaning heap.

Ruby thrust her hands down in front of her, and a shockwave radiated from her, throwing all their attackers off their feet but leaving her allies untouched.

"Joran!" the assassin growled from where he'd taken cover behind the lean-to that Serik had built the previous day. "Order your men to retreat! The cost of winning is too high!"

Joran scowled at the man, but then his eyes flicked over the clearing. More than half of his men were injured. He grimaced, glaring around at them, and placed two fingers in his mouth, giving three sharp whistles. It was the signal for them to withdraw.

Joran stared hard at Kai. The water around her slowed, and she could sense that whatever spell Ruby had used was fading fast. Kai clutched at the wound in her abdomen, blood soaking her clothes as he took a step toward her.

"Leave her!" the assassin yelled. "The poison will finish her off!"

Joran grimaced but turned away from Kai, leaving her bleeding on the ground.

"I have a feeling that we will meet again," the black-haired man said to Ruby.

She couldn't have heard him with everything going on around her, but she stared back at him as if he were an insignificant bug on her shoe.

"*Pray to your gods that we do not,*" she responded in a voice that was unfamiliar to Kai, and her words resonated as if they were coming through the earth itself. Then she turned from him. It was a dismissal.

He smiled at that and stared at Ruby with a mixture of respect and just a touch of excitement. Then, with a wave of his hand and a burst of magic that even Kai could sense, he disappeared into the shadows of the forest.

Her friends stood there, unmoving, watching the trees. Kai tried to sit up, but pain flared in her midsection, and she gasped at the intensity of it. Gav was at her side in an instant, raising her head off the ground. She was so distracted by the pain that she almost missed what happened next.

Serik approached Ruby and placed a hand on her shoulder. "Ruby..."

Ruby flinched, blinking her eyes like she had just woken

from a nap, and looked around. Her eyes had returned to their normal light blue as she stared at the wilder. "Serik? What happened? Where is Kai?"

He frowned.

Kai coughed, turning away from them and closing her eyes. She felt hot all over, like a heated iron was pressed up against her, burning into her skin. There was a cry of surprise and shifting rock. Then a hand took hers.

"No, Kai..." Ruby's words were low and quavering. "Please, you have to survive." Her voice cracked as she spoke, and she squeezed her friend's hand hard.

Kai felt herself smile. The poison was doing its job, just like the assassin had said. Even if she died here, at least she would be surrounded by friends. If she had been traveling with members of the Guild, her injuries were grave enough that they would have left her to die and called it a reasonable loss. Kai herself had had to make decisions like that in the past. It didn't feel good to leave comrades behind, but if they were as good as dead anyway, there was no helping it. The Guild only had one healer, and that woman stayed at head-quarters and didn't go out on missions. If one of them were hurt in the field, they would have to pray that they had a spare potion on hand and that the simple alchemical concoc-tion could heal their wounds. But potions didn't work well on poisons.

Maybe Alek wouldn't have left her behind, but he had already abandoned her once, hadn't he? Joran had been sent here to kill her. Wouldn't that have been at Alek's orders? Maybe he had already turned his back on her too.

But it was different with Ruby, Serik, and Gav. They cared about her, actually cared *for* her. They hadn't known each other for very long, Serik and Gav especially, but she had the feeling that they wouldn't leave her behind. Was it pure luck that they had run into each other, or could it have been fate? Were the gods watching out for her? Kai could feel the tears in her eyes as Serik tended her wound. Gav had laid her head on his folded jacket and taken up her hand while Ruby brushed her hair out of her face, murmuring that she would be all right. Kai never thought that she would have friends like this, and before now, she never understood the need to protect someone else.

These people were good, and they loved her. What more could she ask for?

"Grab my medical pouch," she dimly heard the wilder say. The hands on her face disappeared for a time.

Kai felt like she was floating in a pool of cool water. It was a relief compared to the fire under her skin she'd felt moments before. She wanted to drift, but there was something gripping her hand, keeping her from floating away. There was a feeling in the back of her mind that this pull was important, but she couldn't think of why.

A burning sting in her side brought her back to reality.

"Fuck, that hurts!" she swore, writhing as strong hands held her down.

"Keep her still!" Serik growled, stuffing a green paste that looked like regurgitated grass into her stab wound. Someone had cut her shirt off, and all that was covering her was the strips of linen that she used to bind her breasts.

"What in the hells are you doing?!" she gasped through the pain, trying to get away from him.

"Saving your life!" the wilder snapped.

"It's okay, Kai!" Ruby was holding one of her arms down. Gav held the other and had a knee on her thigh.

"The hell it is!" She twisted as Serik dug into his pouch, pulling out a small vial filled with a bright-orange liquid.

"Open your mouth," the wilder commanded.

Whatever he had looked vile, and Kai didn't want to listen to him, but she remembered how he had tended to Ruby's wounds. Maybe he *could* save her. That place where she'd been drifting before called to her, and she was terrified of going back. Kai had a feeling that if she did, she wouldn't wake up again.

She opened her mouth, and Serik poured the contents of the vial into it. A bitter liquid filled her mouth. She had been right. The concoction tasted the way rotting fruit smelled, and she almost threw it back up.

"That wasn't the potion, was it? Shouldn't you use the potion?" Gav said, alarmed. He forced her flat onto her back again, and Kai glared up at him.

"Do you see how the blood is coagulating around the wound?" Serik said as he pocketed the now empty vial. "There was blue-viper venom on that blade. I don't want the wound healing over with the poison still there. The herbs will draw it out, and the antitoxin will help her body fight it off, but it needs time to work." He stared down at Kai, a mix of worry and frustration in the creases of his face. "You're fortunate it didn't go deeper."

"Yeah, lucky me," she growled back.

"Not that lucky," he said with a scoff. "You won't be able to take the potion until morning." Serik glanced over his shoulder, looking at the entrance to the ruins, then back at Kai. If she didn't know better, she would have sworn there was sympathy on his face. "This is going to hurt. A lot."

The wilder placed his arms under her knees and back as the others moved out of his way, then he lifted her.

She screamed out another string of expletives as he carried her into the ruins. There was something discussed about getting her out of the open in case Joran decided to return, but she didn't really hear it over her own shouting.

It felt like her throat had been turned inside out and dragged along the rocky ground by the time Serik set her down on a pile of blankets Ruby hastily laid out. The wilder shoved the top of a flask into her mouth, and she coughed as burning liquor ran into her stomach. He made her drink what was left in the container, and she wanted to curse him again. She needed healing, not to get drunk!

She opened her mouth to say as much but closed it again with a hiss as he started tending to her shoulder, where she'd been hit with the crossbow bolt.

After a few agonizing minutes, the edges of her vision began to darken. She clutched Ruby's hand in a death grip, but everything felt fuzzy.

"It's okay, Kai." Ruby's voice was the last thing she heard before everything faded to black. "You are going to be okay."

CHAPTER 25

They decided to spend the night in the ruins despite the giant beast that still lurked in Ta'Dormus Deva. Ruby and Gav secured all the doors they could while Serik watched over Kai. Hopefully, they were far enough from the heart of the temple that they would be safe from anything that might go looking for them.

After they had finished with that task, Serik built a small fire, trusting that the smoke would filter out through the holes in the ceiling.

The group was quiet as they ate that night, and it was decided that Ruby, Serik, and Gav would each take a shift, watching and listening for any activity while Kai slept.

Ruby spent her four hours staring at the doorway that led deeper into the temple, fearing that at any moment, that giant black cat-like beast would emerge from the darkness and come after them. It was a relief when her time was up, and she could wake Gav to take over for her.

Even though she was exhausted, she lay awake, staring at the stone ceiling illuminated only by the light of their campfire. She couldn't stop thinking about what had happened earlier that day when she had seen Kai hanging from that tree. Anguish, fear, and rage had washed over her. The next thing she knew, Kai was on the ground, poisoned and bleeding out. She didn't know how they'd gotten there or why their opponents were running away. That man in black had given her a sharp smile before he'd disappeared into the shadows. The ground was cracked, and the tree that those men had hung Kai from was torn in two.

It had been because of *her*, Gav had told Ruby later. She had done those things. But that was impossible. Power like that hadn't existed in Asara for thousands of years. She tried to deny it, but he and Serik were convinced that she had done something extraordinary. The worst part was she couldn't even reliably deny their claims since she couldn't remember the events between exiting the ruins and Joran's men running. Ruby didn't understand what was happening to her.

"Are you still awake?"

Opening her eyes, Ruby pushed herself into a sitting position. Gav was lounging by the dying flames of the fire, looking back at her. Getting to her feet, Ruby approached and settled down on the rubble next to the loresinger.

"How could you tell?" she asked quietly, not wanting to disturb the others.

"You keep shifting around. If you were really sleeping, you wouldn't have moved so restlessly," the loresinger replied. He gazed at the dark opening to the inner temple, much as she had done while on watch. "Are you still thinking about what happened outside?"

Ruby sighed, and Gav turned his blue eyes to her.

"I am, but more that it is unnerving that I cannot remember doing anything." Ruby curled into herself, hugging her knees to her chest. "If what you and the others say is true, then there is some power within me that could take over at any second. That is dangerous, is it not?"

Gav leaned toward Ruby, touching his shoulder to hers. "I'll be the first to admit it was a little unnerving seeing you like that, but you only used your power to help Kai and scare off our enemies. I don't think it's as uncontrollable as it seems."

Ruby didn't reply. She knew he was downplaying the situation to make her feel better, but how could she when she didn't even know herself what was happening?

"I'll just make sure never to get on your bad side. Gods help those who do," he nudged her with his shoulder, drawing a small smile from her.

"At the very least," Gav continued. "Hopefully, this means that we won't have to deal with the Kingfishers again for a time. I think you thoroughly terrified that vile man." He was referring to Joran, the Thieves Guild lieutenant.

"It would be nice to have some peace, would it not?" she said, words slightly muffled with her face still buried in her knees.

"Peace is overrated and boring." He winked at her. "What I'm interested in is the next story. I would prefer less blood and struggle, but I'll be here with you wherever we go. It'll be exciting."

Ruby looked up at him. She knew that Kai would stay with her, but was Gav promising his companionship as well?

The loresinger met her eyes and gave her the slightest nod.

Ruby hid her tears by pretending to be interested in a stone on her opposite side. Once she had a handle on her emotions again, she leaned her head on the loresinger's shoulder.

Gav let out a short, amused breath and allowed her to lean on him until she felt tired enough to sleep.

In the morning, they were all still exhausted, but in one piece. Nothing had come after them during the night. No Thieves Guild. No cat creature. No assassin. As they packed to leave, Serik knelt next to Kai to check on her wound. He gave her the last healing potion that they had, then stuffed the empty vial back into his medical bag.

"You'll be on your feet by the end of the day. The antivenom from yesterday purged the poison from your insides, and this one should do the rest, but I'll have to carry you back to town."

"I can walk on my own," Kai said, indignation heavy in her voice.

"If you try to walk, you'll do more harm than good," he argued.

With a look of defiance, Kai got to her feet but wobbled dangerously. Serik caught her arm, and she snatched it back. She almost did fall over then.

"Stop being stubborn. The faster we can get out of this forest, the sooner you can collect on what was found." He was referring to the pile of gold and gems they had pried from the stones in the altar room. Ruby had told Serik and Gav about it when Kai was sleeping.

Letting out a frustrated sigh, Kai said, "Fine, but if you tell anyone about this, I will kill you." She glared at Ruby and Gav. "You two as well."

Gav placed his right hand over his heart and gave her a solemn nod, and Ruby turned away, trying to hide her smile. Serik turned and knelt, allowing her to climb onto his back.

Kai dug around at the pouch at her belt and pulled out a feather, the focus she used to cast her lightweight spell. She winced, and the feather jerked in her hand, a sure sign that she had trouble focusing.

"Here, let me help," Ruby said as she plucked the feather from Kai's fingers and concentrated on the feel of the soft bristles against her skin. She held her palm up, and the feather dissolved into tiny motes of light. Continuing to concentrate on the effect she wanted, Ruby poured power into the spell. Her legs began to shake as the magic left her, and when she thought it was enough, she pressed her hand on Kai's shoulder, her body absorbing the spell.

Serik stood easily with Kai on his back. She should have weighed no more than a child now.

"I cast a variation of that lightweight spell, the one you used the night we left Valwen," Ruby explained. "The effect is not as dramatic, but it will last longer, hopefully until we get back to town."

"If we hurry, we might be able to get back to the village tonight," Serik said as they picked up their gear. Gav picked up Serik's travel pack. "This time, we know exactly where we are going and what path to take, so it shouldn't be too diffi-cult to get back to Calsith."

That sounded good to her. Ruby was beyond tired of this forest.

When they exited the ruins, there was barely any color on the horizon, and the early songbirds had not started their twit-tering. Serik borrowed Kai's lantern, using it to light their way as they walked through the thick brush of the Caligo Forest. With Ruby's spell active, the wilder had little trouble carrying Kai's small form on his back. Compared to the first time they traversed these woods, they weren't stopping as much as before.

"I'm following the tracks we made two days ago," Serik explained when Ruby mentioned that it felt they were making much better progress. "It's not a direct way back, but it's faster than trying to navigate through the forest." He pointed to multiple sets of footprints. "The Guild left in the same manner. We should keep an eye out for them, just in case."

A little after midday, they reached the remnants of their camp from the first night. It looked like it had been rifled through. Serik's lean-to was mostly destroyed, and the ashes from their first fire were scattered around the little clearing. The wilder set Kai down on a rock and examined what remained of their camp.

Ruby sat next to her, weary from the hike through the trees and the spell that slowly sapped her energy. To maintain the enchantment on Kai, she had to keep feeding the working. It was a slow drain, but they had been walking for hours now, and it added up. Ruby took a drink from her canteen, wiping the back of her mouth with her sleeve. She wanted to pour it over her face but resisted the temptation.

Gav sat on Kai's other side.

"How are you feeling?" the loresinger asked her, sounding anxious.

"Not great," Kai said as she stretched, wincing a little when she raised her arms over her head. "But it doesn't hurt as much as it did. I'm mostly just sore now. A few more hours, and I should be able to walk on my own."

He smiled at that. "I'm sure our woodsy friend would love to keep carrying you around on his back like a child."

Kai punched his arm, and he laughed.

Amused at their bickering, Ruby closed her eyes and took in a deep breath through her nose. It was good that everyone was in high spirits. There had been a nagging feeling at the back of her mind all day that they might run into Joran and his band of thieves again as they made their way back to the village, but it seemed as though those thugs had been equally eager to leave the forest.

"The Guild came through here when they were tracking us," Serik said as he finished searching the camp. "Tore everything apart. An animal wouldn't have caused so much destruction." He looked at Ruby and leaned down a little. "You look tired."

"Magic is draining," she responded, and her voice sounded sluggish, even to her ears.

"Was that spell really so powerful?" Gav asked.

Kai beat Ruby to the answer. "She's been fueling it all day. Spells like that require constant energy." She looked a little guilty, but Ruby just smiled at her.

"I'm happy to do it."

"I think it's safe to rest here for a little while. The Guild tracks go off into the forest from here, so we won't be following them anymore." Serik stared off into the trees. "Hopefully, we won't see them again."

They ate lunch at their former campsite, then continued on the long trek back to Calsith. Around sunset, Kai demanded that Serik let her down, insisting that she felt well enough to walk on her own. Ruby let her spell fade away with a sigh of relief and a slump to her shoulders. Serik gave her a concerned look, but she waved him off. She just wanted to get back to town and have a hot meal.

It was a few more hours before the trees started to thin. Ruby was beginning to wonder if they would have to camp out in the forest again. Perhaps they had underestimated how long it would take to walk back to the village.

"Do you see that?" Gav asked, his voice gaining a measure of excitement.

Ruby looked in the direction the loresinger indicated. Through the breaks in the trees, she could see specs of light. Lamplight. She couldn't stop herself from grinning, even if she wanted to.

They had made it back to Calsith.

CHAPTER 26

It was long after sunset when they finally arrived back at the village. Their pace slowed considerably in the dark, as every step needed to be carefully selected to avoid injury in the uneven and root-filled undergrowth of the Caligo Forest. The night grew chill quickly, and the only thing that kept them going was the promise of a warm fire and soft beds. Ruby wanted nothing more than a nice long bath after their misadventures.

"You're alive!" Raul exclaimed as he nearly dropped his mug when Ruby, Kai, Gav, and Serik entered the tavern. He was sitting at the bar, talking to the innkeeper. "And in one piece!" Raul gave a furtive glance to the six other villagers by the hearth. They all avoided looking at the newcomers. "We had a wager going whether you'd come back or not," the old hunter said sheepishly.

"That's reassuring," Kai said with a scoff. She looked at old man Dorin—the one who had told them the story of his cousin's death—and her expression turned thoughtful, then set her bag down on the table. "I'll be right back," she said before approaching the old man. She knelt beside him, speaking too softly for anyone else to hear.

"Did your friend find you? The one who came after you?" Raul asked, finishing his drink and waving to the man behind the bar to bring him another. "I gave him my spare map. Hopefully, he didn't get lost."

Ruby opened her mouth to ask who he was talking about, but paused. He must have been referring to Joran. In a flash of insight, she realized the Thieves Guild lieutenant had told the villagers that he was one of their companions.

"He didn't come back through here?" Serik asked, looking first at Raul and then at the innkeeper. Both men shook their heads. He must have come to the same conclusion Ruby had. He seemed to mull that over before asking, "Anyone else arrive on the train?"

"Not since you lot."

"I'm sure he's fine," Serik muttered, then louder said. "Drinks for all of us, please, and hot food if you have any left. Do you still have our rooms available?"

Leaving Serik to deal with business, Gav and Ruby settled down at a table in the corner.

"After everything that happened, I can hardly believe we made it back in one piece," the loresinger said as he leaned back in his chair. He lifted his booted feet onto the chair beside him and groaned in relief. "No offense, but I'd rather run around naked in the streets of Valkea than go on another one of those woodsy adventures with you. Let's try to keep our endeavors restricted to populated cities from now on, yes? No more shadow monsters and camping."

"I cannot say that I disagree with that sentiment," Ruby said as Serik slid into the chair next to her. He handed her a large iron key, the same one that they'd had before leaving town two days ago.

"It all depends on how much we can get for what we

found," the wilder said, having apparently overheard Gav's grumbling. "We'll need to buy more supplies while we are here and get train tickets in the morning, but I suppose that's a problem for tomorrow."

Ruby's breath caught in her chest, and she buried her face in her mug to keep her expression hidden. Serik's words made it sound like he was planning to stay with them.

Kai soon joined them, trailing five of the villagers. She stood next to Gav while the farmers and townsfolk crowded their table. Gav seemed bemused, and Ruby raised her eyebrows at her friend, but she wasn't paying attention to them.

"As I was saying!" Kai all but shouted, hopping up onto a chair. "It was huge!" She threw her hands up to the ceiling. "At least fifteen feet tall and teeth like swords! It came out of the shadows, attacking like some massive feline killing machine!"

Kai went on to tell the villagers of their adventures in the ruined temple, leaving out most of the actual details and exaggerating their battles. She didn't mention the Kingfishers, instead substituting them with roving bandits. Gav grinned as he watched her, no doubt entertained by her story and giving helpful commentary when she looked like she was searching for the right words. Clapping and shouting questions at her, the villagers bought more drinks for them as she finished her tale and took a bow.

Ruby smiled. Kai had made their journey sound like a grand adventure fit for the storybooks. The whole tavern was enthralled, watching this brave young woman with rapt attention and adoration shining in their eyes. Even Serik seemed amused by her antics. They wouldn't be famous by any meaning of the word, but this was sure to be a tale that the townsfolk would not soon forget.

Before long, they were already into their third round of

drinks. The roasted vegetables and sliced pork had been eaten quickly, and Ruby was pleasantly warm and full, thanks to the blazing hearth. The crowd of curious villagers had slowly drifted away, and as the night grew later, only one or two remained. Ruby found her mind wandering, pondering the events that had led her to this place with these people.

Would she have made the same choices if she were given the chance to do it again? She thought she would. Even with the hardships they had faced thus far, they were all alive, and Ruby was free to make her own decisions for the first time in her life. She was surrounded by people who cared about her as a person, not her title or the advantages she could provide them with.

"Ruby, are you listening?" Kai's voice broke through her thoughts, and she blinked. Now, she, Kai, and Gav were the only ones left. Kai's pocket watch was sitting open on the table. It was past midnight.

"What?" Ruby rubbed one of her eyes with the palm of her hand. "I am sorry, I must not have heard you."

"You must be tired," Gav said. "You haven't said anything in at least ten minutes."

"I am fine." She waved a hand and picked up her mug again, but it was empty.

Kai and Gav snickered.

She put the mug down. "Where did Serik go?" Ruby asked, ignoring their looks and leaning over in her seat, scanning the room for him.

"Oh, leave him," Kai said. "He probably went to take a piss or something. You'll be able to find him easy enough later." She winked at Ruby.

"That's what I love about you," Gav said as he rolled a coin over his fingers, the metal reflecting light. "Your genteel manner and discretion."

"That's why everyone loves me, loresinger." Kai took a big swig from her own mug, undeterred. Then she turned back to Ruby, a mischievous look in her eyes. "If you really want to get his attention, just crawl into his bed without any clothes on. He won't be able to look away."

Gav dropped the coin he was fiddling with.

Ruby gaped at her friend, scandalized. She couldn't believe Kai had just said that! Despite the thoughts and—though she was loathe to admit—urges she'd had for the wilder, that was not the kind of topic one discussed openly. Ruby wasn't some blushing maiden, but subjects like that were spoken of behind closed doors, and *not* in mixed company. Burying her face in her hands lest it light up the night with its glow, she stammered out, "W-why would you say that?"

"What? It's true!" Kai took another deep drink from her mug. "He's had his eye on you since we met him in the forest. The first forest," she clarified, with a glance at the loresinger. Then she sighed. "Look, I know I was suspicious of him, but he really cares for you, what with risking his life for us and all. I may not like it, but I can accept it." Kai gave Ruby a side-long look and grinned. "With the way he watches you, I bet he would have taken you that night in the cabin if I hadn't been there."

Ruby sank even lower in her chair, praying to the gods that Serik could not hear them.

"She's going to die of embarrassment if you keep that up," Gav supplied with a devious grin on his face, picking up the coin again.

Kai shot him a glare. "And who asked you? You'll know when I'm seeking your input, loresinger." Dismissing him with a sniff, she turned back to Ruby. "He wouldn't turn you down if you went to him. Come on! I bet you haven't had a good toss in the sheets since, well, ever!"

"I think you are drunk," Ruby said as she peeked at her friend between her fingers, embarrassment causing her to giggle.

"I am not," Kai said indignantly. She went to stand, but her words were immediately undermined as she lost her balance and had to grab the edge of the table to keep from falling. "Maybe just a little," she said with a sheepish grin. "Shall we get another drink?"

"Dear *wife*," Gav began, taking one of her hands in his and drawing her attention away from Ruby, "I believe you should drink water."

"Again, who asked you?"

They kept up the banter, but even though Kai and Gav were scowling at each other, Ruby was certain they were both enjoying themselves based on how they watched one another. They reminded her of the groundskeeper and his wife back home on her parents' estate.

After another minute or two of listening to them, Ruby got up and slipped away from the table without either noticing. They had been too wrapped up in a conversation about how they were going to split the jewels and coins that they'd found in the ruins. Kai was shouting about a "finder's fee" as Ruby started making her way up the stairs. The inn had grown cooler as the night went on and the fire died down. The innkeeper was cleaning up, getting ready to abandon them for sleep, and placed a pitcher on the counter if they wanted more drinks. Ruby smiled at him as she climbed the stairs. She planned to grab a shawl from her pack to ward off the chill, and maybe stop by Serik's room to see if he was there.

Before she could make it more than a few steps down the hall, however, the door to Serik and Gav's room opened, and the wilder stepped into her path. He locked the door again with the iron key and only paused when he saw her.

"Ruby? Are you going to sleep?"

Shaking her head, she remembered Kai's words, and heat blossomed across her face again. "I just wanted to get my shawl. It's gotten a bit brisk downstairs."

Serik nodded. "As close to the mountains as we are, I'm surprised it's not snowing."

"Do not speak of it! I, for one, would rather you not curse us. The weather may change to spite you, and we may be stuck here for longer than planned." That made the wilder laugh, and Ruby grinned at him.

There was the sound of footsteps, and the innkeeper approached them, heading for another of the rooms at the end of the hall. Yawning, he mumbled a soft "Goodnight" as he passed.

Ruby stepped toward Serik to get out of the way, only realizing their close proximity after the man was gone. Shuffling back, she cleared her throat. "Kai and Gav are fighting over the split of the findings," she said to fill the awkward silence. "Honestly, between the two of them, I doubt there will be anything left for us."

"I wouldn't worry about that," Serik said, stepping toward her and closing the distance she'd created between them. "Kai has been adamant about taking care of you since this journey began."

Ruby withdrew another foot. "Yes, well, I just hope that we can get a fair deal on the cache. I suppose it is not every day that a broker is presented with a sack full of treasure. I am sure it will take time to liquidate."

"What will you do after we return? Those gems won't last forever, but you should be able to set yourself up with something, get yourself started on a new life." Serik took another step toward her. He was close enough now that she could reach out and touch him.

"Honestly, I do not know," Ruby replied with a shrug. "I

have never imagined a life outside of what was already planned for me." She took a small step back. "What about you? Are you going to go back to 'wildering'?" she asked, trying to keep any emotion out of her voice. "Travel back to the Wytchwood, or perhaps go elsewhere?" She hoped that he would stay with them, with *her*, but she couldn't bring herself to say the words. Given that the Thieves Guild was still a threat to Kai, it was not safe to stay by her side. If he chose to leave because of that, Ruby would not blame him.

"I'm not sure." Hazel eyes studied her face, and he leaned closer to her, close enough that she could smell him. It was intoxicating. "Do you *want* me to stay with you?"

Ruby tried to move away from him again, but her back hit the wall. All she could hear was her own shallow breathing as Serik place a hand on the wall behind her, pinning her there. Reaching up to her face with his other hand, his fingers brushed her neck, his touch warm on her cool skin.

"Serik…" she whispered as he placed one finger under her chin, tilting her head back. He was so close. The wilder's eyes were half-lidded, and his breathing shallow. Their breath mingled together, and the warmth of it made Ruby lick her lips.

He bent his face down to hers, their noses touching. His lips hovered just an inch from hers.

"Do you want me to stop?" he asked her, and she knew that if she said yes, he would let her go and walk away. They'd shared a kiss before, but Ruby felt that he was asking for more than just their lips touching. The two of them stood at the edge of a precipice. If they stepped over, there would be no going back. She could refuse him, and they could keep their relationship as it was, friendly and always with a hint of something more. That was safe.

But it wasn't what she wanted.

Ruby was no stranger to intimacy, but she'd never experienced a passion so strong that it seared all thought from her mind. When Mikel had held and touched her, it felt like she'd been fulfilling the terms of an agreement. A chore that she performed just to make him happy. There hadn't been much emotion, at least, not on her part. After what little pleasure he gave her passed, she still felt no love for the duke, and despite his attempts to retrieve her, she suspected that his desire for her was born more out of his need for control than anything even remotely akin to affection.

This felt right. Serik felt right. No one had told her to do this. No bargains had been made. No papers signed. This was *her* choice. By the gods, she wanted him, and she wanted him now.

"No," she said, her voice barely reaching her ears. "Do not stop."

Serik pressed his lips against hers.

At first, it was a soft kiss, innocent and tender. His touch was gentle as if he was afraid she would break, but when Ruby kissed him back, whatever restraint he had crumbled. Serik wrapped an arm around her waist and pulled her firmly against him, all lean muscle against her supple curves. Ruby's lips parted to allow his tongue into her mouth, and she tasted the bitter drink and some earthy flavor she couldn't define. Something uniquely him.

If she hadn't been certain he wanted her before, the arousal she felt pressing against her through his clothes made her entire body flush with heat. Kai's words rang in her head again, and it conjured in Ruby's mind an image of her lying beneath Serik as he took his pleasure in her. Ruby's hands moved of their own accord, one gripping his shirt as the other wrapped around the back of his neck. His kisses made her head spin, but she couldn't get enough. She wanted more of him.

The hand that had been at her chin moved down her neck

and across her collarbone. Ruby had lost the kerchief that Johana had given her back in Issalden, and her neck and upper chest were bare. His fingers ran along the curves of her breasts, and there was the tickle of metal sliding against her skin as he tugged on the chain she still wore. Serik ran his thumb and forefinger over the pendant, then there was a moment of sharp pressure that bordered on pain, and the chain gave way with a soft *snap!*

Ruby blinked her eyes open. He'd ripped the necklace off her.

"Wha—"

Serik's mouth covered hers again before Ruby could get the question out. The necklace fell from his fingers, and she barely registered the thud of the trinket hitting the floor.

His touch returned to her neckline. Fingers finding the drawstring tucked into her dress, he pulled it apart and slipped his hand inside her gown. Ruby gasped against Serik's lips as he cupped her breast through the thin fabric of her shift, his thumb brushing over the sensitive area in the middle. Ruby arched her back at the sensation of his touch, feeling the burning response that came with desire pool in her stomach and in between her legs.

Kisses that felt like fire on her skin trailed from her mouth to her neck. Her lips, swollen from the kiss, tingled as his teeth scraped against delicate flesh, making Ruby's legs quiver. She let out a low moan.

Serik pressed Ruby back against the wall, kissing her again. Warmth seeped into her as he placed his hands under her bottom and lifted her off her feet. Wrapping her arms around his neck and legs around his waist, Serik turned and walked the few feet to the door of his room. He fumbled with the lock, as his mouth and tongue were occupied by hers, distracting him from the task. After another moment, the wilder pulled his face away to see what he was doing, cursing under his breath.

Ruby took the opportunity to graze her lips along his ear, nipping the soft flesh. A low growl rumbled in his throat as the lock clicked, and Serik pushed the door open, carrying her inside.

"Naughty," he whispered as he kicked the door shut. The room was identical to the one Ruby and Kai shared, with a dresser, bed, and small table with a lit oil lamp casting warm, flickering light over the area. After a few steps across the threadbare carpet, he lowered Ruby to the mattress, placing her down gently as he knelt before her. Lips found her neck, and his hot breath and tongue made their way along her collarbone, then down to her chest. One hand gripped the back of her neck, and the other found the second drawstring at her waist and pulled the tie apart. Nothing keeping it together anymore, the front of her dress parted, exposing her corset, shift, and the tops of her breasts. His eyes roaming from her breasts up to her eyes, Serik gave her a gentle push to lie back on the bed and proceeded to crawl on top of her. Ruby's breath caught, and her heart pounded against her ribs.

Serik tugged at her corset, maneuvering the garment to free her breasts from their confinement. He gripped the soft flesh, squeezing the tip between his fingers and drawing a pleased sound from her. Eyes glistening in the lamplight, the wilder's hand drifted lower, fingers tracing the laces of her undergarment.

Ruby clutched at his shoulders as he lowered his head to her body, a pressure growing deep within her. She sucked in a sharp breath between her teeth as his mouth found the stiff tip of her left breast.

Her mind felt fuzzy. She tried to recall how they had ended up in this situation, but all Ruby could focus on was

Serik's heat, his touch, and how much she wanted the wilder to rip off her remaining clothes and ravish her. She wanted to run her hands over those tight muscles and trace her lips on his skin.

Serik's lips found hers again. Ruby wrapped her arms around him, kissing him back. She wanted him, all of him. If he was this attentive without their bodies even being joined, what would it be like once he took her?

She wanted to know, *now*.

Ruby's hands slid around to the front of his shirt, and she had to stop herself from simply ripping the garment off him.

Before more than two buttons were undone, Serik placed a hand on top of hers, stilling them. Breaking the kiss, he pulled back, breathing labored as if he'd run a mile.

"I really am such a bastard," he murmured.

"What?"

Serik gazed down the length of her before meeting her stare. Ruby had seen that half-crazed look before, the one that drove men to madness and passion. She wanted him to kiss her again, to touch her. Why had he stopped?

The wilder closed his eyes and took a few deep breaths. When he opened them again, he was in control of himself. Serik looked at her, and she could see that behind his eyes, a battle was being waged. He was struggling with an important decision.

Ruby opened her mouth to speak, but the wilder leaned forward and kissed her again, silencing her. Then he laid his forehead on her shoulder and inhaled deeply.

"I want you," he said, his voice barely audible. "I want to feel your skin against mine and hear you cry my name. I want to taste you and bury myself deep inside you while you writhe in pleasure." His words made her face and neck heat. Ruby reached for his shirt again. "—but I can't have you."

That stopped her in her tracks. It had not been what Ruby

expected him to say. She still lay under him, half-clothed, and shocked into muteness by his words. Was he having second thoughts? Were his feelings not as strong as she'd assumed?

Ruby finally found her voice. "Why not?" she asked, trying to keep the hurt and disappointment out of her question.

Serik pushed himself up, one hand touching her cheek. Instead of answering her question, he only shook his head and said, "I'm sorry, Ruby, but I don't want to hurt you more than I already have."

He got to his feet. Taking the time to straighten his clothing, Serik gave her one last long look over his shoulder. Then with a resigned expression, he tore his gaze from her and moved to the door. With a soft click of the latch, Ruby was alone in the bedroom.

Stunned, Ruby just lay there, trying to rein in her emotions. All her life, she had told herself that crying would not help her and tried to resist such weakness, but at that moment, all she wanted to do was run to her room, throw herself on her bed, and weep. She sat up, taking deep breaths to calm her mind and body. She'd offered herself to Serik, and he'd rejected her.

With shaking hands, she fixed her corset and retied the drawstrings at her neck and waistline. Everything was soon back in its proper place. It took her another minute to gather the will to stand and leave the little room behind her.

As she stepped out into the corridor, her foot kicked something that scraped and skittered across the floorboards. Ruby knelt to pick up the silvery object.

It was Mikel's necklace. Ruby held the chain and pendant up to the lamplight, frowning at it.

The clasp was broken.

CHAPTER 27

"What's wrong, Ruby?" Kai asked. "You look like you're going to be sick."

Ruby had decided against going to her room after what happened with Serik. She didn't think she could sleep and didn't want to be alone. So she'd come back down to the tavern. Serik had joined Kai and Gav. She did feel like she would be sick, but plastered a smile on her face and took a seat next to Kai. Serik watched her, but Ruby avoided his gaze.

"I am fine, Kai. Just tired. It has been a long couple of weeks."

"Well, cheer up! We're all a little richer for our efforts, which means we can find a place to settle." She tapped one finger to her chin thoughtfully. "Issalden is out of the question, of course, and we want to stay away from the southwest of the empire since a certain duke will still be on the lookout for you."

Ruby nodded along, half listening. She heard what her friend was saying, but the prospects her future held felt insignificant at the moment. She could still feel the wilder's gaze on her, and as much as she wanted to squirm, she forced herself to remain still, her breathing even.

"I have a few contacts in Lanevin that we can sell the jewels to," Kai was saying. "But I think we should be able to get around five thousand crests, which will mean a little over a thousand for each of us." She winked at Ruby. "It's more than my original fee was. Keeping that key was the right decision, and it wasn't so hard, was it?"

"I could have done without getting shot," Ruby said, picking a mug at random from the pile on the table. She had no idea which one had been hers, but they were all empty. She held it in her lap, not because Ruby wanted another drink, but because she didn't want her hands idle.

Kai clicked her tongue in annoyance. "Why are you still dwelling on that? It was weeks ago!"

Gav raised his own tankard, eyeing the inside and then looking mournfully at the pitcher on the counter. "I'm with Miss Ruby on this. Taking a bullet is no minor injury."

"Miss Violet," Serik corrected softly.

Looking up at him, their eyes met, then she hurriedly glanced away.

"And I was poisoned, but do you see me complaining?" Kai scoffed, then lowered her voice considerably. There was no one left to overhear them, but she still whispered her next words. "What I want to know is what happened in the temple with you, Ruby."

A chill that had nothing to do with the dropping temperature of the inn settled into Ruby. She knew Kai was referring to the odd things that had happened at Ta'Dormus Deva and her lack of memory of their fight with Joran and his assassin. As much as she wanted to argue that the veil breaking, the earthquake, and the murals were a coincidence, it was difficult for her to deny that there had been some sort of connection between the beast that resided there and the weird feeling of déjà vu she'd had the entire time they walked those crumbling halls.

Gav stood and retrieved the pitcher. When he took his seat again, he stared at Ruby thoughtfully as he poured himself another drink. "You know, I have a friend who might know more about this. Do you mind if I write him about it? He works for the emperor, so I'm sure if anyone will be able to help you figure out what happened, it will be him."

"What do you mean 'he works for the emperor'?" Kai asked.

"He's the imperial court mage," Gav said with an arrogant tilt of his head.

Kai rolled her eyes. "Not this story again."

"It's not a fabrication!"

While they argued, Ruby considered Gav's words. She didn't have access to Valwen's vast library anymore, and it was unlikely she would be able to stay in one place long enough to be able to do any in-depth research, at least not in the immediate future. This person could be a solution. She was curious as to why the temple seemed to react to her, and as long as she didn't have to go back, she'd like to know what happened and why her memories were missing.

"All right, I suppose there would be no harm in it," she said, over Kai's teasing. "But do you really think he will know about some obscure temple on the edge of the empire? It hardly seems important."

Gav smiled at her and threw Kai a smug look. "He has access to the royal archives. Like I said, if anyone might know, it's him. Though you should keep in mind that he might not be able to help, and it will just remain a mystery."

Ruby nodded and pushed back from the table. She had something else to focus on now and thought she might be ready to put her mind to it. "I think I will retire then," Ruby said as she headed to the stairs, and Kai jumped up to follow her.

"You can stay if you want to," Ruby told her. "I am all right."

Kai snorted. "I think I've had enough to drink."

The two women made their way to their room. Only when they were safely within the privacy of its walls did Kai continue the conversation.

"What happened, Ruby? You've looked on the verge of tears since you came back downstairs." She watched Ruby carefully. "Did Serik do something to you?"

Images of what happened in the corridor and in his room flooded her mind, and she wrapped her arms around herself. There was no hiding anything from Kai. And why should she? Kai was her best friend. She shouldn't have to keep anything from her, but it was still so fresh.

"He kissed me," Ruby said, touching a finger to her lips and shivering. She could almost feel the heat of his skin against hers. Her lips moved, but no sound came out. She couldn't bring herself to tell her friend about what else she and the wilder had engaged in. After a moment, she finally found the strength to say, "After… more kissing… and other stuff, he told me he could not have me."

"He said *what?*" Kai seemed genuinely surprised. "Did he say why?"

"No, he did not." Her voice sounded bitter to her ears or, at the very least, extremely disappointed.

Kai made a low growling noise in her throat. "I was wrong. He doesn't deserve your affections. Do you want me to stab him?" she asked in all seriousness. "I've had a lot of practice at it, especially this week. Then you can have his share of the loot."

Ruby choked out a laugh. "I fear that would land you in prison for murder."

"Only if I'm caught."

"No, it's all right. If he does not want me, then I cannot force him to return my affections." But he did want her. Hadn't his actions said just that? So why wouldn't he take her? Ruby shrugged one shoulder. "I am sure he has some reason. Maybe he already has a lover."

Eyes narrowing, Kai pursed her lips. "I don't think that's it."

That comment seemed out of place, and Ruby looked up at Kai. She looked guilty. Was she hiding something from her, something about Serik?

"Kai…" she started slowly, "what do you know?"

Kai's lips drew into a thin line. It looked like she didn't want to tell her, but Ruby kept up her intense gaze, and she relented. Sighing, she said, "I don't know the specifics, but he has some history with the duke. *Your* duke."

Ruby wouldn't have been more surprised if Kai had slapped her in the face. "I beg your pardon. He knows Mikel? How? Why did you not tell me?"

"As I said, I don't know the details." Kai looked down at her hands and fiddled with her fingernails. "He let it slip back in Issalden. Serik knew it was the Duke of Ayrilon looking for you. All he told me was that he hates the duke, and he would do whatever it took to keep you away from him." Kai looked up at her again, her eyes wide. "I'm sorry, Ruby. I didn't say anything before because I knew it would hurt. You like Serik, and I thought that if I told you, you wouldn't give yourself a chance with him."

There was a pang in Ruby's chest, an ache that was more than merely physical. Both the man she suspected she'd fallen for and her best friend had kept this from her. They had kept that knowledge—information that she needed in order to make an informed decision about Serik—a secret. If she had known he knew Mikel, maybe she wouldn't have acted upon her feelings and wouldn't be here now, feeling humiliated.

"Ruby," Kai began after Ruby was silent for a while.

"I can't, Kai," she cut her off, voice shaking. "I can't do this right now." She turned away and sat on the bed, holding herself.

Kai didn't say anything else. After a minute, she left the room, closing the door behind her and giving Ruby the privacy she needed to cry.

* * *

GAV TOOK another sip of the diluted liquid this town called ale, watching the retreating form of his two female companions over the rim of the mug. His eyes flicked to the wilder, who was also following the pair ascending the stairs. Both he and the young Miss Ruby had been exceptionally quiet when they had returned from their rooms, and Gav could guess the reason. Serik had done something that he would regret, something that had hurt Ruby.

It wasn't Gav's place to interfere with whatever turn their relationship had taken, but he hated seeing such an exceptional young woman in misery. She had tried to hide her emotions, but the great Gavin Ilias prided himself in knowing the troubles of both men and women. He would get to the bottom of this. The wilder would be a formidable opponent indeed.

"Do you know who is offering Miss Ruby's reward?" he asked nonchalantly, gauging Serik's reaction. "I do."

"Do you?" Serik turned his attention away from the women and focused on Gav, not bothering to correct his use of Ruby's real name this time.

"The Duke of Ayrilon," Gav said without preamble. He'd figured out which duke was after her ages ago. The Dukes of

Ocmura, Ayrilon, and Ashela had been at the top of the list. Ocmura was too young, and Ashela preferred the company of men to women. That only left Mikel Belmont—a fitting match for the illustrious noble lady.

Serik grunted, unsurprised. So, he knew as well.

"Belmont will be furious when he finds out that his runaway fiancée has taken up with a wilder." There, the bait was set.

"She hasn't 'taken up' with me or anyone else." Serik's eyes narrowed at him as he spoke. The man wasn't stupid. He knew Gav was digging.

"I caught you kissing behind the inn two nights ago. Don't lie to me."

The wilder glanced over at the stairs again. He didn't look angry. On the contrary, he looked wistful. Oh yes, he wanted her. "I can't."

"Can't what?"

Serik gave him a flat look.

"Why not? If her parents disown her, and they will after this, what's stopping you?"

Serik's jaw tensed, and his gaze fell to the table, staring at their mugs. "She deserves someone who will really love her. Someone who will care for her without his past interfering. I don't know if I…" He paused, considering his words, then began again. "All I can offer her is more pain."

That made Gav sit up a little straighter. Who exactly was this wilder? "Do you have some connection to the Duke of Ayrilon?"

The wilder remained silent.

"If that's the case, you need not worry. I will not be telling anyone your secret, not even our lovely Ruby. It must be a good one if it means you can't pursue what is so obvious to anyone with eyes." When the wilder still did not speak, Gav sighed. If he wanted to play it this way, so be it. "Let me guess, he's your father. No, you don't look that much younger than the duke. He stole your horse. That would be a shame, though Dream is a nice replacement. Or maybe he killed your father. Oh! I've got it—wrongful imprisonment. Men have killed for less." He grinned. "I can do this all night, Serik."

Glaring at Gav, the petulant man crossed his arms over his chest. What a look! He was close to the truth, Gav was certain. A little more prodding should do it.

"Come on! We've bled together. You know you can trust me."

Serik's glower only deepened. After an awkward moment that stretched into an awkward minute, his mouth moved, but Gav could scarcely believe the words that followed.

"Mikel Belmont is my half-brother."

CHAPTER 28

The next day, they took the train back to Easthollow. As he had done before, Serik reserved them a compartment at the front of the train. This time, Ruby only left to use the toilet or to purchase a snack in the dining car, and Gav or Kai accompanied her. The wilder barely said a word during the trip. He wouldn't meet Ruby's eyes.

Gav and Kai engaged in conversation, making up for the lack of it from their companions. They discussed the treasure again in more detail, where they could sell it, and how much they thought they could get. Once that topic was exhausted, they started talking about what they would spend the money on.

"It's not enough for a house, unless I want to live out in the middle of nowhere, but will provide decent lodgings for a while, long enough to find work that fits my... unique skills," Kai said, then glanced at Ruby. "If you want to finish your education from Valwen, you could hire a private tutor and take the tests. You were only a couple of months away from completing your studies."

"If I take the test and become a true mage, I will have to register with the palace," Ruby pointed out, staring out the window at the countryside sliding by. "Those records are public, and I am sure the government will require my actual name." She wanted to finish her education, she truly did, but she'd realized the unnecessary risk. "Anyone looking for me could just look up those records and see not only that I am registered, but also have access to my address."

"We could set up a dummy address. Then we'll know who comes and looks for you," Kai suggested.

"I already know who is looking for me." The necklace, which she'd stuffed back in her pocket the night before, seemed to gain a few pounds. "I prefer to stay as far from him as possible. Besides, what is the point of my taking the test? It's not as if I can serve as some noble house's court mage."

"No," Kai replied, and her expression was one of patience, the kind one wore when explaining to a child how the world worked. "But you can charge more for your services if you are tested and registered. You'd have the proper credentials to charge guild rates for your spells."

"Oh," Ruby said, not sure what to add to that.

"Just think about it," Kai continued. "We won't need money for a while, but our proceeds thus far will not last forever. You should also consider where you want to live. We could go south to one of the bigger cities. Lanevin is also an option, though it's a little too close to Issalden for my comfort. Or we could leave the country. I've heard Langard is nice."

"The summers are very hot," Serik murmured. It was the first full sentence he'd uttered in the last hour.

"Then we can go elsewhere," Kai shot back at him with a glare. She had been treating him with a tone of hostility since the night before, after Ruby had told her about the kiss. "I hear Fiarna is perfect this time of year."

"Oh, it is!" Gav interjected happily. "It's quite beautiful, and the people there are very nice." His eyes glided over to Kai. "I have a few friends there who wouldn't mind hosting for a bit while we get settled."

Kai's eyes narrowed. "Who said you were coming with us?" But her expression betrayed her words. Even Ruby could see how her muscles tugged at the corners of her mouth as she suppressed a smile.

The conversation went on like that for the rest of the train ride. An attendant came by once to take their orders for supper. Then, after that was delivered and eaten, the same attendant informed them that they would be arriving in Easthollow soon. Ruby was grateful. The ride from Calsith to Easthollow was seven hours in total if one counted the four other stops the train made at various stations in the eastern countryside.

When the train slowed and pulled into the station at Lanevin, the four of them got to their feet and stretched. Kai and Gav had decided to sell one hundred crests worth of gems here. That would give them each enough to set themselves up wherever they decided to go, and the rest of the treasure would be sold over time.

"It's best if the locals don't know that we came across such wealth," Kai explained. "In smaller towns like this, people talk, and the next thing you know, you're the target of an assassination attempt."

The small group went back to the inn they'd stayed at the first night, the *Drunken Lion*, and paid for accommodations. Since it was late, the plan was to rest for the night and take care of their business in the morning.

"Mr. and Mrs. Belin!" the innkeeper said when they entered. "Welcome back!"

Ruby stiffened. She'd almost completely forgotten about their ruse.

The wilder recovered more swiftly than she, wrapping one arm around her shoulders and squeezing her against him. Ruby closed her eyes and prayed to the gods for strength, trying to keep herself from flinching away from his touch.

"Jona," Serik said, his voice loud in Ruby's ear. "How is business?"

"'Bout the same since you lot left town. It's been less than a week. Finished your business already?"

"Yes, you could say that. It was only ever supposed to be a short visit. Violet and I like the quiet of the country, but we really missed the city."

"Violet," Kai said, and Ruby opened her eyes. "Let's get something to drink while the men talk business." She took Ruby's hand and pulled her out of Serik's grip, flashing him a glare that Jona didn't seem to notice.

"Thank you for that," Ruby said once they were out of earshot of the men. She hadn't been prepared to continue the married act and was relieved to be on the other side of the room from the wilder.

Kai gave her a sidelong look. "Of course."

Two rooms were purchased under the guise of the married couples pairing off. Ruby and Kai would share a room, and Serik and Gav shared the other. Kai chose a small table by the front window, one that only sat two. Gav looked confused by the choice, but Serik pursed his lips and chose another table nearby.

After they ate, Kai and Ruby went up to bed. The men didn't try to stop them, but Ruby felt the wilder's eyes on her as she climbed the stairs to the second floor. A tub had been prepared for the women, and they took turns bathing before climbing into bed. Ruby was exhausted, even though they hadn't done much today. Her eyes were heavy, and she closed them, trying not to think too much. Most of all, she just wanted this awful feeling in her chest to go away.

Ta'Dormus Deva haunted Ruby's dreams.

She was back in the old temple, walking through it alone. Leaves crunched under her feet. Unlike in the vision she'd had outside the altar room, which seemed to have transported her back in time, the temple remained as they had found it the other day. Dark, decrepit, and barely standing. There was a damp and musty smell that permeated the stale air. The entire place was lit with a warm glow that seemed to follow her, allowing her to see everything around without the need for a lamp.

The only thing that had changed was the murals.

Instead of the color and images fading into obscurity, covered with dirt and other detritus, they were pristine, as if they had just been created. Ruby could see them clearly, and the woman depicted in them looked even more like her now. It was as if she were staring into a mirror.

Ruby shivered, but unlike in real life, she felt safe here. Confident that nothing would harm her. She continued forward, brushing her fingertips over the smooth mosaic tiles along the wall.

A scent ahead of her caught her attention. It was sweet and earthy. Incense. Someone was burning incense. As she approached the altar room, the smell grew thicker, and she was sure that it was coming from just up ahead.

When she walked through the archway, Ruby found herself staring up at a large pillar behind the altar, one that had not been there when they'd been exploring the temple. But with all the crumbling stone that had littered the floor, a structure such as this could have been here at one point. On top of it sat two women, their legs dangling off the side. They were too far above for Ruby to make out any features, but for some reason, she thought the women looked familiar.

"Hello!" Ruby called out after glancing around nervously. She wanted to make sure that the cat creature wouldn't use this distraction to sneak up on her. There had been no sign of it so far, and she didn't feel like she was in danger here, but it didn't hurt to be cautious.

The women looked down at her, and Ruby took a step back.

They were *her*. Both of them.

The one disparity was that the women on the pillar had golden eyes that seemed to reflect the light. They stared down at her as they scooted forward, slipping off the pillar.

Instead of plummeting to the ground, the two women glided like they were floating through water. Two pairs of bare feet landed softly just out of arm's reach from her.

Ruby looked back toward the entrance, thinking of running, but the archway was gone, replaced by smooth stone as if an exit had never been there.

"Ruby," the woman on the left said, and it was not her own voice that came from those lips. The feminine voice was richer and darker. The features of the women shifted, their cheekbones rising and skin brightening. Both were inhumanly beautiful, with luminous skin, hair as black as night, and those same golden eyes.

"Who are you?" Ruby asked, unable to keep the question back. She was scared, but also fascinated.

"I am you," the woman on the right said with that same dark voice.

"As am I," the other said, almost an echo of her twin. They joined hands, then each held out the other hand toward Ruby, palms up. She hesitated for a moment, then reached out her arms and touched those elegant fingers, completing the circle.

There was a blinding flash of brilliant light, then Ruby opened her eyes.

Echoes of the dream still spinning in her head, Ruby sat up, gazing around the small room. It took her a moment to make out the form lying next to her. Kai was still fast asleep under the blankets, and only dim moonlight streamed in through the window.

Ruby wanted to lie back down and go to sleep, but her mouth was dry, and she desperately needed to use the toilet. Looking down at Kai, she frowned. It was probably all right to go out by herself. She would only be gone for a few minutes, and she didn't want to disturb Kai's slumber. Her friend was normally a light sleeper, and the fact that she was not already awake from Ruby's movements was a testament to how much she needed the rest.

Ruby got out of bed and used a small bit of magic to light the candle on the table. Then she wrapped the light-blue shawl around her shoulders and tiptoed to the door, taking the candle in its little holder with her.

The water closet was down the hall. The lamps on the walls were extinguished. Some light drifted up from the stairs, but it was so dim that Ruby assumed it was just a lamp on the staircase that one of the staff had forgotten to put out. The pale-yellow damask wallpaper seemed to glow as the illumination from her candle touched it. Ruby stepped lightly as she made her way down the hall, determined not to wake any of the other guests from their slumbers.

A floorboard creaked under her foot, sounding loud in her ears. Someone coughed from behind a closed door, causing Ruby to pause, but there were no other sounds of movement. Ruby found the water closet at the end of the hall and did her business quickly, then headed back toward the stairs. A cup of water before going back to sleep would be most refreshing. She was sure that the innkeeper wouldn't mind if she helped herself to a glass.

She had almost reached the end of the hall when she heard a creak from behind her. Turning around, Ruby looked down the corridor, worried that she had awakened one of the sleeping residents. No one was there, not that she could see with the candlelight. She licked her lips. Perhaps she was being a bit jumpy. She was not one to be afraid of the dark, but with everything they had been through in the last few days, it would be unwise to discount anything.

Deciding that the drink could wait until morning, she headed back to her room.

As she reached for the doorknob, an arm wrapped around her from behind, and a hand clamped over her mouth before she could let out a scream. Ruby dropped the candle, kicking and flailing, but whoever had ahold of her was much stronger than she was. Holding her close to his chest, her assailant whispered in her ear.

"Make a sound, and I'll cut your throat."

Ruby stopped struggling, breathing hard through her nose. Her eyes were wide as she tried to turn her head back to see who had ahold of her, but the hand over her mouth kept her face forward.

"That's a good girl," he murmured. "We're going to walk down the stairs and leave the inn. Quiet now." He released her but clamped one hand on her arm, forcing her forward. She stumbled but didn't fall. Guided down the hall by the mysterious man, her mind raced.

Was this another kidnapping attempt by the Kingfishers? That wasn't Joran's voice or that black-haired assassin's. Could Mikel have sent someone else to find her?

Whoever this was, she believed that he would kill her if she screamed.

Ruby walked stiffly toward the stairs. *Think, Ruby! There has to be something you can do.*

As they approached the end of the hall, there was another creaking sound from behind them. It could have been caused by the wind or the settling sounds that old houses make, but whatever it was, the man leading her paused, and his grip loosened for a moment.

Ruby took that opportunity to yank her arm out of his hand and lunge forward and away from the man. Before she could get more than a few steps, she tripped on the carpet, knees hitting the ground hard.

Ignoring the pain, Ruby rolled onto her side and formed a shield over herself just as a dagger came down at her face. It glanced off, and the man cursed as he lost his hold on it, then grabbed one of her legs and yanked her out from the protection of her barrier.

He grabbed her wrist and pinned it to the floor as he fumbled for another weapon.

She kicked out, knocking over a decorative table with a vase that went crashing to the ground, shattering into a hundred pieces and throwing shards of pottery, water, and sunflower petals on them as they struggled. The sound of the vase breaking rang out in the quiet inn, and Ruby struggled to push the man away from her.

Ruby had never seen this man before. It was difficult to make out many details in the darkness, but his face looked lined with years, and she would have placed him in his thirties or forties. He was dressed in formfitting, dark clothes, with a half cloak around his shoulders. The hood was back, and his short brown hair fell around his face, sticking to his skin where it was wet from the vase. His mouth was set in a hard line as they struggled. He was easily stronger than she was, and he held her down with only one hand.

"Help!" she screamed as another dagger flashed at her

face. Ruby jerked to the side, the blade digging into the floor where her head had been a moment before.

"Slippery little eel," he growled. Releasing her wrist, he covered her mouth. "You should have come quietly." He jerked the dagger out of the floor, and she felt the blade's sting on her neck.

There was a flash of blue light, and the man sucked in a sharp breath of pain as his weapon clattered to the ground. Thick, warm liquid splashed onto Ruby's cheek.

"Release her!" Kai's voice rang out. She wore only a light shirt and breeches, and her hair was mussed from sleep, but her green eyes looked murderous in the light cast from her dagger as she called it back to her hand.

The man over Ruby reached for another weapon, but before his fingers touched it, Ruby drove her knee up into his groin. Pain raced up her leg as she connected with something hard, but her assailant let out a startled breath, and his eyes widened. Pushing his hand from her mouth, Ruby gasped for air, only to have it knocked out of her a moment later as the man struck her hard against the side of her head. Pain radiated from her cheek, and she tasted blood in her mouth as he grabbed the front of her dress in his fist and hauled her to her feet, putting her body between his and Kai's.

Ruby's head spun. Her face and knee hurt, and it was enough of a distraction that she couldn't pull on her power. Magic was all about focus, but she could barely think.

The man walked backward, getting closer to the stairs. There were a few more doors until they reached them. Ruby watched his face. He stared past her, presumably at Kai.

He didn't realize that the door behind him had opened.

Serik entered the hall, his short sword in hand, and slammed the pommel into the side of the assassin's head.

The man must have realized someone was behind him at the last second because he released Ruby and moved with the blow. The strike threw him into the wall, but he took considerably less damage than he would have otherwise.

Gav followed behind the wilder, looking much like Kai did, but his eyes were wide and alert. He rushed past the would-be assassin, grabbing Ruby and pulling her away from the altercation as Kai's dagger went flying past them. The man tried to get her back but had to duck a cut from Serik's sword and Kai's dagger. He rolled forward, tumbling past the wilder.

As he came to his feet, Serik swung again, silent in his determined assault. Kai summoned her dagger back.

"He's in the way," she growled, referring to Serik as her eyes moved from place to place, looking for an opening. Gav kept his arms around Ruby, shielding her body with his. His muscles were tense as if he were ready to move her out of harm's way at any second.

Ruby turned to watch the fight, holding her cheek, which felt like it was on fire, but at least the pain was starting to recede.

The man tried to dodge to one side as Serik's blade came down at him, but he wasn't quick enough. The sharpened steel caught the front of his vest and tore through the cloth. A bright green jewel tumbled from the slash Serik had made in his breast pocket. It skittered across the carpet, rolling to a stop near Ruby's feet. She stared at the little jewel and, with a start, recognized it for what it was—a communication gem.

CHAPTER 29

A communication gem. Ruby had learned about them at Valwen. It was an artifact that was enchanted with a magical binding that allowed the little stone to send and receive messages from across the empire. That meant that the man who attacked her could have gotten a message from the Kingfishers to take her—or even be in communication with the duke.

A stunned silence fell over the hallway, and, aside from the wilder's, all eyes were on the gem at Ruby's feet. Serik blocked the path to the others. The assassin cursed and—taking advantage of their surprise—turned and ran.

Ten seconds later, they heard the sound of the front door slamming, and Gav's shoulders slumped as he released Ruby. She looked up at him, and his blue eyes roved over her face. The loresinger winced. Serik looked like he wanted to follow the man, but one glance back at Ruby, and he sheathed his weapon instead.

She must have looked a real mess to cause that reaction from him.

"Are you okay, Ruby?" Kai asked, pulling her attention away from Serik.

"I think so," Ruby said as the events of the last few minutes caught up with her. "Was that… He was…" She couldn't get the words out. Her legs started to shake, and she felt like her stomach was going to empty its contents all over the carpet.

There was a soft touch on her shoulder, and she turned to Serik. The wilder's fingers brushed her cheek where she'd been struck by the assassin. It was tender, and she winced. His thumb brushed her neck, coming back wet with blood. Her blood. Her breath hitched, remembering the sting of the man's blade.

Without a word, he pulled her into an embrace. Ruby broke. Tears welled up in her eyes, and her chest wracked with sobs.

Serik, who had been distant since that night in Calsith, held her tightly against him. After everything that had happened between them, she should have pushed him away, but she was too shaken by the events of the night to care about her dignity. It was the closest she had ever come to death. If Kai had thrown her dagger a moment later, she would be bleeding out on the floor.

"It's all right," he said soothingly as she sobbed into his chest, patting her hair. "You're okay, Ruby."

A door further down the hall flew open, and Jona stepped out into the hallway, holding an oil lamp.

"What happened?!" the innkeeper demanded. Looking them over, his eyes focused on the broken vase.

"There's no reason to worry," Gav said, stepping in front of Ruby and Serik. "It was just a lover's quarrel that got a little out of hand."

Ruby quieted enough to turn her head and look at Gav. What was he saying?

Jona looked like he didn't believe that for a second. "I heard yelling," he said, glaring up at the taller loresinger stubbornly. "And what happened to my floor?!"

The was the creak of wood, and Ruby caught sight of two women watching them through a cracked door. She vaguely remembered seeing the women before. They were the staff for the *Drunken Lion*.

"Ah, that was me," Kai said, looking embarrassed. She glanced over at the women watching them. "I admit, I was a bit confused when I awoke to hear the sounds of their argument and thought something untoward was happening." She held her palm out while she was explaining. The light from her dagger died out, plunging them into shadowy darkness with the only source of illumination in Jona's hand.

The innkeeper flinched at the blatant use of magic, eyeing Kai suspiciously. "You're a mage?"

"I'm a hedge mage," she said by way of explanation. Hedge mages were those born with the abilities, but could not afford training, so they taught themselves whatever spells they could. "I can be a bit jumpy when I feel threatened." Her voice was apologetic. "Not that Mr. Belin was threatening me!" she added quickly. "I just feel a bit protective of my husband's cousin. She is a dear friend of mine."

"We'll pay for the damages, of course," Gav said before the innkeeper could react. "And some extra coin for the inconvenience. Please accept my sincerest apologies," he added, bowing as gracefully as any lord.

There were whispers from the women watching. Jona glared at the door, and the ladies shut it quickly.

"Very well," the innkeeper said. His tone suggested that he still wasn't convinced they were telling the truth. "We can settle your bill in the morning." He looked over Gav's shoulder at Ruby. Kai leaned down to pick something off the floor as he spoke. "Are you sure you're all right, miss?"

She nodded. "Thank you for your concern." Her voice sounded like she had a head cold, but she thought it was convincing.

The innkeeper stared at her for another long moment, then sighed and turned back around, entering his room and shutting the door.

Serik led Ruby into his and Gav's room, the other two following close behind. When they closed the door, Kai turned to it, drawing a rune on the wood with her finger. Ruby felt the tingling essence of her friend's magic, like sipping on tart lemonade, as she cast her spell. Serik released her, and they waited until Kai was finished.

"There, it won't last long, but we can't be overheard for a few minutes," Kai said.

"Why didn't you tell the innkeeper what happened?" Ruby asked Gav.

The loresinger ran one hand through his auburn hair. "Do you really want Inspector Leonte questioning you on why you were attacked *again*?" Gav asked. "That man was suspicious of us at first, but there was no evidence that he could have tried to hold us on. But if it were to happen again, he would be forced to take a closer look. He might even have his men take you into custody 'for your protection.'" Gav rolled his eyes when he said that last part.

"What I want to know is why there was an assassin after you in the first place," Kai said, crossing her arms over her chest and hugging herself. She looked cold, but the room was warm. "He wasn't here to capture you. If you hadn't broken that vase and screamed for help, I would have never woken up."

Ruby looked down at her hands. "He tried to kidnap me first, but I fought him."

Serik was still watching Ruby. "You're lucky he didn't kill you."

"He tried, though," Gav said with a nervous laugh.

Ruby touched her throat and felt the rough area where the assassin's dagger had cut into her skin. It wasn't deep, but it stung when she put pressure on it. If Kai had been a second later…

Her knees felt weak, and she sat on the bed.

"What's this?" Kai asked, holding up the little green emerald. "He dropped it when Serik cut him."

"It's a communication gem," Ruby said automatically. When Kai blinked at her, she continued. "We learned about them at Valwen. Did you sleep through that lecture?"

"Remind me," Kai said with a smirk.

Ruby tried to recall what exactly they had learned about the little magical devices. The lecture about communication gems had been earlier that term, but the subject had been interesting to her, and Ruby had looked them up in the library afterward.

"They are rare," she said, staring at the emerald in Kai's hand. "These gems are magically enchanted to correspond to one paired to it, meaning information put in one gem is sent to the other. You can use it to send a message by either voice or script. It's expensive to make, so there aren't a lot of them around, but many of the noble houses have at least one pair."

Gav made a choking sound, and Ruby turned to him.

He dug in his pockets, fishing out an emerald, almost a duplicate of the one Kai held. "I sent a message to Cosmin," he whispered. "The court mage I mentioned before, to help you figure out what had happened at Ta'Dormus Deva." His expression was one of utter shock. "Why would he do this?"

Kai glared at him. "You only sent that message this morning. There's no way he would have sent someone here by now."

"He has the emperor's ear!" Gav said in a panic and started pacing. "I said he was the royal court mage, right?

That means he has all the power of the imperial palace at his disposal. There are people all over the empire who work for him." Gav ran his hand through his hair again. "How did he know where we were staying? I never told him that."

Kai swore under her breath.

"Magical items like that can be tracked," Serik said for Gav's benefit. "Surely, you knew that."

"O-of course." The look on the loresinger's face told them that he had *not* known that.

"That's how he knew exactly where to find us," Serik continued, running a hand over his face. "And that means that man was a royal assassin."

"The emperor wants me dead?" Ruby squeaked. She'd been thinking that man had been from the Guild, but this was so much worse than she could've imagined.

"Look," Gav began, desperation in his voice as he looked at Ruby. "If we talk to Cosmin or the emperor, I'm sure we can get this all straightened out."

"Oh no. Ruby isn't going anywhere near that man," Kai growled. "If he already sent one assassin to dispose of her, what makes you think he will listen to anything we have to say?"

"Ruby, you can't run from the emperor," Gav implored, ignoring Kai. "He'll find you eventually."

Ruby didn't know what to say. The fact that the emperor —*the* emperor—was after her was enough to turn her blood to ice.

"Why?" she whispered, as if the emperor could hear her words if she spoke too loudly. That was ridiculous, but the fear that clutched at her stomach kept her voice low. "What makes me a threat?"

Gav shook his head, looking bewildered. "I don't know. Maybe it's something to do with what happened at

Ta'Dormus Deva. Whatever the reason, we have to do something before another assassin shows up."

Serik sighed, and Ruby stared at him, praying that the wilder had a solution that didn't include her death. "He's right. Even if it's his fault that the emperor is after you in the first place." He cast a withering glare at the loresinger. "We either need to convince him that you're no threat or leave the country."

"How do we do that?" Ruby asked, her voice sounding small. "How do we convince him to leave me alone?"

"I'll speak to Cosmin. He'll be able to—"

"No, no, no." Kai rubbed her temples with her fingertips. "You've already messed this up once. You can't be trusted to do this alone." She closed her eyes in thought. Moments later, they snapped open again.

"All right, the new plan is that Gav and I take the train to the capital and meet with this Cosmin and find out why the emperor sent someone after you. There has to be a reason for it other than you running away from Valwen—and your fiancé," Kai said, and Gav nodded along with her words, looking relieved. "You and Serik will also make your way south, but on horseback. We already know that if you get attacked on the train again, there really isn't anywhere to run, and with the backing of the imperial palace, it will be more than just the Kingfishers tracking you now."

Ruby and Serik glanced at each other. It would take the better part of two weeks to reach the capital on horseback. Traveling on the open road would give them a better chance to escape and hide if they were tracked, but that would also mean more opportunities for attack. There was also the fact that she would be spending all that time alone with the wilder. Ruby would have jumped at the opportunity a few days ago, but now, the thought made her uncomfortable.

Kai looked back and forth between them. "You both can

handle that, right? You're not going to tear each other apart, are you?"

"She'll be safe with me," Serik said, his eyes still on Ruby. She looked away first.

Kai glared at Ruby until she nodded, then clapped her hands together. "Great! Now that that's settled, let's get some sleep."

THE NEXT AFTERNOON, they all stood together on the platform at the train station. The train was due to leave in the next few minutes, but only Kai and Gav would be on it. They had decided it would be best to split up now and travel separately so that they would not be seen in Lanevin together. Gav and Serik had spent the morning buying supplies after convincing an irate Jona to let Ruby and Serik stay another night. In the end, the wilder had paid the man five crests for the damages and trouble from the night before. The large sum was partially for the innkeeper's silence about the events that transpired under his roof.

Ruby looked sullenly over at the two men as they talked in quiet voices. "Why do you have to go with him?"

Kai sighed. They had already been over this three times this morning, finalizing the details of their scheme, but she smiled patiently at Ruby. "I need to make sure he doesn't fuck this up. It's too important to trust that everything will go according to plan and that the emperor will be so understanding that he rescinds his orders. I'll be able to monitor the situation in the guise of the loresinger's apprentice."

"Maybe I should go with you," Ruby reasoned. "I can explain what happened."

"Don't be ridiculous. We have a plan. It's not the best plan, but it's a good start."

"I know, I know. You made the plans, but I will miss you."

Ruby glanced over at Serik. The wilder was trying not to smile at something that Gav said, but the side of his mouth twitched. Her feelings about Serik felt like a ball of string that had gotten tangled. After his rejection of her in Calsith, she assumed that part of their relationship was over, but with the previous night's events—him holding her as she cried in his arms—she didn't know what to think.

"Just do me a favor and don't get pregnant."

"Kai!" Ruby's gaze whipped back to her friend, and she lowered her voice to a hiss. "Why would you say that? You know what happened between us."

Kai grinned at her. "Because you two will have plenty of chances to make up during the twelve days that you'll be on the road."

"I do not think he wants to rekindle any feelings we may have shared. He has already stated as much." Ruby looked down at her hands.

"Well, if that is truly so, he is an idiot and not suited for you, though I'm not saying he ever was." She took Ruby's hands in her own. "We'll see each other soon! I'm surprised you're not already sick of me. It's been close to two months since we left Valwen."

She would never be sick of Kai. She had already done so much for her. "Are you sure that I cannot accompany you?" Ruby asked again.

"If we aren't able to convince this Cosmin person to relent, I don't want you anywhere near the palace."

"But how will we know if you have succeeded or not?"

Kai pursed her lips in thought. "I'll send a message two days before you are due to arrive in the city. There is an inn on the outskirts of town called Pearl's. You can pick up the message once you arrive. If we determine it's too dangerous for you to stay in the capital, it will be easy for the two of you to turn around and leave again." She put her hands on her hips. "If that happens, tell the wilder to take you out of the country, and I'll come find you. I'm sure he'll do that much."

Ruby wanted to argue that it was just as dangerous for Kai to be wandering around Valkea as it was for her. The Thieves Guild had hired an assassin to find Kai as well. She was sure that the man with the black hair and amber eyes would return.

"I can tell what you're thinking. It's written all over your face." Kai reached out and grabbed ahold of her friend's braid, giving it a tug. "Let me worry about the Kingfishers." She released Ruby's hair. "Without an annoying noble lady to take care of, I might be able to walk around unnoticed."

Ruby grinned and wiped a tear off her cheek. "You are not rid of me yet, Kai."

"Love you," Kai said as she leaned forward to kiss Ruby's cheek. The two women embraced, and the shrill whistle from the train screeched, signaling that it was about to depart.

"Be careful," Ruby whispered. She didn't want to admit it right then, but she was afraid for Kai. If she or Gav were hurt while on this mission to keep her safe, Ruby didn't know if she would be able to live with herself.

Kai took a step back from her, grinning. "You know me. I'm always careful."

Ruby laughed as Gav and Serik approached.

"We must get going, my dear," Gav said to Kai. "Otherwise, the train will leave without us."

"I'm going to be glad when we no longer have to act like we are married," Kai growled in response. She turned away from Ruby and walked toward the train.

Gav bowed to Ruby, much like he had to the innkeeper the night before. "Farewell, cousin. I hope to see you again soon."

Kai rolled her eyes behind him. The loresinger waved as he trotted across the platform and stepped onto the train.

"Take care of him!" Ruby called after Kai, giggling.

Kai winked at her, then hopped onto the train as it started moving.

Ruby watched as the train pulled out of the station, gathering speed and spewing black smoke from the stack on the engine. She stayed on the platform until she could no longer see the locomotive. Serik stood with her.

"Ready to head back?" Serik asked. "We have a long way to travel in the morning."

Ruby wasn't ready for any of this, but she nodded. He held out his arm to her like a gentleman, and she placed her fingers in the crook of his arm. Serik was a comforting presence at her side, even with everything that had happened between them. She squeezed his arm, and he placed his other hand over hers. His skin was warm against hers.

As uncertain of the future as she was, at least she wasn't facing it alone. All she could do now was forge ahead.

ABOUT THE AUTHOR

Accountant by day, writer by night, Vivian Bricker has been penning fantasy stories since she was old enough to pick up a book. She lives near Denver, Colorado, with her husband and three dogs: Hiro, Kalli, and Mira. Free time is hard to come by, but when she has a few extra hours, she likes to paint, practice archery, and run tabletop roleplaying games.

@VBrickerAuthor

brickerandnobles.com

ALSO BY V. BRICKER

The Lanis Chronicles

Runaway

Tempest Hall

Sarah Frost Novels

Coldwave

Realms of Asara

Broken Bonds